APHROCHROME

This book is dedicated to all the people I never knew and might have grown to like, and to the one person I grew to like, but no longer know.

APHROCHROME

Copyright © Jane Emerssen 2022
First published in 2022 by JayStone Publications, Stonecroft, Bassenthwaite,
Keswick, Cumbria CA12 4RL.

www.jane-emerssen.co.uk

Distributed by Ingram Spark worldwide

British Library Cataloguing in Publication Data
A catalogue record for this book is available from the British Library

ISBN 978-0-9574310-3-4

Typeset in Dante by Amolibros, Milverton, Somerset
www.amolibros.com
This book production has been managed by Amolibros
Printed and bound by Ingram Spark worldwide

C J Dacre began writing both fiction and non-fiction under a variety of names after many years working for several different local authorities.

Originally from Carlisle, Dacre's formal education and career progression were both punctuated by frequent moves around the UK. These ultimately provided a rich source of background material on which to draw as an author, resulting in the full-length family sagas *A Necessary Fiction* and the sequel *A Plain and Simple Truth* published under the name Jane Emerssen.

Brought up on a diet of second-hand *Argosy* magazines, Isaac Asimov and Arthur C Clarke, Dacre returned to the world of the imagination with *Walking in Darkness,* a miscellany of previously published and unpublished science fiction short stories.

Aphrochrome was originally drafted several years ago and left sitting on the back burner while other projects took centre stage. Now this has been successfully completed, Dacre is currently compiling a second miscellany of science fiction short stories with the working title *Orange-Coloured Sky.*

ACKNOWLEDGEMENTS

My grateful thanks must go to NASA whose accessible and informative website provided me over the several years involved in the development of this novel with invaluable Lunar data, including more recently details of the 2024 Artemis program envisaging human utilisation of the Moon as the first step towards the eventual exploration of Mars. I have also taken advantage of the most up-to-date information made available on the Martian environment provided by the landers, Curiosity, Insight and Perseverance.

My thanks too go to Emily Lakdawalla on the Planetary Science website for drawing my attention to a 2013 paper published by Silva and Romero in Planetary and Space Science with the daunting title Optimal Longitudes Determination for the Station Keeping of Areostationary Satellites. Without this I would have been totally ignorant of the existence of the four stable and unstable points of Martian gravity where geostationary, or in the case of Mars, areostationary, satellites could be located and maintained over time. I am equally grateful for the excellent poster Mars - Exploring the Red Planet produced by the National Geographic Society, Washington, which enabled me to pinpoint these locations and provided additional data on the two Martian moons, Phobos and Deimos.

On a very personal level, thanks are due to my fellow writer Carol Main Cook for her unstinting support and inspiration during the dispiriting time of prolonged lockdown, and to Jane

Tatam who patiently shepherded me through the hard graft of the publication process to reach a satisfactory conclusion.

CJD
July 2022

ONE

There are many ways to die in space. Oliphant had investigated most of them.

Inside his bulky white sterilised oversuit, he listened to the steady rhythm of his breathing coming back to him over the phones. Standing next to him, encased from head to toe in a similar suit, Senior Security Officer Davron, Head of Security at Shackleton Moonbase, was adjusting his helmet.

Oliphant checked his internal intercom and Davron acknowledged, his voice attracting an echo somewhere in the system.

"Ready?" Oliphant asked.

Davron nodded.

"Then let's get this over with." He led the way from the mortuary changing area, through the ultraviolet shower booths and into the anteroom with its imposing double steel doors beyond. Through the polyplastic laminate insets, the Mortician, shrouded in her sealed silvered worksuit, was waiting to meet them.

"Chief Security Officer Oliphant from ConCorp Regional Security, and SSO Davron," Oliphant announced to the communication panel.

The Mortician palmed the door control with a gloved hand and the doors parted, sliding noiselessly into their casings before closing softly behind them once they'd passed, sealing them off from the rest of the station.

From behind his helmet visor, Oliphant surveyed the room. It reminded him chillingly of one of the ice-caves on Europa, the impression marginally lessened by the ranks of gun-metal grey cabinets ranged along the length of one wall. Ten banks – six high. The rest of the room was a wasteland of eye-watering whiteness – walls, ceiling, floor, dissection slabs – even the flood of light washing over everything from the downlighters.

The Mortician, hindered by the thermal padding of her suit, moved with a deliberate slowness to the wall cabinets. At the control panel adjacent to them, she ran a finger lightly over a list of names and registered the relevant co-ordinates. An almost inaudible *bleep* acknowledged her request.

A drawer, two up from the top of the fifth bank, opened with an elegant slowness and extended to its full depth. There was a small *clunk* as its mechanism latched into the vertical runners on either side. After a reflective pause, it began a stately descent to waist height, stopped, shuddered slightly and was still.

The Mortician beckoned them forward. "Karoli Koblinski," she said through the phones, her voice devoid of any emotion.

As Oliphant moved, a hint of chilled air wafted through the atmospheric filter of the helmet. It had a strange, vaguely unpleasant quality. It reminded him of his distant childhood; of winter afternoons running along a wind-swept Scottish shore – and less attractively, of rotting seaweed.

With practised fingers the Mortician unsealed the black body bag to reveal its contents and held one of the edges back to give Oliphant an unrestricted view. He leaned forward, encumbered by the voluminous folds of the oversuit, several sizes too large, he decided, even for a man of his dimensions.

The dead man occupying the bag was interesting. He must have been somewhere around his late twenties or early thirties, taller than average with a rangy but muscular frame hinting at an underlying strength. Above the sturdy neck and pronounced

Adam's apple, his square jaw had darkened with the stubble of beard that dead men grow. The face itself was remarkable, its features perfectly symmetrical; the nose straight and slim; the mouth finely curved, the blue lips slightly parted to reveal the whiteness of the even teeth beneath. But it was the hair that riveted Oliphant's attention: it was a natural jet-black – not in itself uncommon – but its style was to say the least – eccentric. From forehead to crown, and on either side down to the pierced ears with their gold studs, it was close-cropped; elsewhere it grew long and glossy in thick, luxuriant waves down to his shoulders. Alive, this man had undoubtedly been an eye-catching individual. In death, he still retained the aura of someone very much out of the mainstream.

Oliphant straightened from his examination. He would think about the hair later. "Post mortem scan results?" he asked the Mortician, noticing as he spoke that his visor fogged slightly giving the corpse a passing ghost-like quality.

"Initial findings show signs of concussion caused by the head striking the helmet. Cause of death however was asphyxia."

"Which means?"

"He ran out of air," she said neutrally. "One of the better ways to go, they say."

Oliphant didn't feel the need to pursue this as an option. "Time of death?"

"Life functions ceased approximately two hours before retrieval. Too late for Vindegaard intervention."

Davon cleared his throat. "The full details are in the report if you would like to see them."

"Not particularly, Mister Davron. I'm more interested in circumstances. Times. Places. People."

Davron stiffened visibly at the rebuff, and the Mortician's unblinking gaze wavered briefly, quick to register the tension between the two men.

Damnation, thought Oliphant. That wasn't what I intended.

There were times when he seriously considered the possibility that the multicultural soup of his Russian-Scots heritage had seriously inhibited his social skills. Often, without any intentional effort on his part, he noticed he could produce an instant wariness in the most casual acquaintance – a jumpy nervousness that killed the easy flow of conversation at a stroke. But, he consoled himself, perhaps this was nothing more than a reflection of his perfected interrogation techniques, or how his opinions came across when he expressed them using the ugly syntax of UniCom, spawned as it was from an even less attractive source – InterSlang – the junked together lingo of the international space pioneers way back in the 2190s.

He indicated to the Mortician he'd seen enough, thanked her, and made for the door, motioning Davron to follow.

The comfortable warmth of the changing area with its diffused lighting came as a welcome relief to the chill sterility of the mortuary. Oliphant was keen to rid himself of the ridiculous oversuit. He turned off the internal intercom and released the visor clasps, hoisting the helmet upwards, carefully avoiding his beard. He checked the communicator phones were still in position and replaced the helmet in the sterile unit, setting the decontamination program to run. He was less inclined to be so meticulous with the disposable oversuit, peeling it off in a series of rapid movements and dumping it without ceremony into the recyclation chute. The flap closed behind it with a satisfying *plop*.

Ignoring Davron, he checked his appearance in the full-length mirror by the exit and straightened out the black fabric of his stationsuit, smoothing down the gold-braided epaulettes with their three bars, and the flying-eagle badge above the name-tab on the breast pocket. Leonid James Oliphant: Chief Security Officer, sometimes known to his closest acquaintances as Leo or James, but never as Jim.

Not bad, he thought, studying his image and mentally comparing himself with the physique of the man in the body bag. At fifty-eight he was reaching the peak of his condition: well-built, vigorous, square-jawed with a neatly trimmed beard, he had fox-red hair, and a healthy skin tone that tended to freckle under ultra-violet. His uniform suited him. He carried his rank well, nurturing an easy air of authority acquired from not suffering fools gladly, and a deserved reputation for getting results. Yes – he could be polite – when necessary, but almost by accident he'd cultivated an underlying element of menace in his tone of voice and intensity of gaze. Combined, these attributes were almost as intimidating as the implicit threat embodied in the stun-gun he wore on his hip. On reflection, he thought, maybe he shouldn't be so quick to blame everything on his genes.

He shifted his focus. Behind him in the mirror was the lean, athletic frame of SSO Davron newly emerged from his oversuit. Like a butterfly from its chrysalis, Oliphant thought, testing its wings.

Davron was adjusting his collar and studiously avoiding eye contact. The only hint of what he might be thinking, if any were needed, was the tightness of his jawline and the pinched-in curve of his nostrils. He was clearly not pleased: he might be twenty years Oliphant's junior and subordinate, but at Shackleton he was security top-dog, and visibly smarting at being slighted by the presence of a superior officer giving the orders on his patch. With some SSOs, Oliphant would have enjoyed their discomfiture, but with Davron it was different: it touched a raw nerve in his own psyche, not least because Davron cut an impressive figure and stood slightly taller than himself, which gave him a definite edge. He was better looking too, with his clean-cut features and immaculately groomed dark curly hair. He looked the part, and when he walked, he had the air of a man who was going places – and intended getting there. Given a few more years under his belt and Oliphant suspected Davron would be breathing down his neck ready to challenge him for those gold bars on his epaulettes.

He adjusted his own collar and turned from the mirror. "Ready?" he asked.

Davron nodded and followed him out of the changing area in silence

In the cream-coloured MediCentre corridor beyond, white-suited Medics went about their business lost in a low hum of conversation. The presence of two Security Officers held little interest for them.

Oliphant strode out in the direction of the elevator shafts, Davron pacing him stride for stride, his mouth still firmly clamped shut. There seemed little possibility of a thaw in the atmosphere between them. "Well, Mister Davron," Oliphant asked. "What's the story so far?"

Davron provided the details in a clipped monotone. "Patrolman Friegler discovered Koblinski trapped under a bank of empty dex-racks in Storage Hangar Six during a routine external inspection."

"When?"

"At zero-eight forty-five hours on the twenty-fourth."

"Any signs of a struggle?"

"None visible."

"What do the Sniffers say?" Oliphant asked, casually downgrading the expertise of the Shackleton Forensic Team.

Davron ignored the slight. "Preliminary investigations suggest he was climbing the dex-racks when they fell, taking him with them."

"Why would he be climbing a bank of empty dex-racks?"

Davron's expression remained carved in stone. "We've no idea. There was nothing at the incident scene to provide any clues. Do you want me to arrange a site visit?"

Oliphant shook his head. "Absolutely not," he said brusquely. External walkabouts made his blood run cold. He avoided them whenever possible. Not everyone was a natural Spacer.

"Friegler's logged report is available if you'd like to run through it."

"I'll do that as soon as I've checked out Koblinski's background data. There might be something in his history which'll give us a lead."

They'd reached the elevators at the second quadrant intersection. No one else was waiting. Oliphant thumped the call button, his eyes watching the level indicator but his thoughts drifting. For no particular reason he recalled Koblinski's eccentric hair-style. "Who was he, Mister Davron, this Koblinski? Stores? Maintenance? Techno? What?"

The elevator light blinked, the doors sighed open and they entered the cocooned, softer lighting of the empty interior.

Davron pressed for ground level and kept his eyes fixed dead ahead. "He was a Folkster," he said. The elevator surged slightly, its rapid upward thrust to ground level barely noticeable.

"A Hurdy-Gurdy man!" Oliphant said. making no attempt to hide his contempt for this profession, noticing Davron's reluctance to endorse his highly derogatory description of the deceased.

The elevator slowed, stopped and the doors slid back with a faint hiss revealing the strip-lit ground floor corridor of the Administration and Security Section. Three grey-suited Administrators who were waiting to enter the elevator deferred to the presence of Security Officers and stepped back to let them pass.

"Don't you like the term, Mister Davron? Hurdy-Gurdy?" Oliphant asked as they set off down the corridor.

"I'm not sure I'd describe Karoli Koblinski in those terms, Sir. He was a top-rate performer. Lead male vocalist with The Choralians. Went under the name Karo Deus."

The information meant nothing to Oliphant. He had no truck with Entertainers. They were almost as much trouble as Aberrants: flotsam and jetsam living on the periphery of societal norms with all the potential for criminal activity of one sort or another.

Entertainers were semi-anarchists; Aberrants were total – that was the only difference.

They passed through the open airlock marking the boundary between Quadrants Two and Three without further conversation. Stopping outside the sepia door marked Q3-20. Oliphant palmed the control panel by the casing and released the personalised locking system. The door eased back slowly as if embarrassed at having to reveal a room barely larger than a small store. Like most of the temporary offices in the Administration, Communications and MediCentre complex, it was windowless, soulless and totally claustrophobic.

"Take a seat," Oliphant suggested and eased his way between the standard modular furniture to the automat dispenser set into the opposite wall. He was keen to remove the indefinable flavour of the mortuary atmosphere still clinging to the roof of his mouth. He selected a multi-juice cocktail and downed two in quick succession. "Want one, Mister Davron?" he offered.

"No thank you, Sir," Davron said, edging down carefully into the tight space between the wall and Oliphant's desk occupied by the only spare chair in the room. The door sensors registered the access was clear and closed sluggishly behind him.

Oliphant decided to ignore Davron's continued frostiness and made himself comfortable in the high-backed auto-contour chair, the only available status symbol going spare at the time of his arrival. "Then let's start, shall we?" he said, accessing the data terminal with his security code. The screen cleared and Koblinski's life unfolded before him.

KOBLINSKI: Karoli Tadeus
[90/EEUR/2226/40/FJ937541T]
Status: Male
Profession: Entertainer k/a Karo DEUS

A string of cross-references filled the next two screens listing every connection Koblinski had ever made. A number of these had blocks on them limiting access only to the International Enforcement Agency. Oliphant smiled. ConCorp might be a big-fish conglomerate corporation but in the real world there were still some limits to its power and influence.

The next screen charted Koblinski's career. It was chequered, as Oliphant had expected, painting the usual picture of a drifter straying more than once or twice along the way. From around 2246 there was a string of cross-references that spoke volumes to anyone with even a smattering of inside intelligence on low-grade criminal activity.

Then came 2251 when he'd registered an official five-year partnership with a female – Cassandra Diamantides – vocalist, known professionally as Cass Diamond. For a Folkster, Oliphant thought, a five-year commitment was something out of the ordinary. They must have had a really good thing going. A brief foray into her file told him it had potential – more than just interesting reading to pass the time of day during a bad patch of solar flare activity.

The same year the names Theomenides Xenonopoulos and Umo Manaus appeared, known in Folkster circles as Theo Xenon and plain Umo respectively. Originally billed as 'Calliope's Children', this duo had eventually joined up with Diamantides and Koblinski under the registered name of 'The Choralians'. Oliphant briefly side-stepped into their respective files and mused over his findings.

Umo's background promised rich pickings: a street urchin in Guatemala, he'd innumerable counts of petty crime and was listed as a Prostitute up until '48, by which time he'd reached the advanced age of sixteen years. His list of cross-references was mind-blowing.

Xenon proved more run-of-the-mill. Eight years older than

Umo, on the face of it his background was unexceptional until their paths crossed in '48. They'd registered a three-year partnership only a few months later, renewed in '51 and again in '54. Umo's frequent backsliding into petty crime seemed to have kept Xenon busy pulling him back onto the straight-and-narrow on a regular basis until '51: there were marker-codes showing he'd stood bail, paid fines and generally muddied himself trying to keep Umo's head above murky waters. Beyond '51 there were no further infringements – not even minor ones. Xenon's persistence must have finally paid off. That made him interesting.

A brief description of The Choralians' activities after '51 listed Earthside tours for both that year and '52. They'd gone transcontinental with the exception of Antarctica which meant there was plenty of scope for involvement in just about anything and everything – if they'd had a mind to it. Had they? – he wondered. The data went on to list their specialities. It was dominated by Folkster themes, but strangely at odds with this were occasional 'special' bookings to perform the distinctly tacky entertainment known in the business as 'surger-pop'.

Oliphant scrolled on. Another name surfaced – Miles McMichael, their agent from '51. Oliphant smiled grimly, relishing this find. At last there was something solid to get his teeth into. 'Smiler' McMichael was too smooth an operator to be entirely straight, but somehow nothing ever stuck to him. His hands were always immaculately clean. That was his trade-mark – Mr Spotless. All the Entertainers in his stable suddenly became whiter than white once he took them under his wing. There wasn't so much as a toenail put out of line afterwards. What didn't tie up was the simple fact that around the time Smiler's Entertainers became as pure as the driven snow, an awful lot of nasties began creeping out of the woodwork. Oliphant and his seniors in ConCorp Central Security had already noted that particular point.

He read on, absorbed in the data while across the cell-like room, Davron sat rigidly in his chair, waiting, his face a mask.

In '52 the space tours began: two short-hops to Shackleton Base and then in '54 a long-haul out to Herschel Minor, the leisure station providing service breaks for personnel in the Uranian Sector. The group had contracted to provide in-flight entertainment for the six-month outward run followed by a year on-station and the in-flight entertainment for the seven-month journey back. In late February 2256, they'd boarded the heavy cruiser *Ptolemy* for the return flight. Their brief stopover back at Shackleton was listed for the beginning of September. At that point Koblinski's file came to an abrupt end with the message –

Died: 24/09/56 Shackleton Moonbase
**[Post-mortem report available on application to CentraFile. Authorised
personnel only.]**

A flashing red marker-code blipped spasmodically at the bottom right-hand corner of the screen – the same marker-code that had alerted Oliphant back on Earth to another non-standard death. Recently, there'd been several other fatal accidents on ConCorp stations – more than usual. The causes of death were all different, all apparently accidental, but Oliphant's gut feeling told him otherwise and he'd authorised all subsequent non-standard deaths to be marker-coded. It was beginning to look like these were part of a larger, and as yet unrecognised pattern and Koblinski had just become another piece in the grotesque jigsaw.

Oliphant sank back into the contours of his chair and gave Davron what he hoped would be taken as an attempt to include him in the investigation. "Right then, Mister Davron," he said. "Give me your thoughts. What's the lead male vocalist of a Folkster group doing going external walkabout in Storage Hangar Six?"

Two

When Koblinski's body was found on 24 September 2256, Ben Davron had just completed his first six months as Head of Shackleton Security. He'd also just returned from a spell of much-needed home leave and felt ill-at-ease.

He'd be the first to admit he'd been hungry for promotion. When it came, he'd been elated, but his enthusiasm had been quickly dampened by the prospect of the posting. Not for a moment had he anticipated anything other than an Earthside commission, principally because spacework had never, up until then, been considered suitable for a first-time command. It had been a tribute to the high regard his seniors had of his capabilities that he'd not only been nominated, but ultimately chosen.

Pivotal to most of ConCorp's off-Earth commercial activities, Shackleton was an awesome responsibility, and Davron had every intention of making a success of it. But in his heart he'd have preferred a duty roster that didn't take him from hearth and home for three months at a stretch.

Putting it in a nutshell, he missed Miriam and the children. The twins, Shimon and Esther were twelve now, hovering on the uncertain brink between childhood and adolescence. Over those first six months of his posting, he'd already seen noticeable changes in them both, but particularly in Esther. Maybe the next time, or the time after, he'd arrive home and find her a stranger to him: a woman in her own right. Shimon too was becoming something of a handful, knowing his father wouldn't be there to help exert the restraining hand of paternal control.

The lack of Miriam's presence was something else. There were times when her absence from his bed was a palpable pain to him. He missed her passion; her company; her humour; her vibrant energy. No, she wasn't beautiful in the accepted sense of the term, but her laughter and the excitement she could generate from even the most mundane everyday tasks made her irresistibly attractive. And she missed him too, which only made his absence harder to bear.

"I'll be back in Haifa for Hanukkah," he'd said the morning he'd left, wishing with every atom of his body it were sooner.

Koblinski's death had hit his desk as soon as he'd logged himself back on duty at 0900 hours. Patrolman Friegler had reported the incident fifteen minutes earlier to the Deputy Head of Security, Nadine Tereshkhova, and her message was waiting for him on his return, along with her report on yet another surveillance equipment failure.

By the time he'd kitted out to go external and reached Storage Hangar Six, the Medics were already on the scene along with the meticulous Forensic Team. The body had been scanned and was being prepared for delivery to the mortuary, and then the tedious process of searching for evidence had begun.

He'd barely had time to read the preliminary findings when Communications notified him that CSO Leonid Oliphant would be on-station with the next ferry in two days' time. He would be heading-up the investigation. Why he was coming up to Shackleton was as unwelcome as it was a mystery: his remit according to the *Gazette* was illicit trafficking, particularly the potentially lethal mind-warp products pedalled by MegaJoy Inc. On the basis of initial evidence however, Davron could find nothing to connect Koblinski with illicit trafficking of any sort. The security sweep on departure from the Uranus stations and the double-check on arrival at Shackleton had passed him as clean – and that went for the rest of The Choralians as well. If Koblinski wasn't a mind-warp courier or trafficker, the only possibility was he was carrying information in his head – the most difficult sort of trafficking to detect.

Reduced to a feeling of impotence, Davron had restricted himself to practicalities: he'd booked a VIP Suite for Oliphant in the Carnegie Wing of the Accommodation Unit, arranged for a temporary office to be allocated, and ensured all communication systems Oliphant might need were scrambler-enabled. The fact that the office itself was less than adequate for someone of Oliphant's rank added to Davron's concern. His senior's reputation as a domineering and thoroughly difficult person to work with didn't help.

With what little time he'd got left, he made sure he'd covered all the salient points essential to completing the opening stages of the investigation, points which Oliphant would undoubtedly pick up on if not adequately dealt with, particularly the results of the initial interviews with the remaining members of The Choralians. These however had yielded nothing of substance except the urgent need to call in a Psy-Medic to administer controlled trauma treatment to Koblinski's surviving partner, Cass Diamond, who'd suffered an emotional collapse. Davron hoped Oliphant wouldn't hold him accountable for this.

By 1500 hours on 26 September, Davron had exhausted the limited range of functions he could usefully perform before Oliphant's arrival and reluctantly made his way to the Ferry Terminal to meet his uninvited guest.

Since Duval's propulsion system had become standard on all ferries since the '20s, travel between the home planet and its natural satellite had been reduced to commuting distance. The shuttle service that ran twice a week completed the journey on sub-thrust power in less than a day. As a result, it had become depressingly easy for ConCorp executives of one sort or another to make their presence felt on their nearest company out-station.

The ferry arrived punctually as always. From the Flight Control Room, Davron had watched it manoeuvre down onto Landing Port 2 with a sense of dispiriting emptiness, acutely aware of having to maintain his authority on-station in the face of a high profile presence. Oliphant's arrival seemed to imply the higher echelons of ConCorp Regional Security now lacked confidence in Shackleton's SSO, an implication not lost on others either: Davron had already noticed his subordinates weighing up his reactions to this unexpected turn of events.

Within a few minutes the passengers had disembarked and boarded a lunar geotracker to transport them to the Reception Area for security screening before being admitted to the main sub-lunar complex.

Davron had made his way to the Security Zone, conscious amongst other things that his mouth was dry; his hands were sweating yet strangely cold despite the comfortable 21° Celsius atmosphere, and the fabric of his stationsuit was chafing uncomfortably against the sensitive skin at the side of his neck.

He had never met Oliphant before, and the experience proved every bit as unnerving as he'd expected. As soon as the robust, bearded figure had entered the Reception Area and begun removing his travelsuit with that no-nonsense air of someone with a sense of purpose, Davron had been left with the solid impression he'd be in a permanent state of defensiveness every second his superior remained on-station.

Three hours later in Oliphant's cramped office that initial feeling had intensified rather than diminished. Oliphant had retired briefly to his quarters; cursory introductions were over; the body had been inspected, and now they were down to the nitty-gritty. Oliphant was relaxed, composed, already at home – and waiting for answers. As far as Davron was concerned, he'd have preferred being cornered minus his stun-gun facing a Crazy with a crow bar.

THREE

Oliphant waited with unaccustomed patience for an answer to his question. "Well, Mister Davron," he said after there was no immediate response. "What *do* you think Koblinski was doing in Storage Hangar Six?"

Davron braved the probing with a stiff dignity. "At the moment I've nothing to go on, Sir," he said, a hint of reined-back anger betrayed by the tone of his voice.

Oliphant ploughed on. "Then we'd better start from the beginning, hadn't we? Beside Patrolman Friegler, who else has been questioned?"

Davron's jaw knotted perceptibly and he dropped his gaze to his hands, reeling off the information as it if had been written in blood on his palms. "The stores team and the supervisor on-duty when the body was found and Security Officers Durnig and Cornwall – they were completing a random spot-check at the time –"

Oliphant stopped him. "Why? Was there any indication something out of the ordinary was in the wind?"

Davron appeared irritated by the interruption. "No."

"Then why was a random spot-check necessary?"

Davron looked him straight in the eye, this time with undisguised hostility. "A precaution. When I came on-station six months ago, petty pilfering was on the increase. I decided to bring in random patrols."

"And?"

"The pilfering stopped and I kept the patrols in place – as a precaution."

"Right – so what time did they patrol Hangar Six?"

"Around zero-four-fifty hours."

"Who else has been questioned?"

Davron resumed his account with a dead-pan expression fixed firmly in place. "Roxanne Hu, the receptionist on-duty at the Stage Door Accommodation Unit and of course, the rest of The Choralians."

"Do we know what time Koblinski left the Stage Door Accommodation Unit?"

Davron broke eye contact and there was a long pause before he answered. "Unfortunately – no."

Oliphant made no immediate comment, watching Davron sink into the embarrassment of admitting this monumental failure. "Really?" he said, ensuring his tone made his feelings on the subject quite explicit. "I find that very hard to believe, Mister Davron. What happened to the visual surveillance record?"

The muscles in Davron's jaw tensed. "The system went down at zero-one-forty-five and was out until zero-seven-twenty hours."

"Wasn't that unusual?"

"No. We've had three systems failures with surveillance in the last six weeks."

"Equipment failures or sabotage?"

"Equipment failures – in all cases."

"Any proof?"

Davron eyed him coldly. "If the Technos tell me it's equipment failure, Sir, I have to take their word for it."

"Have you taken this up with CentreTech?"

"Yes – they're still looking into it."

"Okay – so what's the Receptionist's story?"

"She swears she didn't see Koblinski leave. And I can't exactly say she's a liar when there's no record of the external airlock being activated between midnight and zero-eight-hundred hours."

"Well he obviously went out, so the airlock *was* activated. Do you think there's a connection between the logging system failure and surveillance malfunction?"

"None that I know of. They're operated by separate control systems."

Oliphant stored this crucial piece of information for the moment and considered another tack. "What about Koblinski's partner – what's-her-name? Couldn't she come up with anything useful?"

"Cassandra Diamantides? No, nothing we could build on. Koblinski hadn't said anything to her about arranging to meet anyone – and certainly nothing about going external. She'd taken a dose of SoundSleep and turned in around twenty-three-fifteen. The next thing she knew she was being woken up with the news he'd been found dead."

"Does her statement tally?"

"It's valid. No physical indicators she was lying. The mediscan showed traces of SoundSleep in her system consistent with the dose taken around twelve hours earlier."

"What else does she take?"

"Nothing. She's clean. And she's adamant she never touches enhancers – never has and never will. The mediscan and biodata seem to bear this out."

"You mean she hasn't been caught yet."

Davron made no comment.

Oliphant stretched, leaned back in his chair and considered what they'd got to work on. "All right," he said, thinking aloud. "Koblinski disentangles himself from the arms of his beloved some time during the small hours of 24 September and manages to check out from the Stage Door unseen and unlogged. Now how might he have achieved that do you think?"

"Theoretically, it's impossible. As soon as the airlock opens a time-check gets logged."

"Exactly. So if we assume Koblinski hadn't mastered the art of walking through walls, what are we left with?"

"The receptionist was either distracted or absent and he had the means of opening the airlock without triggering the logging mechanism."

"And the only way he could have done that was by having the technical know-how. Looking at Koblinski's file, I wouldn't have said his background gave him an alpha-rating in that particular field, would you?"

Davron agreed with a small nod.

"Let's face it, he was about as remote from being a TechnoPro as it's humanly possible to be. So what does that tell us?"

Davron clasped his hands together, studying the nails carefully before speaking. "Either he went out with someone who had the know-how – or he'd been given the means of getting out himself."

"Agreed."

"But Roxanne Hu swears she didn't see Koblinski – or anyone else."

"What about her down-time? She does take comfort breaks, I presume?"

"Of course. They're mandatory."

"So when did she take them?"

"From memory, once about zero-one-thirty, again somewhere around zero-three-thirty and zero-five-hundred hours – they're all logged – none of them lasting longer than five minutes."

Oliphant weighed up the likelihood of someone overriding the various security systems within that time-scale and decided it was just about possible – just. "Does she follow the same pattern every night?" he asked.

"Roughly," Davron acknowledged. "A few minutes either side."

"Maybe that's all it would take – but whoever it was would've needed to know she had a fairly regular pattern. I'm beginning to suspect Koblinski definitely didn't go out on his own. The time-scale's too tight. Someone had to be with him – someone who knew Hu's shift patterns and had the relevant techno-skills to override all the systems in double-quick time."

"Somebody already here – on Shackleton?"

"I think so. Maybe someone holding down a low-grade posting. Someone who could move around on-station without attracting too much attention. Cleaning Operative – Stores – Maintenance – any one of those jobs. How often do we notice them?"

Davron conceded the point.

Another thought crossed Oliphant's mind. "Was Koblinski wearing his own travelsuit?" he asked.

"No, it was a standard issue from the maintenance locker room."

"And the air-pack?"

"The same."

"Right. And you say his suit and air-pack were checked over for damage?"

"Yes. Just slight grazing on the back of the helmet at the point of contact with the ground. Some abrasions on the front of the suit consistent with the racking shelves catching the fabric."

"No air leakage?"

"None."

"Did it look as if he'd tried to get himself out from under the racks?"

"No, probably because he was either stunned or unconscious. His right arm was pinned down under one of the racking shelves which would have been difficult to shift. The other was broken, twisted under him."

Something wasn't quite right with that explanation to Oliphant's way of thinking. "So he had no way of raising anyone on his communicator either?"

"It would have been impossible."

"Not a pretty choice, was it?" Oliphant mused. "Waiting for help – or waiting to die?" He didn't expect Davron to answer. "So how long does a standard Shackleton air-pack last these days?"

"Four hours max."

"And if Koblinski was dead at least two hours before retrieval, he breathed his last sometime around zero-six-thirty. With that information we assume he left the Stage Door around zero-three-thirty, tying in with Hu's statement?"

"Yes, that's what I put in my report."

"But he wasn't in Storage Hangar Six at zero-four-fifty, was he? The random patrol guys would have spotted him." Another anomaly. "How long does it take to get from the Stage Door to the storage facilities? An hour? And hour-and-a-half?

Davron frowned. "No – half-an-hour at the most."

"So where was he in the interim? And what was he doing?"

There was a long pause before Davron answered. When he did, his voice betrayed his frustration. "Without the surveillance footage, we've no idea."

Oliphant leaned forward and made a concentrated effort to soften his approach. "Ben," he said confidentially, "I think we need to look at possible alternatives. What if he left the Stage Door at around zero-five-hundred with a reduced air-pack."

Davron's expression registered his uncertainty at Oliphant's sudden shift in tone. "That's not possible," he said cautiously. "All air-packs are routinely refilled to maximum after use. Maintenance would have seen to it – no question. It's standard procedure."

Oliphant ventured a smile. "Wouldn't you say we're dealing with a series of events here which don't exactly fit the 'standard procedure' category? I think we have to consider a different scenario, because at the moment all we have is Koblinski going external by some means or other – possibly without a full air-pack – making his way over to the storage facilities – and that's a tough call for someone not used to spacework, wouldn't you say? And once he gets there, what does he do? – He shins up a bank of empty storage racks for no apparent reason and brings the lot down on himself. Doesn't make sense. What about the racking? Was there much damage?"

"Two sections had pulled adrift and twisted. Maintenance are checking if some of the connections had come loose – or been tampered with. Nothing conclusive so far."

"Okay, but could it collapse under a man's weight in zero-point-one-seven gravity?"

"Only under exceptional circumstances, apparently. Loading is done horizontally, so there's no external force outside the racking. They're not designed to be used as ladders. Stress test results show they could potentially become unstable once someone of Koblinski's size and weight reached the fourth tier."

"Any Moonquakes at the time?"

"None recorded. In any case, Dex-racks are specifically designed to absorb them, and storage pallet-loading is automatically suspended during any quakes above three on the Richter Scale."

"This doesn't make sense – Koblinski was only two tiers up."

"I raised this point with the Stores Supervisor. He doesn't understand it either. He said the only incidents of racking malfunction in the past occurred when sections had been knocked out of alignment and a connection had come adrift because a loader had gone out of operational synch. But that's uncommon – and there's no report of a loader malfunction for the last five months."

"Okay, Ben, let's put that to one side for a moment. If we assume Koblinski didn't go external on his own, there must have been a very pressing reason for him to be persuaded to do something so dangerous. And if the person, or persons who were with him in the storage facilities—" He left his comment hanging in the air waiting for Davron to spot the obvious element he'd left unsaid.

Davron caught the drift. "Then that 'person', or 'persons' must have seen him fall?"

"Exactly."

"And left him there."

Oliphant nodded.

"So we're talking murder?"

"It's the only explanation that fits. Looks like Koblinski posed some kind of threat. Or maybe he knew something. Whatever it was, someone wanted to apply pressure – and maybe a tampered air-pack was the means of doing it. Once Koblinski knew he'd only a limited time to get back, he'd want to get the hell out of the situation a.s.a.p." Oliphant eased himself out of the chair with his beaker and helped himself to a third drink. "So the real question is – was the incident with the racking an accident, or something else? Did he fall – or was he pushed?"

Davron looked up sharply. "No – he was *pulled!*"

Oliphant nodded. "I'd say everything points to that. Koblinski was trying to get away – probably hoping to make it to the top of the racks and a clear escape route. But he was out of his depth. He wasn't a Spaceworker. In that suit he'd be clumsy and slow. If you were in his position trying to move around in low gravity – and for the sake of argument you missed your footing climbing up those racks – what would you do if you started to fall?"

"I'd twist and get clear."

"Exactly. And you'd have the time to do it. Koblinski was so damned determined to escape, he hung on until the whole caboodle came down on top of him. "

"But whoever was trying to pull him down could hang on until the last minute and then step out of the way."

"And let the racking finish the job."

"But why kill him?"

Oliphant finished his drink. "That's what I'm here to find out. Director of Security Mendoza is getting worried. ConCorp's

Board of Directors are getting worried. There's been a string of 'accidental' deaths over the last few months – some on stations, others on flightcraft. They don't quite add up and there's no obvious link between them. All genders. Partnered and unpartnered. Different professions. Enhancer users and non-users. There's not even a common denominator in network affiliations – which in my book leaves only one possibility."

"Mind-warp?"

Oliphant nodded. "It's the one possibility that ticks all the boxes."

"But if it is mind-warp, and there's a black market organisation pedalling MegaJoy products out here, ConCorp's going to lose a hell of a lot of Spaceworkers."

"Or end up with a Red Alert that could easily threaten the integrity of an entire station – which is why I've been given *carte blanche* to investigate. It's no reflection on you, Ben. I want you to know that."

Davron showed no sign of being reassured. "Will you need any back-up from my team?" he asked.

Oliphant side-stepped the question. "I'll let you know when it's needed," he said, knowing there was little chance of Davron ever playing anything other than a minor role. "Central Security like to use a Freelance in these situations," he explained, keeping things casual. "They'll pick the best Agent for the job. All I'll get is the code name and re-routed product once they're in place. It's the best way. Direct contacts are too easy to trace – you know that. And we're too high-profile for this type of job. In or out of uniform, we behave differently – and it shows." He ventured a smile. "Hardly covert material, are we?"

Davron shifted slightly in his chair, but said nothing.

Oliphant realised he was wasting his time trying to smooth down a ruffled ego. Feeling the claustrophobic effect of the small office and Davron's tangible regret beginning to gnaw at him, he decided to move on. The clock on the opposite wall flicked over to 2003 hours. He pushed himself up from behind his desk and straightened his uniform. "I'd like to have a talk with this Cassandra Diamantides," he said, taking the conversation off at a tangent. "What state is she likely to be in now? Coherent? Capable of answering a few questions, do you think?"

Davron acknowledged the end of the interview by getting to his feet. "I can ask the Psy-Medic to bring her here if you like," he offered.

Oliphant shook his head. He wanted a change of surroundings, not the prospect of more than two people in his office at once. "No, I think I'll pay her a visit in her own quarters. She might be less on her guard and easier to interrogate. Anyone with her?"

"Theo Xenon. Do you want me along?"

"No, if you don't mind. I'll get in touch later. But thanks for your help by the way." He hoped his smile would take the edge off Davron's casual dismissal, but from Davron's expression, it didn't seem very likely.

FOUR

Cassandra Diamantides lay on her disordered bed, her eyes closed. Behind her eyelids she listened to the silence, conscious of its straining demands on her, and the void which refused to be filled; conscious of wanting to feel pain, and being unable to register anything except the experience of living the moment – of listening to her heartbeat.

She knew Theo was with her, holding her hand. His presence was a tangible reassurance, bringing with it a balm which flowed from his touch into her veins. She was adrift, but somehow safe. He had been there since she could remember; since the Psy-Medic had administered the trauma regulator. He had become Eternity itself.

She opened her eyes slowly, seeing through a thin mist, and turned her head to look at him. In the subdued lighting of the sleeping area, she could just make out his features; his expression betraying inner, unspoken fears; his own pain. Theo, her new guardian. Theo, whose colouring and fine-boned features mirrored her own so closely.

"You're awake," he said softly. "You've slept a long time."

She listened to the sweet comforting rhythm of her mother tongue made more beautiful by the dark resonances within his voice, and let it wrap around her like a protective cloak. It eased the vague disquiet lingering in the corners of her mind. "Yes," she said at last, unable to manage more than the simplest of replies.

"Do you want me to stay?"

She nodded, the effort to say more too great.

He stroked a stray lock of hair from her forehead and smiled down at her. His eyes were lost in shadow, but she pictured them, liquid brown, filled with compassion. Karoli's had been grey, she remembered vaguely, occasionally tinged with a steely hardness. Sometimes he had needed that strength.

Now there was Theo. Theo. She said his name over and over again in her mind, like a kind of mantra, as though by saying it she would be protected from everything. Theo. Theo.

She closed her eyes again, trying to picture Karoli as she last remembered him. But his features refused to solidify: he had become a blur, a dull memory with no focus, lost to view behind a veil of sedation; a shifting mirage. Gone. A dull ache encircled her heart.

From somewhere far away came the sound of a door buzzer; an intrusive sound repeated twice more, each time a little longer; more insistent.

She felt Theo rise from the bed; her hand being placed on the coverlet, and a sense of coldness wash over her at the loss of human contact. She shivered. There was a pause, and then the sound of men's voices. One she recognised – Theo, his tone soft and lilting, like his singing voice, even when speaking in UniCom; the other – more demanding, with an underlying harshness that brooked no contradiction, its tones crudely emphasised by the communicator. There was the sigh of the door opening and the second voice entered: a disembodied baritone with a tendency to roll his 'r's very slightly in a way that refused to be identified as belonging to any particular language.

She slowly opened her eyes again, a vague curiosity stirring. The bulk of a tall man was silhouetted against the brighter light flooding through the doorway of the living area. He was standing on the threshold of her sleeping quarters; legs slightly apart; hands planted firmly on his hips. It was a disturbing vision: mysterious;

oddly exciting. It was talking at her, this voice from the silhouette, demanding her attention.

Her mind tingled softly in reply, playing strange songs in her head. They sang of the sudden stillness of a storm, and the silence of the earthquake; of danger and delight.

The voice and image began to coalesce into a complete entity; into something which profoundly unsettled her; something to be wary of; something she needed to think about very carefully.

FIVE

Oliphant stood in the doorway addressing the darkness beyond. "Cassandra Diamantides?" he asked sticking to UniCom. There was no answer. "I'm Chief Security Officer Oliphant. I want to ask you a few questions." There was still no answer. He turned up the lighting level a couple of notches and advanced into the sleeping area, ignoring the protestations of the man behind him who'd opened the door.

From the incredible disorder of an unmade bed, a gypsy of a woman was lying on her side enveloped in a scarlet kaftan fringed with gold-coloured tassels, watching him with large, intensely dark, but vacant eyes.

As soon as he stepped across the threshold into that room, Oliphant realised he was unprepared for this meeting. She had been a name on a potentially interesting file, nothing more. A Folkster. Now, in her presence, he was aware she was a great deal more. She seemed to generate a personal electricity; a force field he could almost touch, even in this reduced physical state; a potency he hadn't bargained for.

She was a profoundly disturbing sight, lying there, shimmering like a heat haze under the glow of the side lights. The soft folds of the fabric lay draped across her figure with all the voluptuousness of a Pre-Raphaelite painting, and her terrible inertia was in stark contrast to the disorder of the tumbled white sheets and the deep blue coverlet around her.

The warm closeness of the room only added to his sudden

sense of disorientation. A strangely aromatic fragrance invaded his nostrils, evoking images of startling clarity: deep, unexplored sensuality and intense physical pleasure. It made his spine tingle.

She was still watching him, expressionless, her face dominated by those large wide-spaced eyes beneath curving brows and a mass of jet-black hair that lay in confusion around her on the pillow. She remained perfectly still. One slender arm, the colour of dark ivory, had sometime earlier escaped the confines of the tasselled fringes of the kaftan and lay at rest, waiting, like its owner, for some hidden motivation, some unknown trigger, to come to life. For a moment, Oliphant wondered if it were wise to waken this slumbering vitality, this dangerous doll: its potential was almost frightening.

How old was she? He mentally recast the data on her file. Born sometime in 2230, he remembered. Roughly twenty-six. Her eyes looked older, her potency older still; as old as Eve.

"She cannot answer you," the man behind him insisted for a second time.

Oliphant turned and cast a critical eye over the speaker. He had similar features to Diamantides: a good-looking man if you liked the sort, somewhere in his early thirties with spaniel eyes and long lashes, a slim straight nose and generous mouth. His dark brown, almost black hair was worn in the same fashion as Koblinski's, the mane not so much tumbling in waves as curling back on itself around his small ears. Two slim gold hoops threaded his right lobe catching the light, and a large-linked gold chain encircled his neck. His clothes were no less eccentric. He wore a loose-fitting jade-coloured tabard covered in a bold design of exotic gilded birds over a full-length white muslin shift, and his feet were bare. The effect was stunning, but more of the barbarian than the Greek.

"And you are?" Oliphant asked him abruptly.

"Theomenides Xenonopoulos," the man replied simply in his softly spoken way. "Theo Xenon. A Choralian."

"Keeping her company, are you?" Oliphant nodded in the direction of the prone figure on the bed.

The man coloured, either through embarrassment or anger, Oliphant couldn't decide which.

In the brief silence that followed, there was the rustle of movement and Oliphant turned, instinctively his hand already sweeping downwards towards the gun on his hip. But there was no need: the woman was stirring with an exquisite slowness.

Like a dancer in slow motion she uncurled, sat up, and slid her feet over the side of the bed. The kaftan shimmered and slipped across her body as she moved. Two finely-boned feet planted themselves firmly on the floor as she stood up, a little hesitantly – straight, head erect, her hair wild about her face, her eyes still fixed on him as though in a trance. Their eyes met. Hell and damnation, Oliphant thought, his mind reeling through half-remembered stories of Medusa or Medea, no matter which: of enchantment. This woman could be anything she wanted to be – if she turned her mind to it.

She walked with a floating motion towards him – and passed him – into the living area. The fabric of the kaftan whispered like a breeze playing among the stems of tall grasses. After her came the scent that curled his toes, a sensation he'd almost forgotten: it reminded him briefly of Tina, and the warm summer nights of his misspent youth making love under the open sky.

He turned and followed her into the living area, aware there was something strangely different to the place compared with his own accommodation in the Carnegie Suite. There was an odd starkness he wasn't accustomed to. And then he realised why. The wall panes were blanked out. There were no images on any of them. Nothing: a functional cream-grey barrenness relieved only by the sparse and basic dark-brown station furniture. The room had been placed in mourning.

Walking ahead of him, she selected the low couch facing the

outer door and sat down with great dignity, lifting her feet onto it and arranging the kaftan around her. Xenon took up station behind her, his hands resting on the back of the couch. The picture was complete.

How many times had these two arranged themselves for holograms? – Oliphant wondered. It came naturally to them – even now, under pressure. He remained standing, facing them, keeping his hands on his hips. "I need some answers," he said, addressing his remarks to the woman.

Her eyes flickered briefly under his gaze but did not look away. "Yes," she replied after a moment's pause, her voice easy on the ear, low and husky, the sort that spoke to you across a pillow. "You must forgive me, I thought I'd told Senior Officer Davron everything." She spoke the words slowly, with care, almost caressing them, giving UniCom an entirely new dimension.

Oliphant folded his arms. "I think you can tell me more," he said, still hearing the sound of her in his head and feeling it merge with the visual image in a most dangerous manner. UniCom had no right to sound so seductive. How much of this sensuality was induced by the trauma regulator? – he wondered. How much was professional persona? How much was really *her*?

The dead expression in her eyes was ebbing away, the dark pupils beginning to contract. She was concentrating. The regulator was loosening its hold for the moment.

Behind her, the man was uneasy. "Please –"

"Mister Xenon," Oliphant interrupted him. "If you want to stay during the remainder of this interview, you'd be well advised to keep silent. Unless, that is, you can add anything that might be relevant to my inquiries."

The man stiffened perceptibly.

"How well did you know Karoli Koblinski, Miss Diamantides?" Oliphant continued.

The sound of Koblinski's name visibly hurt her: she looked away for a moment. Xenon's hands gripped the back of the couch.

"We were official," she said at last.

"That only tells me you had a commitment, not how well you actually *knew* him."

Her dark eyes were troubled. "I'm not sure what you mean."

"Was he secretive?"

She tilted her head backwards and made a small clicking sound with her tongue.

"Is that a 'yes' or a 'no'?"

"No!" The vehemence of her answer was echoed in her eyes.

"So he told you who he was going to meet in the early hours of 24 September?"

She frowned, clearly distressed.

"Did he, or didn't he?"

"No," she confessed, her voice suddenly so low he could barely hear it.

"So he was secretive."

"Never before!" she fired back at him, her earlier vehemence firmly in place again.

Xenon's hands shifted to her shoulders, giving her support. "Karoli did not keep secrets from us."

"Did he ever use MegaJoy products? Mind-warp for instance?"

Xenon's expression registered genuine shock at the suggestion. "No! None of us do!"

"What about your partner, Xenon? What about what's-his-name – Umo? He's tried just about everything else."

Xenon faltered briefly but held Oliphant's gaze when he answered. "Once – before I knew him. That's all."

"You'd like to swear to that?"

Xenon's denial died on his lips, replaced by a look of hopelessness.

"No doubt time will tell," Oliphant commented and returned to questioning the woman. "You take SoundSleep, don't you?"

"We work strange hours. Sleep is often difficult without it."

"So you wouldn't be aware of much once you'd taken a dose?"

She agreed with a small acquiescent nod.

"Was there anything unusual about Koblinski's behaviour that night? Something that didn't seem important at the time?"

The tilt of her head and click of the tongue again.

"Maybe in the last few weeks? Since you arrived at Shackleton for instance?"

She considered this for a while, her fingers distractedly caressing the tasselled fringes of the kaftan. "No," she said at last. "Not since we arrived here."

"Any other time?"

She turned and looked up at Xenon. "Do you remember, Theo? About three months ago?"

Xenon seemed unwilling to be drawn into the recollection of it. He merely nodded.

Oliphant pursued the opening, keeping up the pressure. "What happened?"

She turned back to face him, her fingers still playing with the tasselled fringe. "We were on the *Ptolemy* – sometime in April." Her voice had developed a dream-like quality in its reminiscing. "We'd left Herschel Minor in January. We'd been on-station for a year and we all wanted to come home. Space is a difficult place," she added, lapsing into silence for a moment, gathering her thoughts. "The flight back was seven months. By then we were all on edge. Umo was very unhappy."

"Any particular reason?"

"Space frightens him."

"Understandable. So what happened in April?" he asked, nudging her memory.

She began again. "Miles McMichael – our agent – arranged this stopover on Shackleton without our knowledge. None of us wanted it, but he insisted. The demand ratings after the transmissions from Herschel were so high, he said, we couldn't afford to miss the publicity. Mister McMichael can be very persuasive," she added with a slightly nuanced tone that betrayed an underlying meaning. "So we gave in."

"Did anyone else put pressure on you?"

"No."

"Not even Koblinski?"

"No! He was angry with Miles for suggesting it. Very angry."

Oliphant pulled over one of the upright chairs from the side of the room and sat astride it, leaning his forearms heavily against its metal back. From that position he could look her squarely in the eyes and watch for the lies to register. "So that was the only reason you came to Shackleton?"

The woman looked right back at him, unmoved." Yes," she said.

"Was there anything special about the shows you were supposed to give here? Something more demanding perhaps?" he asked, because he sensed there was.

Unexpectedly, she laughed: a low sound that came from deep within her diaphragm and made the hairs on the back of his neck stand on end. It threw him off-guard momentarily but confirmed his hunch. "Was it surger-pop?" he probed.

Her laughter died as quickly as it had sprung to life. She riveted him with her gaze. Xenon had turned to marble.

So, it *was* surger-pop – the aural equivalent of drug-induced surging using electronically enhanced music to manipulate the heart and alpha-wave rhythms of an audience, combining them with the visual stimulation of an erotic performance. The result was the fine-tuning and focussing of the senses into an orgy of mass sexual hysteria. It was tacky, low-grade entertainment of the worst kind, reminiscent of the late Twenty-first Century. It appealed to the young, the emotionally immature and indiscriminate. Its occasional performance on ConCorp's stations was tolerated only as a useful means of defusing the frustrated sexual energy space tours could generate. But it needed careful handling under controlled conditions. Station Commanders were authorised to distribute suppressants such as Bromidox in the drinking water afterwards.

"Well – was it?" Oliphant wanted to know, still waiting for confirmation of his assumption.

Those deep unfathomable eyes, now very much on a level with his own across that small space dividing them, unwaveringly held his gaze. She gave a small, almost imperceptible nod.

"From which I gather you don't much like it," he said, making it a statement rather than a question.

She reached up to clasp Xenon's hand. He held it firmly.

"Was that why Koblinski didn't want to do the stopover?"

"Have you ever seen a surger-pop performance, Mister Oliphant?" she asked him frankly, her head tilting slightly as she spoke.

"A couple of times," he replied, keeping a neutral tone to his voice. "It's not to my taste."

She smiled at him weakly, scrutinising him closely for some moments before making the startling comment, "No, I don't suppose it is. I imagine your tastes are more traditional."

Her observation unsettled him. Unbidden images hovered briefly in the corners of his mind, inviting others. He brought himself up short, keeping such stray thoughts in check. He pressed on, as if her observation hadn't been made. "Was there anything in particular that caused him concern?"

She nodded. "My costume," she said. "A special request from a sponsor to see me wear it."

"Do you have it with you?"

"No. Miles collected it after our last tour here three years ago."

"Had this sponsor seen you wear the costume before?"

"I don't know – but he knew of it."

"You're sure it was a 'he'?"

"Oh yes."

"Does he have a name?"

"Miles never mentioned it."

"Why was that, do you think?"

"Because he was someone wanting to keep a low profile."

"What was so special about this costume then?"

She shrugged slightly. "I don't know," she said looking him straight in the eyes again. "One surger costume is much like any other. They're designed to over-emphasise the figure – to be revealing – to come apart, of course." She was so matter-of-fact it reminded him of the tone adopted by Morticians describing mutilated bodies at post mortems. To be specific, it reminded him of Karoli Koblinski on the slab.

"Something must have made this one different," he suggested.

She considered this possibility but came to no definite conclusion. "It emphasised the breasts," she said after giving the matter some thought. "But they all do, Mister Oliphant. Like this." And without a trace of embarrassment she cupped her breasts in her hands, lifting them upwards towards him, the lovely shape of them straining against the fabric of the kaftan.

Nothing afterwards could undo the effect of that simple action. His concentration wavered just for an instant, his gaze slipping automatically to encompass what she had been demonstrating. It was only a moment's folly, he told himself repeatedly in the months that followed, but it might as well have lasted a lifetime. The image of her burned into his memory with all the permanence and pain of a branding iron. If Xenon had not been there, he feared he'd have lost his reason in that strange, intoxicating atmosphere.

She showed no signs of registering his discomfort. Instead, she regarded the overall effect she was attempting to illustrate and seemed dissatisfied with the result. "No," she said, "There's more emphasis," and she removed her hands allowing the kaftan to fall naturally into place again, obscuring the delights so generously revealed to his hungry eyes only moments earlier. She was frowning. "It's in the construction," she added.

He struggled to resurface from the sudden hammering of blood at his temples. "Construction?" he said, trying hard to concentrate on what she was saying.

"How it's made," she explained, as if talking to a curious but simple-minded child. "I have a similar costume with me – if you really wish to see it?" Her ownership of such a thing clearly embarrassed her.

Oliphant maintained an appearance of detached disinterest. "Yes – it might be helpful," he said. What he thought was something entirely different.

Xenon offered to get it. There was the sound of a closet door being opened and closed in the sleeping area. Oliphant abandoned the comparative safety of his chair and rose to meet him as he reappeared holding the offending garment.

The costume was garish: the lower bodice and hip-hugging floor-length skirt sported an array of fluorescent patches overlapping one another in riotous disorder, the whole held together in unexpected places by slim strips of contact fastener which Xenon proceeded to undo at random, like a salesman demonstrating the essentials of a product to a would-be purchaser. Under the woman's gaze, Oliphant tried to remain objective, but the most obvious feature of the design was bizarre – two silver-sequined peaks jutting out from the upper part of the high-necked bodice. It was impossible for him to imagine the softness of her lovely breasts crammed into the confines of such ridiculous structures.

Xenon handed over the costume, draping it delicately over Oliphant's hands: the fabric was sensuously silky to the touch, like the smooth snake-skin of a rainbow boa; the cones were hard and unyielding, like armour plating.

"You can remove them," the woman said, and reached up, taking the offending outfit from him and prising off one of the cones with a quick twist. It came away with a small ripping sound.

Watching her perform this task, he experienced a fleeting but exquisite mental image of what would be revealed to an ecstatic audience under very different circumstances.

She had read his thoughts. As he reached forward to take the cone from her, their fingers touched. Their eyes met. That was all it took. "The male costumes are no better," she said very quietly, shattering his fantasy into a million pieces, and he saw Xenon turn away.

She relinquished her hold on the cone, her attention still fixed on his face. Their fingers parted, the spell was broken for a moment and he was able to turn his mind again to more urgent matters. Under the silent gaze of his audience, he inspected his acquisition. The cone had a soft padded inlay inside the solid construction. He ran his fingers over the fabric, feeling the seams: between the outer shell and the inlay was a very obvious hiding place for a multitude of possibilities. "What was going to be special about the performance this time?" he asked, but the break in his questioning had allowed the regulator to reassert its control: her alertness had dimmed, her vitality beginning to ebb away, her attention drifting elsewhere. There was little time left before she would be of no further use to him. "Was it to do with the cones?"

She nodded, her eyelids growing heavy. "I had to give them to someone."

"Who?"

"The sponsor," she said with a small sigh, resting her head against the back of the couch.

"And Koblinski didn't want you to?"

"No. He was very angry."

"She's tiring," Xenon warned.

"I'm nearly done. What happened about the costume?"

It took her a long time to answer: she was slipping away from him fast. "Karoli said he'd speak to Miles when we got here. "

"Did he? Did he contact 'Smiler'?"

The use of McMichael's nickname reanimated her briefly. There was a thin smile on her lips that lingered for a moment. "I don't know," she whispered and closed her eyes, finally out of his reach.

"Do you know?" he asked Xenon.

"No. Karoli would have dealt with it."

"When was the performance scheduled?"

"For tomorrow night."

Oliphant placed the offending cone on the table. It was time to leave. "Thank you for your help, Mister Xenon," he said, adding without knowing why, "I hope Miss Diamantides will forgive my abruptness."

"I'll tell her, Mister Oliphant."

"Please do."

On the threshold, something made Oliphant turn to take one last look. Diamantides was asleep, her head resting against her shoulder, her face half-hidden by the dark mass of her hair. In her lap, constrained by her delicate hands, the incongruous costume lay disembodied, trailing downwards onto the floor, its obscenity vying with the chasteness of the kaftan. Behind her, Xenon remained standing, sentry-like: on guard and impassive.

It was hard to imagine either of them embracing their partners in a frenzied erotic routine designed for public consumption. No, he corrected himself, it wasn't hard – it was unimaginable. On the other hand, he discovered, it was relatively easy for him to imagine himself embracing Cassandra Diamantides for his own personal gratification in the sweetly-scented seclusion of her own room.

Nodding briefly to Xenon, he took his leave, and was glad to be gone.

Six

After his interview with Cassandra Diamantides, Oliphant's first thought was it would have been wiser to return to his comfortable accommodation in the Carnegie Suite and take a much-needed cold shower. Instead, he put duty before personal comfort and took the Route 5 underground glidetrack between the Stage Door Unit and the ACM Complex. His determination to keep his mind on the job in the face of considerable temptation made him feel marginally better about what had proved to be a thoroughly disconcerting experience.

The glidetrack was empty, sliding almost noiselessly through the bright, echoless tunnel, the centre strip-lighting a brilliant white ribbon running as straight as an arrow ahead of him into the distance.

It was getting late: 2235 hours. There was little activity. Those on the late shift were about their business either in the mineral extraction plant or inside control rooms. But most Shackleton personnel were tucked up for the night keeping to Earthtime. Such little rituals helped to make life on the satellite less alien, even though regular meteorite showers and solar radiation had imposed sub-lunar living as a matter of course.

Watching the glidetrack for want of any other occupation, Oliphant slipped into a reverie thinking over what Diamantides had said about Umo Manaus's fear of space. Not everyone could cope. If he were honest, he would have to admit he didn't handle long-term space postings all that well himself. At least at

Shackleton a space tour could be interspersed with regular spells of home leave.

On the outer stations – Jupiter, Saturn and Uranus – Oliphant knew ConCorp was having problems. Personnel sometimes went space crazy. Gaia Deprivation Syndrome they called it – GDS for short – a condition ranging from minor depression to full-blown mental dysfunction. In some cases, those who'd completely lost their marbles had needed de-animation for transhipment back to Earth and long-term readjustment therapy afterwards. Some had even walked off-station, stepping out into the void as if they'd been setting off for a casual evening stroll. The most recent case, it was rumoured, had been in February that year, involving a Senior R & D officer on Herschel Major – although such incidents were no longer given headline treatment to reduce angst spreading to other personnel. It crossed Oliphant's mind that if The Choralians didn't tranship soon, Umo Manaus might become another statistic to add to those who'd opted for the great cosmic walkabout.

The flashing red sign ahead gave him advance warning of the dismount pad approaching for access to the ACM Complex. He stepped off the track to the sound of the airlock doors hissing open at his approach. The slightly metallic tang of the Complex atmosphere greeted him.

Out in the main corridor of Level 1, he took the first available elevator up to Ground Level, sharing it with three Administrators in their nondescript pale-grey uniforms going off-duty after a late meeting. Their conversation died when he entered, their casual inspection of him registering the significance of his uniform and its insignia, and rendering them silent for the remaining few seconds it took to reach their destination. They let him leave first, and he heard them resume their conversation when they judged him to be sufficiently out of earshot. One of the perks of the job, Oliphant thought. Perfect silence in claustrophobic conditions.

The next sepia door down from his own miniscule office was labelled in red – Q3-15/19 SECURITY. Underneath, in less intimidating capitals were details of the sections: Reception, Control, and Administration and the names and titles of the three Senior Officers of Shackleton Security: Ben Davron, Nadine Tereshkhova and Harry Ndabe.

The door to the Reception opened automatically at his approach and slid back into its casing behind him with a soft sigh. Ahead of him was the large laminated polyplastic screen from waist height up to the ceiling, with its communication ports guaranteed to withstand just about everything from small side-arms fire to anti-personnel heavy-duty stuff. In the spacious, well-lit office behind the screen, three officers were seated at consoles making random infra-red sweeps of the processing areas and landing port maintenance hangars.

Oliphant noticed his arrival had registered on a monitor in front of the nearest officer. She acknowledged his arrival and got up to greet him. She was an Amazon of a woman, of indeterminate age with very short grey hair and angular features, about as attractive as the lunar landscape, but an interesting way of walking. Her name tab identified her as Security Officer Erica Carson. She opened the communication port Oliphant had selected and he could hear the faint hum of equipment in the background.

"Is Senior Officer Davron still on duty?" he asked, sticking with standard UniCom for the moment.

Her pale green eyes scanned his insignia and widened slightly. "Yes, Sir," she said crisply. "I'll let him know you're here." The communication port went dead.

She swung back to her desk, leaning across it to access the internal communication channels. Her rump, encased in its black uniform, thrust itself in his direction. For a moment, his mind rolled away, thinking of soft red fabric encasing other curves. Pulling his attention back to the present, he concentrated on the officer's lips forming his name soundlessly on the far side of the screen. There was a brief pause and then her voice came over the open channel again. "Access is now available, Sir."

Set into the wall adjacent to the screen was a solid metal security door. It clunked open and swung back in an elegant arc. When he stepped through into the corridor beyond, Davron was standing waiting for him in the doorway to his office.

"I wasn't sure I'd still find you here, Ben. Shouldn't you be off-duty?"

Oliphant's attempt at geniality fell on stony ground. "Officially – yes," Davron replied without smiling. "There were a few outstanding admin matters I needed to go through." He might just as well have added – 'I've wasted most of the day on the Koblinski case which you've successfully pulled from under me' – but he merely showed Oliphant the way into his office and indicated the nearest of the visitors' loungers.

Oliphant sank gratefully into its auto-contours, taking in the room with a practised eye. It was spacious and tidy: a place for everything and everything in its place, uncluttered by unnecessary status furniture or management 'toys'. "I won't keep you long," he said.

Davron shut down the console on his desk and settled back into his chair, adopting the air of authority appropriate for his position as Head of Security. He seemed in no hurry to ask Oliphant why he'd come.

There seemed little point, Oliphant decided, in waiting for Davron to defrost. "I've got a lead," he said casually without giving anything away. "Can you run an incoming mailcheck for me – for a package – sometime between 1 July and 24 September?"

Davron reactivated the console. "Sender?"

"McMichael Entertainment Agency. It might have been logged as something else – MEA possibly.

"Recipient?"

"Leave that blank will you. I want to pick up anything from the McMichael stable."

Davron studied the results. "Three deliveries – 16th and 28th July for Dream's Kingdom – they did a summer season here," he added, as if the notion of seasons was somehow relevant in a seasonless environment. "The last one was 20th September for -"

Oliphant detected the slight hesitation. "Let me guess," he said. "Cassandra Diamantides?"

Davron nodded. "Addressed to her under the name Cass Diamond. Do you want me to run a contents and scan check?"

"And any data on who collected the delivery if that's been logged."

There was a brief delay while the data came up. "Contents – 'Costume for performing artiste'. Scan – all clear."

Oliphant wasn't happy. "So whatever came in with that costume didn't show up on the analysis scanners."

"Or maybe they just didn't recognise it," Davron suggested. "A new product?"

"Could be. Looks like it."

"That's all we need – something dangerous on-station we can't detect."

"Any record of when the costume was picked up?"

"Collected same day – "

" – by Karoli Koblinski?" Oliphant cut in,

"Is that what you expected?"

Oliphant nodded, satisfied his hunch had paid off. "I've been looking for patterns in these non-standard deaths, Ben. But with mind-warp as the link there's a string of possibilities out there to build on. I'm certain Koblinski's murder fits into one of them – and I'd like to share my thoughts with you on what we might be dealing with." It would do no harm, he'd decided, to mollify Davron's wounded pride a little and maybe keep him on-side and less hostile in future – just in case.

Davron sat back in his chair without comment, waiting to be informed.

With no sign of an immediate thaw, Oliphant began reeling off what he had in mind. "I'm thinking aloud here, Ben," he said, conscious he was laying on the bonhomie a bit thick as he said it, " – but this is how I see things. We're looking at the possibility of Pushers who've stepped out of line and had to be disposed of. Couriers who've become liabilities – or were muscling in on the action. Users who got careless and overdosed accidentally. Or possibly Vulnerables who've been blackmailed into becoming Couriers and then stopped playing ball."

"So where did Koblinski fit into this?"

"I'm not sure. But from what I've gathered with my little chat with Diamond and Xenon, I'm pretty sure he knew a mind-warp product was in that outfit when it arrived. What I don't know is what he intended doing with it."

"Do you want me to initiate a station search?"

"For the outfit?" Oliphant shook his head. "I think we can safely say we wouldn't find it just lying around waiting for us to pick it up. It most likely got shoved down a convenient recyclation chute at some point – either by Koblinski – or whoever killed him. Diamond said she'd never seen it."

Davron was looking him straight in the eye. "Do you believe her story?" he asked, almost casually.

There was something in his tone which Oliphant resented – the implication that he could have been swayed somehow by Diamond when he interviewed her – or worse still, that he might be a gullible fool. With some effort, he let it pass, thinking it was more to do with his own perception of events in that sweetly-scented room than Davron being critical of his interrogation of her. "In her state, I don't think she was up to stringing together a fabricated story," he said, reassuring himself as much as Davron.

"What about this so-called 'sponsor'? There's no proof he existed, is there?"

Oliphant had to agree. "But we can't discount the other factor – the involvement of someone already here – and not just the low-graders. We might even have a rogue Security Officer working for this network." He added this just for the hell of seeing Davron's reaction to the idea. "Especially if we're looking at someone tampering with security systems."

Davron didn't blink, but Oliphant could tell what he was thinking.

"Yes, I know it's unlikely, Ben—"

"I'll check who was on duty on the 20th anyway."

"Okay. Keep it low key. Don't want to raise suspicions, do we? Let me know if you find anything."

"Of course."

Oliphant eased himself out of the lounger and headed for the door.

Davron's voice followed him. "And if there's anything else I can do—"

"Yes – of course. I'll keep in touch." But he left knowing perfectly well he would do nothing of the sort.

SEVEN

By 0900 hours the following morning, Oliphant had submitted a report on his preliminary findings to Shackleton's Station Commander, Josephine Deneuve. It was a matter of courtesy. He informed her simply that Karoli Koblinski's security file would remain open until certain aspects of the circumstances surrounding his death had been satisfactorily explained. He also indicated, as politely as he could, he was unable to elucidate further for the time being, as this would jeopardise wider investigations. SSO Davron would relay any further information as and when it became available.

Josephine Deneuve was a dynamic, extremely forceful woman. Oliphant preferred to keep her at indirect communication distance, not least because she was too well-acquainted with his last official partner, Lorraine Fousseau: they were old Academy friends and still kept in touch on a fairly regular basis.

Lorraine had stuck it out with Oliphant for two three-year contracts before deciding she couldn't stand the strain of being a Security Officer's partner any longer. "I've tried," she'd said. "I've tried and failed." She'd disliked the long separations, the erratic schedules and the increasing intrusion of the seamy side of life into their domestic world.

In '39 their two children, Vicky who was four at the time, and Alex who was still a babe in arms, had been the subject of a bungled snatch by a group of very young and very inept amateur terrorists operating out of Toulouse. Oliphant, as a newly promoted Senior Officer in charge of anti-terrorism operations for ConCorp at the time, had soon run them down. He'd dealt with the case efficiently and dispassionately – as he would have done with any other incident – but it had been the last straw as far as Lorraine was concerned. Almost immediately afterwards, she'd taken the children and moved to Orleans, effectively ending the second contract almost a year before it was due to expire. He hadn't pressed for compensation. Two years later, she'd contacted him to let him know she'd set up a new official partnership with Gregor Bukhov, a peripheral member of the wealthy Bukhovski drinks clan and a financial adviser for the TransGlobe Bank. She would no longer hold him to his contractual obligations as far as the children were concerned, she said. Access, of course, would still be permitted, but Oliphant had read between the lines. He'd become a dangerous connection. Direct links with Lorraine and the children during the intervening years had dwindled on both sides to the sending of birthday greetings and little more besides. He'd also taken the necessary decision – as far as he saw it – not to intrude into their new life: it was no good for them, and no good for him. But Josephine Deneuve had always thought otherwise, and made her feelings very plain to him whenever their paths crossed. They had crossed fleetingly in '46 when she'd attended a station management course held at Regional Security and she'd harangued him at length about his duties as a father. From then on, Oliphant had avoided meeting her face-to-face with an adroitness he was almost proud to acknowledge.

Fifteen years on, Lorraine and Gregor were still contracted and very happy by all accounts, or at least they were according to Josephine.

After filing his report, Oliphant had turned his attention again to the security files of the surviving members of The Choralians. He wanted to memorise as much as possible: to immerse himself in their histories; to absorb them. He was beginning to get an inkling as to what had made Karoli Tadeus Koblinski tick; now he wanted to feel his way into the minds of the rest of them. Somewhere, he was certain there was a clue which would put the final pieces into the Koblinski jigsaw and complete the picture, and if not that, then something that would provide him with the essential pointer he was looking for – the need to identify the right type of Freelance he'd need to ask for to act as an undercover agent.

When Davron had originally told him they were dealing with Folksters, Oliphant realised he'd made rapid assumptions which had blinkered his whole approach. He'd lumped Entertainers into a neat, single all-purpose category: people with weird habits; even weirder thought processes – if any; a predisposition to deviation of all sorts; and were, by and large, intellectually without any merit whatever. Now he was having to rethink his entire strategy. The Choralians didn't fit snugly into his glib suppositions. Far from it. Perhaps Umo didn't quite match up to the others: he was the runt; an overgrown kid from the look of his file who'd never had the benefit of formal education at any level, sampling just about every known vice in the book. He was the obvious weak link, both on his own account and Xenon's, who'd taken responsibility for him.

There was also Cass Diamond in the mix. She remained a problem – in more ways than one. Not a weak link in herself perhaps, but her adoptive mother, Hippolyta Diamantides, was another story. Trawling through her file, Oliphant had uncovered a messy history. Once a successful Folkster group leader, she'd sunk into an erratic existence, apparently adopting the foundling Cassandra in a moment of altruism and drunkenness. After that her life had gone into freefall. She'd died at the early age of thirty-eight addicted to an adaptive mind-warp program implanted in her cerebellum. It provided the sexual stimulus she must have craved even when she was no longer in virtual reality.

In a nutshell, Hippolyta Diamantides had died from an excess of orgiastic ecstasy, totally warped out of her mind. Cassandra had been sixteen at the time.

Oliphant cast his mind back to Davron being so adamant that Diamond never touched mind-warp. With her background, it made sense, but equally it had provided her with a lot of access to Pushers and others of that ilk at some time in her life. It made her a target, and it made her vulnerable – if not an actual Vulnerable herself.

The thought lingered. Oliphant sat back in his chair and pondered long and hard. Had she been Koblinski's weak link? Had he been protecting her? Had he *died* protecting her? Memories of her flooded into his mind again for the umpteenth time, and with them the notion that if he'd been in Koblinski's place, would he have just as willingly put his life on the line for her as well? He began to think it wasn't such an implausible idea after all.

His reflective mood was shattered by the jarring insistence of the door buzzer. He wasn't expecting anyone and the interruption was unwelcome. Irascibly, he activated the door monitor. When the panel cleared, it revealed Xenon waiting in the corridor, his long hair hidden beneath a nondescript grey cap and no gold earrings visible either. There was someone standing behind him, head down. Same type of cap.

Oliphant opened the communicator Link.

Xenon announced himself in his elegant, softly-spoken UniCom. "I would like you to speak with Umo, Mister Oliphant," he said. "He has something he wants to tell you."

Oliphant let them wait for a moment before releasing the door mechanism. He'd learnt never to rush an interview with an enthusiastic potential witness, and he watched the tension in Xenon's face become more pronounced as the seconds ticked by. When he finally activated the access control, Xenon hastily removed his cap and ushered Umo ahead of him until he was jammed up against Oliphant's desk. The scent that had pervaded the atmosphere in Cass Diamond's quarters wafted across the space between them.

Never having seen Umo Manaus in the flesh, Oliphant had no real appreciation of the person in front of him. For all his twenty-four years, Umo had all the appearance of an adolescent boy of no more than fourteen. His frame was compact, sinewy but slight, barely reaching up to Xenon's shoulders. The fingers clutching the cap he had hastily pulled off in Oliphant's presence were slender – almost feminine in appearance, and were clutching at the fabric as if his life depended on keeping a tight grip on it. With the cap off, a thick mop of blue-black hair in the style of an old-time Amerindian had been revealed, and the face beneath the heavy bang across his forehead echoed his ancestry: skin the colour of burnished copper; dark, slightly Asiatic eyes; high cheek bones, and a wide, generous mouth. He was licking his lips nervously.

Oliphant observed them from behind his desk, keeping them waiting. He was curious: they were both dressed sombrely in forest-green leisuresuits in stark contrast to the outlandish stage costumes on their hologram publicity threads. Anyone knowing them from their publicity, or from their performances, would have been hard pressed to recognise either of them – which was possibly why they'd felt safe enough to cross the public areas of the station so openly.

The atmosphere in his office was noticeably claustrophobic once the door had closed, the pervasive scent giving the air recycling system a hard time. With his only one spare chair available, Oliphant decided to keep them both standing: he could watch their responses better if they had no alternative but to occupy the limited space directly in front of him, and that would give him the distinct advantage of spotting any collusion between them.

"Well," he asked eventually, breaking the silence after surveying them long enough to maintain their nervousness. "What is it that Umo wants to tell me?" He addressed Xenon. Umo it seemed was over-awed, incapable of speech. There was a fine slick of sweat on his upper lip.

Xenon immediately put his arm around Umo's shoulders. "I know you had great doubts yesterday," he began. "About Umo." He spoke slowly, apparently choosing his words with care, his gaze steadying, becoming more intense, as if wanting to emphasise the truth behind what he was about to say. "I have talked with him this morning. He has promised me he will answer your questions truthfully. I have told him you would authorise a Statement Rating if necessary."

Manaus looked scared witless at the prospect. The cap came in for more pummelling.

Oliphant was intrigued: he'd never mentioned such a drastic possibility. Why was Xenon saying that he had? The man's gaze was unwavering, speaking volumes: he was asking Oliphant to play along with that possibility. That was interesting. All right – he thought – I'll play your game for a while and see what turns up. Shifting slightly in his chair, he gave Manaus the benefit of his full attention and addressed him directly. "When I say the word 'mind-warp', what do you take it to mean?"

Manaus stiffened, his eyes darting backwards and forwards between various unconnected points in the room. He glanced up nervously at Xenon and then back at Oliphant before making any attempt to reply. "Programs," he whispered in halting UniCom.

"Louder boy – I can't hear you!" Oliphant boomed, the sound shuddering against the thick fragorboard walls of the room before it was lost in their moonquake sound-absorbent surfaces.

Manaus visibly shrivelled. "Programs," he repeated, slightly more loudly, his voice strangely high and piping, like a plaintive reed blown in the wind. It was downright unnerving.

Oliphant was momentarily taken aback by its childlike quality.

Xenon had read his thoughts. "He is a castrato, Mister Oliphant," he explained evenly. "The Enforcers in Guatemala, you understand – when he was seven. That is why he is afraid of you."

Oliphant mulled over the information: none of this was recorded on Manaus's security file. Perhaps, as the Enforcers were often the main source of ConCorp intelligence, it was easy to understand why. He sat back in his chair, giving Manaus more space and changed tack. "What sort of programs?" he asked, less forcefully this time.

Manaus gulped visibly. "VR," he said.

"Ever used a VR program?"

Another gulp. "Once. Long ago. Many years now."

"What about combos – hallucinogenics?"

Xenon cut in. "He has taken them in the past," he said simply, his hold on Manaus tightening perceptibly.

"I'd like him to answer for himself, Mister Xenon, if you don't mind."

Xenon lapsed into a dignified silence. Manaus was beginning to tremble.

"What do you take, Manaus?"

"Combos," he confessed.

"When was the last time?"

"The outflight to Uranus."

Now that was interesting in itself, thought Oliphant. "How did you get hold of them?"

"There was a man," Manaus said, his UniCom becoming so stilted it was bordering on the unintelligible. "He saw space frightened me. He offered me a combo if I went with him."

"So you took up his offer?"

Manaus coloured visibly.

"How many times?"

Manaus looked down at his hands still clutching the cap. "Three," he said.

Oliphant noted Xenon's grip on Umo's shoulders was as tight as the clenched muscles on his face.

"Who was the man?"

Manaus shook his head and began twisting the cap in a series of small jerky movements. "I don't know. He told me to call him 'Angel'."

"Describe him to me."

"All in black. But no gold – there," and he pointed to the gold trim on Oliphant's uniform. "No badge. Not Security."

"Besides what he was wearing, Manaus, what did he look like?"

"Tall. Strong. Maybe thirty years. I don't know. Not old. Moved like a panther. Hair – all white -" he stopped suddenly, fear etched into his face. "His eyes – no colour. Evil."

It was a stunning description, Oliphant thought. Not the sort of high profile visibility a Trafficker would choose to adopt. He wasn't entirely convinced Manaus was telling the truth, but he let him run on.

Manaus was starting to struggle with his confession. "Theo found out – the third time – about Angel and me. About the combo." He glanced up at his protector, his smooth childlike face distraught with anguish at his betrayal.

"How did you find out, Mister Xenon?"

Xenon's face was a rigid mask of dignity under duress. "The third time – this 'Angel' used neuro-rods when he took his pleasure. They cause spasms – as you may know," he added. "It's impossible to hide such things."

Oliphant agreed. "And at the time, you couldn't report the assault because of the illegal use of the combo?"

Xenon nodded.

"Did you ever see this 'Angel' yourself?"

"No."

"Do you remember seeing anyone who remotely matched his description at any time during the outflight, or after?"

"No."

Oliphant turned his attention back to Manaus. He was sure there was more if he could only prise it out of him. He needed to rack up the pressure again – but not too much. He waited a moment before resuming his questioning, filling the time by tapping his fingers against his pursed lips and smoothing down his beard. It was a practised art. Manaus had gone back to twisting the cap, now badly misshapen in his hands. "Manaus, have *you* seen this 'Angel' at any time since the outflight?"

Manaus quivered.

"When?"

"On the *Ptolemy*. Coming back." Tears were beginning to seep down his cheeks. "He said he wanted me again – as a casual during the flight back. We were to meet next day – in one of the storage areas. He would have a combo for me." It was a long time since Oliphant had seen anyone look as frightened as Manaus did at that moment.

Xenon cut in. "This 'Angel' said he would make me 'disappear', Mister Oliphant, if Umo told anyone about their 'arrangement'. He said no one would ever know what had happened to me."

"Blackmail?"

"Yes."

"Did you keep the appointment, Manaus?"

"Yes. That's when Karoli discovered us."

Oliphant's interest went up several notches.

Xenon took up the story again. "I knew something was wrong because Umo had started acting strangely. I told Karoli. We'd been in space so long, I was afraid Umo might be going crazy. I never suspected …" His composure faltered for a moment. "Karoli said he would find out if Umo was keeping anything from me."

"And presumably he did?"

Manaus nodded. "Yes. He followed me – to the storage area. Told me to leave. So I ran away. He came to me later and told me there would be no more trouble. I could forget everything. He didn't say why. He promised he wouldn't say anything to Theo."

"Did he keep his promise, Mister Xenon?"

"Yes. And Umo seemed more settled, so I stopped worrying."

"So you knew nothing about the reappearance of this 'Angel'?"

"Nothing, Mister Oliphant. I swear."

"Which begs the question – why has Manaus told you about this now?"

"Because I asked him. After what you said last night, I wanted to be clear in my own mind. I wanted to know if he knew something he hadn't told me."

"And he confessed everything. But why now?"

With an astonishing act of self-control, Xenon looked him straight in the eye. "Because I told him of your arrival here, Mister Oliphant. Chief Security Officers do not usually trouble themselves over accidental deaths."

Oliphant made a mental note of Xenon's depth of understanding.

"But they do if that death might be suspicious," Xenon was saying. "Ever since Karoli died, Umo has been troubled over the incident on the *Ptolemy*. He thinks Karoli's death was not an accident."

There was a noticeable silence for a moment. Oliphant had never expected to have his suspicions confirmed by someone as unlikely as Umo Manaus. "Have you seen this 'Angel' since you arrived at Shackleton?"

Manaus shook his head.

"But you think he might be behind Karoli's death?"

"Yes." Manaus's voice had once again been reduced to a piping whisper.

Oliphant pushed back his chair and stood up. "Well – thank you both for coming and being so frank with me," he said, operating the door control to show them out.

But Xenon wasn't willing to be dismissed so quickly. "Was Karoli's death an accident?" he asked, the frank, open look in his eyes asking more than his words.

Oliphant wasn't prepared to say anything more than he had to. "There are a few aspects that still need to be cleared up, Mister Xenon. Until they are, it would be better not to speculate one way or the other." And for reasons he wasn't entirely sure about, he added, "As soon as there is anything definite, I'll let you know. And if you feel there is anything else I should know about in the future, please contact me."

Xenon paused on the threshold. "Are we in any danger?"

"Not as far as I know."

Xenon nodded and stuffing his hair back under his cap, he ushered Manaus out of the office.

Once the door had sighed shut behind them, Oliphant settled back into his chair and considered the turn in events. He still wasn't sure about Manaus's story, but the implied threat of a Statement Rating – and the effect it had had on him – seemed to confirm he was telling the truth.

So who was 'Angel'? How did someone so conspicuous manage to become so invisible and move around ConCorp facilities at will? Multiple identities? Disguises? They had to be in the mix somewhere. But the big question was what had happened between this man and Koblinski once Manaus had left the storage area? Had Koblinski and 'Angel' struck a deal? A trade-off? Was 'Angel' working in cahoots with McMichael, or someone else? Or was it the other way around? Everything had suddenly become a lot more complicated.

Oliphant stirred himself. He needed to get something organised – fast. A complex operation like this needed official sanction from a Regional Commander. There were contacts to be made, and the best undercover agent to be found to infiltrate McMichael's organisation without raising any suspicions. Getting the right person would be difficult, but not impossible.

It was then, while he was engrossed in working out the best strategy to adopt, that for no reason at all Xenon's words came back to him. *Are we in any danger?* And for the first time, it occurred to Oliphant that possibly they were.

*E*IGHT

Davron was taken by surprise to find Oliphant preparing to leave on the ferry due out that afternoon: he'd expected the CSO to stay longer than five days, perhaps even a couple of weeks. This unexpected turn of events left him with mixed emotions – glad in one sense to have him off his patch sooner rather than later, but less than delighted he'd been kept at arm's length from the CSO's investigations for the past two days. Oliphant had been shut away in his office asking not to be disturbed unless it was vitally important, with his communication Links almost permanently open.

Yes, Davron had to admit he'd been kept 'informed', after a fashion, but it hardly amounted to anything more than superficial intelligence. Manaus's revelations had been reduced to a couple of carefully worded neutral sentences, and it had been almost on sufferance that Oliphant had endorsed the idea of a personnel check to see if anyone matching Angel's description might still be on-station. It had proved negative, a fact which didn't seem to surprise Oliphant in the least.

But it hadn't stopped Davron persisting. He'd poured over the passenger lists for the outflight to the Uranus stations and the return journey on the *Ptolemy*. Beside The Choralian entourage, sixteen duplicated names came up. Checked against CentraFile holograms none of them bore the remotest resemblance to Manaus's 'Angel'. Equally galling were the crew listings – completely different for both flights.

"None of this makes sense," Davron had insisted. "This man was supposed to be on both flights. Manaus is obviously lying." Oliphant had smiled in that maddeningly superior way he had of making Davron feel inadequate. "No, I don't think so, Ben. This 'Angel' can make himself 'disappear' as well as other people. I'm told angels are quite good at it."

Davron hadn't been in the mood for such humour.

"This man's a living shape-shifter," Oliphant had emphasised. "We're not just talking about using doctored eye lenses here – or wearing a new body-form, second skin or funny wig – although he probably did. No, we're talking highly sophisticated data manipulation – different names and holograms, different file references and fake histories. And what's more, Ben, we don't know how many identities this man has under his belt. Let's face it, we've come up against forged ID tags and matching biodata before, haven't we? So we can take that as a given along with the new stuff – technological know-how – how to override security systems – managing to get flights as a last-minute unlogged replacement crew member – or passenger. If there's a damned loophole in the system, Ben, someone somewhere out there will know how to make use of it."

But beyond theorising on the multiple possibilities facing them, Oliphant had seemed uninterested in pursuing the matter further. Shackleton had ceased to play a role in the complex scheme of things: his concerns apparently lay elsewhere. Precisely where, he'd not seen fit to share with him, and contrary to the wishes of both Station Commander Deneuve and himself as Head of Shackleton Security, he'd authorised the immediate transhipment of The Choralians earthwards on compassionate grounds. They'd been given the highly unusual, possibly irregular, permission to travel by freighter, and were packed and gone the afternoon of Manaus's confession, taking with them the embalmed body of Karoli Koblinski. Their sudden, and unannounced return

Earthside, Oliphant had explained, was to relieve them of the burden of facing a massive crowd of grieving fans who'd otherwise have gathered at the Kalgoorlie Ferry Terminal to meet them.

Irritated by Oliphant's attitude, and determined to be involved regardless, Davron had initiated his own investigations. The results had been so completely negative, they'd only added to his increasing sense of frustration. The missing stage costume hadn't been found, despite an exhaustive search – just as Oliphant had predicted – and the detailed scrutiny and analysis of the banking credits of all officers on duty around the time of Koblinski's murder, had revealed nothing to show they'd received so much as a single dollarouble that could be labelled a back-hander. Every entry on their statements was accounted for and totally unremarkable. It was even more dispiriting to discover they appeared to run such well-regulated financial lives, it was possible to predict their statement entries with unerring accuracy.

That afternoon, already kitted out in his travelsuit, Oliphant was in the Security Office taking his leave, and Davron was fully prepared to admit he couldn't wait to see him to go.

The CSO had the air of a man whose thoughts were travelling ahead of him, with little use for any idle chit-chat in the meantime. "I've cleared my room over at the Carnegie," he announced without any preamble." Thanks for your help, Mister Davron." He extended a gloved hand and Davron shook it automatically.

Goodbye, good luck and good riddance, Davron thought, but out of expected courtesy and nothing more, he intended to accompany his CSO at least as far as the glidetrack Access Point. They'd only made it part way down the corridor when his personal Link bleeped and a taut female voice summoned him in precise UniCom. "Officer Carson, Sir. Incident Room report just in."

Oliphant, walking slightly ahead of him, gave him a brief nod of acknowledgement. "You'd better see what she wants," he said. "She's not the sort of person I'd keep waiting." And with that he'd continued down the corridor, his brisk strides eating up the distance to the Access Point for Route 1 heading to the collection point for Departures.

Davron watched him go before opening his communication Link. "Davron here, Officer Carson."

"Disturbance on the production line in the Mineral Processing Plant, Sir. One operative running amok causing extensive damage. Alpha Squad already on site."

"Containment authorised," he replied, glad of the action. "Tell the officers I'll be with them in three minutes."

He set off towards the Route 2 glidetrack at a run, his hand automatically dropping to check the stun-gun on his hip, finding its presence a considerable comfort. If he was going to be cornered by a Crazy with a crow bar, he wasn't going to be unarmed.

NINE

The Garrison Clinic was a fortress: a neat complex of white-walled, functional buildings and low, red-roofed bungalows set among well-manicured lawns and luxuriant flowerbeds filling the air with scents of honey and thyme – but a fortress nonetheless.

It occupied the flat ground at the head of a secluded valley, tucked neatly away from the hustle and bustle of the main Corinth to Patras coast route, and surrounded by electronic surveillance systems designed to detect and deter any unauthorised visitors using unorthodox methods of entry. Around its perimeter, a deceptively innocuous but potentially lethal lattice fencing was patrolled twenty-four hours a day by the Clinic's private security guards: anonymous helmeted men in equally anonymous khaki uniforms. Beyond the perimeter, other invisible barriers secured its isolation from prying eyes.

Access to this peaceful haven was restricted by the simple expedient of having no overland route to any centre of habitation or major highway. Its Maintenance Operatives and more professional personnel lived on-site in separate enclaves, and a fleet of half-a-dozen Clinic skeeters operated out of the helipad on the eastern fringe of the complex providing the only means of regular transport in or out of the area. Everyone and everything came and went through this single terminal: patients, staff, stores, equipment – absolutely everything. It made the control process that much easier.

The remoteness of the Clinic emphasised its lack of interest in being the object of public scrutiny. Dr Elgar Garrison, a tall, distinguished looking gentleman of Britannic stock and Norman ancestry was both its inspiration and Director. He was a lean man – now in his late fifties with gaunt features, short iron-grey hair flecked with white at the sides, a thin-lipped smile and deep blue eyes. Twenty years earlier, he'd been regarded by the R&D gurus of the time as one of the best brains in his field. The zenith of his career had culminated in a research doctorate at the renowned Saragoza University Genetics Department, a post he still remembered with mixed emotions – those of the deepest affection and the bitterest gall.

In all social health matters, Garrison had consistently maintained that the end justified the means. It was a philosophy which gained him many friends among the elite band of third generation Social Engineers who were continuing the process of making giant strides in drastically reducing global population figures up until the mid-'30s. But equally, it was a philosophy which generated powerful enemies, not least the Guardians of Life movement. In 2238, these self-styled moralists, as he saw them, had become the active majority on the University Council. His methods were put under the microscope of popular opinion at the time with a thoroughness it was hard to fault – even by his own standards. He couldn't deny it, they'd built up a compelling case against him: emotional, but compelling. Within six months, he was forced to resign his position, and at a stroke he lost everything: prestige, power, recognition and respect.

A man of considerable financial standing through his many patents, combined with an almost facile ability to make astute investments, he sank his accumulated wealth into establishing a private Clinic. He still had sufficient influence to obtain a licence to continue both his practice and his research with the blessing of a Research Commissioner interested in receiving the potential benefits of such a clinic himself. Three years later, the

Garrison Clinic was opened, quietly and without ceremony, and the Commissioner hadn't been disappointed with its services. Subsequently, the international network of the rich and famous had ensured the Clinic's continuous supply of patients who were seeking unorthodox genetic or other answers to awkward and inconvenient medical problems. Equally lucrative was Garrison's discreet treatment of those in high places who'd scrambled their brains with the latest combo-drug, Supercharge.

Success encouraged him to expand his already diverse research programme. He gathered around himself colleagues of a like mind who didn't feel the need to be over-scrupulous in their attitude towards overcoming the genetic or psychological dysfunctions of the human race. More than ten years on, well-established and well-recommended by those who knew, the Garrison Clinic was able to offer a whole range of fringe treatments to anyone willing and able to pay for the services available. His success rate would have been the envy of the medical establishment – had they known of it – which they did not. Garrison's sphere of power and influence had shifted from the scrutiny of the public eye to the domain of the quiet word and discreet arrangement. He'd grown to appreciate these changed circumstances and the greater freedom that went with them.

In the early hours of the morning on 23 March 2256, almost six months before Karoli Koblinski met his sudden end in Storage Hangar Six on Shackleton, Elgar Garrison's communicator Link buzzed distractedly by his bed. He became aware of its intrusion into his dreams only gradually, opening his eyes to the all-pervading darkness of his private rooms under the laboratory, and registering the urgency of its summons with a vague sense of unease. He snapped his fingers to activate the night-light, his thoughts still lingering on the fast-fading dream he'd been enjoying.

"Dr Garrison." The voice at the other end of the communication line sounded tense and distinctly out of breath.

"Yes – what is it, Hogan?"

His Chief Technical Officer on duty was beginning to gabble. "I think you should know there's been a – a break-in."

Garrison was suddenly very wide awake. "Where?"

"In the Restricted Area …three experiments have been taken. Security are carrying out preliminary searches."

Garrison swung his long legs free of the coverlet and sat up, noting the time on the headboard clock. 0246 hours. "Which three, Hogan?"

"Thirty-five, Thirty-six – and Forty." There was a noticeable hesitancy in revealing the last.

Garrison went cold, despite the controlled heating. A small shiver crossed his shoulders and travelled the length of his spine. "You're sure they've been taken?" he asked, clinging to a vague hope. "They haven't just wandered out of their areas?"

"No – they've definitely been taken," the voice confirmed. "Security found an electronic over-ride on the perimeter fence and a blocker on the sound wall. There's a similar device on the emergency exit and blinders on every interior spy-eye."

Garrison fumbled for his slippers. "Give me five minutes, Hogan. I'll be with you directly. Alert all relevant staff for me, will you?"

Five minutes later, in a state of acute anxiety, his pristine white over-tunic thrown hastily over his sleepsuit, Garrison was in the closely monitored facility of the Restricted Area. Hogan was waiting for him. A man in his mid-forties, usually bustling and robust, he looked as though he'd just seen an apparition which had foretold him of his rapid demise in the not too distant future.

"Show me," Garrison demanded.

Hogan led the way down the central corridor of the facility, the automatic lighting springing to life in his wake. In sealed rooms on either side, sleepy animals blinked black-eyed at them, unaccustomed to the sudden onset of their day in contradiction to their body clocks.

At the far end of the corridor, closest to the emergency exit, the additional security door leading into the ultra-sensitive area stood open. The first enclosure was empty. Thirty-five and Thirty-six, the chimpanzees Garrison had been patiently reconstructing for the last two years had gone. There was only the sound of the air ventilation unit filling the place. Three burly security guards were standing in the doorway, hands on hips, looking uncomfortable.

Garrison felt bile rise into his throat. Next to the chimp enclosure was the separate apartment which housed his most precious experiment. The door was ajar. The large cot in the sleeping area had been slept in, but the sheets were cold. The cupboard behind the door was empty and the door through to the wash room was standing open – a testimony, if any were needed, to the patent lack of occupation. And on the table in the living area, the electronic game from the night before sat mute, its potential only half-realised, waiting for its owner to complete the set.

Garrison turned slowly, taking in the surroundings which had become a part of his life for the past three years. Their familiarity had suddenly become strange – meaningless.

By the cot, he bent down and felt beneath the pillow. The entertainment system Forty loved so much had gone. He straightened, trying to focus his mind on what might have happened while he lay blissfully asleep, ignorant of the disaster being enacted two floors above him. "He went with them," he said, barely able to comprehend what he was saying. "He went willingly. He took his ES with him – for company."

Hogan nodded, seemingly embarrassed by the simple truth of this statement.

Garrison concentrated on his breathing. "When could it have happened?" he asked.

"Sometime after eleven. The last security check was clear."

"And no one saw or heard anything?"

Hogan shook his head. "They're running a perimeter search now, but they don't expect to find anything 'til daylight."

Garrison sat down heavily on the chair he'd occupied only eight hours earlier and stroked the control button on the game console. It blipped back at him, activated and ready to go. "So it could have been almost four hours ago," he said staring at the screen. "That's a long time."

Hogan didn't reply.

Garrison didn't notice. He was contemplating what *modus operandi* had been used this time. When the Genetic Rights Movement had attempted a break-in three months earlier, they'd used geotrackers across the rough terrain, ignoring the lack of recognised land routes. They'd parked them well back, outside the range of any sensor, and come in on foot with a range of sophisticated jamming devices. On that occasion they'd been repelled by a combination of the malfunction of one of their jammers and sharp-eyed security guards making a random search of the outer defences.

Garrison watched the frenetic activity of the yellow blob on the screen before him with a fascination he found hard to explain, but his thoughts were truly elsewhere. Perhaps the previous attempted incursion had only been a dummy run. It seemed possible. The GRM was noted for its operational thoroughness in planning action.

His interest in the blob faded. He stroked the control button and it vanished from the screen with a plaintive *blip*. Four hours, he thought. Over the inhospitable terrain, infra-red guides would have led the intruders out of the immediate area without any difficulty, and even the lumbering progress of a geotracker would put sufficient distance between them and any pursuers. Yes, it had been well-planned.

What would they do with their prizes? – he wondered. Did they realise what they'd stolen? Possibly. Possibly not. With luck the chimpanzees might survive if they were set free. That was something of a comfort – and at least, they could never breed – not without mutational assistance – and no one but himself was likely to be able to give them that. But his pride and joy – what would become of his pride and joy? Forty was vulnerable and precious; more precious than he dared to think about. Did the GRM have any idea just how precious?

He looked up at Hogan, and caught the man's pitying expression. "Do you think he went willingly?"

Hogan shrugged, unable to give an answer.

"How did they coax him out of here? I don't understand it."

"Maybe they said the right words to him ... he likes to please ... Maybe they didn't take him. Maybe he just went out through the open door ..." But his attempts to find an explanation trailed off, lacking conviction.

Garrison felt a great surge of emotion sweep over him. "I want him back, Hogan! Do you hear? I want him back!" On the table top, his hand had contracted into a solid fist. "And if there's no sign of him after the aerial search is completed, I shall bring in Palatine."

Hogan looked distinctly worried. "What about the Enforcers, Dr Garrison?"

Garrison's fist came down hard on the table top, his anger overwhelming his self-control. "For heaven's sake, man, I don't want them anywhere near this! He's an experiment, isn't he? And he's mine!"

"I just thought – "

"Don't think! We need to get him back – here – where he belongs! And I'll do whatever it takes! Do you understand?"

Hogan was just staring at him, white with fear.

TEN

By noon on 23 March 2256, the updates on the desk monitor in Garrison's office overlooking the gardens confirmed what he'd already suspected – that the security sweep had proved abortive.

The raid had been carried out with meticulous thoroughness. There were tracks suggesting three geotrackers had been parked more than two kilometres north of the Clinic, well hidden by the rising ground closer to the perimeter. Like commandos, the raiders had apparently accessed the site on foot and left the same way. There were no signs of any struggle. When they left they must have either carried or walked their acquisitions through every security barrier unhindered. Once clear of the complex, they'd apparently picked up the geotrackers and headed due north to meet the main Corinth to Patras highway where all signs of them had simply vanished. A grid-search at dawn by the security skeeters had failed to find any trace of them, which suggested another mode of transport had been waiting to pick them up at some point on the highway – destination unknown.

Garrison leaned back in his chair contemplating the scene beyond his window: the immaculate lawns fed by spring rains; the fountain, the clear sunlight catching the water spilling over its shell-like plinths in lazy rivulets; and the massed brilliance of the rhododendrons, already in full bloom, a riot of colour. All this peace, he thought, strangely at odds with the turmoil in his soul.

The door buzzer broke into his reverie and Hogan announced himself. Garrison had half a mind to send him away. At that moment, he'd have preferred the silence of his personal grief to the need for conversation. He felt tired to the last atom of his being and in no hurry to be interrupted – particularly by bad news.

Hogan had a strangely deflated look about him, Garrison thought, a difficult feat for someone not usually given to such a visible display of hopelessness. The skin around his eyes was inflamed and puffy through lack of sleep; he was unshaven; unkempt, and an air of exhaustion hung about him like a lead weight. He sank down heavily into the nearest chair by the window without waiting for permission, in itself totally out of character. "There's no news," Hogan said wearily, "But you probably knew that already."

Garrison chose to ignore the lapse in etiquette. "Yes – Security have just informed me," he said, quite unable to add anything further at that point: his mind had become a perfect blank, filled only with a black despair and little else except for a dull pain that was persisting behind his eyes.

Hogan leaned an elbow on the window sill next to him and propped his head in his hand. "Where the hell have they gone?" he said, addressing the tranquil scene of sunlit lawns beyond the panes. "Geotrackers don't exactly break the speed barrier."

Garrison inhaled deeply to clear his brain and tilted his chair back a little further in the hope it might somehow help him to relax. "I think we can safely assume they used a cargo transporter once they reached the highway," he said, feeling a sudden certainty this was what must have happened. "All they had to do was drive the geotrackers into the back of the container under cover of darkness and – *poof*," he added, with a little wave of his hand, "gone. A high-speed exit in either direction. Nothing to say where. Quick. Efficient. Flawless." He closed his eyes, trying to blot out the dull ache that had lodged itself behind them.

Hogan sighed. "Quite an operation," he said.

Yes, thought Garrison. Quite an operation. Well planned, well executed and well targeted. Too well targeted, perhaps. The thoughts flitting idly to and fro coalesced, took hold, and grew until he could ignore them no longer.

He opened his eyes and pushed the chair forward into a slightly more upright position, regarding Hogan with a mild curiosity. "Why do you think they chose them?" he asked casually. "Why Thirty-five, Thirty-six and Forty? Why none of the others?"

"Nearest the emergency exit?" Hogan suggested.

"Yes," Garrison agreed. "Not the main exit. Doesn't that strike you as odd?"

Hogan frowned, looking none the wiser. "Easier access?"

"Oh, you couldn't say that," Garrison objected. "Not really – not from the outside. The emergency exit presents far greater access problems, wouldn't you say?" He was beginning to think Hogan was being particularly dim-witted not to have come to this conclusion himself.

"You mean the external stairs?"

Garrison leaned forward across his desk to emphasise the point. "Yes – the external stairs, Mister Hogan. Metal stairs. Potentially noisy stairs. Two flights of them – with automatic safety lighting to disable as well as the security systems. And then there's the emergency door to deal with. It has to be forced because it doesn't open naturally from the outside. And all this has to be done with considerable speed and silence before they can even enter the premises. Why take such a monumental risk to break in if they just wanted to snatch a couple of our experiments – any experiments? All they had to do was surprise the Duty Officer at the main entrance. That would have been so much easier, wouldn't it? They could have accessed the main lobby in a matter of seconds. In fact," he added, more for his own benefit than Hogan's, "I must take that point up with Security. Extra precautions need to be put in place in future."

"Maybe they didn't know there was only one officer on duty?" Hogan suggested.

"Possibly."

"And maybe they didn't want any witnesses. No violence. It would be safer in the long run."

"Perhaps," Garrison conceded, "Although they haven't been too scrupulous about such matters in the past."

Hogan just frowned, possibly accepting the truth of this observation.

Garrison sighed, his thoughts momentarily distracted by the distant sound of an approaching stores skeeter making its presence heard through the half-open window. He turned his head to watch the pilot bring the machine down in a graceful arc to the helipad behind the waste incineration block, the sunlight glancing off its fuselage in a blinding shaft of silver. Unacceptable thoughts intruded into his mind again and refused to go away. He turned back to Hogan. "How many people in this facility know about Forty?" he asked pointedly.

Hogan stirred himself and gave consideration to the question. "Only those on the secure list," he said. "Apart from yourself there's just the Technical Medics – Bakhara, Montagu, Gomez, Terrence – and the Cleaning Operatives, but they're contained in the staffing compound when they're not on duty and have no access to outside communication."

"And there's you, Mister Hogan." Garrison reminded him.

Hogan looked embarrassed. "Yes, of course – me."

"I'm not suggesting anyone might have purposely breached what's required of them, you understand?"

Hogan was taken aback by the suggestion. "Unthinkable," he said vehemently.

"Yes, well – unthinkable or not – isn't it possible someone might have been less than mindful of their responsibilities when off-duty for example? – say when they've been in the restaurant area for instance? The bar, maybe? A casual remark possibly? Just in passing to someone else not on the list?" Garrison made sure he made this sound perfectly possible.

Hogan began to look distinctly nervous. He sat upright, thrusting his hands onto the seat of his chair to steady himself. "No – never," he said, obviously keen to dispel such an unacceptable notion, but showing visible signs of catching the drift of where the questioning was leading.

"Mm," Garrison said, rising from his position behind his desk and walking with slow deliberation towards the window next to his Chief. He stood for a while studying the view, noticing one of the Clinic's current residents, still in his sleepsuit at such an hour, was admiring the blooms of the particularly fine bright-pink rhododendron in the centre bed. "Mm," he repeated, anticipating the likely effect of what he was about to say. "Well, Mister Hogan, I think we have to accept that someone has been very loose-tongued. Someone on the secure list has been responsible for an information leak. Someone on the secure list has either direct – or indirect connections with the Genetic Rights Movement." He cast a glance in Hogan's direction only to ensure he was engaging fully in what was being said. "I therefore propose to ask all of you," he went on, "- including you, Mister Hogan, to make statements to Security this afternoon. Based on these, and in consultation with Chief Security Officer Conrad of course, I intend to authorise Statement Ratings on each of you afterwards."

There was only the briefest pause before Hogan was on his feet. "That's monstrous!" he protested.

Garrison turned to face him. "Not from where I'm standing," he said crisply so that Hogan was in no doubt whatever there would be no exceptions in this case. "One of you has undoubtedly spoken out of turn. Perhaps not intentionally – I would honestly like to believe that – but nevertheless, out of turn." He quit his station by the window and returned to his desk. He remained standing however, adding his full height to the authority of his words. "I need to know who that person was."

Hogan had started to sweat, beads of perspiration visibly

standing out on his forehead. "But we were all A-One vetted ..." he began.

"That was in the past," Garrison reminded him. "Times change. People change. Circumstances change. Nothing stays the same. I'm fully aware of this, but I need total confidence in my staff here, Mister Hogan, and at the moment, I'm not in that happy position."

"What about Palatine?" Hogan blurted out, colour suddenly rushing back into his face. "Can you trust Palatine?"

"Palatine has no knowledge of Forty, Mister Hogan. At least -" he added as an afterthought now that anything was possible, "not as far as I'm aware."

Hogan's face had turned almost purple. His breathing had become fast and highly audible, anger fighting with tiredness and undisguised fear. "And you should keep it that way," he choked out, lurching against the leather-topped desk and covering Garrison with a fine haze of spittle at such close proximity. "Call in the Enforcers!" he urged with a desperation Garrison had never seen him exhibit in all the years of their long association. "It's their job to hunt down criminals – activists – not Palatine's!"

Garrison sat down to avoid any further contamination from Hogan's heightened emotional state and turned his attention instead to the desk monitor, consigning the unwelcome message recording the failure of the security sweep to the data dump. His patience was beginning to evaporate. "Mister Hogan," he said, feeling what he was about to say had already been rehearsed and shouldn't have needed to become the subject of further discussion. "I've made it quite clear I've not the slightest intention of letting experiment Forty become public property. You may not like Palatine's methods, but you have to admit they are usually effective. Regardless of whether or not your Statement Ratings provide a useful lead, I shall certainly need someone who is effective in returning Forty to this Clinic as soon as possible."

Hogan started to back away towards the door, visibly shaking and barely able to control himself.

Garrison verbally helped him on his way. "I expect all of you to report to Chief Security Officer Conrad at fourteen-hundred hours," he ordered. "That should give you sufficient time to draft your written statements on your whereabouts between twenty-three-hundred hours yesterday and zero-two-thirty this morning. Mister Conrad will arrange the times for you to undergo your respective Statement Ratings." He input a string of access codes and brought up the work rotas for the day on-screen. "Thank you, Mister Hogan. You may go." He looked up from the screen and pressed the door control.

Without another word, Hogan turned and stumbled out.

The door sighed shut behind him. The room relaxed into silence. Garrison waited a moment than flicked open his communication channels. Conrad answered almost immediately.

ELEVEN

Hardcopy data from the Statement Ratings lay strewn across Garrison's desk. He viewed the incomprehensible graphs and jargon-riddled analysis with some unease, feeling – unusually for him – out of his depth. The sense of outrage at having to resort to such a methodology only added to his discomfort.

Hogan and Conrad were sitting opposite him, an incongruous pair: Hogan, in his crumpled white suit, unshaven and slumped in his seat unable to keep his head from lolling forward every now and then; Conrad in his immaculate black dress-uniform with silver piping around the collar and cuffs, sitting erect, and alert as a wolf.

Whatever Hogan was thinking, his anger and humiliation still burned visibly in his features. There were tight lines around his mouth, and when on occasions he took the opportunity to glare in Garrison's direction, his eyes were red-rimmed and watery. Garrison was left in no doubt that their previously good working relationship had been irreparably damaged. No matter, he told himself, it had been necessary.

Lack of sleep was playing havoc with his own concentration, he decided, trying to turn his mind to what his Chief of Security was saying.

A snake-eyed man in his early forties with grizzled, close-cropped hair, Conrad was not averse to a little violence, if it provided the necessary stimulus to elicit information. He was reeling off a summary of his findings from a portable on his lap in a cold, dead-pan voice. He finished, and after a suitable pause added casually, "Which means your information leak came from Montagu."

Garrison looked up from the bewildering array of data in front of him, his former anger now reduced to the familiar dull ache behind his eyes that had refused to budge for two days. Conrad was nothing if not thorough, he thought. A man in black with a mind to match. "So where are the indicators?" he asked mechanically, scanning the mass of information that blurred in front of his eyes.

Conrad leaned forward across the desk. With a well-manicured finger he pointed to a red-circled figure and indicated the corresponding leap in the graph line opposite. "Here," he said. "A subliminal memory trace."

"What exactly does that mean?"

"No overt recollection of the incident."

"Are you actually saying he can't *remember* doing it?"

"Not at a conscious level."

"Well I suppose that's some consolation – but does it help at all?"

Conrad smiled faintly. It was a rather unpleasant smile to Garrison's way of thinking. "It helps *you* to know you don't have a real bastard on your staff – just a careless loud-mouth. It helped *me* to follow a new lead."

Garrison was beginning to wish he could terminate this interview as quickly as possible. He was suddenly very weary of Conrad – of everything.

"Once the trace was identified," Conrad was saying, getting into his stride, "it was just a matter of repeating the process – at a higher level of course – to lift Montagu's subconscious into his consciousness. Loosen things up a bit, if you like."

What an appalling man, thought Garrison. Necessary, but appalling, and with some effort he kept his expression devoid of anything that might betray the extent of his revulsion.

From the depths of his chair, Hogan stirred and glared at Conrad through blood-shot eyes. "You mean you strung him out," he said, with a voice that Garrison barely recognised – a rough, rasping sound, distorted by the use of drugs and neural probing.

Conrad raised one eyebrow glancing briefly in Hogan's direction. "Different methods achieve different ends," he said smoothly and turning back to Garrison added, "Neural probing at a higher level. Veracidrine. A bit of this, a bit of that. It's what *you* wanted." And there it was again – that dreadful smile.

Garrison had no need of reminding. He turned his mind away from the ugly reality. "So, Mister Conrad, what do we know?"

Conrad casually spread the hardcopy across the desk top as if it were a deck of cards. His eyes skimmed over several pages, apparently reading it upside down with little difficulty, until he came to the relevant information he wished to enlarge upon. "Montagu talked to someone visiting the Clinic during this time-scale – here," he said, indicating the date-fix on a graph, "and this provided the basis for further investigation. The results are available on this." And he undid the top pocket of his uniform, drawing out a vid cover-slip. "It's encrypted of course," he added, handing it over to Garrison. "For additional security."

Garrison studied the object that now lay in his hand and frowned at it. "And what precisely is this?" he asked.

Conrad looked at him as though he considered the question hardly worthy of a response. "It's the statutorily required visual record of Montagu's further interrogation," he said in his most infuriating tone. "You can use the sound-only option if you prefer," he added, implying a contempt for Garrison's sensibilities which was not lost on his listener.

Garrison gave him the benefit of a stony, fixed stare: that he should want to watch, or even listen to, a form of official torture, was quite beyond the pale. He was offended by the very notion. "Précis it for me, will you?" he said stiffly, putting the wretched thing and its contents to one side on the desk. Even touching it was a kind of contamination he wanted to avoid.

Conrad leaned back with a superior nonchalance and crossed his long legs. "If you prefer," he said, as though the matter were of supreme indifference to him. "Montagu's 'contact', for want of a better word, is someone who visits the Clinic on a regular basis – but not to any set time-scale. From the data available, it appears nothing specific was said to this person. Perhaps it was nothing more than an off-the-cuff remark," he added. "But whatever Montagu said, it drew attention to those three experiments as potentially interesting."

"And you've established who visited the Clinic during the period in question and who might have had contact with Montagu?"

"There's no one individual that can be identified at the moment." Conrad explained, exhibiting a small irritation that this was the case. "There were three visits by personnel from the Waste Containment Executive; two from TMI – Techno-Maintenance International, and a couple of reps from BPI – Bio-Products Incorporated."

"And you can't be any more precise than that?" Garrison said, feeling a small frisson of satisfaction at Conrad's frustrated expectations.

Sensing perhaps that he was being purposely needled, Conrad paused before giving Garrison his answer. "As I explained," he said crisply, "what we uncovered was a casual, non-specific conversation which took place about six months ago. But we can be absolutely certain that Montagu had the opportunity to meet personnel from all three of these organisations."

"I see," Garrison said and sat back to survey Hogan, noticing he was no longer taking any interest in the conversation: his eyes were glazed.

"With your authority, Dr Garrison," Conrad was suggesting "Clinic Security could take the matter further – unless you intend to bring in the Enforcers of course."

"I think under these particular circumstances, Mister Conrad, I shall do neither," he said with heavy emphasis. "These experiments are a vital part of our research and development programme. For patent reasons, this matter must remain in the private domain – and, much as I admire your thoroughness, Mister Conrad, I believe some of the enquiries might require greater resources than Clinic Security has at its disposal."

Conrad level-gazed him for a moment and then nodded, seeming to accept the situation. He unwound himself smoothly out of his chair and straightened his uniform. "Can I take it then that you won't be needing me further at this stage?"

"Not at this stage," Garrison confirmed. "Thank you for your help with this matter."

Conrad nodded and made for the door.

"By the way," Garrison asked casually, "Does Montagu know that he's breached the Clinic's Confidentiality Code?"

Conrad turned. "He does now," he said, his face expressionless.

"And what is the condition of his cognitive processes at the moment, would you say?"

There was a raised eyebrow in response to this. "What condition do you expect him to be in, Dr Garrison?"

"I expect you to answer my question, Mister Conrad."

Conrad didn't even blink. "In that case – less than adequate."

"And how long will it take for him to recover from the heightened probing?"

"You would have to ask a Psy-Medic to answer that question, Dr Garrison. I only carry out procedures – as requested. It may take a month – maybe a year." He paused to reflect. "Maybe never."

Garrison looked into Conrad's soulless eyes and was irritated with himself for asking: he'd already known the range of possible outcomes.

"Anything else, Dr Garrison?" Conrad was asking.

"No – thank you, Mister Conrad."

Conrad came crisply to attention, turned smoothly and left.

There was silence after he'd gone. Hogan remained hunched in his chair, head bent, his breathing audibly laboured. Beads of sweat still clung to his high forehead and glistened in a shaft of down-lighting.

The silence became suffocating. "How do you feel?" Garrison asked, realising almost immediately his question didn't deserve an answer.

Hogan lifted his head slowly. "How the hell do you expect me to feel?" he rasped. "Glowing with health? I feel bloody lousy, if you really want to know. Bloody lousy."

"Yes – of course. I'm sorry."

Hogan made an attempt at laughter. "You aren't sorry – you're just bloody embarrassed. Well, at least I'm still sane. That's probably more than can be said of Montagu, isn't it?"

There wasn't much Garrison could say to that. He cleared his throat and let some silence come between them again for a moment. "I'm pleased it wasn't you who was responsible for the leak," he said at last, hoping this might in some small way be a consolation to Hogan.

His Chief simply glared back at him, his truculence more tangible in his silence than in anything he might have said.

"Regardless of what you believe, Hogan, I am truly sorry this was necessary, but security in the R&D wing must be watertight. There's no place for tittle-tattle, intentional or otherwise. A breach of confidentiality has to be tracked down, however unpleasant for those who are totally blameless."

Hogan was studying the visible tremor that had set up in his hands.

"I had to authorise the Ratings – you must see that. I *had* to find the leak."

"And you'll bring in Palatine to do the rest, I suppose?" Hogan commented, his concentration still fixed on his hands.

"Of course! Forty is an extremely valuable asset. His loss is incalculable as far as our future development work is concerned. He's unique. It's imperative he's found and returned here as soon as possible – and not just for our sake either," he added meaningfully. "I don't need to spell it out for you surely?"

Hogan shifted uncomfortably in his seat and turned his head slowly towards the window, his attention caught by the silhouette of a butterfly fluttering softly against the pane.

Garrison sighed and wished he could find a polite way of asking Hogan to leave: there were other more pressing matters he needed to attend to. Hogan however showed no sign of going anywhere. Garrison cleared his throat again. "I need to deal with Montagu," he said, wishing Hogan would take the hint.

Hogan didn't respond.

"The Clinic cannot afford to retain personnel who divulge experimental programme data – or to let them go without the necessity of ensuring they do not jeopardise our work in future."

The butterfly lost interest in its futile quest to enter the room and flew away. Hogan's attention drifted back to what Garrison was saying. He nodded, a haunted look flickering briefly across his face. "Yes – I understand what has to be done."

"Good. I will instruct a Psy-Medic to initiate the necessary erasure procedures as soon as possible."

Hogan's eyes met his for a moment. "How much?" he asked.

"As much as necessary. I don't wish to send the man back to his family totally de-animated of course, but it's essential that all recollection of his time here is erased."

"And how will you explain that to his family?"

Garrison was surprised by the question. "Explain? Good heavens, Hogan, there's no need to explain! The Clinic has every right to initiate erasure procedures for gross misconduct. That point is made perfectly clear to everyone who joins the experimental programme. It's in the contract. Montagu accepted those terms just as you all did. Which is why – if you haven't noticed before – I pay you all very well, very well indeed." He felt deeply offended by the need to mention this. Hogan's attitude was beginning to irritate him. It was time for action. "Now, if you'll excuse me, I need to get on. Let me have a revised duty roster with effect from today, will you?" he ordered. "And reallocate Montagu's work-load while you're about it," he added bitterly.

The order registered in Hogan's mangled thought processes. He dragged himself out of his chair with painful slowness and leaned heavily against the desk for support. "When do you want Montagu's quarters cleared?" he asked.

Garrison wondered if the man had completely lost all his initiative. "Now, of course," he said briskly. "He'll be confined to the MediCentre secure wing until arrangements can be made for him to be transhipped home."

Hogan was still hovering, seemingly unwilling to leave.

"Is there anything else?" Garrison asked.

"I was just wondering," Hogan said, seeming to be casting around for the right words. "Well – if any of the rest of the team wanted to leave – voluntarily, I mean – for any reason – would it be the same for us?"

Garrison looked up from an analysis program he'd just activated on his monitor. "What are you talking about?"

"Erasure." The word triggered a nervous tic at one side of Hogan's mouth.

"Good heavens, man – I thought we'd just covered that point! It's in everyone's contract!"

Hogan blinked and made a grunt of acknowledgement.

Scrutinising his Chief Technical Officer with renewed interest, an unpleasant thought insinuated itself into Garrison's mind. "You aren't thinking of leaving, are you, Mister Hogan?" he asked casually.

Hogan shook his head.

TWELVE

Like the Garrison Clinic, Miles McMichael's personal kingdom lacked nothing except accessibility. It was perched on the barren, rocky plateau of Philomos, an isolated, insignificant little island in the Ionian Sea, heaved into existence during the great 'quake of 2160. There were no exquisite sandy beaches, no inviting secluded bays: its flanks were craggy rock faces, rising sheer and forbidding on all sides from the bedrock deep in the restless sea. And like the Clinic, the only access to this secluded spot was via a skeeter, the helipad marked out on an area just outside the main complex.

Smiler's business associates who might visit – other agents, financiers and potential clients – were housed in his guest wing, each with a personal suite of rooms with lavish facilities, attended by individual staff allocated to provide basic services. Additional specialists were available on demand to offer more exotic, possibly less obvious requirements. Smiler's reputation was spun out of the knowledge that he liked to cater for all tastes, but he never did anything without a reason. His gifts usually came at a price.

The complex's reception areas were impressive: grandiose beyond necessity; opulent to the point of vulgarity. Marble was used as if it were little more than commonplace polyplastic: floors were of polished rosso antico, warm to the eyes, but cool to the touch. On them floated islands of deep-piled carpets in dusky purples and gold. Groups of high-backed loungers were ranged in close proximity to one another for intimate conversations – or other alternative social interactions. Their leather, with the creamy smoothness of a Parian sculpture, was draped in exotic wraps of Persian designs and colours. Near them, low side-tables in glossy black marble had legs carved in the style of miniature Doric columns, while exquisitely moulded replicas of ancient bronze statues stood guard at the doors holding alabaster bowls filled with sweetly-scented rose petals. On three sides of the room, the highly-polished walls of white marble streaked with delicate grey tracery, gleamed in the afternoon sun, while the fourth was a continuous line of gossamer-light curtains veiling the panoramic full-length windows that opened out onto an expansive terrace. Out from its balustrade, visitors could admire the breath-taking beauty of the setting sun on the dappled turquoise waters below. To the south, a colonnade covered in abundant vines led to a palatial flight of curving steps which descended to reveal another expansive terrace, surrounded by a backdrop of tamarisk, ceanothus, sweetly scented daphne – and high walls. Here a large oval swimming pool lined with blue and green tesserae in pastel hues dominated the space, and around this a range of loungers offered bathers the option of lazing in the sun or the more private facilities available in the recesses set into the walls.

Smiler rarely visited this version of Paradise, preferring his own private quarters situated well away from any visitor's prying eyes. Access to his personal apartments was limited to only the select few. His office suite however, attached to the main complex, was open to all. He took pride in showing it to everyone, filled as it was with the latest technology and management gadgetry of every kind, all individually tailored to meet his very particular needs, allowing him to be completely independent of any outside interference. And as no one shared the fortune he'd amassed from his Entertainer empire, it was indeed his, and his alone to do with as he pleased.

"I have total control," he'd once bragged, eager to impress Cassandra when, despite Karoli's enthusiasm, she'd had her doubts about joining his agency. "I don't pay staff I don't need. Got enough of them looking after my guests," he'd added slurring his words and downing another exotic cocktail, knowing she'd understand precisely what he meant, and in doing so badly misjudged her reaction.

Cassandra had travelled only once before to Philomos – with Karoli, Theo and Umo – and she'd been glad to leave. For all its opulence, from the very beginning she'd sensed there was something unwholesome about the place and the man who owned it. But, despite her misgivings, she'd let Karoli convince her the McMichael Entertainment Agency was the one to sign up to – anyone who was anyone was already under his wing. Coming back to this place on her own rekindled all her old doubts and anxieties. But Smiler had been insistent – the invitation was specifically for her, and only her – without any explanation as to why Theo and Umo hadn't been included.

Theo had understood her reluctance. "But if that's what McMichael wants," he'd said, "you'll have to go." But it left her feeling very vulnerable, and very alone.

On the outflight, the skeeter pilot did nothing to ease her disquiet, seemingly determined to engage her in conversation, despite his position as one of the favoured few on Smiler's personal staff. As such he was required to be a functionary and nothing more. She ignored him for the most part, but he was unstoppable and not above openly weighing her up, even to the point of mentioning he'd seen one of The Choralians' surger-pop performances. "Hey, you really gave me a blast that night," he said, giving her a meaningful sideways glance. "Wouldn't mind watching that again some time."

"I'll tell Mister McMichael, if you like," she said, knowing if she did, Smiler wouldn't hesitate in dismissing him. It had the required effect, but didn't stop him continuing to evaluate her potential. Keeping him at bay for the rest of the flight made concentrating on other matters difficult: on maintaining her dignity; on feigning an interest in the barren white outcrops of the islands below; on being mentally alive – and alert.

They touched down. One of the service boys was waiting to greet her on the helipad, the wind from the skeeter blades catching at his short white tunic and whipping it about his limbs. He graciously offered his hand to help her down and took her travel bag, showing the way to her quarters with deferential little bows and expansive hand movements. He was good-looking, olive-skinned with dark, liquid eyes and long lashes, still very much in his teens and anxious to please. An exotic aroma of expensive essence hovered around him as he moved. Inside her guest suite, he gave her a tour around the array of facilities available with the same little rituals and smiles, avoiding too much eye contact in case this should be taken to mean he was being too forward. He would be available for her pleasure only if she wished it.

The doors onto her balcony had been left open, the light fabric of the curtains rippling in lazy folds, like cobwebs caught in the breeze. In her pleasantly cool bedroom a message marker flashed intermittently on the wall screen. Smiling shyly, the boy indicated its presence and bowed, pausing for a moment just in case she should require anything further. She thanked him briefly and he left without a word, tactfully accepting his services were not required for the moment.

For a few minutes, she'd no desire to do anything except indulge in the coolness of the evening breeze wafting through the open doorway. She removed her travelsuit and wearing only her lightweight second skins stretched out on the wide expanse of cream coverlet, breathing deeply, absorbing the clear tanginess of the sea air, savouring the light-headed sensation it produced that was so different from the recycled atmospheres of space existence. She never wanted to smell or taste that strange, lifeless air again.

But what had to be done could not be put off for ever. Smiler would have seen her land; he'd be waiting for her to respond to his message. Reluctantly, she pulled herself upright and activated the screen. The geometric MEA logo dissolved into its component parts and coalesced into Smiler's unlovely features beaming out at her from his pre-recorded memo-vid. He was perverse enough to rejoice in his nickname because, as he was very eager to explain to all and sundry, it made him sound avuncular, but he was not a pretty sight. He was, to put it bluntly, repulsively grotesque: a huge, over-fed individual with putty-coloured features and multiple double chins. His beady, blood-shot eyes peered out at the world with some difficulty from their puffy sockets set in his mottled cheeks, and his bulbous blue-veined nose sat awkwardly above his thick, blubbery lips. A shock of grey-white hair swept backwards from his high-domed forehead, curling behind his fleshy ears in exaggerated greasy waves that hid his neck from view. Taken as a whole, he looked remarkably like a misshapen beached whale with seaweed on its head, and a great deal older than his fifty years.

His dress sense was as grotesque as the man. The garish image smiling out at her was dressed in a striped scarlet and lime-green undershirt, which did nothing for his skin tones and played havoc with the transmission pixels.

In a voice that had got lost in the mountain of flesh only to emerge as a wheezing gravelly croak, he said, "Hi sweetie. Glad you could make it." He'd chosen to speak in English. From anyone else, Cassandra would have taken this recognition of her polyglot abilities as a compliment. But not from him. She'd have preferred him to stick to UniCom. English gave him the opportunity to be too familiar, something she'd no wish to encourage.

"I know you must be pooped out after your journey," he went on in his dreadful, vulgar vernacular, "So give yourself the night off. Relax. Have a swim. Watch a vid. Whatever you like. If you need anything special, buzz for Tobar. He's the lovely boy you met at the helipad. Isn't he a sight for sore eyes? You might have gathered he's not so good at conversation though. Well, that's because he's a mute – but you can ask him for anything. He's very obliging," he added, making it sound obscene. "Okay?" The expansive smile split across his monumental face, leering at her. "But don't keep him up too late, sweetie. He needs his beauty sleep too. See you in the conference suite tomorrow – say at ten? 'Bye for now." And his image faded out to be replaced by the MEA logo and soft, indefinable musi-tone.

She turned off the screen, sickened to her soul, and stepped out onto the balcony and into the late afternoon sun. Out of the cooling shadows, nothing stirred. Even now in late October, the heat poured into her. She leaned against the marble balustrade and closed her eyes, breathing in the warm scents of the air. The skeeter had gone; there was a blissful silence, only the breeze sighing in the rock crannies and the occasional slop of a wave on the rocks below. Even the sea birds were silent.

Everything was at peace – except for herself. Inside, she was edgy: listening; waiting; uncertain what to expect. Why had Smiler been so insistent she should come alone? She'd no power to decide The Choralians' future without Theo and Umo – and she'd made this very plain – or thought she had. But he'd still insisted.

"Look, sweetie," he'd wheezed over the vidLink two days earlier. "I've got this guy – completely new. I'd like you to take a look at his demos – see what you think."

"Miles, what are you saying?"

He'd smiled awkwardly but not convincingly. "Well – you know ..." And he'd trailed off leaving it unsaid.

"It's too soon, Miles," she'd protested. "It's only a month ..."

He'd shaken his gross head and wagged an admonishing podgy finger at her. "Listen, my treasure, you're Entertainers, okay? You've got a grieving public out there waiting for you. They're all heart. They want to feel your pain. They want you to share it with them – good and hard." He'd paused to recover his breath and let her reflect on this. "Look, sweetie, this guy might be just what you Choralians need to get back on the road again."

Feeling cornered, she'd retaliated. "If he's that good, Miles, then we should all see his vids – not just me."

He'd screwed up his face into a mask of fabricated embarrassment. "Yeah, well I know that, sweetie, but let's face it, it's you he'd be working with. I mean, you'd be the one ..."

Almost at breaking point, she'd been unable to tolerate his easy disregard for her dignity a moment longer. "No surger-pop!" she'd said flatly. "You understand, Miles? No surger-pop! No more!"

He'd had the temerity to shrug off her refusal with one of his odiously coy smirks. "Oh, come on, sweetie," he'd wheezed. "No offence meant. You're a professional. I'm not asking you to plug him in straight off."

But she'd known that was precisely what he expected her to do.

He'd gone on, ignoring what must have been her very visible anger. "He's just too good to lose, that's all. Come on over to Philomos and let me show you his demos. That's all I'm asking. You can look them over, think about it, take them back and chew on it with the other guys and let me know. What do you say?"

She'd wanted to say, "Go to the crows!" but she also knew she couldn't keep Theo and Umo cooling their heels much longer. They needed to be working even if she didn't. She'd agreed, her anger draining away, leaving her exhausted. Almost as an afterthought she'd asked him, "So what's his name? – this guy who's too good to miss."

"Jason – Jason Raymer – Jay for short – and you're going to love him."

That, she thought, was the most tactless thing Smiler had ever said to her.

THIRTEEN

The image on the vast wall-screen in the conference room faded into blackness. Smiler was lounging back into his couch and helping himself to a ripe pear from the fruit bowl at his elbow. "So what do you think of him, sweetie?" he said, sinking his teeth into the soft flesh and letting the juice run down his chin.

The morning sunlight slanted downward from the high narrow windows along the eastern side of the room, lighting up the voluminous expanse of white toga he was wearing over a lurid pink full-length tunic. From this enormous heap of fabric protruded his wide, unlovely, sandalled feet. Cassandra decided, on reflection, he looked more like a walrus than a whale – a walrus with a smug, self-satisfied expression on its face.

She'd no intention of immediately answering his question. Instead, she adopted delaying tactics, picking out a choice peach from the selection available and caressing the soft down on its skin as she gathered her thoughts. She'd been very careful to maintain a neutral expression during the vid play-back, keeping in check anything that might betray what she was thinking. Smiler had been watching her closely, looking for any reaction to the sound and image of the man on the screen.

Once the performance was over, Smiler had launched into his sales pitch, reeling off all the reasons why Raymer was someone The Choralians couldn't afford to turn down. She'd listened in silence until he'd finished, but now he was waiting for her answer.

She knew what was expected of her: she was to wax eloquent on what a truly fantastic catch Jason Raymer was; on how brilliant Smiler had been in getting hold of him, and how remarkable Raymer was as a potential Folkster – to say nothing of his stunning good looks. She could deny none of these things, but equally, her only genuine response was a persistent underlying unease – something she couldn't clearly identify beyond a vague concern that refused to be dispelled.

"Oh, come on, sweetie," Smiler was urging, feigning hurt. "Don't tell me you can't see he's got a load going for him?" His tongue travelled across his thick lips with a terrible anticipation.

"Does he enjoy your company?" she asked maliciously, taking a bite out of the peach for good measure.

Smiler's expression slipped into one of annoyance for a moment before being rapidly replaced by his dreadful unctuous smile. "Now that was naughty of you, sweetie," he said reproachfully. "You know he's not my type."

There wasn't much to be gained by antagonising him unnecessarily, she realised. Jason Raymer was a grown man, somewhere in his late twenties, early thirties maybe. Smiler liked his companions much younger. So why, she was asking herself as she casually finished the peach and let the attendant youth at her elbow offer her a warmed, damp towel to wipe its juice from her hand, was she so reluctant to say what was blindingly obvious? Why was her enthusiasm for this good-looking man, with his superb Folkster singing voice, and obvious musical talent with a variety of instruments, dampened by an abiding anxiety that refused to budge? Was it simply that she couldn't overcome her suspicion that Smiler wanted the obvious physical attractiveness of Raymer to lead on to other things, despite her refusal to engage in any future surger-pop performances?

Smiler helped himself to another pear. "The Choralians need to get back on the road, Cassie," he said, his tone of voice taking on a slightly sharper edge. He was running out of patience, and she knew why. From a purely business point of view, Smiler was losing money. No doubt he'd already got a scheduled tour up his sleeve for The Choralians, and Jason Raymer was the obvious answer to his prayers.

Cassandra could feel herself beginning to panic. She realised she'd not discarded the peach stone: she was clutching it in her hand, its sharp point digging into the soft flesh of her palm.

Smiler munched his way through the second pear with careful deliberation and discarded the core onto the table top beside him. "What's holding you back, sweetie?" he said, reverting to avuncular wheedling. "Don't you like the way he moves?" And he activated the replay before she could answer, this time on low sound. "Just look at him!" he said, waving a trunk of an arm in the direction of the screen. "He'll have audiences screaming for more first time around."

"The way he moves is less important than the way he sounds," she retaliated, clutching at straws and knowing it. "We're a Folkster group, Miles. I sometimes think you forget that."

"Hey, don't play hard to get with me, Cassie. This guy's got a great voice."

"Then why haven't we heard of him before?"

Smiler frowned. "Because he's fresh on the professional scene, sweetie," he explained with exaggerated emphasis. "New. Brand new," he added for effect.

"So how did you find him, Miles? Is he a favour you owe someone?"

Smiler looked hurt beyond imagining. "I don't owe favours to anyone," he said, his tone conciliatory. "Except you," he added. "Why do you think I got him for you?" And he smiled horribly.

She clutched the peach stone harder, the pain reminding her to keep alert. "What do you want me to say, Miles? That he's perfect? All right – he's perfect – except I know nothing about him. So what was he doing before you 'discovered' him?"

Smiler sighed. "What does it matter, sweetie?" he said, wearing the pained look of a martyr.

His reluctance goaded her. "What precisely?" she insisted.

He studied his podgy fingers, still apparently reluctant to give her an answer. "Social engineering," he said at last, avoiding her gaze.

If she'd been asked to guess, it would have taken a thousand years for her to come up with that reply.

Her expression must have said it all: he shrugged apologetically. "Did he practise, Miles? Don't tell me he practised!"

He shifted his great bulk around on the couch, still visibly uncomfortable. "For a while," he conceded. "But only for a while," he added hastily. "Nothing major, believe me. Administration – that sort of thing – nothing operational, you understand."

"It's still loathsome, Miles. I wouldn't want to be anywhere near him."

Smiler's previous embarrassment evaporated with lightning speed. "I wouldn't get so hung up on his biodata, Cassie," he said, the edgy tone of voice rearing its ugly head again. "Okay, it's not to everyone's taste – but no worse than Karoli's was – or yours." And he looked her straight in the eyes as he said it.

Her revulsion flared briefly into anger. Trust Smiler to bring that up now, of all times, and with all her heart she wished Karoli had never persuaded her to let Miles McMichael into their lives. He was nothing but a leach, sucking them all dry, using their flaky pasts as silent levers to make them do this, or that – or whatever. It wasn't exactly blackmail, but it was too close for comfort. She dug the peach stone harder into her palm.

The silence between them was punctuated only by the faint sounds from the unobtrusive vid speakers.

Smiler shifted his position again, dolefully watching the screen, his huge head propped disconsolately on the wedge of flesh and bone that constituted a fist. "I thought you'd be grateful I'd looked out someone for you," he said, sounding hurt, peevish almost, turning his attention from the screen to examine the finger nails of his other hand for a moment. "Chances like this don't happen too often," he added, eyeing her from beneath half-closed lids. "And I don't intend passing up on this one." His meaning was perfectly clear.

"So we have to take him, whether we want to or not? Is that what you mean?"

He pulled a face. "Face facts, Cassie. If The Choralians don't get back on tour in the next few weeks, your public's going to latch onto someone else. We've already lost that vid contract to the Mohawks. It was worth a packet. I could sell this guy to anyone. I'm offering him to you."

She could feel the noose tightening.

"Look, Cassie, I've an instinct for these things. I know a marketable product when I see it. I don't give a honk if Jason Raymer is straight off the back of a maintenance operative contract. I don't care if he was cleaning out cess-pits in some Aberrant backwater – he's got what it takes. Okay, he's an amateur. Been doing solo stuff for the last three years. Learning the ropes. Low grade openers, Cassie. Never had the right agent."

Until now, she thought. No one but Miles McMichael would touch a guy with social engineering on his biodata.

"This is a great move for The Choralians," Smiler was saying, the familiar wheeze back in place as he shifted his position once more. "You can mould this guy just the way you want him." And he turned up the sound again.

She got up from her couch, feeling the sudden need for fresh air. The marble floor had a reassuringly solid feel beneath her feet. Jason Raymer was crooning softly from the screen, nursing a choraladian like a lover, his strong tenor voice sliding moodily through its performance, accompanied by shimmering notes that sent a shiver down her spine. At the split second she glanced at his image, he seemed to look right through her. It was like being hit in the solar plexus. She caught her breath and turned away. "I can't sell him to the others on the basis of a cheap demo, Miles," she protested. "It's not enough. It's not even a basic hologram or VR. He could be all electronics and no reality." She headed towards the open doorway onto the terrace.

"Sure, I know that," his gravelly voice trailed after her. "I just wanted your first impressions."

She walked out into the cleansing breezes of the morning air, eager to escape Smiler's malign presence. Her head was becoming strangely light, floating away from her. Behind her she heard him heaving himself onto his feet, his thick-soled sandals scuffing against the smooth marble in time to his wheezing progress towards her. She leaned hard against the balustrade for support and threw the peach stone as far as she could, watching it drop away into the sea in a graceful arc.

He came up close, so close she could feel his breath on the side of her face and smell the dreadful sweetness of his scented hair oil. One fat paw settled on her shoulder. Inwardly, she flinched.

"Would you prefer to see him in the flesh – so to speak?" he suggested crudely.

She moved away from him, intent on escape, although she'd not the faintest idea how she might achieve this. He was blocking her way. Steadying herself, she began a sedate progress along the remaining length of the balustrade, running her hand over the cool stonework while her mind free-wheeled seeking some way out.

He shuffled behind her like an obedient dog.

Her progress took her to the north end of the terrace to where three flights of marble steps led down to a walled area encircled by a colonnade surrounding a central fountain. Water trickled from a small pitcher held by a statue of a beautiful gilded youth as he stooped to empty the contents into the pool. But as she began to descend, her eyes caught sight of another figure, a man in a simple beige tunic over a pale cream leisuresuit leaning nonchalantly against the first pillar, arms folded, face averted, his attention apparently held by the ripples on the pool. She stopped in her tracks.

"Cassie," Smiler wheezed from the top terrace. "Wait for me."

The man by the pillar turned at the sound of Smiler's voice.

Cassandra had no need to guess his identity. Even without his make-up, his Entertainer persona and wild-hair piece, the set of the grey-blue eyes and ready smile were enough.

"*Kalimera*," he said, extending a hand as she came down to the bottom step.

A nice touch, she thought, weighing him up. High on his right cheekbone, a small scar showed like a silver crescent against a background of golden tan. Yes, a nice touch, she thought, for a social engineer, but a little too pat, perhaps. She took the hand, aware of its warmth and the scent of patchouli that wafted over her as she did so. It was an exotic scent for a Caucasian: out of place and slightly at odds with the sombre dress and the sobriety of the style in which he wore his natural tawny-coloured hair: it lay in lazy, careless curls reminiscent of those on statues of ancient Greek athletes. This little charade is to impress me, she thought. Was its artlessness quite so ingenuous at it seemed? She sensed it wasn't, but a perverse curiosity made her decide to play along for a while.

Smiler was still making his inelegant progress down the steps behind her. "Cassie, my sweet," he croaked, labouring to catch his breath and not succeeding very well. "Let me introduce you to Jason Raymer."

She forced her mouth into a smile. "*Kalimera*," she said, and released his hand, thinking of social engineering. "*Kserete Elinika?*"

He smiled disarmingly. "Only a little," he confessed, slipping into UniCom. "You have the advantage of me."

"If you prefer UniCom, I'm happy to use it – or English," she added suspecting this was his natural language.

"I'd prefer English," he said, giving her the benefit of his smile again.

She nodded her assent and turning back to Smiler, decided she was no longer prepared to hide her contempt for his duplicity. "What a surprise to find Mister Raymer here," she said caustically.

For once Smiler looked awkward, his bulk trying to reduce itself in size, and failing.

Quietly fuming, she turned and strolled casually around the pool, selecting a marble bench in the shade and sat down, waiting to see what would happen next. Smiler puffed after her and slumped onto the nearest bench available. Raymer was left standing at the bottom of the steps. "Will you not join us, Mister Raymer?" she asked, indicating the only other available bench by the side of the fountain. From her vantage point, she watched him move to the appointed spot. There was an easy litheness to his movements – like a dancer's – like Karoli's – just like Karoli. She shivered at the thought: Karoli's ghost was still too close.

He sat down, perfectly poised, and waited.

She let her attention be drawn to the patterns made by the light flickering across the surface of the water. Her heart was hammering its objections in her brain. She wasn't ready for this.

Smiler was still wheezing. Raymer continued to sit motionless, his expression one of patient expectation.

"Miles has shown me your demo," she managed at last, looking him squarely in the face, her voice strangely controlled under the circumstances, she thought. "A little primitive, perhaps, but impressive."

He acknowledged her assessment with a small nod.

"He tells me you're looking for your first professional break." It was half a question, half a statement, and she wondered if he would rise to the bait and sell himself – or would he rely on Smiler for his sales pitch.

"I'd like to think I had something to offer."

Too glib, she thought. "And have you?"

A look of surprise fleeting crossed his face. "I think so."

"Good. Then let me hear you sing. Here. Now."

He was visibly off-guard. "Now?" he repeated.

She nodded. "Yes. Now."

He frowned, glancing across at Smiler, apparently seeking guidance.

"Cassie wants to see if you're as good without the electronics," Smiler explained, still wheezing.

"Okay. Fine. Anything in particular?" he asked her.

"Any Folkster-style ballad will do."

"Right," he said with a little smile. That winning smile. A smile to capture an audience, she thought. He relied on it a lot.

He stood up, moving to a spot further away to where a vigorous vine had been encouraged to entwine itself around one of the colonnade pillars so that when he turned to face her, he was framed in vine leaves and bunches of dark, bruised-looking purple fruit. He'd chosen his position well. He paused, gathering himself. There was a moment's silence, then he began to sing.

His fine tenor voice was well pitched, each syllable clear, even there, where the acoustics had nothing to offer even the best balladeer, the sound rising to be swallowed up by the infinite openness of the sky.

The language was strange to her – Fatingu probably – the latest cultural vogue-tongue developed from a mish-mash of aboriginal languages to promote international music sales. Its use had sprung up during the time The Choralians had been on their Uranian tour, and she recognised the edge Raymer's knowledge of it gave him. It was something she'd have to turn her mind to.

She was increasingly drawn into his performance. The tune was hauntingly beautiful, its inner sadness tinged with undying hope. It would have been easy to lose her objectivity. Something else she would have to consider. Forcing herself to concentrate, she took a mental step backwards and began to evaluate him at a very practical level: the way he controlled his breathing; how he looked as he sang; the way he moved to add meaning to the words; and how he controlled the emotion behind the words so there was no need to understand the language. Yes, it was all there: everything. He was just what Theo and Umo would want to see – and hear. And yet ... And yet ...

He'd finished, taking the song up onto a high note, the last tones dying away on the breeze, leaving a void in their passing.

She let the silence hold the stage for a moment, then nodded approvingly, her approbation soured by the sight of Smiler's satyr-like grin.

"Would you like me to sing another?" Raymer was asking, eager to please.

She shook her head, turning again to watch the patterns of light dance across the surface of the pool.

Everything was happening too quickly – and much too soon.

FOURTEEN

This time Cassandra didn't care whether the skeeter pilot was giving her the once-over or not. Her nerves were at breaking point. Not a moment had passed since the unexpected meeting with Raymer that morning when she hadn't been forced to marshal every ounce of energy to keep her outward and visible self controlled and calm. Inside, she'd been twisting and turning, trying to find some way – any way – to escape what she increasingly saw as the inevitable. But there'd been no way out. Smiler had been all affability in his appalling way, but his meaning had been unambiguous – The Choralians were on their way out if she – or they – didn't accept the premise that Jason Raymer was to become a member of their group – and soon.

"Sure, you talk it over with the other guys," Smiler had said as she boarded the skeeter, his podgy hand hoisting her up into the passenger seat. But she knew there was nothing to talk over. She was trapped – they all were: she was taking back not just a demo vid and an enhanced hologram version Smiler had produced for her, but an uncompromising ultimatum as well.

It was simply a matter of the bottom line for Smiler: he'd a business to run. The Choralians were a marketable commodity. Human emotions had no place on his balance sheet. "Look, sweetie," he'd told her, "I understand – but you've had a clear month to do your grieving. I need commitment. You get a good cut of the takings. But – if you're not happy with what I'm offering, I can let you go. Just say the word and I'll get in touch with my lawyer." And there it was – the threat of breach of contract and an impossibly expensive get-out clause that none of them could afford. Karoli had bound them to the McMichael Entertainment Agency in good faith, never imagining the consequences would outlive him.

Smiler waved her off from the safe distance beyond the perimeter of the helipad. As the rotors began to spin, he was already waddling back to his apartments, summoning one of his young attendants hovering around in the background to follow him.

"Everything okay?" the pilot was asking her above the whine of the engine. He was watching her intently.

She nodded, persuading herself she was perfectly calm.

"Need anything?" he persisted.

"No, thank you."

He shrugged, visibly disappointed she'd no intention of engaging in small talk.

They took off.

Through gathering tears, she watched Philomos and the massive complex Smiler liked to call home, receding into the golden brilliance of the evening light spilling out across the Ionian Sea to the far horizon.

The skeeter turned sharply and headed eastward into the encroaching darkness settling over the mainland.

FIFTEEN

Between tours, Theo and Umo returned to their simply-furnished apartment in the Aktichoria on the coastal highway between Athens and Sounion.

Aktichoria were now recognised as properly constituted communes of Creatives: Artists, Writers and Entertainers. It hadn't always been the case: they'd originally sprung up at various locations dotted around the globe as these new bohemians gravitated together for their mutual benefit and protection.

After such a long absence, Theo took comfort from closing the door and keeping the world at bay. The apartment had never been so inviting, nor so welcome, its familiarity a source of joy, a small light in the surrounding gloom. Here at least he could try to unwind, with the assurance that within the community everyone's privacy was paramount. Comfort and support were gladly given, but only when they were openly sought. Neighbours learned to be discreet and tolerant, never pushy.

It had been a long time since Theo had felt so weary: the tour and its fateful stopover had drained his vitality. Umo was attentive, trying to make amends as best he could in every way possible. But Theo couldn't forget. Nor could he dismiss the distressing thought which persistently lingered at the forefront of his mind – that Umo's weakness had possibly been the cause of Karoli's sudden and terrible death. And sometimes he feared most of all that Umo could read these thoughts as surely as if he'd written them into the lines on his face.

The dreadful inertia that had engulfed him for days on end at the beginning of October was made worse by the lack of any immediate plans or future schedule. They were all directionless. Cassandra seemed unwilling, or unable, to make the first move and it worried him. Since their return, she'd become almost a recluse in the apartment she'd shared with Karoli, tucked away in the anonymous labyrinth of the Aktichoria in Athens. She'd wanted no one's company but her own; no one to share her grief or anger. Time was passing and they all needed to be doing something – anything – but it was still far too soon for her.

Smiler's suggestion she should fly over to Philomos had briefly raised his hopes, but when it came to it, he'd failed to find the right words to assure her the trip might turn out better than she'd feared. Now she was back, his earlier optimism had been dashed, replaced by a gnawing anxiety at her unwillingness to talk over an open Link.

"I'll tell you everything when I see you," she'd said. "Please don't ask me to explain. I'll come tomorrow."

In the early hours, he'd left Umo sleeping peacefully in their bed and roamed the apartment, unable to settle for more than a few minutes at a time. Eventually, he'd fallen asleep on a couch only to be woken again by the autumn rain that set in shortly before dawn. He'd dressed hurriedly for no other reason than his mind was racing and he needed some occupation to distract himself. Searching around for something else to do, he'd made a fresh batch of sweetened lemon juice for her when she arrived, and waited, passing the time watching for her from the window.

An hour later, the rain had given way to passing showers, and hearing a skeeter approaching the helipad, he went out onto their balcony into the fresh morning air. Shortly afterwards, a figure in a silver plexiwrap rain cloak threaded its way down the path between the bougainvillaea and newly emerging cyclamen and autumn flowering crocus. Her face was obscured by the hood, but he recognised her by the rhythm of her walk. It was a troubling image, the fitful early morning light playing against the silver fabric of the cloak, smudging its outline. Fleetingly he saw her as he might see a ghost wandering between the flower beds.

She didn't look up to wave to him as she usually did.

Theo took her cloak and offered her a glass of the sweetened lemon juice. She accepted it with a small nod of thanks and sank onto a couch, mute and unapproachable, clutching her travel sack. She looked exhausted, black circles around her eyes.

Umo, still only half-awake and tousled, came into the room, and sensing all was not well, retreated to the corner and curled up in one of their wicker chairs, from where, like a household cat weighing up a dangerous situation, he continued to watch intently while making himself invisible.

"Smiler's found us a replacement for Karoli," she suddenly announced, pulling a vid cover-slip from her travel sack and pushing it into Theo's hand. "There's a hologram option attached." And she sat back on the couch, concentrating on the lemon juice while he activated the code.

Jason Raymer sprang into their lives.

The hologram was a brief distraction, but it wasn't long before Theo became aware her thoughts were locked into some personal, private agony. At intervals, her hands clutched one another seeking mutual support; she bit her lower lip incessantly, and although her eyes were fixed on the image that floated in front of them, with its beguiling voice and eye-catching vitality, there was a vacant expression in her gaze which disturbed him.

Once the performance ended, she got up from the couch abandoning the now empty glass, and moved over to the window, hugging herself closely. Her silhouette against the emerging morning sun, blurred at the edges by the intensity of the light, only magnified his earlier image of her wandering like a lost soul through the world of the Shades. It brought back too, with a startling clarity, the unwelcome memories of Shackleton and her reaction to Karoli's death.

The room slipped back into silence. From the courtyard below, came the sudden shouts of children coming out to play. Cassandra seemed deaf to their shrieks of laughter,

The spell she was under needed to be broken. "What's wrong?" he asked as gently as he could. "He's good. Very good."

"For a Social Engineer?" she queried. "That's what he was, Theo – before Smiler 'discovered' him."

He was embarrassed by her outburst. "We're none of us perfect," he said simply. "Whatever his past, he's an Entertainer now. Can't you accept that?"

She turned from the window. "But I don't *know* him, Theo. I – I can't explain it – it just doesn't feel right"

He understood. Raymer hadn't been their choice – hadn't been *her* choice. He'd been imposed – an unknown quantity – but if he were only half as good as his demo, it seemed worth making the effort to accommodate him. "Cassandra," he said gently, "We need to get on the road again, you know that."

There was suddenly fire in her eyes. She fixed him with a ferocity that took him by surprise. "But do we need the *Ivanov*?" She almost spat out the word as she said it.

There was the familiar fathomless silence that always follows unwelcome news. From the corner of his eye, Theo saw Umo freeze in his seat, and felt a cold hand brush against his own heart. "The *Ivanov*?" he heard himself saying. "After Herschel?"

"Yes," she said, her anger blazing. "Another space tour!"

"When?"

"The New Year."

Theo glanced briefly at Umo and saw the panic in his eyes. His own stomach crawled into a knot and refused to untie itself. "Are we heading for Mars?" he heard himself ask.

She nodded. "And Shackleton to start with. I can't bear the thought of it."

"How long on *Ivanov*?"

"Two months," she said. "Two months on that – " She stumbled over a word to describe it. " – warehouse."

"And the Mars stations?"

"Six months."

From the corner of the room Umo began moaning softly.

Theo tried to ignore him, his brain racing through the implications of what she was telling him. "So there'll be another stopover on *Ivanov's* return run – and Shackleton again?"

She nodded. "Another month."

Heaven help us, Theo thought. Effectively another year in space. "How many shows a week?" he asked, his mind leaping ahead to the logistics involved in another space tour.

"At least three."

"That's impossible!"

She laughed, but it had a fractured sound to it. "Not according to Smiler. He wants new songs, new routines, new costumes. Everything. He's throwing money at us with a virtually unknown lead male vocalist – and," she added, tears beginning to spring into her eyes, "he wants to know by the end of the week whether we'll sign up or not."

"And if we don't?"

"We're finished. He'll hit us with breach of contract none of us can afford, and give the tour to Raymer as a solo with the Aztecs as his backing group."

"As simple as that?"

She nodded, turning back to staring out of the window.

"Then we don't have much choice, do we?"

"None at all." Her voice had gone flat; emotionless.

For several minutes strangely disjointed ideas jumbled formlessly in his mind producing nothing but a series of voids. McMichael's logic defeated him. Umo's monotonous droning was distracting.

"None of this makes sense, Cassandra," he said, addressing her back still resolutely turned towards him. "We should be going global if we're such hot property. Why space?"

"Money, of course," she said, some of the old fire stirring briefly again. "He's arranging live coverage of the tour with VR spin-offs. It's worth a fortune apparently."

It still didn't make any sense. "But he could get that from going global surely – with bigger audiences."

She gave a small strangled laugh. "He said he didn't care about bigger audiences, Theo. Smaller venues make it more 'intimate', he said. More immersive." And Theo could imagine him saying it.

He glanced across at Umo who'd suddenly stopped moaning. Instead, he was rocking backwards and forwards distractedly on the edge of breaking down. Theo knew exactly what he was thinking: that somewhere out there, Angel would reappear.

Outside, the children were called in and the pattering of the rain replaced their laughter. Cassandra quit her station by the window and returned to the couch, trying to regain her composure.

Theo sat next to her. "Has Raymer been screened for spacework?" he asked, grasping at straws that might buy them some time.

"Of course. The all-clear came through apparently before I'd even set foot on Philomos." She laughed mirthlessly. "Do you know what Smiler said to me, Theo? He said a year isn't so hard to get through – imagine that! There speaks a man who's never even been as far as Shackleton!"

Theo glanced across at Umo. "We all know just how long a year can be," he said, and hated himself immediately for saying so.

Umo swallowed hard. "This time I will try – I promise," he said, choking on his words. "No combos. I promise." He coloured up and averted his eyes.

Theo didn't need to ask him for anything else. Implicit was

the understanding there'd be no casual liaisons either. He turned back to Cassandra. "What about you?" he asked gently. "Should you be going back to Shackleton?"

"I passed the psy-debrief, didn't I?" she said bitterly. "What did the report say? Short-term trauma ..." She trailed off, leaving the sentence unfinished.

"Do we have any bargaining counters?"

She shrugged. "I didn't notice any."

Umo offered no opinion.

"Then perhaps we'd better find some. We can't take on a space tour without some safeguards – especially with a newcomer."

"Such as?" she asked caustically. "A drop-out clause? What use is a drop-out clause on a Mars station?"

"Not much, but I think we need it," he insisted. "We've every right to pull out if things go wrong. What if Raymer falls apart on us? We don't know if he'll stand the pressure long-term. Psy-tests aren't everything. Look at the Crazies who walk off-station. Nothing is certain. We have the right to be cautious after ..."

She looked away from him quickly, but not before he saw the tears springing into her eyes again.

With all the tenderness he could muster, he reached out and stroked the dark mane of her hair. "For you, Cassandra," he said, turning her face towards his, brushing away her tears, "there must be no surger-gigs with a newcomer. McMichael owes you that much."

"And what if he says 'no'?" she asked.

"I'll plead your case," he said softly, wiping away the trace of fresh tears. "In the courts if necessary." He'd already decided he'd sacrifice his last dollarouble if that's what it took.

Sixteen

The rehearsal studios on Philomos were carved out of the rock beneath McMichael's conference area. Sound-proof and buried so deep, they existed in isolation from his other activities, but were close enough to give him the opportunity of keeping an eye on proceedings whenever it suited him. And it suited him often, particularly when a new face was in the mix. He liked to feel he knew his artistes, and their 'little ways', as he was very fond of telling them. To Cassandra however, his unfettered enthusiasm for dropping in on The Choralians' rehearsals was a torment.

That afternoon in early December, his presence at their dress rehearsal was particularly unwelcome. He'd collapsed in an untidy heap on a couch in front of the raised area like a snowman left too long in the sun, nodding his approval at everything and grinning lop-sidedly. He'd come to gloat; to have his choice of Jason Raymer confirmed and to hammer home what a brilliant agent he was to have discovered him. Cassandra found it hard to conceal her contempt.

Giving him a wide berth, she took up position in the darkness to one side of the pools of white light flooding the area where Theo, Umo and Raymer were well into the opening instrumental. The sound, amplified through the enhanced peri-system, shivered the air, strangely disembodied and quivering. Yes, it was good; hypnotic.

The Costume Designer, Adrian hovered around her like a persistent gad-fly, fussing over the finishing touches, apparently dissatisfied with everything. By this stratagem he strove hard to elicit words of praise for his creation, but only succeeded in being annoying. He was justifiably proud of his workmanship: the soft fabric of her costume flickered from the deepest blue to darkest green, rippling like the surface of unfathomable watery depths as she moved. He'd pinned the folds at her shoulders with large silver-studded brooches, leaving her arms bare. The effect was artless simplicity that was nothing of the sort: the cloth fell in soft folds across her breasts, gathering in at the waist and flowing outward again with the curve of her hips to swirl and lap seductively around her ankles as she moved. He stood back to admire the effect and frowned again, still unhappy it seemed with some aspect of the hemline. He motioned her to turn around, making no attempt to speak across the barrier of exotic sound. She turned slowly to appease his professionalism, and caught Smiler eying her with undisguised satisfaction.

The appalling man had been lavish with his generosity – however much it irked her to think of it. The costume was just one of many equally gorgeous creations he'd commissioned and financed himself. "I owe it to you, sweetie," he'd said. "I owe it to all of you. Wanted to show it," he'd added in that infuriatingly faux confidential manner he adopted when he was pretending this was a little secret between them, as if she were totally ignorant of the newscasts blaring out how much their contracts were worth, and the level of his personal investment in the upcoming tour.

He heaved himself up from the couch, hindered by his pea-green kaftan, and padded across the floor towards her. "You look fantastic, Cassie," he wheezed above the torrent of sound swirling around them. And then, shoving himself up against her, rasped into her ear at close quarters, "There's a lot of influential guys out there, sweetie." He motioned towards the little knots of onlookers he'd brought with him, now buried deep in the shadows along the walls. "They've got an interest," he added. "Know what I mean?

Give them what it takes, eh?" And he patted her on the shoulder, grinning obscenely.

She'd stiffened at his touch, and the Costume Designer, on his knees in front of her adjusting the hemline, tutted in annoyance. Smiler looked down at him as if he were nothing more than a small dog yapping at his heels. He bent over and patted him indulgently on the head. "Don't fret, Adrian, it looks just great," he assured him before shuffling back to his seat and easing his vast bulk onto the couch again.

Raymer began the solo introduction for the next piece and the lights dimmed to a soft amber so that everything about him was golden. All eyes were on him. Yes, she thought, he looks magnificent, and sounds just as good: his notes were faultless; his rendition as perfect as anyone could ask for. He knew he was good, and she hated him for it. As she stood awaiting her turn, his voice ringing in her ears, it was as if someone were busily tearing out her heart. 'Comfort Zone' had been Karoli's song, composed by him especially for her. She'd never wanted to hear anyone else sing it, but they'd been so short of time to produce so many new pieces, Smiler had said they'd no alternative but to use it to fill the programme. It was one of The Choralians' best-known lyrics. Her only consolation was that Raymer made no attempt to mimic his predecessor's performance: he brought his own interpretation to the words without losing their integrity. Quite a feat. Perhaps Karoli would have approved. Perhaps the ghost she so often felt was watching them would be satisfied.

The music rolled on, spilling over her, Raymer's voice like aural golden rain. Smiler was shouting at her again. "He's good, Cassie. Didn't I tell you you'd love him?"

She turned her back on him to hide her anger. At the most basic level it was unforgivable to interrupt a performer – any performer – in rehearsals. But he'd gone one step further: he'd given Raymer the impression there might be more than a singing partnership in the offing.

Adrian was continuing to fuss around her, evidently still smarting from the indignity of Smiler's patronising little show. His persistence in making minor adjustments here and there, combined with the heart-rending memories the song was conjuring up for her, suddenly became intolerable.

"Leave it," she ordered him curtly, unable to bear his attentions a moment longer. He looked up, startled, and with an expression of being mortally offended, bustled off, complaining bitterly to himself.

With the memorable throbbing vocal climax that had given the song its popularity, Raymer brought 'Comfort Zone' to an end. General applause broke out around the room from the shadowy figures hugging the walls, taking their supposedly 'sneak preview' shots to accompany their reports on just how fantastic The Choralians were going to be on their next tour. Raymer bowed slightly, acknowledging the recognition he'd made his mark, and with a quick half-turn, darted dramatically off-stage to change.

The applause died down. The lights dimmed and Theo and Umo took their places to run through the tuning-in routine for one of their new pieces. A few minutes later, Raymer was back in his new costume. There was a pause, then the lights blazed and the three of them sent the music soaring. It was an intoxicating blend of shimmering sound and colour – of their costumes reflecting kingfisher blues and greens interlaced with gold and silver. The effect was breath-taking. Theo and Raymer sang the main theme, their voices perfectly balanced, interleaving with the variations on their choraladions, while Umo soared in counterpoint to spine-tingling heights, the thin, eerie notes of the paparingo pipes interspersed with his own clear treble ululating in reply.

Smiler was on his feet again. "Fantastic! Absolutely jigging fantastic! You Choralians are definitely going places," and he began applauding even while they continued singing.

Cassandra caught her breath. Yes, she thought bitterly, you've seen to that, haven't you? – Shackleton – *Ivanov* – the Mars Stations. But at least we're going on our own terms – no surger-pop.

She'd denied Smiler the one thing she knew he really wanted. He'd shrugged his vast shoulders and put on a mask of being very hurt that she should even suggest such an idea was in his mind, but it had been almost too easy, and that was unsettling. But at least it felt like a small triumph in a lost war – the *Ivanov* tour.

The crescendo of the piece pulled her back from her reverie and cued her in. She stepped forward, her costume moving in a strangely sensuous motion against her skin, caressing her tenderly like a lover, and the old ache heaved itself up inside her again, momentarily making her heart stumble. The notes of the choraladions swelled. She let the music take her and sank her mind into the sound of it, subduing her will to the rhythms which sang in her soul. I am first and foremost a Folkster, she said to her aching heart. Everything else must come second.

The introductory chord was struck and she was out of the darkness and into the spotlight – into another world, the lights dazzling, blinding her, obscuring the audience from her view as they waited, spell-bound.

The rhythm changed: a huge, thundering, rolling wave of sound crashed onto a hidden shore and dispersed, drawing back and gathering itself up again for the next onrush of curving foam. The instrumental introduction from Raymer and Theo enfolded her, sucking her into a magical whirlpool of light and sound. A mer-child's song, one of Raymer's collection in Fatingu: sad; unutterably sad, and full of longing. She sang it for Karoli, drawing her voice from the depths of the dark ranges to the crystal clarity of the upper reaches. The notes came easily, the melody flowing like the sea itself, remorselessly lifting and dipping, carrying her forward.

She sustained the final soaring note and cut it on cue. As the echo faded, there was a moment's total silence, then loud, spontaneous applause and whooping and stamping from the hidden onlookers. Smiler was yelping and clapping his approval, swaying unsteadily as he struggled back to his feet.

A huge adrenalin surge put a sudden fire into her face. For the first time in months she realised she'd enjoyed the simple pleasure of singing again. Perhaps it was reaction to feeling too much grief for too long; perhaps it was the triumph of a song well sung; or perhaps it was just the sheer pleasure of the music itself. She turned to look at Raymer, suddenly aware she was seeking his recognition of the quality of her own performance. He smiled back, very ready to give it.

Somewhere in the back of her mind above the clamour of shouting and clapping around her, she could hear warning bells jangling uncomfortably close. Her heart stumbled again, catching her breath, and she turned from him to hide her disquiet, prompting Theo to begin the introduction to the next number.

Not yet, she heard her inner voice warning her. Not yet.

SEVENTEEN

By late December, preparations for their space tour were almost complete. In those last few precious days on Earth, The Choralians had gone their separate ways: Raymer to Sparta to say goodbye to old friends; Theo and Umo to the privacy of their Aktichoria near Sounion, and Cassandra to the seclusion of her apartment deep within the Plaka.

The approaching New Year filled Theo with a sense of foreboding: anxieties pressed in on him from all sides and woke him in the early hours, leaving him sleepless. Once he was awake he could no longer remember what had troubled him, his dreams fading into a lost world. All he could recall was that Cassandra had been in danger and he'd been struggling against all the odds to reach her. He'd find himself covered in sweat, his heart rate soaring, and the outcome of the desperate rescue unresolved.

On New Year's Eve, he took the decision to call her: it suddenly seemed important to tell her she could turn to him, no matter how inadequate he felt he might be. He'd try to be stronger, as he'd learnt to be for Umo; to become perhaps the essential rock to cling to. But she *must* know he'd be there for her in her hour of need.

It took him some time to overcome his natural hesitation to intrude on her solitude, knowing how much she valued the personal freedom of those final days before the intense, suffocating closeness space demanded. She didn't answer when he tried to contact her, but he left his message that morning and waited. He must learn patience: she'd call him in her own good time.

The *son et lumière* celebrations continued well after midnight, and when Theo and Umo returned to their apartment, her reply on the Link said simply, "Come and see me."

And so he had. The following evening, he paid off the hovertaxi and it whooshed away, lost in the swirl of lights from other taxis with city permits, and the sound of its motor merged with the rest, like a high wind blowing through trees in summer. Except it was winter, and a cold, fine drizzle leached out of a leaden sky and made him hurry, pulling the hood of his raincloak more tightly about his face.

It took him only a few minutes to reach the alleyway leading to her apartment but when he came to the entrance he stopped, unable to go further until he'd steadied himself. His heart trembled like a lover's, and he could hear the rhythm of it thumping in his head. He stood in the chill dampness, feeling the cold pinch his cheeks and lips, and wondered whether he'd be able to carry through the promise he was about to make.

The Warden admitted him after verifying his identity and checking to see whether he was welcome before giving him access to her apartment lobby. She came out to greet him dressed in a plain, deep blue kaftan over her second skins, looking lovely in that artless way of hers; unadorned; her thick, lustrous hair loose about her shoulders and falling in soft wisps around her face. She embraced him tenderly, lightly kissing him on the cheek and filling his nostrils with her perfume.

"You're wet," she said, threading her arm through his and leading him down the brightly lit lobby into her apartment. "Let me take your cloak."

He undid the clasp and let her take it from him as she showed him into the familiar softly-lit living area, scented candles filling the air with a waxy sweetness. The large lounge-cushions were scattered in a circle around the central hearth as usual, and the hologram blaze purred invitingly in the grate, sending patterns of light and shade dancing onto the walls, its flames coiling upwards into the dark bronze interior of the canopied flue above.

"Make yourself comfortable, Theo. I'll bring you some mulled wine."

He chose his usual place and settled back into the cushion, listening to her moving around the preparation area. It was strange to be back, surprised he no longer expected to see Karoli sprawled seductively on the cushion opposite. He'd been a strong, attractive masculine presence, and it unsettled him to think how quickly his image had faded. A little over three months, that was all. Was it the same for Cassandra? – he wondered. Probably not.

Her return with two generously-filled glasses balanced on a small tray brushed aside his troubled thoughts. "To the New Year," she said handing him one, and settling down on the cushion next to his. "And to whatever it brings," she added, her dark eyes giving nothing away as to what she might mean by this.

"To Twenty-two fifty-seven," he agreed.

As they drank, the firelight captured in the rim of his glass gave the illusion she was encircled by a halo of flame, suffusing her skin with an almost feverish brilliance. The image conjured up the half-memory of his dream. He lowered the glass and the halo vanished, but her brilliance remained, her face lit up by the warm cast of the flames. How long, he wondered, before Jason Raymer found it impossible to ignore her potency? And how long before she was unable to ignore Jason's easy charm and willingness to please?

"What's wrong, Theo?" she was asking him.

His heart stumbled, "I needed to tell you something."

"Is it about Umo?"

"No, it's not about Umo – although I'm worried about him. You know why."

She nodded. "Then what is it?"

He struggled with the words he'd rehearsed so carefully during the skeeter flight down from Sounion. They seemed in no hurry to form themselves into meaningful sentences. "I – I ..." he began, suddenly embarrassed by what he'd intended to tell her.

She was waiting for him to go on.

"I just wanted to say this – because I might not get the chance once the tour starts." He paused, wanting to add emphasis to what he was about to say. "Cassandra, I want to tell you – I'll always be there for you."

"Why do you need to tell me what I already know, Theo?"

"I just felt the need to say it, that was all."

She smiled at him, reaching across and patting his hand affectionately.

"We *know* what life is like in space," he stressed. "We know the pressures. We've lived through them. Jason hasn't. Becoming Jay Raymer – out there in the spotlight with an audience cheering for more – it won't change a thing. He might need help. Don't feel you have to carry him on your own."

"Do you think he might need carrying?"

"I don't know," he said, unable to articulate his fears as well as he wanted to. "But whatever happens, Cassandra, you have to put yourself first."

She placed her emptied glass with exaggerated care onto the low table beside her. "Yes, I know," she said, drawing up her knees and hugging them close as she stared into the firelight.

Theo left the silence undisturbed for a while before he asked, "Has there been any word – from Mister Oliphant?" He tried to make it sound as casual as possible, not wanting to give the impression he placed any great store by her answer. But he did.

She shook her head without looking up, her concentration still on the dancing flames.

He was disappointed. He'd expected something because Oliphant had left a deep impression on him. There'd been a solidity about him; a steely determination; something that could be relied upon to uncover the truth and ensure that justice would be done. And beyond that, there was the way he'd seen Oliphant's attitude to Cassandra change, softened by her presence, an unexpected humanity about him, compassion almost, despite the bluff exterior. And he'd glimpsed it again in Oliphant's office when Umo had confessed to so much and revealed the existence of the malign 'Angel'. Yet despite all this there'd been no word. It was strange.

Cassandra sighed, cutting across his thoughts. "Perhaps he has nothing to tell us, Theo. Perhaps Karoli …" Her sentence remained incomplete, her concentration slipping back to the flames.

He didn't press her: it would have been unkind to play into her fears that Karoli may have been involved in mind-warp trafficking, however unlikely this seemed.

Unexpectedly, she stirred herself. "Perhaps two weeks at Shackleton won't be too hard," she said with a small, brittle laugh.

He swirled the remaining wine around the glass a few times before draining it. "Do you think we're ready?" he asked, because he wasn't sure.

She was serious again. "Yes, we're ready. We have the right material and the right combination." She paused, tilting her head backwards, running her hands through her hair. "Raymer was a good choice," she added, "Even if I'd never admit it to Smiler. He's got style, moves well, plays well – what more could we ask for?"

Theo contemplated his empty glass. "Nothing – as long as he can take what space does to you." Why did it unsettle him so much that she always referred to Jason as Raymer? Never Jason – or Jay. Raymer. Always Raymer. Was it her way of keeping her distance from the man? Was it a conscious attempt at self-preservation?

"Yes," she was saying, "I suppose it all comes down to space," adding with a sad smile, "But if we're honest, Theo, it comes down to that with all of us, doesn't it?"

Umo, he thought. She means Umo. But she didn't say it.

The fire continued to purr, flickering cheerfully, its manufactured warmth mingling with the wine in their veins.

She reached out to him again and took his hand in hers, her dark eyes fixed on him with that terrible seriousness that could melt his heart. "Sometimes," she said, her face incredibly beautiful to him at that moment. "Sometimes, I wish we could have been partners, Theo. It would have made life so much simpler."

He turned away from her, watching the shadows dancing crazily against the walls and across the ceiling, contorting and twisting themselves in a frenzy of movement. "Yes," he said, hearing himself sigh as he said it, knowing just how impossible such a notion was. "Yes, I suppose it would."

EIGHTEEN

A chilly January morning pinched their faces as Theo and Umo left the comfortable warmth of the monorail and transferred to the shuttle service at Glyfada Transcontinental Freight Terminal. Cocooned again for a few precious moments, Theo was outwardly watching the comings and goings at the various hangar stops along the way, but was inwardly remembering earlier days. Karoli had been with them the last time they'd travelled this route. His absence now was a reminder, if any were needed, of the dangers which might lie ahead at Shackleton – and beyond.

They alighted at Hangar Nine following the signs to the glidetrack down to the departure bays where travellers and exporters had their manifests checked over by Outflight Customs before loading was authorised.

The pedestrian access gate opened as they approached and they stepped through onto the raised metal walkway high above the loading bays into a world of noise and confusion. Looking down from their vantage point, it was all too easy to spot which bay The Choralians had been allocated. Amidst a blaze of floodlighting from the rafters, the extent of the chaos below them was disconcerting. Insulated metal packing containers had their polyplastic boxes off-loaded, and lighting gantries, sound systems and instrument cases littered the area, as though a mighty wind had blown through the bay intent on destruction. Outflight Customs Officers were ordering loaders to move cases from one location to another without any apparent rhyme or reason, and raised voices mingled with the mobile baggage loaders' screeching and wheezing as they manoeuvred on the silicone floor. The cacophony reached deafening proportions.

Theo viewed the uncoordinated activity with alarm. Even allowing for a very large miracle and some immediate positive action, he couldn't see how the loading could be completed before the scheduled afternoon outflight to Kalgoorlie's Lunar Ferry Terminal and the rendezvous with the rest of the crew hired for the tour.

He scanned the area in desperation, looking for anyone he might recognise. "Cassandra!" he called out several times, raising his voice above the din to a pitch where it hurt his throat.

A figure in khaki overalls and peaked cap, deep in earnest conversation with a skeeter pilot near a batch of opened boxes, turned and looked upwards.

"Cassandra!" he called again, running down the access steps and waving in the hope it might be her. Umo followed him.

The figure disengaged itself from conversation and waved back.

"What's going on?" he yelled over the noise when she reached him. "Where's Tregorran?"

She pulled them both into the lee of a nearby container where normal conversation was almost possible. She was in a fiery mood. "Our so-called Transportation Manager is drunk out of his mind."

"Drunk? He's never been drunk before. Why now?"

"Perhaps he doesn't want an *Ivanov* tour either," she said caustically. "I could forgive him that – but not the rest." She pointed to the open boxes, some of their contents lying on the floor next to them. "He's not completed a single manifest check," she explained. "Customs are furious. We're having to unpack everything, list the contents and repack them. Krodalt and Farrance are doing their best. Argosti has gone into melt-down over the costumes." She indicated a distraught figure sitting with his head in his hands on a nearby box. Argosti was the only person Smiler's

Designer would trust to oversee packing his precious creations on-tour, and like Adrian, he was apparently prone to excessive bouts of emotion.

"Is *anything* loaded?"

She shook her head. "No – and now it seems Ransome, one of our new Technos, has gone AWOL."

"Does McMichael know?"

"Not yet. I've had my hands full with Argosti. I kept hoping Ransome would turn up."

"Cassandra – forget about this, I'll take over transport management. I've done it before. I'll contact McMichael and tell him what's happened."

"What about a replacement for Ransome?"

"I doubt he'll be able to find anyone at short notice – but he might. Let's just concentrate on getting the loading done on time. We've got six hours before ETD. Umo can help with the costumes. I'll explain to Argosti."

Four hours later, Theo straightened from the long hours bent double, and eased his shoulder muscles. Krodalt and Farrance were still overseeing the last of the boxes to get them through Customs.

Cassandra left Umo with Argosti and came over to join him. Several stray strands of unruly hair had escaped her peaked cap and she looked weary. "Any news from Smiler?" she asked.

"Not yet." Theo massaged the base of his neck and surveyed the hive of industry around them with tired eyes. For the first time he realised Ransome and Tregorran weren't the only ones missing. He double-checked to make sure he wasn't mistaken. He wasn't. "Cassandra, where's Jason? There's only two hours to ETD. He's cutting it a bit fine."

"Perhaps he thought he was doing us a favour keeping out of the way"

"Maybe, but we could have done with an extra pair of hands."

"Tell him when you see him."

"I will." He stretched, trying to unknot a shoulder muscle. At the far end of the hangar, he spotted two figures apparently advancing in their direction. Their direct line of approach contrasted with that of the baggage-loaders weaving between the loading bays and the external doors to the ferry. One of the figures moved with that unmistakable swing of the hips and loping stride. Jason Raymer had arrived.

His companion was smaller, with a very obvious uneven gait, each step a deliberate movement that seemed to require concentrated effort to achieve it. Theo watched their approach, his words of welcome dying on his lips.

Cassandra turned and stared. "Raymer," she whispered.

"And someone else," Theo added.

Raymer had the air of a man taking a small child or a pet animal for a walk, while his companion turned to look up at him every now and then from the depths of a travelsuit hood, as though seeking reassurance.

Raymer smiled as he drew closer. "Sorry I'm late," he said apologetically in UniCom, his tone bright and untroubled. "I hope I haven't caused any problems. I travelled up from Sparta and – well, you know how things go."

Cassandra was transfixed, studying Raymer's anonymous friend with guarded, questioning eyes.

Theo studied him too.

"Let me introduce you," Raymer was saying. "This is Lazar. Lazar Excell. He doesn't speak UniCom, I'm afraid – only English – but as Miles said, we're a Techno down, what does that matter? Lazar's a Pro, so I thought he'd be useful – as a stand-in until things get sorted, of course. A month, maybe six weeks at the most." His grey-blue eyes looked hopefully between the two of them, his smile still firmly in place.

Theo wanted to say a great many things all at once, and failed to find a single satisfactory starting point from which to achieve his purpose. Instead, he stalled, conscious of needing to be tactful. "Can we sort out his travel docs in time?" he asked, sticking to UniCom.

"No problem," Raymer assured him. "It's all done. Miles got him fast-tracked. That's why we're a bit late." He continued to look between the two of them, his smile beginning to fade. "Look, I hope you don't mind me stepping into the breach on this one. Miles said things were pretty urgent."

Cassandra turned back to Theo, uncertainty written all over her face.

Theo made a conscious effort to smile, trying hard not to stare either too hard or too long at the newcomer. "Has McMichael met Lazar?" he asked, absolutely certain this was impossible.

Raymer looked slightly uncomfortable at the question. "Well – not personally," he conceded.

"Has Lazar had a psy-test?"

A glimmer of uncertainty crossed Raymer's face. "Miles said it wasn't necessary for a temp under three months. Was he wrong?"

"No," Theo assured him, keeping firmly to UniCom and feeling a small knot of panic gathering in his stomach. "But I think we need to talk over a few things – just the three of us. Umo can baby-sit," he added, indicating Lazar was the baby in question. At the same time, he kept his general demeanour as unruffled as possible, a considerable feat under the circumstances, he thought.

NINETEEN

Inside the brightly-lit interior of the diner in Hangar Nine, the ubiquitous musi-tone burbled contentedly to itself in the background, looping through its endless indistinguishable melodies unnoticed.

The lunch-break was over, the diner deserted, the shiny red polyplastic tables and matching back-to-back seating all cleaned down and tidy; the grey polished floor swept and gleaming. Cassandra made straight for the first enclosed alcove by the entrance and sat down ahead of Raymer and Theo.

The Diner Attendant busily buffing up and reloading the automats looked up on their arrival. She must have been fresh out of academy, Cassandra thought: a chit of a girl with a sulky expression and too much body for the size of her red-and-white checked uniform. She briefly registered their presence with evident irritation, sensing they might interrupt her routine maintenance schedule. "We're closed," she said abruptly before noticing Raymer, her eyes widening visibly at the sight of him. "If you wait a minute," she added, her attitude suddenly less hostile, "you can place your order then."

Cassandra glared at her. "We're here to talk," she said, in no mood to be trifled with.

The girl shrugged, giving Raymer a lazy evaluation of his possibilities before retreating to continue buffing up the automats.

Raymer sat down on the opposite side of the table, looking relaxed and completely unfazed.

Cassandra was in no mood for casual conversation. "What are you playing at?" she demanded, automatically choosing English.

Raymer appeared genuinely bemused by the question. He sat back, apparently in no great hurry to answer. "Look, I'm sorry," he said, although he didn't sound it. "I thought you'd be pleased I'd found someone to help out. Miles was."

"And how did *you* know we were a Techno down?" she challenged him. "We only found out when he didn't turn up this morning."

"Well, I can't help that," he said, shrugging off her tetchiness. "Miles asked me a while back to let him know how I felt about the tour before I left. I did as I was told. I contacted him on the Link last night. We talked. I said I felt great. He said he'd just heard this guy Ransome had given back-word and he was having problems finding a replacement."

"Then why didn't he let us know?"

Raymer frowned. "He said he didn't want to worry you unnecessarily."

"And what did you say?"

"I said I thought I could get a stand-in on a temporary basis. He was fine with that. I said I'd let him know as soon as I could – and that's what I did – this morning. That's all. No great mystery." He stopped, looking quickly between them and picking up on their shared animosity. "Look, if I'd thought you'd make such a big thing of it, I wouldn't have bothered. I thought I was helping you out." He sounded peevish.

"Well thank you for your efforts on our behalf, Raymer, but *who* is he?"

"No," Theo cut it. "*What* is he?"

Raymer shrugged. "All right, I owe you some sort of explanation, I suppose. But he'll be fine, I promise."

Cassandra remained unconvinced. "Be straight with me,

Raymer. Is he one of your social engineering Non-people? One of the Unacceptables? I thought they couldn't happen any more. Or am I wrong? Are the Social Engineers still helping to remove the ones that got away?"

The muscles in Raymer's jaw tightened perceptibly. It took him a few moments to make any sort of reply. "I can assure you he's *not* an Unacceptable," he said, his voice quite low and thick, as if it were sticking in his throat. "And you know damn well I got out of social engineering a long time ago."

"Perhaps you got him out too," she suggested, pressing the point because there had to be some sort of answer which would make better sense to her. "Is that the idea now? Ship them out? Lose them in space, perhaps?"

Raymer's open palm came down on the table top with some force. "Stop it!" he said through clenched teeth, his sudden display of anger all the more vehement for being so unexpected. The Diner Attendant looked up and stared across at them, curious to know more. Raymer hunched his shoulders, obscuring himself from her gaze. "Lazar wasn't born like that," he added, keeping his voice lower. The Diner Attendant lost interest.

"No?" Cassandra parried. "Then what happened to him?"

"An accident on a construction site," Raymer explained. "Sometime in 'fifty-three. He was on an engineering project. I'm not sure of all the details – and he doesn't remember them. A loader came off its tracks apparently. He got crushed under it. Lots of broken bones, fractured skull – something like that anyway. Okay, it affected his speech and he can't walk so well, but Cass – I swear to you – he's not a Dummy." He was quite emphatic on this point. "He's absolutely all there when it comes to being a Techno. He's a Pro – honestly."

Theo leaned forward. "Jason, you must know, we can't take him just on your say-so. Not on a space tour. It would be absolute madness."

Raymer's expression slipped into deadly earnestness. "I *know* his work," he stressed. "It's the best. I guarantee it. I wouldn't have suggested him to Miles if I'd had any doubts. I agree – it would be madness."

Cassandra took up the challenge. "How do you know his work?" she asked, sceptical that Raymer had the faintest notion of what he was talking about.

"I know because he's employed by a friend of mine who runs his own technobusiness – outside Sparta. I've spent some time there. All right?"

"I see. And your friend was happy to lend you Lazar for a space tour at the drop of a hat, was he?" It sounded highly unlikely.

"Yes."

"Just the thing for him, was it?"

"He reckoned it would give Lazar more experience."

"How very thoughtful," she said witheringly, unable to mask her incredulity. The story sounded vaguely plausible, but not quite plausible enough. She searched Raymer's face, seeking out the lie, or even the half-truth, hidden somewhere in that earnest expression and the strength of feeling he was generating.

Raymer was studying her with an equal intensity. "You don't believe me, do you?"

She smiled back at him and shook her head slowly. "No," she said, "but do go on. It sounds fascinating."

A look of exasperation passed briefly across his face. "All right – let me start again," he said, with an air of frustrated patience. "I have this friend – Guido Servione. I've known him for more than seven years. He owns the technomaintenance business I told you about, operating mostly in Near Eurasia. He's been aiming to expand the business and thinks the time's right to do it." He paused to study their faces before continuing. "Okay, he'd like to get into the Entertainment field – "

"Ah," Theo cut in, " – and he thought solving our little problem would be a useful way of getting one of his Technos into the network. Am I right?"

Raymer acknowledged the point with a shrug.

Cassandra leaned across the table, forcing Raymer to look her in the eye. "So the arrangement wasn't just for our benefit, was it?"

"Does it matter?" he asked. "We'd be a Techno down without him."

She evaluated his steady grey-blue gaze. Was it a challenge? Was it conviction? She wasn't sure. It could have been either. "True," she said eventually. "But it might have been more helpful if you'd made all this clear right from the start."

"You didn't exactly give me the chance."

She sat back, and regarded him coolly. Point taken. "So how long has Lazar been with your 'good friend' Guido Servione?"

"About nine months," he said, ignoring her sarcasm.

"And before that?"

Raymer gestured his ignorance in the matter. "I can only tell you what Guido said – that Lazar'd been testing logic systems at his last place. That's all I know. Of course, if we'd access to his security data that would be different, wouldn't it? – but we don't." He gave them both a tight little smile.

It was a facetious comment that didn't go down well with Theo. "He has an ID card, I suppose?" he asked casually.

Raymer laughed in his face. "Of course he has! How do you think he'd get emergency travel docs without one?"

"Okay, but as far as I can see, we only have your word he's a good Techno. We know nothing about his history – and more important to us, Jason – whether he'll be able to cope – even for a few weeks – up there – in space."

Raymer blew out his cheeks and shook his head in disbelief. "Oh come on!" he said, suddenly raising his voice again and attracting the attention of the Diner Attendant for a moment. "Didn't you notice his skin tone?"

133

Cassandra was reminded of the sallow complexion beneath the hood, with all the appeal of new putty. "Are you telling us, he spends his life in the workshop?" she said casually. She was throwing his earlier facetiousness back in his face, not expecting him to agree with her, so the effect of Raymer's nodding assent to her guesswork threw her completely.

"As near as damn it," he informed her, his earnest expression firmly back in its place. "You don't understand, do you?" he said, his voice reduced to a hoarse whisper. "He *knows* he looks like that. That's why he stays out of sight. Indoors. All the time. It's the only way he feels safe."

"So you think a space environment won't worry him?" she said, making sure he picked up on her incredulity.

Raymer sat back in his seat. "He'll probably have less hang-ups than the rest of us," he said, folding his arms as if the discussion were closed as far as he was concerned.

Perhaps he was right, Cassandra thought. And yet …And yet, the doubts lingered.

At her elbow, the doubts in Theo's mind lingered more strongly. He was leaning forward again, his gaze fixed on Raymer with an intensity Cassandra had never seen before. "Say we accept your word he's a TechnoPro, Jason," he said. "Say we accept he *might* be able to cope with a space tour better than the rest of us put together. Okay – but is he *right* for us?"

Raymer looked puzzled.

"Let me spell it out for you," Theo said bluntly. "I'm talking about prejudice. Plain, ordinary prejudice, Jason. It exists. We know. And why do we know? Because we meet it all the time."

Raymer said nothing.

"Do you know what some people call Entertainers?" Theo asked. "Maybe you don't. You're new to this. We're called Hurdy-Gurdies. It's not a term of affection," he added.

Raymer shrugged off the description with a stifled laugh.

Theo persisted. "If you find that amusing, Jason, you won't for long if you stay in this profession," he warned. "Prejudice is alive and well. We spend our lives trying to prove we're not what people think we are. Our image matters."

Raymer's smile vanished. "You mean Lazar's the wrong image for The Choralians?" His inflection was highly critical.

Theo remained unfazed. "Yes, I'm saying exactly that. We're a Folkster group, remember? We're expected to be the Beautiful People, and at the moment we're very high profile. Whether you like it or not, Lazar could never be described as 'beautiful'. Put that alongside what appears to outsiders as impaired brain function, and out there at Shackleton and on the *Ivanov* things could get very rough for him. Do you understand what I'm saying?"

Raymer nodded, perhaps realising at last there was more than just one problem in taking Lazar with them. "Okay," he said. "I get the message."

Evidently, Theo wasn't sure he had. "Don't fool yourself, Jason. He'll be a very easy target for anyone who likes to prey on Vulnerables. *We know.*"

"We had a problem on the last tour," Cassandra explained simply. She'd no intention of bringing Angel's abuse of Umo into the conversation.

"If Lazar comes with us, he's going to need protection," Theo warned. "You can't pretend he won't."

Raymer looked away briefly and nodded, some of his earlier bravado knocked out of him. "I know. I've already promised I'll look after him. Guido wouldn't have let him come if I hadn't. He can bunk up in my quarters – look after the instrumental maintenance side and leave Krodalt, Farrance and the rest of the crew to handle stagecraft. That's their province anyway."

Cassandra looked him straight in the eye. "You think of everything," she said pointedly.

Raymer held her gaze briefly. Again, the challenge – or the

conviction – she still couldn't decide which. But whichever it was, Jason Raymer was undoubtedly a fixer – something she would have to watch.

"Just make sure his travelsuit hood is up when we're out in public," she said, emphasising the absolute necessity for this. "And you'll have to school him on how to stand better – and walk in a straight line. In fact, Raymer, you need to make him almost invisible, because right now he's a liability."

Raymer nodded his agreement to her terms.

The doors to the diner eased back softly into their casings. Through them, along with a swirl of noise and the metallic tang of overheating engines, came Umo and Lazar, their arms around one another. They made an incongruous pair: Umo, lithe and dark, perfectly formed, his eyes alert, watchful, his movements animated; Lazar, pale and listless, his straight brown hair hanging forward across his forehead from its erratic hairline, his body slightly at odds with itself beneath the thick layer of outer clothing – and his eyes …childlike and trusting.

"Friends," Umo announced cheerfully in his stilted English. "Us," he added triumphantly, pointing between himself and Lazar. He beamed, a happiness radiating from him which sent warning bells clamouring in Cassandra's head. She turned to see Theo look downwards at the table top, his hands clenching shut on themselves in front of him. She could only guess at what he was thinking.

TWENTY

It was common knowledge among the ranks of ConCorp's Security personnel that the Northern Regional Sector's C-in-C had allowed Oliphant considerable latitude when it came to choosing his Earthside home base. The excuse was that the peripatetic nature of Oliphant's job description, running down illicit trafficking, meant that it didn't much matter what location he chose: he'd never be static for long. No one was surprised when he didn't opt for the prestigious, sumptuously furnished complex of the Regional HQ in Bern: it didn't suit his personality. But rumour had it that some of his immediate superiors preferred to keep him at arm's length in any case, so no eyebrows were raised when he elected to operate from ConCorp's less conspicuous, but nonetheless important, Divisional HQ based on the perimeter of the wind-swept air terminal of Benbecula in the Hebrides.

His executive suite, in what many thought of as a God-forsaken place, was nonetheless comfortable enough for a man of his tastes. Defying the Atlantic gales, it was one of only a handful of third-floor offices in the whole building, its large single-paned window facing east overlooking the sheltered quadrangle with its well-kept hardy shrubs interspersed with pink gravel walkways. Set into the sloping roofline on the adjacent wall, a smaller version provided sunlight whenever it could, even in winter. The office itself was functional with its standard furniture, workstation and essential VR conference booth. Retractable opaque sliding doors separated it from a less Spartan environment, theoretically for the purposes of personal relaxation, or for entertaining VIPs, although no one could remember when anyone had taken the trouble to visit. Oliphant rarely opened the doors except to access the small corridor that led down to his sleeping quarters.

At that time of year, when the Hebridean sun barely heaved itself above the roofline of the building opposite, long slices of white winter sunlight lanced through his southern window, illuminating a collection of Gordenochek murals he'd chosen to hang on the only wall-space available. They were geometric collages of extraordinarily intense primary and secondary colours fabricated from woven textiles. They were loud – some said vulgar – but he liked them: they reminded him not everything in life was black and white.

Despite his solidly northern heritage, the short winter days of cheerless sun, and long, bitterly cold nights of the encroaching mini-Ice Age, could subdue his spirits, particularly after a few days confined to quarters by the bleakness of the weather. Hells bells, he'd ask himself, how do those poor devils cope with the limitations of life in space?

Taking advantage of a break in the weather, he'd just completed a brisk walk around the air terminal perimeter fence after a particularly hearty lunch, hoping to rid himself of an unwelcome lethargy.

His door buzzer sounded as he was hanging up his great coat in the walk-in office closet, and Junior Security Office MacFadden announced himself over the communicator.

Oliphant glanced in the mirror, giving his hair and beard a last critical evaluation and straightened his uniform. "Enter," he instructed, activating the door control.

JSO MacFadden presented himself and saluted crisply. Oliphant surveyed him with a critical eye and mentally congratulated him on his appearance and bearing.

Andrew MacFadden was the latest in a long line of JSOs

purposely seconded to Oliphant to knock into shape. The theory was that anyone who survived a six-month stint under Oliphant's tutelage would survive anything. MacFadden was younger than most, only just twenty, red-headed, freckled and still on the gawky side, his legs having outgrown the rest of him a few years earlier. But he had the makings of a fine officer, and Oliphant was prepared to give the lad a chance, perhaps because he reminded him of his younger self, although he'd never admit to this. Most juniors who came his way were glad when their time was up; few had ever felt the need to thank him for the experience – and he never expected to receive it. MacFadden however seemed less intimidated, or more able to hide the fact, Oliphant wasn't sure which. Not that it mattered: all he was interested in was a Junior Officer's potential. Now half way through MacFadden's secondment, Oliphant was beginning to feel they had the makings of a good team.

"Well, MacFadden," he said, seating himself comfortably in the high-backed chair behind his rosewood desk and readjusting his collar. He was finding the internal heating overpoweringly stuffy in comparison with the bracing air outside, "What have you got for me?"

MacFadden remained stiffly to attention, head up, green eyes steady, his square chin forward. "A report just in on Operation Misfit, Sir," he said, the rich burr of his accent a welcome relief to Oliphant's UniCom-weary ears. "Channel Ten scrambled. From Regional Commander-in-Chief Lattimer. You asked me to report directly it came through."

"So I did. Sit down, MacFadden. You're giving me neck ache."

With the barest flicker of an eye lid, MacFadden did as he was told and sat ramrod straight in the interview chair immediately to his right.

Oliphant accessed Channel Ten on his monitor, tripped in the scrambler decoder and skimmed through the information scrolling up in front of him. "Right," he said feeling justified in what he'd set in motion. "Looks like the Freelance is well and truly in place.

Any last minute hitches reported from our eyes-on-site?"

"None, Sir. The tour has now got its full complement. The recording crew were the last to be picked up at Kalgoorlie before take-off." He paused to check his watch. "The ferry should be touching down at Shackleton in eighteen minutes our time, Sir."

"No problems reported with security checks?"

"None, Sir."

"Mm. Well we know what that means, don't we?"

"Yes, Sir."

"It confirms what we already knew – there's at least one loophole in our mighty corporation's security systems if it's possible to mask multiple identities without triggering existing scanning procedures." How many others were managing to slip through the net if one person could do it so effectively? – he wondered. Too many, was the suspicion that refused to go away. "When do we expect the next report?"

"Not certain, Sir. His reporting opportunities are likely to be limited."

"Yes, well we half-expected that, didn't we? If he's part of a team, he can't go swanning off on his own too often without drawing attention to himself."

"Do you want the twenty-four hour alert initiated now, Sir?"

"Yes, it's imperative once he's on Shackleton. SSO Davron's on standby."

"Do you expect any action on Shackleton, Sir?"

"No – not really. I'm putting my money on everything staying quiet until The Choralians are aboard the *Ivanov*. But I could be wrong – so if anything big starts, I want to know about it – and I want to know about it fast. That means immediately, MacFadden, because when this particular balloon goes up, you and I will be going where the action is – whether the Regional Commander likes it or not. Understand?"

The young man's head came up smartly. "Yes, Sir."

TWENTY-ONE

With MacFadden dismissed, Oliphant sank back into his earlier lethargy. Operation Misfit had been hastily put together three months ago, and he'd known when he'd submitted his proposal to his Regional C-in-C, Bradley Lattimer, that it was an under-developed string of possibilities that would require constant re-evaluation and flexible action. In other words, it was far from perfect.

Lattimer was high profile and definitely going places. A man of towering authority and physique to match, he was two years older than Oliphant and had the advantage of coming from one of the most senior Enforcer ranks before joining ConCorp Security. It was widely understood he was the natural successor to the Director of Security, Salvador Mendoza, when he stepped down in two years' time.

There'd never been any doubt in Oliphant's mind that his operation would be sanctioned: the mere suggestion of mind-warp trafficking on any ConCorp space station would have sent the Board of Directors and the investors into freefall. They might all have been as high as kites on Supercharge or combos themselves in their free time, but they knew where to draw the line as far as Spaceworkers were concerned.

And on the basis of data already to hand, he'd also known he could have asked for almost unlimited resources and had them allocated without so much as a raised eyebrow or minor quibble. But his requirements had been modest: requests for flexibility of roles and interdepartmental cooperation rather than making a bid for open-ended finance. And it had all been granted, no questions asked, just as he'd hoped.

The fly in the ointment – and to Oliphant it was a very big fly – was Lattimer's insistence that with security systems comprehensively compromised, and doubts about the trustworthiness of personnel at all levels, it was imperative there should be absolutely no direct contact between the chosen Freelance and the operational team. None whatever. All reports were to be re-routed through several unmanned global and satellite relay stations with different scrambling systems to prevent any Listeners picking up intelligence. The transmission routes would be automatically selected at random every time a new report was filed. Similarly, contact with the Freelance by the operational team was to be strictly limited to emergencies only, and would require authorisation at Regional level using Priority Protocols. The result was that any action to be taken had become less of a hands-on and more of an arm's-length example of an extremely covert operation.

Lattimer had effectively removed Operation Misfit from Oliphant's immediate control and reduced him to the status of an operational overseer, and that irked him; irked him in the same way it had obviously irked Davron when Oliphant had effectively pulled the rug from under him. Nor did it help that Oliphant's best contact, Guido Servione, had come up with the anonymous 'exceptionally brilliant' Freelance – codenamed 'Phoenix' by Lattimer.

"That's all you need to know about him," Lattimer had said, apart from the fact Phoenix was already using an alias. And to make doubly sure Oliphant didn't stray beyond his remit, Lattimer had instituted a security lock on all in-depth biodata for the new personnel joining The Choralians' entourage.

Given no say in the matter, and no information on what role Phoenix would play, Oliphant was left feeling deeply uneasy.

He'd been given oversight of an operation with one hand tied behind his back. Doubts began to creep into his mind where none had existed before. Doubts about Servione himself. Could he be trusted? – even after so many years? Servione, with his international technomaintenance business; a chancer; a Freelance himself who'd made the break and set up his own stable. And that raised a further question – What did Servione know about Phoenix? – because Oliphant had been stone-walled when he'd tried quizzing Servione for more information.

"Don't ask questions I won't answer," Servione had said bluntly. "It was made pretty clear that if I didn't sign a Deep Silence Declaration, ConCorp's Security Panel would've encouraged the Enforcers to pick over my business accounts and contacts' lists to their hearts' content. So I'm not going to spill any beans, Oliphant, even for you. Just accept Phoenix isn't your average Freelance, okay? That's all you need to know."

But no Freelance was ever 'average' – or lily-white for that matter. Scratch the surface and they were all counterfeit to some extent – like Phoenix. None of their histories or lifestyles stood up to much scrutiny. Sometimes, he reflected, it was better not to know – or to care – especially if they became disposable …

Yes, they'd lost a few good ones over the years. None of Servione's, he had to admit, but good ones all the same. It didn't necessarily happen as a matter of course. Circumstance always played a part in what eventually pulled them off the rails – or laid them out cold on a mortuary slab – sometimes both. He'd known it to be something quite simple, like being in the wrong place at the wrong time, or getting too emotionally involved with a target. At other times it could be more complex: a series of events that gradually sucked them into situations they no longer wanted to get out of – or couldn't. Either way, it was bad news – both for them and their operation. Strange to think Karoli Koblinski's demise seemed to have followed a similar pattern.

His mind drifted from Koblinski back to Phoenix: someone with a vague history; someone whose skills could be accepted for what they were and perhaps no further questions asked. Hurdy-Gurdies were notorious for keeping their personal histories to themselves and their most trusted inner circle.

Pulling himself back into the present, Oliphant dumped the operational data he'd been scrolling through listlessly and accessed the security files. Lattimer had been as good as his word: all the biodata for the half-a-dozen or so newcomers to The Choralians' outfit was limited to what would register on their security tags, and nothing more. A bright red 'Access Denied' notice barred any further enquiries, and offered no further options to pursue.

To soothe his ruffled ego, Oliphant accessed the biodata he knew was still available to him.

DIAMANTIDES: Cassandra
[89/EEUR/2230/VR257832Q]
Status: Female
Profession: Entertainer k/a Cass DIAMOND

He'd read it all before. Read it and re-read it, trying to match the cold data to the warm living entity he'd met. A foundling. No true identity beyond herself. Another mystery. In an age when so much was regulated, basic human interaction could still outwit the system. It always would.

He sat back and closed his eyes, remembering the image of their meeting as fresh and as potent as it had been four months earlier: their only meeting and yet she lingered, a vivid image in the recesses of his mind, emerging at unexpected moments with all the clarity of a newly-minted hologram.

His thoughts wandered, imagining her as a young girl, not the mature woman of twenty-seven. He could picture her running wild among the trailers: barefoot, vibrant. She'd grown up in a world of drifters; a world of music and dancing and self-imposed rules on how to survive. She'd seen her adoptive mother reduced to a wreck and dead before her time. Cassandra Diamantides might have no known origin, but she was a powerful entity in her own right. She had presence. She was something out of the ordinary.

He opened his eyes briefly to look out of his window, surprised how easy it was to conjure her up. And when he succumbed to the temptation of letting his mind wander again, there she was, directly in his line of vision, draped in the vivid scarlet and gold kaftan; her hair a wild, black halo around her face; her hand extended towards him; those dark eyes meeting his with that terrible frankness as she gave him the cone and their fingers had touched. And there it was – the spark that had passed between them – like invisible lightning.

Was she the innocent dupe? – he wondered – or a magnificent actress? He might never know.

He rested his head against the back of his chair closing his eyes again, remembering the way she moved: gliding, flowing, her hips swinging easily; the shape of her breasts thrust forward beneath the silky fabric, tantalisingly close; and the low spine-tingling sound of her humourless laughter that still echoed in his brain even now. And there too was the figure of Xenon, standing guard behind her, their faces so similar they fused together in his mind: inseparable.

For a while, he contemplated a future where it would be possible to self-generate VR fantasies, acting out imaginings like waking dreams. But the notion paled. For him, he realised, nothing would replace the living warmth of human contact or the interaction of human chemistry, not VR programs nor the pathetic artificiality of surger-pop. All just games to cheat the senses, and for what? For cheap momentary physical thrills and emotional emptiness. Nothing lasting. Nothing of merit.

He opened his eyes again to the image of the monitor still

displaying her security data, the white lettering standing out boldly now in the encroaching half-light. He logged-out and stood up, stretching to loosen his limbs, becoming aware of his aroused physical need. He could do with a partner. Perhaps Stella Bonner over in Data Protection might be free for the evening – they'd had a casual arrangement before and it had suited them both at the time. But somehow even the thought of Stella's stimulating repertoire didn't ease the yearning ache he was experiencing. He needed more than the simple physical release she could offer him. Cassandra Diamantides had touched him, and disturbed his soul. Had Koblinski felt the same?

He crossed over to the bay window and stood for a while watching the comings and goings of colleagues in the quadrangle below. The sun was already dipping, plunging the gravelled area under his window into intense shadow. Lights from the lower offices flickered nervously into life. His own followed suit. Brusquely, he ordered them to shut down. He wanted darkness.

Above him the colours of the Hebridean sky were deepening into dusky, darker hues, and in the blue-blackness, the first stars twinkled fitfully in the cold, clear air. Outside the cocooned atmosphere of his office, a diamond-hard frost was setting in, and the first sliver of a full moon came into view to the south-east of the HQ building. It rose with an elegant slowness, intensely white against the blackness of the sky until its full roundness was complete, suspended like a silver coin on an invisible thread against a backcloth of spangled black velvet. It hurt his eyes to look at it.

The Moon. Shackleton. Shackleton and Cassandra Diamantides. Contradictions. Intense cold and intense warmth. Frost. Icicles. Silver cones. The warm breasts beneath them. Her breasts. Close enough to touch.

He turned from the window, angry with himself. He could no longer pretend: the only partner he really wanted – and not just casually – was out of reach.

TWENTY-TWO

Freshly showered, Cassandra lay sprawled on the crumpled coverlet of her solitary bed, staring up at the creamy flatness of the ceiling and the dull glow from the recessed lighting panel above her head. Shackleton. The Stage Door Accommodation Unit. A different room. A different time. But still Shackleton.

Karoli. Karoli's presence lingered like a forlorn ghost.

She rolled over onto her side, hugging the pillow closer for comfort, remembering their last night together only four short months before. Sometimes it felt like a lifetime ago; sometimes only yesterday. She ached from the memory of it, her body hot with the need for him.

She was surprised how his loss could suddenly overwhelm her, filling her with a burning passion and emptiness at the same time. If she closed her eyes, she could still see him looking down at her, his magnificent moody eyes consuming her as they always did before they made love. And they'd made love often, not just as part of a grotesque public performance, but as two people wrapped up in an intensely physical relationship. How often she'd thought she might dissolve under that determined gaze. How totally exquisite he could make her feel by simply looking at her, and her body would respond long before his hands had even begun to caress her.

The flow of desire began to circle within her, her breasts tightening, the soft palpitations increasing in intensity between her thighs, seeking the hardness of the man who was no longer there.

She snapped open her eyes and sat up, tossing her hair back from her face and gripping the edges of the bed for support, waiting for the desire to ebb. Bromidox would dull the need, she thought. But it wouldn't help her come to terms with her loss. She needed company; she needed someone to talk to. Now.

She swung off the bed and strode over to her clothes closet, eyeing the contents critically. It was still mid-afternoon, a time at odds with itself. The rehearsal had ended, or rather her part in it. Theo, Umo and Raymer were running through the instrumental pieces one last time; Krodalt and Farrance were putting the finishing touches to the integrated sound and lighting systems with the help of the new Technos, and the recording crew were fussing around like mother hens over their new-born chicks.

In the hugeness of the Armstrong Hall, she'd suddenly felt the need to escape; to leave them all to get on with whatever they needed to do; to be alone. Perhaps Karoli's ghost had been up there on the stage. Perhaps Raymer's presence had been too much for her – an affront to Karoli's memory. But now suddenly, the urge to be solitary had evaporated. She was on edge: fidgety; eager for company.

Still staring into the clothes closet, she pulled out her scarlet and gold-fringed kaftan and slipped it over her head, flicking her hair free of the neckline. In that brief moment, she caught sight of herself in the full-length mirror on the inside of the door. The image alarmed her: she was dishevelled; her face glowing, still flushed from her shower and the reawakening of a passion she could no longer share with the man she loved. Her eyes had become intensely dark, the pupils gleaming like polished jet.

Perhaps because it was Shackleton, and the furnishings and fittings had a familiarity she'd have preferred to forget, an unwelcome recollection sprang into her mind. Suddenly, she remembered wearing the kaftan when Oliphant had interrogated her. She'd never recalled that singular meeting so clearly as she did then, standing in front of that mirror staring back at herself. Small pieces of the scene flitted through her mind: the frisson of awareness as he stood silhouetted against the light in the doorway; his incredible unwavering gaze; his abruptness; his solidity; the fiery colour of his beard and hair; the small, but nonetheless perceptible change in him when she'd tried to describe the effect of the cones – and yes, afterwards, that brief moment when their fingers had touched.

She lifted her hands slowly and cupped her breasts, seeing for herself in her reflected image the effect of this simple act. Her heart jolted. The curve of her breasts strained against the fine weave of the fabric, the nipples clearly outlined; inviting. She lowered her hands, still staring at the glass – horrified. She'd been under the influence of the trauma regulator, she told herself. It had reduced her ability to monitor her actions; to give proper consideration to what she was doing. But the effect was undeniable: she'd given Oliphant an open invitation, not on stage as part of a public display for everyone to enjoy, but in a private room, at close quarters. Had he thought her actions had somehow implicated her in Karoli's death? Had he suspected she was prepared to 'buy him off' with a casual liaison if he got too close to the truth? Or had he simply thought her a pushover for anyone who might express an interest in that direction now her partner was dead? The possibilities frightened her.

She wrenched off the kaftan, and picking the nearest leisuresuit available, scrambled into it, slamming the closet door shut to trap the image of the seductress inside, safely out of sight and beyond reach. Her heart-rate had rocketed; her breathing had become rapid and uneven, and she knew without a shadow of a doubt that if she did not escape from that room immediately, with all its frustrated sexuality, she would probably scream.

Out in the brightly lit, empty corridor, the musi-tone played softly to itself, unappreciated. She moved in a kind of dream, simply moving in order not to think.

At the first door, she automatically pressed the buzzer, her mind ignoring the red light above the lintel telling her no one was inside. She pressed again, unwilling to accept the simple truth she already knew – that Theo and Umo were still in the Armstrong Hall. She waited a few more moments before moving on to the next door – Raymer's – a green glow shining from its indicator.

She pressed the buzzer and waited, still breathless.

The door didn't open immediately and no one answered her summons. Instinctively, she knew someone was watching her on the monitoring panel. Was it Angel? For a split second she was prepared to make a run for it.

Suddenly, the door slid back into its casing, making her start.

She hovered on the threshold, ready to flee if necessary. But no one stepped forward, or invited her in. Standing against the far wall was Lazar, anxiously cradling the shell of a choraladian close to his chest. On the table next to him, its working parts were spread out in meticulous rows, with assorted tools ready to hand. Even more incongruously, several handset monitors were linked up to the power conduit on the adjacent wall, their screens registering strings of incomprehensible data.

For a moment, neither of them moved, Lazar staring back at her from his dull, expressionless face. He looked like a badly dressed dummy in a shopping mall window, his bulky silver and emerald-coloured leisuresuit several sizes too large for his slender frame. His appearance was comical, not in the sense of being funny, but of being foolish.

Something seemed to click in his mind. He took a hesitant step forward, stumbling slightly against the chair he'd been sitting on. "Cass come in?" he asked hesitantly, his voice a tremulous soft murmuring that defied adequate description. "Only me here. No Jay," he added, as if no one ever wanted to see him – always someone else. It seemed to register indescribable isolation – and loneliness.

She hesitated, fearing her desire for company had been turned on its head.

"Cass welcome," he insisted, carefully placing the choraladian casing back onto the table top, and indicating the lounger next to a neo-urban artscape on the adjacent wallpane.

Despite rising misgivings, she accepted his invitation. He sat down again on the small upright chair beside the table. "I working," he informed her, as if it were important she should know this. The place was a mess: on every available flat surface, instrumentation of one sort or another lay in various stages of either being reconstructed or dismantled.

He was waiting patiently for her to speak, and when she found herself unable to think of a single thing to say, he simply sat and stared at her.

Compelled to start some sort of conversation, she said the first thing that came into her head. "I – I wondered how you were settling in – I mean, do you mind – being here?"

He gave this some thought before shaking his head solemnly.

"You don't mind space?"

Again, the shake of the head. "Like home," he added.

Rapidly running out of small-talk, Cassandra pointed to the choraladian. "Is it faulty?" she asked.

He pondered this for a moment, then turned his attention to the visual display on the nearest monitor before replying. "No, I am learning how it works."

"Raymer says you're a TechnoPro."

He nodded.

From the array of parts littering the table top, Cassandra had serious doubts. "Can you show me?" she asked, simply to give herself time to think how to extricate herself from the situation she'd so successfully got herself into.

He nodded again and carefully began reassembling the various components into the casing. His movements were slow but deliberate: methodical. He dropped nothing. He mishandled nothing. There was an assurance about each move that belied his outward appearance. Within less than five minutes, the choraladian was complete.

"Does it work?" she asked, tempted to believe it might not.

He cradled it once more, his delicate fingers seeking out the buttons tentatively, stroking them like a blind man feeling his way around old-time braille script. The instrument hummed into life. He played a few chords, tried a scale or two, and began to wail softly to himself with half-closed eyes. The music was execrable; the pitch perfect.

Cassandra sat immobile, hypnotised, the notes from the instrument and his quavering voice weaving and interweaving with one another like a banshee in torment. It made her shudder. It was music to raise spirits by. The dead would surely answer his call.

"That's wonderful," she said, raising her voice to cut across the performance she desperately wanted to stop at all costs. "Really – very good."

He ceased in mid-flow, the unearthly music dying away to a soft moan. With great care that almost amounted to tenderness, he placed the instrument back on the table, stroking its gilded surface as though it had spoken to him and he was acknowledging its words. His eyes lifted to hers. "I can stay?" he asked. "Cass let me stay? Jay say you will let me stay if I am good."

"It's not just up to me, Lazar," she explained.

Lazar shook his head. "Jay say Cass is the boss."

She smiled at him. That was nice to know, she thought, because sometimes she wondered if Raymer's compliance to her wishes hid a ravenous ambition. She changed the subject. "Do you miss your family, Lazar?"

His eyes swivelled back to the choraladian. He shrugged.

"Do they miss you?"

A moment's pause before another shake of the head. "Not remember."

"Oh, of course. Sorry." And then because she'd run out of things to say, she said. "I heard about your accident. Were you in the MediCentre for long?"

He thought about this then shrugged again, his shoulders heaving themselves up around his neck as if they were being hoisted by an unseen winch. "Good Doctor," he said, with a small but definite flicker of visible emotion. "Made me well."

Not well enough, she thought. She smiled at him. "What was he like?" she pressed him, because she was curious. "Your Doctor."

The question seemed to bewilder him. He frowned, the first real physical change she'd seen in his features.

Her interest grew. "Was he tall – short – fat – thin?" she suggested light-heartedly, and for good measure asked, "Can you remember his name?"

He shambled to his feet and turned away, hugging himself, the leisuresuit shrinking inwards to reflect the true size of its occupant.

She watched with an awful fascination as he began shuffling slowly up and down the room in the same posture, head bent, his eyes watching the silent progress of his shoes across the sable-coloured floor. It was an eerie sight: a mind out of step with itself; a body ill-at-ease with its component parts, his movements suggesting a whole range of contradictions she found impossible to reconcile. Was she witnessing a genuine reaction? Or was it a profoundly disturbing act put on for her benefit?

Lazar was still mumbling softly and shaking his head as though in earnest conversation with an unseen third party.

"I'm sorry," she said, realising she must put a stop to this dreadful display. "I shouldn't have asked."

But it didn't stop him. He shuffled on, turned and stumbled back again, slower now, head still bent with his lank hair drooping over his lifeless face, the low mumbling dropping to a continuous monotone.

Realising it would take more than words, she stood up and intercepted him, grasping him by the shoulders as he shambled past. He stopped, like an antique clockwork toy, his eyes still downcast, his arms still embracing his narrow ribcage in a grip of iron.

With all the gentleness she could muster, she lifted his chin, bringing up the blank emptiness of his face to look at her. "I'm sorry, Laz," she said softly. "Please, don't be upset."

He gazed up at her with soft, hazel-coloured eyes: unflinching, strangely cognisant at that moment. He blinked. "Laz," he said slowly, with that tremulous voice that sent a shiver through her. "Laz," he repeated, as if he were savouring the sound of the word. "Laz."

She swallowed hard, aware she'd unintentionally dislodged a distant mangled memory from somewhere in his broken brain.

He stepped back and stood straighter so she had to loosen her hold on him. He was nodding, making something clear to himself. "I not upset. I your friend," he announced and stepped forward again, putting his hands on her shoulders as if this confirmed the fact.

Taken by surprise, she didn't move. "Of course you're my friend," she found herself saying automatically. As close as they were now under one of the downlighters, she could make out the fine tracery of scar tissue that covered his forehead like a damaged web, and the small dimples beneath the skin where the structure of his skull had been repaired. A deep furrow, like an erratic graph, echoed the chaotic progress of his hairline, and the skin that covered his distorted features had the strangely lifeless appearance of translucent parchment.

Standing there, open and unguarded, his defences down, he was the picture of absolute vulnerability, and there was suddenly something about his defencelessness that demanded her protection. "I'll always be your friend, Laz," she said, not having the slightest notion why she should make such an outrageous statement.

Then to her shame, he smiled: a beautiful lop-sided smile full of small china-white artificial teeth. The sort of smile intended to please, to coax, to placate. "Laz happy," he said, wrapping his arms around her, and burying his head between her breasts as though she were his mother.

She was suddenly very frightened at what she'd done.

Unexpectedly, the door from the corridor slid into its casing with a sigh, letting in the musi-tone and Jason Raymer, his face and tunic spangled with sweat from the exertions of the rehearsal. Their eyes met: hers facing him across the top of Lazar's head; his briefly registering shock and surprise by turn.

Hearing the door open, Lazar disengaged himself and stood proudly in front of Raymer, head up. "Cassie my friend," he announced, his voice more animated and vibrant than she'd ever heard it before. "Cassie say Laz," he added, as if to underline the fact.

Cassandra didn't know what to do, or say, aware of the incongruous picture painted for anyone entering the room the moment before.

Raymer managed a stiff smile, letting the door close behind him. "Good. I'm glad," he said in English, and then directing his words at Cassandra, added more sharply in UniCom, "I hope you know what you're doing."

She accepted the rebuke. It was the first time he'd asserted himself so openly. But then, she reflected, he'd every right to: here she was in his private quarters without his invitation, apparently indulging herself with a Vulnerable. She moved back to sit on the lounger, avoiding a piece of equipment on the floor, and trying to conceal the acute embarrassment she was feeling. "Can we discuss this?" she asked, keeping to UniCom as a matter of necessity.

Raymer nodded. "Cassie and I want to talk, Laz," he said quietly, using English again. "You go next door, yes?"

Lazar nodded and complied, like an obedient robot.

Once the door to the sleeping quarters had closed, there was a moment's silence. Raymer took the opportunity to push aside the choraladian and perch on the edge of the table. He wiped his forehead with the back of his hand but seemed in no hurry to start a conversation.

She cleared her throat. "I didn't realise – " she began.

"Realise what?" His tone was neutral but there was a hint of antagonism in his grey-blue stare that was slightly unnerving. "That Lazar has feelings?"

"No, I didn't realise how much he needed friends."

Raymer swung a chair out from under the table and mounted it, leaning against the back exactly as Oliphant had done, she remembered, only the posture was different, less intimidating – but only marginally.

"I know how it must have looked – when you came in," she said.

"How did it look?" he challenged her.

"I wasn't trying to – " But the words trailed away into nothing, dying in her mouth.

He cocked his head to one side, raising an eyebrow. "Trying to do what exactly?"

She looked away, studying the neo-urban landscape on the wallpane, feeling acutely uncomfortable under his gaze. "Trying to take advantage of him," she managed at last.

"What *were* you doing?" he asked.

"I was just talking. I needed to talk – to someone – to anyone. Shackleton's getting to me, I suppose."

"Well I hope you realise you've probably done something you may regret."

"It wasn't intentional! I was talking for the sake of it."

"About what?"

"About his family – his accident – the MediCentre."

"And?"

"What the Doctor was like – oh, I can't remember exactly! Why do you want to know?"

"Did *you* mention the Doctor, or did he?"

"He did. Is that important?"

Raymer shrugged. "I don't know," he said getting up from the chair and peeling off the sweat-soaked tunic that clung to him, leaving his skin glossy under the downlights. "I don't ask him questions any more," he added, flinging the stained garment across the back of the chair, his attention deflected by the monitors on the table. He stood surveying them, hands on his hips. "I just accept there's a lot I don't know about him. He's an enigma with a lot of pieces missing. Sometimes he's incredibly lucid. Others – " He shrugged again glancing across at her, the severity of his expression softening a little. "He's good at his job. I suppose that's all that matters to us."

"Yes," she agreed, wondering if his interrogation of her was over. "He was learning how the choraladian worked when I arrived."

Raymer picked it up and inspected it closely, his head bent, his hair falling forward around his neck and ears. He'd let it grow at the back. Like Theo. Like Karoli … He was sideways on to her and didn't notice her studying him, his semi-nakedness a matter of apparent indifference as far as he was concerned: he was lost in thought. He played a few notes, humming softly, and seemed satisfied with the sound. The downlights shone along the muscles of his shoulders and the sides of his arms, and drew a gleaming golden line down the curve of his spine. He was quite smooth, a fact that suddenly imprinted itself sharply on her mind, and lingered. He would be beautiful to touch …

She got up quickly, interrupting her thoughts. "I must go," she said hastily. "We both need time to get ready. Tonight's important."

He straightened and replaced the choraladian on the table. As she passed him to reach the door, he caught hold of her hand. She stiffened involuntarily and he let go immediately, putting a decent space between them.

"I'm just a bit jittery," she said, trying to explain herself. "First night nerves. The usual."

He gave her a weak smile. "I understand," he said softly and opened the door for her.

"Thank you," she said, skirting past him to leave.

His voice followed her, forcing her to stop short as he spoke. "Cassandra – I won't let you down tonight – I promise. I know I'll never be Karoli. I won't try to be, please believe me. But I'll give it the best I've got."

She nodded and walked out quickly through the open door.

Twenty-three

The Festival of Light was over and Ben Davron was back on-station picking up the threads of the Koblinski case as instructed. Oliphant had given him only the barest of details. "Lattimer wants to keep things tight," he'd said. "He doesn't want anyone outside the Security Panel knowing the identity of the Freelance. So I know as much as you do, Ben. 'Phoenix' is part of the tour – that's all. I don't like it either, but we have to live with it."

Davron thought otherwise. If something went wrong, Shackleton Security was his responsibility. Ignorance was more likely to be a hindrance than a help if he were forced to contain a difficult situation, and getting zapped by a stun gun wasn't everyone's idea of an acceptable inconvenience when working undercover.

Quietly seething, he'd reluctantly taken on board Lattimer's injunction to watch every performance – or rather, watch the audience watching every performance. "Nothing obvious," Lattimer had stressed. "A low-key operation – routine monitoring, a Senior Security Officer just keeping an eye on things. Forget about the Freelance. We need to track down this 'Angel'."

But Davron couldn't forget about the Freelance. If he could spot him, he'd make damned sure he wasn't in the firing line if things got nasty.

Determined to do things his own way, he took himself over to the Armstrong Hall and strolled around introducing himself to the new Technos, asking if everything was 'okay'. He'd already met Raymer and his pathetic pet Vulnerable when they'd arrived on-station and discounted them. The same went for Argosti and his diminutive, but earnest young apprentice Chimala. None of those four could operate as effective Freelances: they were either too visible; too petulant, or too emotionally fragile.

Of the new Technos, Ballinger, he discovered, was abrasive and seemed permanently ill-at-ease, his concentration never resting on anything in particular for more than a few seconds at a time. Meriq seemed disinclined to talk and had the unsettling habit of staring intently straight ahead when the peri-phones were clamped to his ears, so it was hard to know whether he was really listening – or watching – or both. Staines on the other hand was a run-of-the-mill Techno, full of himself and eager to show it. Maybourne, Krodalt's latest assistant and in his early twenties, stuck to Krodalt like glue and showed little initiative. Banks was around the same age, competent, but indecisive, worrying over minor details and noticeably driving Dunnock mad. Of the two Sound Recordists, Ortona had been at Shackleton with other Entertainer groups in the past. Proud of his product, he liked to have his work appreciated. Glaister, his new assistant, was still learning the ropes and less voluble, but wasn't above giving as good as he got when provoked.

Later, back in his office, Davron had to admit that frustratingly he was no nearer identifying the Freelance than before – and no one had given him the slightest hint they were anything more than they seemed – but, he reflected, that was to be expected.

That night, unenthusiastically following Lattimer's instructions, he unobtrusively joined the sea of casually dressed Spaceworkers filling the Armstrong Hall. The buzz of conversations was loud with the occasional whoop and yell from the over-enthusiastic. The pre-tour advertising had done a good job. The word was out: The Choralians were back – better than ever. The atmosphere was electric.

Despite the aircon functioning at full throttle, the hall was warm with the press of bodies, and Davron chose to mount his vigil close to the ventilation duct nearest the access pay-point. From this spot, he had an uninterrupted view of the whole tiered seating area and most of the stage; it also allowed him to discretely scrutinise every new arrival as they logged-in their credit rating. Sitting behind him, his deputy, Tereshkhova, ran a double check on the security files for everyone who filed through. But there was nothing. Zilch.

His frustration grew. He realised he'd been hoping against all probability that he might strike it lucky – just this once – and turn up something to show for his efforts. It would have been deeply satisfying. But once the capacity audience was seated, with no hint of anything out of the ordinary, his optimism evaporated. He felt he'd been wasting his time. Equally disconcerting was the suspicion that the station's security checks had triggered an alert somewhere in a covert surveillance system and Angel had been warned off. Or perhaps he'd chosen not to come to the performance. Or perhaps he wasn't even on-station.

The lights suddenly went down and the performance began. It was an assault on the senses. With difficulty, he braved the barrage of sound and light bombarding him from all sides, attempting to keep his mind focussed on studying the frenetic responses of all six-hundred-and-fifty cheering, screaming and waving fans. But the only emergency turned out to be the need to call in the Medics to evacuate three enthusiasts who'd let the proceedings get the better of them.

The instrumental intro over, an expectant hush filled the auditorium. From the blackness on-stage came the first rays of light, expanding slowly in the shimmering blues and greens of the sea. Raymer, Xenon and Manaus, in costumes reflecting the light were almost invisible against the dappled backcloth. They set the scene: a Folkster number with its slow rhythm and plaintive melody. The music was hypnotic, almost magical in quality. Davron found himself drawn into the sound, compelled by its beauty to submerge his senses and drown in it.

Centre stage, a single white spot expanded slowly to reveal Cass Diamond, her dark hair loose about her shoulders and threaded with silver-sequinned ribbons that caught the light and dazzled the eyes. Her arms were bare, her supple body swathed in a haze of blue-green silken cloth: an exotic creature from the depths of the ocean. Davron couldn't take his eyes off her. She moved like the sea: swaying, rippling to the rhythm of the music, hypnotising him.

And then she began to sing: a mer-child's song – in that new, but strangely evocative vogue language of Fatingu. Her voice spiralled upwards with the music until the whole arena was engulfed in exquisite, lambent, sound and light. It made his spine turn to jelly, and the hairs on the back of his neck prickle against his collar.

Almost imperceptibly, the music shifted into another key and the rhythm began to change. Davron had never experienced anything quite like it: he began to feel disembodied; floating; remote. The sound swelled in his ears, making him quiver. The lighting flickered fitfully, like moonshine on a wide expanse of heaving, rolling water. Her voice, combining with the music and light, seemed to climb inside his brain until his whole consciousness was concentrated on the sight and sound of her. He could hear the rhythm of his heartbeat rising: steadily, remorselessly, increasing his pulse rate. Adrenalin flowed. His eyes locked onto the movement of her body: swaying; inviting. He was being seduced, a hair's breath away from surging.

With a supreme effort, he fought to tear himself free of her image, clamping his hands over his ears to block out the siren's song. His heart was jumping and stuttering alarmingly. Blackness lingered at the corners of his vision for a moment and he gasped for air, fighting back unconsciousness. He pulled savagely at his collar, yanking it open and staggering backwards, steadied himself against the solidity of a pillar, hoping Tereshkova wouldn't notice. Breathe, he told himself. Breathe slowly.

His vision cleared. He looked about him, feeling foolish and highly visible. But not even Tereshkova was watching him. All eyes were focussed on the stage as if everyone had gazed on Medusa and been turned to stone. The centre of the universe had shifted. At its core was Cass Diamond enveloped in light, her voice and the music swirling around her. It felt dangerous.

The last bars swelled to a crescendo, vibrating through the very fabric of the hall. As the final notes died away, there was a pause, then the lighting levels rocketed to full power, breaking the spell and the brief silence was torn apart by six-hundred-and-forty-seven acolytes stamping and clapping, cheering and screaming for more. And they got it.

Davron kept his fingers stuffed in his ears, feeling weak and disorientated. The solidity of the pillar at his back gave him strength, but only just. In the end, it was only when the third encore began that he felt he had enough self-control to listen again.

The music had changed: there was none of the dangerous mind-play of the earlier pieces. It was up-tempo, a song dedicated to life and love – the eternal theme, as Cass Diamond described it to the adoring audience in her introduction, her voice crooning over the sound system, luring them all into her web.

A traditional Folkster tune, it was lively, easy to memorise and everyone was encouraged to join in the chorus. Davron quickly recognised it from the few opening bars: it was one of The Choralians' best known songs – a duet – one in which Karoli Koblinski would have played a leading part – if he'd lived.

Davron's curiosity stirred. He eased himself forward a little to get a better view of the stage. Just how well would Cass Diamond cope with the contradictions? Would memories rise up, like ghosts? Would she be able to carry it off?

Jay Raymer stepped forward and joined her centre stage, freeing his hair from a restraining band as he entered the spotlight, tossing his glossy mane back from his shoulders: self-assured; totally confident. It was almost a challenge. Here I am, it said. I'm not Koblinski, but his successor. I'm even better.

The applause and cheering died down, and the song began.

To Davron, it was as if Koblinski had never been; as if Raymer and Diamond had always sung together, their harmony lifting and shifting in tune with one another, merging like molten metals into a single mould. They smiled fondly, held hands and flirted, driving the audience wild.

Davron could feel his chest tighten, and the thought uppermost in his mind was just how much had Cass Diamond really known about Koblinski's last few hours? How much heartbreak had she truly suffered? Who was the real Cass Diamond? Was she the traumatised woman he'd interviewed four months ago, or the vibrant, sensual being on stage now with her new singing partner – perhaps already more than just her singing partner – bowing with him, accepting the roar of approval from the crowd?

His blood was raging in his head. Leaving Tereshkhova to monitor the exits, he stumbled out of the hall into the foyer, his anger eating into him.

He was no stranger to deception. Half his operational life was wrapped up in it one way or another. Criminal deception: the petty pilfering; the smuggling; the occasional large-scale attempt to cream off ConCorp's profits into private accounts. But this deception was on a personal level: it destroyed his faith in himself. Cass Diamond had made a fool of him. He'd been content to take her verbal statement at face value. Why had he been so easily convinced she knew nothing, when she might have been holding back vital information? Why had he been so gullible?

The answer was simple. Because he'd wanted to be. Because at the time, her reaction to the news of Koblinski's death had been so extreme, her seeming fragility and vulnerability had beguiled and bewitched him.

Now he was not only angry at his lack of professional thoroughness, he was angry at his emotional response to an attractive and undoubtedly powerful woman. Angry too when he remembered how Oliphant had been so resolute before his visit to her room, and how suddenly he too had been prepared to wrap up his Shackleton enquiries, giving The Choralians the all-clear to tranship with only the most cursory investigation of their respective stories.

His rage now turned fully on her, with her easy ability to play the anguished innocent. If she wasn't a liar, then she was certainly a cheat, her closeness to Jay Raymer blatantly displayed for everyone to see. Easy come. Easy go. A jigging Hurdy-Gurdy.

TWENTY-FOUR

"Did I give it my best?" Raymer was asking her.

His question followed her down the corridor as their made their hurried escape from the Armstrong Hall into the sanctuary of the secure Stage Door area, courtesy of half-a-dozen burly Security Officers. The drumming of stamping and clapping was still thundering in her ears, and the press of bodies demanding autographed holograms still lingered in her nostrils.

Theo and Umo had gone ahead and she let Raymer catch up with her. "You know you did," she said, mocking him, but the thought crossed her mind – what else could she have said? That he'd outshone Karoli? That his rendition of that special song had been fresh, vital and everything she'd have wanted it to be? It would have been the truth – but she couldn't bring herself to say it.

He was looking very pleased with himself. "Do you think Smiler will approve?"

"Of course he will."

Oh yes – Smiler would be well-pleased. Raymer had matched the expectations placed on him, perhaps more than matched them. Meanwhile, ConCorp's communications systems were taking the enhanced 3D format and distributing it through Smiler's multi-media networks to fans back on Earth, and out there, on stations in the depths of the Solar System. She could imagine him rubbing his fat hands at the prospect of a healthy return on his investment.

They'd reached the door to the dressing rooms. He opened it for her in an act of old-fashioned gallantry. "I think I'd rather know that *you* approved," he said.

She noted the slight inflection in his tone of voice, but if he were looking for more fulsome praise, she denied him the pleasure. "I've said so, haven't I?" she said casually. "Get changed. I'll meet you in the bar."

He looked slightly embarrassed at the rebuff, like a schoolboy caught out insisting on extra praise from his tutor.

Half-an-hour later, showered and thoroughly refreshed, she joined the rest of the crew in the exclusive privacy of the Artistes' Bar. The atmosphere was buoyant, everyone elated: laughing; joking; talking much too loud. The mood was infectious and she caught it, finding herself daring to feel happy without the burden of guilt. Karoli would have understood, she hoped. Success that evening had been crucial: the first show with a new lead singer had to go well, or the rest of the tour could have hung in the balance. Smiler had to be satisfied.

"Great product," Ortona was yelling at her over the hubbub. "Fantastic. Zillions of hits on the recording!"

She acknowledged his enthusiasm, unable to understand the expansive jargon-riddled explanation that followed on the technical brilliance he and Glaister had added to the performance.

Krodalt and the rest of the Technos gave her the thumbs-up as she wove between their exuberant huddles to reach Theo, Umo and Raymer at the bar. "Terrific," said Krodalt, not usually given to saying much at all.

"You were amazing," Staines said as he stepped back to let her past. "Never seen anything like it," his observation accompanied by a nuanced smile that reminded Cassandra not to engage him in too much conversation in the future.

Raymer made room for her, shifting onto another bar stool. "Looks like we pleased everyone," he said and nodding to the barman, placed his order. "A Burmudan Brandy for the star of the show, Lexi, if you please. Make it a double, will you?"

Cassandra allowed herself to smile at his silliness: alcohol, like mind-warp was forbidden on-station, but the synthetic versions were passable, and no one could possibly get drunk or morose on any of them.

With elaborate courtesy, Raymer handed over her drink and called for a toast. "To a successful tour," he said. Theo and Umo raised theirs in reply and the conversation moved on to which songs had produced the best audience reaction. Fatingu was declared the best choice for any future material, and so it went on.

Conscious of Staines's earlier interest and Raymer's enthusiasm, Cassandra chose to lean against Theo, like others lean against trees for security. Sipping at the brandy, she let her gaze roam over those in the bar and was suddenly aware that someone was missing from the celebrations. "Where's Lazar?" she asked casually, his absence from the group, who'd accepted him without any questions asked, was suddenly noticeable, in the same way that a commonplace piece of furniture, so often taken for granted by the very mundaneness of its function, is suddenly not there, and the place it occupied seems to draw attention to itself.

"He's in our quarters," Raymer chipped in. "Too many people, he said. I didn't want to force the issue."

She was sorry he'd excluded himself: he was safe in their company. "He really should be here," she said. "He's part of the team."

"That's what I told him," Raymer said.

Umo, buoyed up by the overwhelming success of the evening, was unusually voluble and eager to give his opinion. "He mend my choraladian very well," he said, clutching his half-drunk Paradise Cocktail. "Okay – if he not want to come, I take him a drink, yes?"

Up until that moment, Cassandra had been feeling relaxed and comfortable with Theo's arm lightly encircling her waist. With

Umo's words, she felt his grip tighten, just a fraction, and heard the conviviality of his laughter die upon his lips.

"I think he should be persuaded to join us here, Umo," she cut in quickly, anxious not to allow Umo the chance of being alone with Lazar. "Theo, see if you can persuade him to come. Tell him Cassie asked for him especially."

Theo disengaged himself from her, giving her the smallest of nods, understanding her motive and being grateful for it. He quit the bar with Umo in tow and Cassandra watched them leave, knowing the tight-knit closeness of the party atmosphere had been broken. So be it.

Time passed. She waited patiently, sipping her brandy and consuming a small bowl of cashew nuts abstractedly. Raymer had been accosted by Ballinger and Staines and was deep into technical details of the performance at the far end of the bar. Ortona and Glaister had drawn into their circle Nyagan, a Shackleton Techno seconded to The Choralians for the duration of their stay, and the rest of the Technos were still clustered around Krodalt involved in a convoluted and detailed discussion on whether this adjustment or that should be made to the staging to achieve an even better result. At a small table at the side of the room, she spied Argosti fretting over the state of the costumes as usual, and his diminutive young assistant, Chimala, only on his second space tour, wide-eyed and visibly excited by the whole experience. Yes, we're got a good team, she thought.

Banks had appeared by her elbow, waiting for the barman to finish tidying away some used glasses. "Hello," he said. He'd never approached her before on his own and was visibly nervous about speaking to her. He was a gangly young man with floppy fair hair, and as Cassandra discovered, once he'd got over his initial shyness, he was eager to demonstrate his extensive knowledge of every aspect of The Choralians' professional careers. He was determined she should be impressed by the extent of his accumulated wisdom.

For the want of anything better to do, she listened politely while he regurgitated a steady stream of publicity data far-removed from the reality of The Choralians' individual true histories: a fantasy world conjured up by Smiler in one of his more creative marketing moods.

Banks's enthusiasm was boundless, but increasingly wearisome. Her attention wandered. Idly, she watched the others talking animatedly amongst themselves and suddenly felt strangely isolated – removed from the scene. A lethargy settled on her spirits, intensified by the seemingly endless details Banks was reeling off like a looped announcement on a glidetrack. Politely as she could, she interrupted him. "Charlie, I hope you don't mind – I'm feeling a little tired," she said smiling at him, and seeing his disappointment added, "Do something for me, will you? I don't want to break up the party. Just say I've popped out for a moment if anyone asks you where I am. Thanks." And she patted him on the arm to make him feel he'd been taken into her confidence.

With a sense of relief, she slipped out of the bar unseen and boarded the underground glidetrack to the Accommodation Unit.

The corridor on A floor was empty, abandoned to the musi-tone and the bright downlights that dropped pools of brilliance onto the geometric flooring. The indicator light outside Raymer's quarters glowed red, the one above Theo's showed green. She stopped in her tracks outside Raymer's door with a single thought in her head. Where was Lazar?

As if in answer to her question, Theo's door opened and Theo emerged, the sound of a muffled conversation drifting after him. "Looking for me?" he asked.

"I wondered what had happened. Where's Lazar?"

"We couldn't persuade him to join the party, I'm afraid, so we invited him in for company. I hope you don't mind. I haven't spoilt your evening, have I?"

"No, not at all."

He looked relieved. "That's all right then. I thought you might want to spend some time with Jason anyway," he added. "Celebrate your success together."

"No – he's talking with the Technos anyway," she said, unsettled by the notion Theo imagined it would be Raymer and not himself that would become the focus of her attention in future. She'd made strenuous efforts to keep Raymer at arm's length off-stage, and she'd no intention of letting him get closer. "It was a great show, Theo – I just want some time to myself to get over it."

He nodded. "No memories to keep you awake?"

"No."

"I'm glad for you." He embraced her briefly. "Sleep well," he said, tenderly. "Tonight was a new beginning. Let the past rest undisturbed."

"I will."

"Good night then."

"Good night, Theo – and thank you." She kissed him lightly on the cheek and they parted. As she turned, she heard his door sigh shut.

The short space between their two rooms suddenly seemed to stretch into infinity. Her legs felt strangely weak, unwilling to hold her up as the great unstoppable wave of anti-climax and tiredness began to wash over her. There'd be no need for SoundSleep: she knew emotional and physical fatigue would embrace her as soon as she lay down.

Almost stumbling against the door to her quarters, she was suddenly very aware that the occupancy indicator was a steady, deep green. She steadied herself against the doorframe and studied the offending light with a creeping sense of disquiet: she could think of no one who should rightfully be in her quarters at 0217 hours: it was well beyond the limit when Maintenance Operatives would be on duty.

A shiver travelled along her spine. She stood motionless,

conscious the monitoring panel might well be operational, and whoever was inside was probably watching her every move. Her mind began to race through the possibilities that might lie beyond the sepia-coloured door. For a brief moment she wondered if she were on the wrong floor – a stupid notion of course – only moments before she'd been talking to Theo further down the corridor, and here was the door's reference code staring back at her, stippled clearly in stencilled alphanumerics – A-20. There could be no doubt she was definitely outside her own quarters.

So who might be watching her? Angel? She remained paralysed, staring at the door.

TWENTY-FIVE

The door slid back. The light from the corridor spilled into a darkened, silent interior. Cassandra remained frozen to the spot.

"Why don't you come in?" a man's voice demanded.

She flinched, hearing her breath coming in sudden uncontrollable sobs. She couldn't have moved even if she'd wanted to.

A tall, menacing figure suddenly strode forward out of the darkness and grabbed her by the arms, pulling her roughly inside from the comparative safety of the corridor. She heard the door sigh shut behind her, locking out the musi-tone and replacing it with the heavy breathing of an adrenalin-fuelled man. He jerked up the lighting.

She stared up into his face, bewildered by the ferocity she saw there. Somewhere beneath the anger was SSO Davron.

"So you've not brought him back with you then?" he snarled at her.

"Who?" she asked, trying to make sense of his question.

"Your latest man," he snapped back.

"Raymer?" She was incredulous. "No – No – why should I?"

"Why shouldn't you?" he challenged her, his grip on her arms tightening. "Or were you expecting someone else?"

"No – I wasn't expecting anyone."

"Not 'Angel' perhaps?"

"No!"

"Oh, so you *do* know him?" he said, dragging her closer.

"Only what Theo told me."

The muscles in his jaw kept knotting and unknotting. "Don't lie to me!" he spat back. The intensity of his fury shrivelled up the last of her momentary relief her unexpected guest wasn't Angel. Now she was facing something worse – and she recognised it from years before, when she'd been much younger, in a world with its own rules, or lack of them. It was dangerous, and needed very careful handling.

"I only know what Theo told me," she repeated.

Davron's eyes had narrowed, the blackness of his pupils intensified by the terrible closeness of his face to hers. "You're lying, Cass Diamond. You think you can play games with me, don't you? You think I'm a soft touch, but you can't fool me twice."

He was shoving her now, pushing her backwards. She stumbled over chairs and other pieces of furniture that suddenly seemed to litter the room. All she could think of was the immediate necessity of staying upright, and not to fall. It was the first and cardinal rule of survival. *Stay on your feet.*

Somewhere in the back of her mind, her rational self was analysing the situation. Crying for help was out of the question in a sound-proofed room. Wrestling herself free wasn't an option either. He'd finally pinned her against the wall, the suddenness of his onslaught rendering counter-attack impossible. Besides, she told herself, no one in their right mind countenanced offering violence to a Security Officer: it simply gave them the excuse to retaliate.

Violence: the one luxury still available to Security Officers and Enforcers – and denied to other people – especially in the space environment.

With her back slammed against the wall and his full weight against her, he gave her an extra shove, knocking the breath clean out of her. "Now, tell me again about Angel," he hissed in her ear, spraying her with fine spittle. "Everything. From the beginning."

Winded, she was unable to speak.

"Now!" he demanded.

"I don't know him," she insisted, her voice barely recognisable to herself.

He wound her hair around one hand and pulled hard. It brought tears to her eyes.

"I don't know him," she repeated.

"But you know of him, don't you? Did your precious Karoli Koblinski work for him? Was he running combos for him? Supercharge? Mind-warp maybe?"

"No!"

There was another savage yank that reminded her of so many others in her past when she'd fought to retain a shred of dignity in circumstances where none existed.

"So it *was* you then – *you* sold Koblinski out to Angel! Easy come, easy go. There's always someone else."

"No!" It was a terrible thought.

"Was Angel your contact?"

"No!"

"Who is he?"

"I don't know!" The pain encircling her head was becoming unbearable.

"You lying little jigger!" His lips curled in contempt.

With a flick of his wrist he pulled her head backwards, his face so close to hers she could feel the heat of his skin. He called her every dirty name she'd ever heard, and more besides, grinding her even harder against the wall, the rough fabric of his uniform grazing the skin at her throat.

He hates me, she thought, fighting back tears. He hates me enough to harm me. Why? What was driving him? What was the purpose behind these useless questions? Where was the mild-mannered, respectful man she remembered treating her so sympathetically four months before? Had he discovered something damning against Karoli that implicated her? She couldn't imagine what, but whatever it was, he wanted to make her talk. What small torture would he choose? The stun gun at close quarters perhaps? No, her rational self argued, that would produce massive bruising, even on a low setting. Take her for a walk outside on the surface perhaps, with all the terror that would induce in someone totally unprepared for the enormity of space? No, that could result in total mental dysfunction. No, he'd never be mad enough to do that.

And then, looking into the depths of his eyes, she realised precisely what he was contemplating. It was suddenly written there quite plainly. She'd seen that expression before, way back in one of the trailer camps when she was sixteen and life had become a hand-to-mouth existence. Live entertainment had been going through a rough patch. Everyone was having Experience Rooms installed in their homes – the must-have highly desirable acquisition everyone wanted. Who needed the real thing when you could plug into virtual reality? Destitute, her mother had resorted to combos. Combos cost credit, and credit was the one thing Hippolyta Diamantides hadn't got. But she'd got her adopted daughter, and Cassandra had become a commodity, if the price were right. And the price had always been right.

And here she was again – looking into a man's eyes, and behind them, a man's mind.

She needed to confirm his intentions, to prepare herself for what was to come. Yes, he was ready to do it. She could feel the hardness of him pressed up against her. His free hand came up to the thin fabric at the neck of her leisuresuit, pulling at it savagely. Soon it would tear. She was surprised how coolly she could distance herself from his frenzy; from his physical touch; from his verbal assault. Perhaps her past had left her partly immune; perhaps she couldn't bring herself to believe this man would carry out such a threat.

Perhaps there was something in her expression that reflected her thoughts; maybe he had a momentary stab of conscience, or the sudden realisation of the enormity of the offence he was about to commit hit him. For no specific reason she could think of, the stream of invective suddenly stopped. He blinked, and in the space of that blink, the veil of insanity seemed to lift from him.

His weight no longer crushed against her so violently; his hold on her hair lessened fractionally, and the hand at her neck stopped in its tracks. He blinked again, as though clearing his mind.

As the moment of supreme danger passed, her understanding of the situation suddenly became crystal clear. His anger had nothing to do with Angel. Nothing to do with Karoli. Nothing to do with anyone except herself, and this man's perception of her. It was entirely personal. Davron must have watched the performance. He'd seen her perform with Raymer.

A well of silence had opened up. It needed filling quickly – but with the right words. "I loved Karoli," she managed, barely able to whisper. "Raymer – Raymer and I – we sing together – that's all. We give people what they want to see."

He seemed to digest this information slowly.

She forced herself to look into his eyes without fear, trying not to give him any signal that might be misinterpreted.

Very slowly, he released his hold on her and stood back, keeping an arm's length distance between them. The blood which engorged his face began to drain away. He was becoming recognisable as the man she'd once known.

What mattered immediately was to maintain essential eye-contact. "I swear to you," she said, finding her voice still catching in her throat, "what you saw on stage was a performance – nothing more. Isn't that why we're called Hurdy-Gurdies? – because we're mechanical? Wind us up and we'll do anything?"

He didn't move, still gathering his composure, studying her, perhaps seeking out the trace of a lie to justify his actions. "You're not partners then?" he asked. It sounded like a challenge.

"No."

He looked away from her, and stepped back, straightening his uniform, trying to re-establish his dignity.

She remained leaning against the wall, giving him no reason to imagine she might make a bolt for the door. "I'm not lying to you. I never have," she said quietly. "I don't know who Angel is. I didn't know Karoli knew him. All I know is that Karoli died – and maybe – maybe Angel killed him."

He was studying the toes of his shoes. "Yes," he said, before looking up at her again. "That's what Oliphant thought too."

Oliphant. *Oliphant*. His name conjured out of nowhere suddenly made her feel weak.

Davron cleared his throat. "You know what I was going to do, don't you?" he said quietly.

She nodded.

Abruptly, he turned away and righted one of the chairs he'd knocked aside in their disordered progress across the room. He sat astride it facing her, just as Oliphant had done when he'd interrogated her, just as Raymer had done, the back of the chair a barrier between them – a defence; a shield.

For the first time she realised the full extent of her power. They were all in some way afraid of her: Oliphant, Raymer – and Davron. She could possess them all, at any time. It was a revelation. All she had to do was to give the necessary signal.

"What will you do?" he was asking her.

She didn't understand.

"You're within your rights to file an official complaint. I have to accept that." His unexpected frankness was disarming.

"What could I say?"

"The truth. It was a straightforward case of unprovoked assault. You have your rights as a citizen."

"There were no witnesses," she said, keeping things simple. "– and I have no interest in blackmail, Mister Davron."

He stood up suddenly, putting the chair tidily away under the table. "I have a partner – back on Earth – in Haifa," he said, addressing the table top. "I miss her very much. I'll leave the matter in your hands."

She didn't know what more she could say. She was beginning to feel faint and just wanted him out of the room.

The door buzzer startled them both. Neither of them moved.

"You'd better see who that is," Davron said quietly.

When she activated the monitoring panel, it revealed Jason Raymer.

Davron shot an accusatory look in her direction, throwing all her assertions back in her face. She shook her head vigorously to deny all knowledge.

Taking a deep breath, she pressed the communicator. "Hello, Jay," she said, trying to control any shakiness in her voice. "I didn't expect you." And then, because she'd no real alternative, she added, "Come in."

Raymer's smile vanished when he entered, realising she wasn't alone. His expression betrayed momentary shock and then ill-disguised suspicion. "I'm sorry," he said. "I didn't realise you had company."

For a split second, she saw the scene as Raymer saw it: Davron standing to attention adjusting his uniform; herself dishevelled, and signs of disarray about the place.

"I was just leaving," Davron said stiffly, the image of an efficient SSO. "Thank you for being so frank with me, Miss Diamond." He nodded in her direction, and briskly took his leave, evaluating Raymer as he left. The door sighed shut behind him.

Raymer was frowning. "Cass, are you all right?" he said, reaching out to hold her.

She moved away from him, pulling out the upright chair

Davron had occupied and slumping down onto it. The last thing she wanted right then was another man putting his hands on her.

"Yes, I'm all right," she managed, trying to sound convincing while her vision blurred and darkened at the edges alarmingly.

"You don't look it. I'll get you some water."

She heard the water being run and the sound of it filling a beaker, but it seemed to be a long way off. The next thing she knew he was shoving the beaker into her hand and helping her drink from it.

"What was he doing here?" he asked, taking the next chair out from under the table and sitting close to her. Much too close.

"He wanted to clear up a couple of things about Karoli," she lied, studying the depths of the beaker and wishing the dreadful buzzing in her head would go away.

Raymer choked off a half-laugh. "I don't think so, Cass. What else was he after?"

She shook her head, glancing up at him: his smooth features; the concern in his grey-blue eyes; the small crescent scar just visible in the downlight. And the notion came into her head Jason Raymer was jealous, and he didn't believe her. "I was standing too long," she said dismissively. "That's all. I'm just tired." Adding for good measure. "Are you going to interrogate me too?"

He backed off. "No – no – of course not. It's just … well, you both looked … strange, that's all."

"I had trouble explaining myself. Let's leave it at that. So – why are you here?"

"I didn't see you leave the bar, Cass. I just came to see if you were okay. I know tonight's been a strain for you."

"I'm fine, Jay. As I said, I'm just tired – and you don't have to be my keeper," she added wearily. "It doesn't come with the job." She got up to refill the beaker.

"I know that. I just wanted to know if you thought I'd handled things right tonight." He was looking up at her, and for the first time she was acutely aware Jason Raymer wanted to make himself available, if she cared to take him on.

Under different circumstances she might have succumbed to the temptation to try him out: the success of the evening; the excitement it had generated; the great surge of adrenalin that a responsive crowd inevitably produced; and most of all, the intense loneliness she felt at Shackleton without Karoli. But Davron's reaction to her performance had put the idea right out of her mind. "You know what I think, Jay. I've told you several times already," she said, making a move to activate the door control, hoping he'd take the hint. "The tour's going to be a great success. Better than we could have hoped for. Now, please let me get some rest. Theo and Umo are entertaining Lazar. Why not join them?" She hoped it didn't sound too much like a casual dismissal, but she'd had enough of explaining, cajoling and generally trying to get herself some space. But more than that, she suspected Davron would be hovering outside, watching, waiting to see how long Raymer stayed with her. The sooner she could get him out of her quarters the better.

He got up, mercifully prepared to recognise he'd chosen the wrong time to press home any advantage he might have been hoping for. "Of course. As long as you're okay."

She activated the door and moved aside to let him pass. "Good night, Jay," she said.

"Good night."

He left, and with an overwhelming sense of relief she closed the door behind him.

With what little strength she could muster, she fumbled her way into her sleeping area and collapsed onto the bed, fully clothed, feeling no need to resort to SoundSleep.

In the half-reality that existed between wakefulness and sleep, her fevered imagination roamed at will. She half expected to hear the door buzzer again, and to find Oliphant waiting to be admitted, announcing his presence in that strange combination of Russian-Scots UniCom that still hummed in her ears: intimidating yet oddly attractive. She could see him so clearly in her mind's eye: a solid figure, his fox-red hair and beard lit up by the downlights, hands on hips. Disconcertingly too came the realisation that if by some extraordinary chance he'd come, even then, when she was bone tired to the point of collapse, not only would she have let him in, she'd have asked him to stay – and even more perversely – made him more than welcome.

TWENTY-SIX

Ivanov 3 was fast approaching the Moon heading for Mars on the outward leg of its journey away from the Sun. With its central zero-gravity docking hub, this grotesque H-shaped travelling warehouse had become synonymous with 'drawing the short straw' as far as Spaceworker personnel were concerned. It was boredom personified orbiting the polar regions of the Sun and the inner planets.

Way back in the infancy of space exploration, it had proved far more economical to tranship bulk payloads destined for elsewhere from Shackleton. Low-level gravity and the minimum power thrust needed for the gigantic Shackleton bulk loaders were the two main factors. The two loaders, prosaically known as L-1 and L-2, could shift the equivalent of fifty ferry-loads of cargo in one go into the holds of a heavy freighter.

In the interval between *Ivanov's* annual flypast of the northern and southern hemispheres, stores were transhipped from Earth to Shackleton using the regular ferry services. The vast sublunar hangars, which had originally been the site of the first mine workings, were stacked high with provisions, equipment, maintenance and building materials awaiting its arrival.

Specialist equipment, materials and fragile goods were usually transhipped direct from Earth to mega-stations using one of ConCorp's heavy cruiser fleet. *Ivanov* dealt with the humdrum; the mundane, the non-perishable, and the non-volatile cargoes – a tramp steamer in all but name.

Historically, it had the doubtful distinction of being the oldest ConCorp's space vehicle still in service. Parts of it dated back to the very early days of ConCorp's first ventures into space almost two centuries before. It had been built in the standard space station design of its time with two cylindrical arms sticking out at 180° from a central hub. One arm housed the essentials for personnel living on-station; the second was reserved for warehousing, It was generally agreed the two areas should be kept entirely separate.

Ivanov's main energy source came from solar cells deployed from its two arms like erratic dorsal fins on a badly designed fish, and the whole structure doggedly rotated around its axis to maintain sufficient gravity to keep water in the bath tub, and other liquids firmly in their rightful place.

The station's history was chequered. Originally known only as CT1 – Cargo Transporter 1 – it had been renamed *Ivanov 1* to commemorate the Chief Engineer in charge of the original project back in the heady days of the late 2090s, almost fifteen years after the original date set for the inauguration of Stage One of the Martian terraforming project. *Ivanov* was to provide essential stores for ferries to supply the first base camps on the Red Planet, filling the awkward gap when Earth and Mars were badly aligned. It had the attraction, it was argued, of reducing direct flight-times from the home planet in these circumstances, which were both long-winded, and consequently expensive.

Right from the start *Ivanov* was dogged by problems. Initially, an industrial dispute during its construction delayed its completion by six months. After commissioning, a series of apparently minor, but nonetheless potentially lethal structural faults showed up. These took a further six months to rectify before the first skeleton crews came on board. Subsequent hiccups with the recyclation and aircon units resulted in even more delay in reaching fully operational status. By the turn of the century, *Ivanov* had acquired the reputation of being a less than successful project.

Once in orbit, further problems quickly manifested themselves, exacerbated by the ill-timed inauguration of the wildly ambitious programme to exploit the mineral content of several larger asteroids on the fringes of the asteroid belt nearest to Mars. Remote robotic mining from a Mars base was the only viable option. Unfortunately, the harvesting and transportation of mined products proved an intractable problem because it was entirely dependent on the construction of essential processing plants on Mars itself. Sadly, these projects were already badly behind schedule, with the slippage rate showing no signs of improving – and if anything getting worse. As a result, for most of its two-year orbit, *Ivanov's* cargo holds were only ever half-full.

Unable to justify such a massive expenditure to an increasing number of critical high-powered investors, the ConCorp Board had cobbled together an attractive package making *Ivanov* available to any scientific or research institute keen to take advantage of ideal laboratory conditions in space. Within six months of this being marketed, ConCorp had a list of prospective clients which threatened to overwhelm *Ivanov's* original function as a travelling warehouse.

About the same time as *Ivanov* began to be a more viable economic proposition, it became clear the original concept was flawed. Despite careful strategic planning, Technos working on the terraforming project always seemed to need essential equipment or replacement components when *Ivanov* was swinging outwards towards the asteroid belt, and Mars was on the far side of the Sun – or vice-versa – an awkward distance of roughly 500 million kilometres. Consequently, freighters were still having to be launched directly from Earth to bridge the gap, adding further delay and expense to the project. Frustration reached gargantuan proportions.

It was eventually decided the only way around the problem was to place four micro-stations, roughly equi-distant apart in areaostationary orbit above the Martian equator. Safely positioned approximately three-thousand kilometres inside the orbit of the diminutive Martian moon Deimos, these would act as service, accommodation and more importantly, provisioning centres. Here, essential equipment, stores, research teams and Technos could be housed in relatively safe and controlled environments that weren't available on either of the Martian moons. Teams could not only access the Martian surface whenever they wanted to, but could take the opportunity to make exploratory trips to the nearest asteroids on reconnaissance missions.

By 2120 *Ivanov* had completed transhipment of the large prefabricated planar panels which provided the basic construction units of the first Mars station, and by 2130, Lowell was fully operational with its complement of fifty assorted personnel.

Fourteen years later, Gio and Schroter were up and running, coinciding with Phase One of the Mars Plantation Programme which was aimed at testing the viability of genetically modified conifers to increase oxygen levels. Three years later, and Anton, the last of the Martian Quartet, as they became known, was in orbit.

Activity on Mars went up a couple of notches, and with it an increasing number of Spaceworkers on medium-term contracts. The mineral processing plants came on-stream and the highly controversial systematic spraying of the polar ice caps with carbon combustion products was underway. The demand for warehouse capacity increased. As a result, R & D facilities on *Ivanov* came under pressure and were finally withdrawn as individual leases expired.

ConCorp began to look further afield. By 2160, plans were afoot to extend their empire as far as Jupiter and Saturn, with longer term projections taking in the Uranus and Neptune sectors when the time was ripe. Humanity, it was loudly proclaimed, had to get to grips with the inevitable that one day – even if it were millions of years into the future – the mild-mannered yellow dwarf star it relied on for life itself was going to turn nasty, swollen and red. Future generations would need an alternative to the Blue Planet to call home, so it was better to start looking sooner rather than later. All of which meant that *Ivanov 1* was obsolete.

Like the rabbit out of the magician's hat, *Ivanov 2* provided the short-term answer. All that was required was the construction of an enlarged outer envelope using the new lightweight titaniplastic alloy in the familiar planar panel configuration to double its original cubic dimensions. For once, the project went without a hitch, and within a single two-year orbit *Ivanov 2* had a shiny new outer casing and more elegant solar fins.

Those who were geeky enough to study *Ivanov's* developmental stages, said that just like Topsy it grew and grew. The Jupiter and Saturn mega-stations, plus the robotic base established on Titan, became a reality when Duval's revolutionary propulsion system punched holes in space-time travel schedules, and the Uranian mega-station Herschel was no longer a pipe dream. *Ivanov* was increasingly in demand, not only to re-provision the Quartet, but to restock long-haul freighters and cruisers heading for the outer stations.

By 2200, *Ivanov 3* was on the drawing board, the additional parallel arms and the extended hub section giving the station its distinctive H-shape. Twenty years later, *Ivanov 3* was fully operational. Impressive, ConCorp liked to call it, with its expanded storage areas and updated accommodation and recreational facilities, but at its heart it remained what it had always been – a functional warehouse looping endlessly around the Sun on a two-year cycle shifting stuff from here to there. Entirely transputer controlled, it required no navigational or piloting skills; demanded little intellectual input from its loader crews, and reduced the administrative role to stock-control and personnel functions. As such, it remained the most dismal posting for any Spaceworker – with the possible exception of the Flight Maintenance Operatives who had the more stimulating role of servicing incoming ferries, freighters and additional random cruisers.

Taken all round, it badly needed a bit of life injecting into it to relieve the monotony of existence on board – and The Choralians were there to provide it.

TWENTY-SEVEN

Oliphant pushed back into the autoform upholstery of his chair in the VR conference booth and stretched with the slowness of a cat, enjoying the experience of easing the tension out of his shoulders. It had been a long morning. Carefully, he prised the communications visor away from his face, trying to avoid catching his beard in the adjuster straps, and returned the visor to its storage compartment. Absent-mindedly, he massaged his forehead where the skin had been left feeling hot and prickly.

He was allowing himself to be mildly self-satisfied. An increasing number of both small- and large-scale mind-warp trafficking networks were being rolled up. Mai, the SSO running a string of agents in Seasia, had cleared out three Family-based operations in the last month. Bolivar had completed a similar sweep in the Americas, while Felixon had exposed embezzlement on a grand scale in one of ConCorp's Energy Divisions funding illicit activities in the Levant.

Whatever successes were being achieved globally however, one thing was certain: his position as CSO co-ordinating action to dismantle mind-warp networks was unlikely to be redundant any time soon. Like the regenerating heads of the Lernaean Hydra, no sooner had one organisation been snuffed out when another sprang up in its place. The task was Herculean without the possibility of having Hercules' success: it boiled down to supply and demand – and there was plenty of both.

He left the booth and strolled over to the window, glad to give his eyes a variation in focal length. Momentarily, he was distracted by the progress of a pretty cadet as she crossed the quadrangle, her helmet held purposefully under one arm, her long legs striding out with an easy, almost indolent motion that hinted at a hidden ability to spring into action if necessary. She disappeared into the side entrance leading to the refectory and Oliphant returned to more sobering thoughts.

The door buzzer hummed and MacFadden announced himself. "I saw your Link had cleared," he said.

Oliphant checked his watch. "Sorry for keeping you waiting, MacFadden. The conference went on longer than I'd expected. Has Phoenix reported in?"

"Yes, Sir. I forwarded it to your monitor from the Decoding Station as you instructed."

"Have you read it?"

"Yes, Sir."

"Good." Oliphant settled once more behind his desk and brought up the data, scanning it quickly. It was a carefully logged, precisely worded account of activity on the *Ivanov* over the last few days. Detailed, but mundane. "Sit down, MacFadden," he said, turning the screen so MacFadden could read it more easily. "What do you make of it?"

MacFadden pulled a face, something he'd never have dared to do a few weeks earlier. "There's not much to go on is there, Sir?" He scanned the material a second time. "No sign of this 'Angel' so far – and no open talk about anything we'd be interested in. Perhaps everyone's being careful with so many new faces around?"

"Maybe," Oliphant conceded. "If you were dealing in a highly dubious commodity, would you be bringing in an outsider any time soon?"

"Probably not, Sir."

Oliphant scrolled through the report again, beginning to

suspect that Operation Misfit might be a hiding into nothing. "What's the significance of the marker against paragraph two?" he asked. He hadn't noticed it on the first read-through.

MacFadden blushed. "I put it there, Sir. I hope you don't mind."

"I don't mind as long as you tell me what it's for."

"To be honest, Sir, I didn't know if it was relevant or not."

Oliphant re-read the paragraph, feeling in his bones that MacFadden may have stumbled on something. "What made Mister Davron interrogate Cass Diamond?" It was a question he was asking himself rather than MacFadden.

"I don't know, Sir, but could it have anything to do with Mister Davron's resignation?"

"What? When?"

"It was listed in this morning's Gazette, Sir. It came up while you were in conference."

Oliphant brought up the Gazette pages, scanning them quickly.

"Page five, Sir," MacFadden offered helpfully.

There were three officers listed under the Resignations heading: Benjamin Davron, Senior Security Officer, Shackleton Moonbase, was the second.

"A bit unexpected, Sir?"

"Absolutely. Take a break, MacFadden. I'll meet you in the squash courts in an hour."

MacFadden got up, saluted crisply and left.

Calling up Scrambler Level Four on the Link, Oliphant requested ForcePlan Enquiries.

A fresh-faced young woman smiled back at him from the monitor. "Irma Gullman, ForcePlan Enquiries," she said brightly in her best UniCom. "How can I help you, Mister Oliphant?"

"I notice Senior Security Officer Davron's name appears in the resignation list this morning. Can you tell me if his resignation's confirmed?"

She consulted her data file. "Yes, Sir, as of yesterday."

"In that case please give me access to his debriefing file under Security Regulation 97b."

A hint of concern at his request flickered briefly across her face, but it was gone by the time the access code came up on his screen. "Is there anything further you require at this stage, Sir?"

"No thank you, Miss Gullman. I'll call you later if there is." He smiled at her as if it were an everyday occurrence for a Security Officer's file to be accessed under Security Regulation 97b. It wasn't, but with Oliphant's remit outlined in bold lettering on the screen in front of her, it would have been more than her job was worth to mention it.

The debriefing file came up as soon as he input the request.

DAVRON Benjamin.
Date of request to terminate contract: 14-01-57
Reason for request: See subsections 2(a) and (b) below.
Date of discharge: 28-01-57

Oliphant smoothed down his beard. A discharge with fourteen days' notice, not the standard termination period of three months, was interesting in itself. That Davron had made his request only two days after the incident mentioned so casually in Phoenix's report, made it even more interesting.

Oliphant brought up Phoenix's report again to refresh his memory. It amounted to little more than there was some talk that SSO Davron had questioned Cass Diamond about her former partner after the opening night. There was no further information and the rest of the paragraph dealt with sundry other events, including an argument between Argosti and Staines over damage to one of the costumes. Trivia.

Choosing another line of enquiry, Oliphant accessed Davron's official log for The Choralians' first night. All he found was a simple one-liner. 'Interviewed Cass Diamond. No further action.'

But it was a one-liner Davron had omitted to send to Oliphant. Why? The more he thought about it, the more he became convinced something had happened during that interview which Davron wanted to play down.

He went back into the security file, increasingly uneasy. The debriefing officer's notes under the subsections mentioned were succinct. They were followed by a precis of a Psy-Medic's report, the full text of which was unavailable even to Security without medical clearance.

Davron had given two reasons for his resignation. The first was operational: he didn't feel the duties and responsibilities at Shackleton Moonbase had matched his expectations. He felt he'd not been entrusted with overseeing investigations within his jurisdiction – a clear reference to the Koblinski case. He'd wanted more fieldwork and less administration which was increasingly reducing his ability to function as a good field officer. He recognised the fieldwork element could only be achieved by taking demotion, and he felt this left him in an untenable position.

The second reason given was domestic and personal: he wanted a ground posting nearer his family which ConCorp Security couldn't guarantee, and consequently he intended to apply to the International Enforcement Agency which had a Regional HQ in Haifa.

What stood out was that neither of these reasons would have secured a reduction from the standard three month notice period to fourteen days.

The précis of the Psy-Medic's report however recorded 'Early signs of GDS'. Gaia Deprivation Syndrome: a gamut of psychological disturbances associated with spacework ranging from mild feelings of claustrophobia to full-blown mental dysfunction. If anyone wanted to get out of spacework fast, implying the onset of GDS was the way to do it. ConCorp had become almost paranoid about the condition. Hadn't the Board just sunk a few million dollaroubles into the Stollard Institute to investigate ways of overcoming it?

With GDS diagnosed, even in the early stages, discharge would be authorised as soon as practicable. But tying in the data from Phoenix, Davron had left Shackleton the day after The Choralians transhipped to the *Ivanov*. It seemed a little too pat.

Something was wrong. Yes, he knew Davron had felt he'd been side-lined over the Koblinski case, and perhaps he'd genuinely found the long periods of separation from his family increasingly difficult, but none of that was enough to ditch a promising career at short notice. Which left the GDS diagnosis.

GDS didn't strike overnight: it came on slowly and started to manifest itself in changes of behaviour that were easily identifiable. But in all the time Oliphant had been at Shackleton, Davron had never shown the slightest sign of becoming even mildly space crazy. On the contrary, he'd seemed perfectly at ease with his sub-lunar existence. As such, the diagnosis made no sense, which immediately put it into the 'useful excuse' category. Davron had just wanted out – and fast.

The more he thought about Davron's decision, the more Oliphant found his mind looping back to paragraph two – the interrogation of Cass Diamond. And the more he thought about that, the more uneasy he became. Had Davron uncovered evidence of connivance or involvement in mind-warp trafficking that had led to her door? And if he'd found solid evidence, why had he kept it to himself?

Other possibilities sprang to mind, none of them much comfort. Once the evidence had come to light, had Smiler stepped in to safeguard his investment in the tour? Had he offered Davron an inducement to ensure The Choralians' safe passage up to the *Ivanov*? Had this inducement involved Davron making a speedy exit from ConCorp employment? Even less palatable was the possibility Davron had been offered a slice of the action. In the

Levant perhaps? Hadn't Felixon just rolled up an operation there? Wasn't there a ready made vacuum just waiting to be filled? Which meant he couldn't afford to rule out the possibility that Davron could be bought. There'd been times in the past when he'd made that mistake, and turned a blind eye when good officers had been lured into going for easy gains on the other side of the fence.

Somehow in Davron's case, however, the theory didn't stack up: he was ambitious and wanted the kudos of success, not money. Here was a guy still smarting over not being brought into the heart of the Koblinski investigation; his reputation had been put on the line. He'd done everything Oliphant had asked of him and he'd drawn a blank. All his reports had confirmed this. Had Davron decided Cass Diamond was the key to the whole mystery? Maybe he'd persuaded himself that if he leaned on her hard enough he'd get the answers he was looking for. Had he leaned? The thought lingered.

Oliphant suddenly felt his face burning. He could picture the scene, and his mind went wheeling away to another time, to another room at Shackleton, and his own reactions to Cass Diamond. She was there in his imagination again. Their fingers touching. Her dark eyes looking right through him. The scent of exotic perfume filling his nostrils. Her sensuality that had caught him off-guard. Is that what had happened? Had Davron lost his reason when he'd been alone with her? Was it so improbable? No.

With the Link to Regulation 97b still open, Oliphant scrolled down to the last entries on Davron's service record. There was nothing that might have raised questions about his conduct. If Davron had given Cass Diamond any reason to report him, she'd remained silent. Had he waited to see if she'd file a complaint against him, and when she hadn't, was that when he decided to resign? His stress levels must have been sky high, and could have been easily mistaken for early onset GDS. It seemed the most logical explanation.

Ben Davron had sacrificed his career on the altar of Cassandra Diamantides.

Oliphant shut down the monitor and took up his favourite spot by the window. The reluctant late January sun shone weakly from a watery sky, casting pale shadows on the gravel below, while sudden gusts of wind rippled across the pools of water left by an earlier squall. The bleakness of the scene seeped into his Northern soul, turning his mind to melancholy and sombre introspection: he wanted to salvage something positive from the wreckage of Davron's career. He could come up with very little, except that Cass Diamond was capable of far more than he'd ever allowed for: she'd the capacity to control the responses of others – and in that he'd yet to meet her equal. In a different life, she'd have made a good Freelance.

Outside, the sun gave up the unequal struggle, finally extinguished behind a bank of angry steel-grey clouds. Thin rain was already blowing in on a brisk wind.

He swung away from the window, conscious he'd let time slip by. It was almost 1400 hours and MacFadden would be waiting for him.

TWENTY-EIGHT

Eleven months is a long time when every second is filled with frustration, and each day comes and goes without a single piece of news to gladden the heart. For most of the time since the theft of his precious experiments, Elgar Garrison had tried to keep his mind preoccupied to lift his spirits, but it had proved an almost impossible task. Even the urgent request to provide an extensive restructuring programme for a certain Marco Vincente, had done little to relieve his sense of melancholy.

Marco was the youngest of the numerous nephews of Hannibal Vincente, the current influential Chairman of the ConCorp empire. Marco was an indolent youth, easily led and lacking his uncle's ability to choose his friends with discretion. His vast inherited personal wealth had attracted an unsavoury set of companions, all hangers-on keen to help him spend his fortune in as many dissolute pleasures as possible. And Marco had been willing to oblige. It was hardly surprising therefore, that at nineteen, Marco had the mind and body-cell condition of someone several decades older, and his life expectancy had plummeted from the average five-score-years-and-ten to a couple of years, at the most optimistic of estimates, down to a few months at the worst. To put it bluntly, Marco Vincente was coming apart at the seams.

Understandably, in view of the family's global prominence, Marco's indulgent uncle had been at pains to ensure his nephew's urgent restructuring was not only the best that money could buy, but also the most discreet. The Garrison Clinic had been the obvious choice. It had also given Garrison the opportunity to remind Clinic personnel to follow contractual protocols, and the price to be paid for careless talk.

Marco's ultimate downfall had been an overdose of Supercharge. The treatment and therapy programmes were of necessity long-term. They'd begun with a prolonged period of detoxification under de-animation pending neurosurgical intervention. For several months, it had been necessary to keep Marco in a cryogenic coma. Most of his digestive system by then was defunct, and there was extensive damage to both kidneys requiring cellular revitalisation. Most of his brain had required similar attention to restore his ability to function, even at a basic level. One thalamus was so grotesquely disfigured, it had needed total replacement with a synthetic substitute, and the remaining partner had been rescued from a similar fate by an inhibitor implant to curb any uncontrollable urges to indulge in excesses of any kind in future.

Most of the restructuring had involved tried and tested techniques which not even the Global Council for Medical Ethics could have objected to. But there were other aspects of Marco's treatment, particularly Garrison's choice of blood substitute – a bio-synthetic concoction with genetic enhancers – which had been the subject of heated medical debate two years earlier, and finally banned on the grounds it was fundamentally unsafe. Garrison had been unimpressed by the arguments: it had no known side-effects, except for a reduction in immunity to certain infections, but these could be easily overcome by pseudo-leukocyte absorption techniques. It was unfortunate the Council had already decided to ban these interventions as well on the grounds that insufficient medical trials had been undertaken by recognised research establishments to warrant granting a licence to would-be practitioners. Garrison considered this to be short-sighted and an affront to medical progress. So he ignored the ban.

During those long months when Marco's well-being had become a twenty-four hour, seven-day a week concern, Garrison had managed to keep his frustrations at arm's length, but by December 2256 Marco was recuperating, and the loss of the experiments had once again become uppermost in Garrison's mind. He had time on his hands and was increasingly morose. Grimly, he toured the laboratories every morning checking the limited progress in the R & D Unit, Hogan's dour presence at his side still harbouring undiminished resentment. The foetal material had been returned to the cryogenic facility; the precious bank of mutated genes was similarly 'on ice'; everything was biding its time; waiting. Waiting for Forty to come home.

By the New Year, Garrison had become permanently depressed, his research programme shrinking to concentrating on the genetic malfunctions of the remainder of the animals housed in the Restricted Area. These sad creatures were not of his making: they were the result of Nature's misplaced enthusiasm for trial and error evolution. He'd acquired most of them from conservation reserves who were keen to off-load their freaks without too many questions asked.

Garrison did not consider himself uncaring: he abhorred animal cruelty: it was unforgivable. In his facility he was proud to say there were no Nineteenth Century horrors. No creatures were tied down by restraining harnesses, their vital organs laid bare, probed, palpating helplessly in a half-existence, being neither dead nor alive, but somewhere in between: just being. He was repelled by such barbarity. His experiments were providers and recipients of cells, that was all. True, his work had produced occasional unintended consequences as he accidentally replicated what Nature had already managed to achieve, but he loved them. He loved them all. He regarded their disordered genetic codes as precious gifts to enhance his knowledge; to open his mind to understanding how to overcome life's 'little difficulties'.

True, his animals lived an artificial existence with only the minimal semblance of natural surroundings. True, their only daylight was the pseudo-sunlight beamed down to them from the ultra-violet phosphor glows above their pens. Their food was largely synthetic and without any similarity to their natural fare, and the air they breathed was a rarefied and thoroughly filtered concoction devoid of contamination. But as Garrison often reminded his critics, his animals would never have survived at all in the real world. Nature would have de-selected them by predatory means or starvation. What hope had the two-legged zebra? The limbless baboon? Or the spineless panther? – he would argue. And at the back of his mind as the New Year limped into its second week, he could hear a sad rejoinder – *What hope had Forty?* All of which served to remind him of Palatine and the slow, remorseless persistence of the Palatine Enterprises network as it acquired data, filtered it and picked out pieces that might interest him.

Palatine had accepted the commission without so much as a raised eyebrow when Garrison had made his initial approach ten months earlier. But this was hardly surprising, he reflected: he had after all put together a very attractive remuneration package, including half-a-million dollaroubles as a purse to pay out *bona fide* informants, allowing Palatine the freedom to act as paymaster – as long as detailed accounting records were regularly produced for his scrutiny.

"I don't want you to be tight-fisted," he'd said over the restricted Link to his office. "If the information is sound, I want you to pay well. It encourages others."

Of course, he hadn't been entirely frank with Palatine about Forty's potential – just his importance to the Clinic's developmental programme. Palatine might be discreet, but Garrison was under no illusions: any professional Ferret was never to be completely trusted – and Palatine was no exception. Besides, there were Palatine's other business ventures – like Supercharge distribution. But as Palatine always pointed out, theirs was a very symbiotic relationship: one supplied at a profit; the other made a lucrative business out of detoxification programmes.

"We are two sides of the same coin, are we not?" Palatine would say, smiling indulgently at him. And Garrison could not but agree.

But progress in the investigative process remained painfully slow. So slow, Garrison's interest barely altered by a micro-metre on the morning of 16 February '57 when he returned to his office from a routine laboratory tour to find a sealed message in his receiver tray. He glanced at it, noting with almost casual indifference the presence of the scrambler identification code on the flap. He'd received too many in the past few months which had lifted his hopes, only to dash them again when he read the contents.

He retrieved the packet and listlessly activated the desktop reader to scan it, automatically inputting the relevant codes when requested and waiting for the string of incomprehensible alphanumerics to be reconstituted into reasonably comprehensible English. A lethargy had settled about him that refused to budge.

So far Palatine's network had cleared all three Reps from the Waste Containment Executive who'd visited the Clinic almost a year ago. Tracing the Reps from BPI – BioProducts Incorporated – had taken longer. BPI had introduced a new state-of-the-art data security system that needed painstaking unpicking before contact grids could be constructed. Meanwhile, work on tracing the Reps from TechnoMaintenance International – TMI – had proved even more difficult because data maintenance was their forté, and they had protocols in place which were regularly updated using a combination of obscure algorithms and random blockers.

"Some things take time," Palatine would say when Garrison had tried to hurry up the process, and that lazy smile would spread across her remarkably symmetrical features.

Palatine. Livilla Tullia Palatine – Tullia to her closest acquaintances, including Garrison. On the surface she was a successful businesswoman, running a top-rate personnel agency providing temporary high-grade staff on short-term contracts as Systems Consultants. Below the surface, she was something else, her business connections allowing her access to a multitude of organisations. Combined with her Professionals, as she called them, she also ran a string of less visible communications experts – Hackers who, given enough time, could run rings around any security log jam in their path and leave no trace of their passing. Her extensive organisation provided her with an intelligence overview that ConCorp Security and the International Enforcement Agency would have been proud to own. So apart from her distribution of Supercharge on the side, it wasn't too difficult for Garrison to imagine industrial espionage as another of her less visible commercial activities.

Tullia was not what Garrison would describe as a beautiful woman, not within the accepted meaning of the term. Her features were possibly a little too bold: her mouth a fraction too wide; her eyebrows too arching above intense aquamarine eyes; her nose perhaps a little too long, although exquisitely sculpted. But the symmetry was perfect, one half of her face the mirror image of the other, the dark auburn hair sweeping back from her smooth forehead up onto the top of her head in a crown of coiled, luxuriant splendour.

She was strangely ageless, existing in a time zone anywhere between thirty and fifty years of age. And there was an undeniable 'something' about her that even Elgar Garrison couldn't fail to notice, despite his lack of interest in sexual liaisons of any dimension: it was both innate and acquired. Occasionally he'd allow himself the luxury of imagining how she might look with that great coiled mass of hair set free to fall in a tumbling mane. It must surely reach down to her waist, he thought, or even further, an area of total mystery because they'd never actually met, his knowledge of her anatomy entirely limited to what was visible in the confines of a Link monitor. Sometimes, when idle thoughts had led him to stray too far into the realms of fantasy, he'd allowed himself to muse on the possibility she had no legs at all.

The alert button on the scanner was winking at him, pulling him back into reality. He switched modes and accessed the unscrambled message. It unscrolled slowly, sentence by sentence.

He surveyed it with tired eyes, and perhaps because he expected so little, the information lying in front of him came like a bolt from the blue.

Possible connection, he read. *New data suggests TMI involvement with Genetic Rights Movement. Managing Director, Guido Servione reported meeting with GRM activist Marcia Mitchell in Bergen yesterday. Have arranged for TMI activities over the last twelve months to be accessed and assessed. Will report progress as soon as this is available.* It was signed simply *LTP.*

Twenty-nine

A month into their stay on *Ivanov* and Cassandra was on edge. There was something about *Ivanov's* dimensions that unsettled her: it had none of the intimacy of the accommodation on a flightcraft, or even a micro-station. *Ivanov* was huge, and yet strangely more claustrophobic, like a vast, terrible prison. The living accommodation units were larger than on other stations, but the furnishings were the same standard issue and therefore out of scale, appearing small and mean, huddled around the walls as if embarrassed by their inadequacy.

By contrast, the wallpane options were excessive. She'd quickly tired of the seascapes that were too reminiscent of Smiler, safe on his island stronghold, and later abandoned the seasonal variations of a seemingly endless choice of landscapes enhanced by diurnal programs, because they were too realistic. They'd made her yearn to be outdoors with the sun on her face and the wind in her hair. Ultimately, she'd chosen the safest options: a veined cream marble on every wall with the exception of a single pane of a summer skyscape with passing clouds and randomly programmed flights of birds. Watching the swallows swoop and soar had given her the mental lift she'd increasingly needed.

She'd ignored the VR facilities altogether.

The holograms on offer had been equally problematical. Too many. She'd chosen only two. The first, the life-size bronze of the Poseidon of Artemisium, mistakenly named as Zeus until regaining his rightful place in the Pantheon after much academic argument, poised at the very moment of hurling the trident that had long since slipped from his grasp. He was a symbol of controlled but terrible power nonetheless that made her feel safe. The second, the marble bust of Pallas Athene, a calming image to combat the fears she refused to openly acknowledge, but often left her sleepless at night.

It was one of those nights. She awoke suddenly, her pulse thudding, her blood raging through her veins.

She threw aside the coverlet and sat up, snapping her fingers to activate the glowlight beside the bed. It hummed softly into life, filling the room with a pale golden luminescence and deep shadows. The clock said 0325 hours. Above her, the aircon whispered like a summer breeze but the atmosphere felt dense, and she struggled to fill her lungs with enough of it.

Panic, she thought. Pure panic. Nothing else. *Ivanov* was becoming oppressive.

She sat bolt upright on the edge of the bed, expecting something to happen, but had no idea what. She got up, desperate to do something; anything. Her brain was refusing to faze down, her mind running in an endless loop. I'm strung out, she thought. We need more material. Much more.

Deep down was the nagging fear that when they needed it most, inspiration would desert them, and no one would pay good credit for the same numbers night after night. It was what she dreaded most: that *Ivanov* would exhaust them mentally and physically; that the continuous strain of two, sometimes three shows a week would take its toll and the tour would be a disaster.

Padding around the place like a caged panther, she pulled herself up short and sternly told herself to calm down. It worked for a moment before her memory went into recall endlessly trying to complete a verse that had defeated all of them the previous evening.

Everything had been going so well. Theo had produced a

new melody on a choraladian and Umo had embellished it on the paparingos. Raymer had suggested a possible theme and it had begun to take shape – with the startling exception of the last line in the third verse. It had defied every attempt to complete it. After an hour, it was clear they were getting nowhere. UniCom had defeated them.

"Bloody soulless language," Raymer had said, unusually impatient. "I say we take a break. We're just going round in circles."

For once, Cassandra had agreed with him. "It's late. We're all tired. Let's try again in the morning."

So they'd called it a night in an atmosphere of irritation tinged with despair.

Now, distractedly standing in the middle of her room with her mind only half-engaged, she hummed the tune again, giving no thought to the obstacle lying in wait at the end of the third verse. The chorus was good. She broke into song to get the feel of it, and liked it the more she sang it. The second verse. She altered the emphasis slightly and preferred the effect. She sang it again to be certain. Back to the perfect chorus. By now she was in full song, fighting to make the notes ring out against the acoustically dampening effect of the fragorboard walls. Third verse. It swelled out from her, the words springing naturally into place as though they'd been there all the time waiting for her to release them.

"...Give me what I need, not what I ask for, can't you read my mind?"

The notes of the last line died on her lips into silence as she rethreaded the words silently to fix them in place.

Exultant, she accessed the Link to Raymer's quarters. There was a buzz, then Raymer's voice, heavy with sleep.

"Hello," he said dully.

"It's Cass, Jay. I've got the line."

For a moment there was silence, then the sound of him stirring and sitting up. "The line?"

"Yes – the last line. The last line of the third verse. I've got it. Shall I sing it to you?"

"Now?"

"You're not interested?"

"I'd be more interested if I wasn't half asleep. Can't it wait?" Her irritation must have shouted at him through the silence when she didn't reply. "Laz is asleep, Cass. You'll wake him up. Just say the words to me, will you?"

"That's pointless! It's the emphasis – the sound – the whole thing. If I can't sing it, it'll sound all wrong. Forget it." She could hear him sigh. "Do you want to hear it or not?" His lack of enthusiasm irritated her.

"Yes, okay. I'll come over."

She stormed around the room waiting for him. How long did it take to walk a few steps down the corridor? – she asked herself. After what seemed a small age, her buzzer sounded and she let him in.

He was thoroughly dishevelled: his hair was tousled, his eyes barely focussing. He'd thrown his silver kimono haphazardly over his sleepsuit; his feet were bare, and a night's growth of beard shadowed his face.

"You look a wreck," she said, speaking her mind. "Do you want a drink?"

He slumped onto the couch and yawned. "No, I want to go back to bed. This is a hell of a time to wake anyone."

She regarded him coldly. "Perhaps I should have wakened Theo instead. He'd have been more appreciative."

"Perhaps you should have," he retaliated, relenting almost immediately. "No, I didn't mean that." He pulled a face, rubbing his eyes and forcing them to remain open. "Okay then – let's have it."

"Do you really feel up to it?"

He blew out his cheeks. "No, but let's have it anyway."

She tried to subdue her irritation and revive the emotion she'd felt earlier. She closed her eyes, hearing the music playing in her head. Then, humming the chorus aloud to lead her in, she began to sing the third verse.

"... Give me what I need, not what I ask for, can't you read my mind?"

It was so easy. She finished the whole song, opening her eyes at the end of it, triumphant.

He was now very much awake, all traces of sleep quite washed from his face. He was no longer slumped on the couch, but leaning forward, arms propped against his knees. His gaze was concentrated on her, unblinking, as if he couldn't get enough of the sight of her, and his features had a tautness about them she'd glimpsed occasionally when they'd finished singing together and stepped forward to receive the applause.

Had she sung to him? – or for him? What nuances had she put into the song intentionally or unintentionally? Did it matter?

"What do you think?" she asked, aware that her voice was suddenly husky and her throat had gone dry. "About the song," she added, not knowing why this needed to be said.

Her voice broke the spell he seemed to be under. He looked down at his hands briefly. "It's perfect, Cass," he said quietly. "Just perfect."

She caught the meaning of what he'd read into the words; in her choice of him and not Theo to sing them to; in him being with her alone in her room.

Slowly, she sat down on the lounger opposite him, pulling her robe around her and mulling over the conscious and unconscious processes that had contrived to produce this situation. She saw herself as he was seeing her: as dishevelled as he was, her hair no doubt in wild confusion; her colour, probably heightened by the singing; the passion of the song still throbbing in her veins.

He was still looking at her, his face devoid of any expression, just waiting. Waiting to be called.

She cleared her throat, feeling very foolish. "I ... I had to ... The words just came – suddenly," she added, trying to sound rational. "I thought you should hear them."

He nodded.

Silence again while he continued to look at her with those enigmatic grey-blue eyes. Still waiting.

She got up from the lounger, listening to her heart-beat quicken. Why was she pretending? Images of him were flashing through her mind's eye: the gleam of light along his spine; the sleek smoothness of his skin; the perfection of his body; the way his singing could send shivers running through her. She'd wanted him from the first moment she'd laid eyes on him standing by the pool on Philomos.

It had just been a matter of time, she realised; of choosing the right moment without knowing it. Theo had known. Davron had known. Karoli was dead and all the wailing and anguish she could raise would never put him back into her bed. Perhaps *Ivanov* had been the catalyst. At Shackleton, Karoli's ghost had been a constant companion, whether she'd admit to it or not. But in this place, in this monstrous sealed warehouse whirling through space, there was an emptiness within her that wanted to be filled – and Jason Raymer could fill it. She needed him. Now.

He'd got up from the couch and was standing facing her, the silence between them an almost living, tangible thing. He wouldn't make the first move, she realised.

"Can you read my mind?" she asked him.

A smile hovered briefly around his lips. "I'd like to think so," he said softly.

"Give me what I need, not what I asked for ... that's what I said."

He nodded.

"It's need. Just need."

"Yes, I understand."

"I'm not in love with you."

"No. I know."

"Do you mind?"

He shook his head.

She took him by the hand and led him into the sleeping area. He didn't resist, nor did he help her as she peeled away his clothing. He let her take the lead in everything so there should be no misunderstanding: this was her decision. But in the end there was no passivity on his part, no holding back with the intimacy of his caresses as they lay sprawled across the tumbled sheets and she led him into her.

The rough stubble on his face chafed against her neck as he began the sweet persistent thrusting that would drown her in a world of fantasy and forgetfulness; a world in which Karoli no longer played a part. Her mind was filled with memories of long-ago casual partners; the shifting of scenes; the shifting of faces and the bodies that went with them. And then came the fantasies as her pulse quickened, fantasies with no part in the reality of what was happening in the here and now: Davron stripping her in his frenzy and finding himself consumed; the exultant triumph of enclosing the man and drawing him on to his inevitable conclusion; the indulgence of undiluted physical pleasure just for the sake of it.

And then, without warning, at the moment of total ecstasy as she cried out, the most profound image of all – not of Raymer striving to please her, nor of Davron humbled, nor even of Karoli – but of Oliphant, steadily gazing into her eyes; his voice – deep, resonant, thick with passion and utterly compelling, urging her on.

THIRTY

Sometimes it's the smallest, almost imperceptible shift in emphasis, a glance, a word, which marks a change in circumstances: an insignificant something which separates the time before from the time after. In such a way Theo sensed the relationship between Cassandra and Jason had changed: there was a closeness he hadn't seen before. Not that it was highly visible, because it wasn't, it was just that he was so finely attuned to Cassandra and her moods, he saw the difference. Others could have been forgiven for not noticing. In public, she maintained an even greater distance between herself and Jason than ever before, but in more private moments, there was a familiarity which spoke of more than friendship: a certain look; a smile; a casual remark with a deeper, less obvious meaning. And then there were the occasional lapses when she spoke of him not as Raymer, but as 'Jay'.

The liaison was nothing more than Theo had expected, the inevitability of it simply a matter of time. But as the days wore on, what left him vaguely troubled was her unwillingness to drop the charade: she was always alone in the mornings.

Jason seemed content with the situation: he held back, not crowding her, perhaps because he had his own commitment to Lazar. But Cassandra was more alive now on-stage; almost electric in her intensity, and no one cared much as to why: they were only grateful the *Ivanov* tour was a huge success.

There'd been the song, of course – the song with the troublesome third verse. She'd sung it with a vibrancy that illuminated the words. She sang it to Jason, and he sang it back to her. And that had been only the beginning. Other songs followed, the two of them generating new material at a frenetic pace: older Folkster-style numbers Karoli would have enjoyed; other more primitive rhythms and themes; new choreography. There were more rehearsals; more refinements; Krodalt and Farrance expected to produce stagecraft effects at the drop of a hat; and the constant adaptation of existing costumes that drove Argosti into regular hissy-fits. But it was exhilarating; alive. And messages from McMichael were ecstatic.

Theo watched his own place in Cassandra's life diminish. He felt neither resentment nor sadness, perhaps because he'd seen it coming for so long; it was merely a completion of his expectations; a natural outcome. He understood better because he saw the need to play another, older role that Karoli had played – that of Minder.

Whether Theo liked it or not, Lazar's attachment to Umo was growing, and with Jason more preoccupied with Cassandra, Lazar had naturally gravitated towards Umo as a small child might to a slightly older brother. Theo watched as Umo blossomed, able to take on responsibility for the first time in his life, showing Lazar how to play some of the wind instruments, even helping him to learn the simpler tunes.

Lazar was an earnest, methodical learner. His face occasionally bore traces of animation when he managed a performance particularly well. He was eager to please and easily crushed. To be in his company was like tending a fragile flower whose petals had a tendency to fall at the merest puff of wind, and to be constantly aware he was different; unpredictable, and possibly more capable than he seemed.

Gradually, Theo's fears that Umo was becoming increasingly involved with this strange half-person subsided. Umo seemed dedicated to take his role no further than being a teacher and mentor, and more importantly, Lazar provided a useful distraction, keeping Umo's attention deflected from the consciousness of being in space, and the dreadful closeness of infinity beyond *Ivanov's* smooth exterior. For that at least, Theo was glad: it allowed him to be occupied elsewhere.

Theo saw himself become someone else; someone slightly removed from the mainstream of events, and yet at the same time pivotal to the comings and goings around him. He discovered the role of tour co-ordinator came easily. He could manage any crisis, whether this was the unexpected cost of additional requirements not covered in their contract, or liaising with *Ivanov's* First Officer Ricovic over the need for extra on-station Technos to help revamp the Ariadne Hall if there was problem with equipment. He could even deal with McMichael, deflecting his more outrageous suggestions with a diplomacy that masked downright refusal to comply.

He noticed his new role had enhanced his status among those who'd previously regarded him as little more than a minor member of the group. His opinion was actively sought by everyone and acted on, almost without question. It was a strange sensation. Like being elected to play God.

Mid-March arrived. The following week they were scheduled to join one of the Minnow flightcraft out from Lowell specifically to collect them. Mars and its Quartet were four days away on a direct flightpath at Duval maximum velocity. *Ivanov* would lumber on, reaching its closest flypast four months later to unload the contents of its cavernous stores onto ferries from the four stations, and fill its holds with Earth-bound products in return. And as Mars began to swing away from *Ivanov's* orbit, The Choralians would tranship back onto it for their return journey to Earth and the worst would be over.

Except ... the previous evening the performance had included two new pieces. The audience had loved them, particularly the final song – *Making the Most of It*. That night, to Theo's experienced eyes, Cassandra had been more provocative in her rendition than at any time since Karoli's death. It had been a stunning performance, and it had become clear afterwards, from the clamorous stamping and exuberant whistling, that some of the audience had witnessed one of her surger performances in the past. They'd screamed at her to take them with her; to give them everything; now – now – now! A near riot had developed and Security Officers had finally been called in to restore order.

She'd come off stage visibly shaken, avoiding everyone, disappearing hurriedly into her dressing room and refusing to join them later at the Artistes' Bar. Theo noted Jason made no attempt to follow her. Later, everyone agreed the least said the better.

The following morning, Theo was alone finishing his latest report to McMichael when his door buzzer sounded. Umo had agreed to join Lazar and Jason in packing some of the spare instruments ready for transhipment and he wasn't expected back for a while. When the monitoring panel cleared, it was Cassandra waiting outside.

When he let her in, she made straight for a lounger, perching precariously on one of the arms, fidgeting with the plaited silver bracelet on her wrist, while her gaze roamed the room with a restless, fierce energy. "I suppose you've guessed," she said, raking back her hair from her face. "About Jay and me?"

Theo sat down opposite her. "It was inevitable, Cassandra. You're only human."

She laughed, a laugh tinged with bitterness. "I knew you'd say that." She paused to study him, her hand still caught up in the thickness of her hair. "How long have you known?"

"From the beginning. I know you too well not to notice the change. Do you love him?"

"No. He doesn't touch my soul. He's not Karoli."

He could tell there was more she wanted to say, and he'd already guessed what it would be.

She was nervously fiddling with the bracelet again. "Has Smiler called?"

"Not yet."

"But he will, won't he? After he sees the performance." She was beginning to tremble.

"Yes, I think he will."

"I won't be pushed into a corner," she said defiantly.

"We said no surger performances. It was agreed."

"But that was before, wasn't it?" Her colour was rising as she spoke. "I had the excuse. No partner – casual or otherwise. Now ..." She pressed her hands over her eyes as though she could shut out reality. "I thought we could get away with it, Theo. I thought if we kept our lives separate it would work out. But it hasn't, has it?" She sounded desperate.

"No," he said simply. What could he tell her that she didn't already know? That if the sound systems had been recalibrated to the critical alpha-wavelengths and the last song re-choreographed, they'd a surger-pop performance in the making. *Making the Most of It*. All that was needed were the costumes and body paint, a small matter Miles McMichael would overcome with no difficulty at all.

Theo felt a lump rise in his throat. He hated the sight of her as a spectacle of crude frenetic motion; the loss of individual control; the abandonment of self to rhythm and basic instinct for voyeuristic and self-induced sexual pleasure; the debasing of herself to titillate the appetites of others; and the sheer physical and mental exhaustion that came afterwards from artificially created coupling. "You don't have to do them," he insisted, hoping to ease her mind. "Your relationship with Jason is your own business."

She suddenly got to her feet and began pacing the room. "I'll give him up. It'll be for the best."

Theo rose and stopped her in her tracks. "No, don't do that, Cassandra. You're a good team. You're producing first-rate material."

Her eyes went very dark. "We don't need what we produced last night."

"Don't take all the blame, Cassandra. I watched the rehearsals. I should have seen that number had surger potential. I should have warned you."

She was coming close to tears.

He held her close. "We're only on Ivanov another week. Two more performances, that's all. You're both working on other material. Keep to basic Folkster ballads instead. When McMichael calls, I'll handle it. Don't worry. Understand? I'll speak to Jason if you like."

"Thank you," she whispered, burying her face in his shoulder. "Thank you for always being here when I need you."

His apotheosis was complete.

THIRTY-ONE

Homer Strendl knew what he wanted from life: prompt payment for services rendered. He'd had little trouble achieving this.

A small, weasel-faced man in his mid-forties with a swarthy complexion darkened still further by the blue-black shadow of his facial stubble, he had a talent he willingly exploited to the full. It had been his special knack since he was eight years old in down-town Prague: something he'd picked up from a Techno-Freak whose clandestine workshop he'd frequented more often than his schoolroom. Homer was a smart kid. He'd learnt fast. By the age of fourteen he'd become a Hacker-Supremo operating out of an anonymous backroom in a shabby suburb of the city, building up a string of interested clients and beginning to earn serious money.

Homer could hack into any system anyone might care to mention. He might not always be able to crack the scrambled code, but he could always lay his hands on the raw data, and given time, he could work out who'd sent it and who'd received it. His unofficial paymasters paid him well to be their disinterested Listener.

Homer was always happy to oblige. With glowing references, he'd become a Communications Officer on ConCorp's payroll, reaping the financial benefits of his office twice over: firstly from his regular salary; secondly by manipulating ConCorp's communication systems.

He was good. So good, he could set up branch lines of external recording facilities or additional communication channels, and remove them at will without anyone being any the wiser. He could hack into someone's personal Link, use it for his own purposes and let them pick up the tab. He could paralyse the user counters on supposedly sophisticated secure Links, transmit and receive at will, then unfreeze the counter and disappear without a trace. He could access confidential databanks using his own highly developed decoder, scan what he wanted, then leave behind false echoes for the Tracers to tie themselves in knots over afterwards. He was proud of his work. It was the best, which was why his latest unofficial paymaster was Livilla Tullia Palatine.

Homer had volunteered for a stint on the *Ivanov* at Palatine's suggestion. He'd worked for her before and she'd been more than satisfied with his product, which was why the remuneration package she'd offered had outbid her nearest rival's by several zeros at the time.

With a permanent shortage of enthusiastic personnel for an *Ivanov* tour, Homer's accession to the post of Communications Officer was swift. Once on-station, his world had become the Communications Centre, a grand-sounding name for a medium-sized room with three walls engulfed in control panels, multi-coloured screens, communication relays and emergency back-up systems. Dust-free with a temperature modulator permanently in operation to combat the tropical conditions generated by the electronics, the place nonetheless managed to feel overly warm, with a permanent odour of hot metal and polyplastic, both of which mingled uneasily with less definable body odours.

The job was thoroughly tedious, restricted out of necessity to mundane operational reports and maintenance duties on Links which rarely needed attention. The only flurries of excitement were during transhipment operations, or visits from Minnow flightcraft operating within the Inner Planets. During the many hours left unfilled however, Homer had plenty of time, and even more opportunity, to eavesdrop on personal communications. Which was precisely what Palatine wanted.

"There are deep hummings an independent organisation is building up a space distribution network for MegaJoy products," she'd explained. "The word is that *Ivanov* is to play a starring role. We need to know who they are, and how they intend getting their goods past Security. Monitor everything, Strendl – and I mean *everything*. Give me anything that looks even slightly out of the ordinary. What you do with anything else that might interest you is your business."

So he'd listened and filtered information meticulously for months, and in the process discovered just about everything there was to know about every member of the crew. He was privy to their innermost thoughts expressed to their nearest and dearest back home; he'd a shrewd idea who managed their finances well and who didn't; who was setting up unofficial arrangements with whom for the duration of the tour; who was creaming off the odd box of cargo here and there; and who was disaffected enough to keep on ice just in case they became a useful source of information in the future.

After only a few short weeks, quite apart from the funds Palatine kept for him in a coded account, he could have kept himself in unaccustomed luxury for the rest of his life simply from the proceeds of blackmail alone. But he knew better. Going down that particular route would have blown his cover – and that was priceless.

With his head bent over the communication consoles, a strand of lank, dark hair permanently flopping forward across his face, and his narrow features locked in deep concentration, Homer had merged into the background, keeping himself to himself: listening, sifting, and passing on his knowledge.

For almost six months there'd been only the occasional tit-bit. It had worried him. He'd begun to expect Palatine would grow restless, or even worse, begin to query his abilities, but she seemed unfazed by his lack of hard material, content to leave him in place: inconspicuous; part of the scenery; a time bomb waiting to be activated.

Then in late January The Choralians had come on-station, and everything had changed. For Homer, life had suddenly provided him with a feast of fascinating possibilities to pass on to his grateful 'employer'.

It started almost as soon as they arrived.

What happened next was a pure fluke. Janek Zabinak, the young blood Communications Officer who worked alternate shifts to Homer, was a Choralians' fan. So much so, he'd practically bored Homer to death with a ceaseless barrage of verbiage on just how fantastic they were. As a result, it had almost been the end of the world for Janek when he realised he'd be on duty the night of their first performance.

Homer didn't give a tinker's toss about The Choralians: they weren't his sort of poison. So it had been no hardship for him to make the offer to double up his shift and take on Janek's as well. He never slept much anyway.

Janek could barely contain his gratitude. He offered Homer a whole range of compensations which Homer said he'd think about, some of which he might just be interested in, like making up a threesome with the good-looking Maintenance Operative Gerda Dumas who was Janek's current unofficial, and who spent a lot of time in the Communications Centre when Janek was on duty – presumably communicating with him in a variety of fascinating ways.

So with Janek and a large slice of on-station personnel in the Ariadne Hall for the first night performance, Homer had settled down to a relatively quiet stint.

And that was when it happened – about an hour before the first performance – a Whisperer.

Homer had been doing what he always did, scanning the systems in a methodical double-sweep followed by a random-choice program of his own devising: his 'magic box', as he liked to call his piece of techno-wizardry. It had barely begun the random program when he picked up the trace. Someone had hacked into *Ivanov's* communication system from an internal access point and was transmitting a scrambled impulse message.

Time had been of the essence: the message was already underway and could have stopped at any moment. Homer's only hope was that he could get enough of it on record to work out the potential access point and possible sender. The destination would have to wait until the next message – and there would be a next message – of that he'd been certain.

The message, whatever it said, was brief. From the time he'd begun recording to the sudden cessation of transmission there was barely twenty seconds. Homer reckoned that allowing for the time taken to complete his last routine sweep, the whole message could have taken no more than around half a minute.

A quick job then. Something along the lines of 'arrived safely', or 'in place' – and no frills.

Homer tingled with anticipation. He flipped open his memo pad, logged in his personal scrambler code and copied in the message. At last he'd got something for Palatine which was definitely out of the ordinary. All he needed now was time to work on the material.

He began systematically checking the profile of every communication outlet on *Ivanov*. There were two-hundred-and-fifty possibilities. At four checks a minutes, he was facing more than a solid hour's work if the profile ended up being the last one on the list – and that was providing no one, or nothing, interrupted him.

After almost fifty minutes, he made the match. The profile belonged to outlet R-28 situated in a maintenance storeroom in the accommodation area. Exultant at his find, he accessed the logging record for R-28 and found exactly what he expected – a negative use indicator. So someone was using similar techniques to his own, and then subsequently erasing the evidence.

He went back to the recording and put it through its paces, working and reworking the impulses in the hope of getting the feel of the piece. Persistence always paid off, but sometimes, as he'd found out occasionally in the past, plain good luck worked just as well.

He'd been working methodically for nearly two hours when he came up against a block he recognised and rather wished he hadn't – the latest refined version of a ConCorp security program for high-grade intelligence.

High-grade intelligence. Homer pondered the possible consequences of making this discovery while he was trapped in the confines of *Ivanov*, and decided they could be seriously damaging to his health. He became very hot and bothered, yanking open the top fastening of his crimson stationsuit in something approaching a full-on panic attack. A fine slick of sweat had already emerged on his brow and upper lip, and begun to edge its way down his face between the bristles to the corners of his mouth. He licked at the saltiness, suddenly aware of how cold he felt despite evidence to the contrary. *High-grade intelligence.* Someone with access to a state-of-the-art ConCorp security program was up on *Ivanov* and reporting in – not on the official closed communication Link, which any child of three with an ounce of know-how could access with a hairpin – but by hacking into a storeroom outlet. This wasn't one Security Officer having a cosy chat with a buddy: this was something else – someone working with the blessing of ConCorp Security – which made it heavy stuff.

He'd been rumbled: there was always that possibility, no matter how careful he'd been. New counter-surveillance gadgetry and programs were being developed all the time and it wasn't always easy to keep ahead of the game.

He checked the clock. 2140 hours. Janek would be back within half-an-hour or so. Immediate action was needed. Hastily, he copied the message into his memo-pad, paralysed the counter on an unused Link he'd found, and transmitted the data to the predetermined listening post he'd been allocated, from where all his Palatine material was collected and evaluated.

There was a few tense moments before receipt of the material was acknowledged and he could unfreeze the Link, clear the line and wait for something else to happen.

There was nothing for several days: a silence in amongst the clutter of trivia that he found unnerving. He waited for the axe to fall, but nothing happened. He began to hope nothing would.

For the want of something to do, he put a personal marker on R-28 so he could be alerted to its use when he was off-duty, a move that produced an uncomfortable flurry of activity one evening when the marker suddenly activated and he leapt out of his shower to ensure the memo-pad was responding. Frustratingly, he was treated to a mundane conversation between two Maintenance Operatives discussing the merits of the latest exerciser in the multi-gym, a contraption Homer regarded with acute distaste.

Still dripping, he was about to return to the shower when the marker was suddenly reactivated and a scrambled message began. Whoever was transmitting had been waiting for the Operative to leave the storeroom. Homer waited with a quiet satisfaction: this time he'd got the destination code recorded.

The message was short, barely a minute's duration. Another routine signing-in maybe. Homer felt better immediately: he mightn't be the object of attention after all. He watched the Link clear and returned to the shower, relishing the prospect of identifying the destination code more than sluicing down his thin and unremarkable body.

Swathed in an oversized purple kimono he'd acquired some time ago from a grateful client who'd never actually met him, he sat at the little table in the relative comfort of his personal accommodation and began working on the destination of the message. He already knew it had to be a ConCorp Security destination, but whether this would be an identifiable location, or a listening post similar to his own, was something else. He input the profile for comparison against the illicit stock of existing Security locations in his data bank – and came up with nothing. The general public register drew a blank as well, which he half-expected. So – the destination was unregistered, like his own. It was probably buried in some unremarkable systems location, the data passing through a maze of other listening posts before it landed at its final destination for transcribing. He'd expected as much. It would have been too neat, too easy to find himself routed straight into ConCorp Central Security. All he'd got was a letter box.

There was silence again for several days and then the pattern was repeated: same length of message; same destination. And again, a few days later. Never the same time; never the same interval between transmissions; but always the same outlet. Homer passed it all on to Palatine but felt frustrated.

By the second week in March, there'd been a total of ten outgoing messages, all the same length, and nothing coming in. Homer needed some action. Off-duty during a Choralians' concert, he decided he'd probably be able to nose around the accommodation units without too much trouble. He reached level R without a hitch and found the place deserted.

Humming tunelessly to himself in time to the musi-tone, and pretending not be interested in anything in particular, he was scuffing his way down the corridor to R-28 when one of the doors ahead of him sighed open. The shock of actually finding someone still in the area almost stopped him in his tracks. He was torn between turning on his heels and getting the hell out of the place, or simply carrying on as though his presence was nothing out of the ordinary. He opted for the second choice by default, his indecision having already taken him a couple of steps closer to the door.

Whoever he'd imagined he was going to come face to face with, he was totally unprepared for what happened next. Out of the doorway shambled a slight figure in a stationsuit several sizes too large, clutching what Homer recognised as a musical contraption he'd seen on one of The Choralians' advertising holograms. The figure stopped, suddenly aware of someone close by, and turned to look at him.

Homer was greeted with a facial expression he'd never seen in his life before and had no great wish to see again: a total blankness looked him squarely in the eyes from a putty-coloured face beneath a wildly erratic hairline. It gave him the creeps. He stopped in his tracks.

The blankness gave way briefly to a flicker of shock, then anxiety, both vanishing into the blank nothingness again almost as quickly as they'd appeared – like snow landing on a warming plate.

Homer attempted a weak smile of acknowledgement. The figure took a step backwards, hugging the instrument closer, fearing perhaps that it might be taken from him. Then, without making any attempt at conversation, it turned away and shambled back into the room, all interest in its earlier expedition quite gone. The door promptly sighed shut.

Homer wasn't sure what to do for the best. From his position in the corridor, he could just make out the code on the now closed door. R-25. Better to stay out of range of the visitor monitoring panel, he reckoned, so he could still reconnoitre the corridor from his existing vantage point. What was immediately obvious was the clear diagonal view from R-25 to the storeroom if anyone used the visitor monitoring panel. The same probably applied to R-29. But the door with the best view was R-27, slap-bang opposite R-28.

Seemingly without a care in the world, Homer turned round

and sauntered nonchalantly back down the corridor to his own quarters several levels down, and promptly set about accessing the room allocation lists used for emergency evacuation procedures.

Who the hell was holed up in R-25? The list gave him two names: Jason Raymer and Lazar Excell. He was already well-acquainted with Raymer: he'd have had to be both blind and deaf not to have noticed the name on the hologram ads, and heard it repeated often enough on the information systems – not to mention the frequent eulogies from Janek. But Lazar Excell was something else. A Freak – and a pet Freak at that. Who knew what those Hurdy-Gurdy men fancied off-stage? Homer decided to keep that tasty tit-bit to drop on Janek the next time he was boring him to shreds about those jigging Choralians. Take some of the gloss off them.

He helped himself to a multi-juice cocktail and sat back, feeling in his gut he'd got something that might lead to the Whisperer. When he accessed the data again, he came up with the names Gary Maybourne and Charles T Banks in R-27 and Bart Ballinger and Martin Staines in R-29. They didn't ring any bells, but a quick run through the list of The Choralians' technical crew had Homer almost dancing with joy. Technos! All of them! Bazang! It was like winning the Global Lottery twice in one day! He switched straight into his personal, very private Link and reported his findings to Palatine. At last he felt he was beginning to get his teeth into something interesting.

A couple of days later, he was pleased to see his unofficial credit level boosted by a generous bonus for his efforts.

THIRTY-TWO

After his brush with the Freak, Homer's capacity for listening increased dramatically, even though there was no traffic on the R-28 outlet immediately afterwards. In moments of quiet contemplation, it occurred to him his little walkabout two days earlier might have interrupted a potential transmission, but he dismissed the thought as wild imaginings. The Freak didn't look capable of fathoming out the complexities of sophisticated hacking. Still, he reminded himself, it was never wise to rule out any possibility.

Just to be sure, he'd set up markers on all three rooms with easy access to R-28 and inserted automatic recording facilities to pick up any transmissions. It was a simple matter for him to re-route any traffic through his personal systems before looping them back into the main *Ivanov* communications Link. He wasn't too optimistic he'd get anything useful, but there was always the chance that he might.

It was still quiet. Communications through normal channels were strangely silent on R-25: Raymer didn't seem to be the communicative type. There were a couple of outgoing transmissions from R-27, both by Maybourne to his girl-friend back in the U.S, confined to lovey-dovey small-talk and little more, while Ballinger in R-29 had more exotic topics to discuss with someone in Australia he liked to call 'Trixie'. There was nothing on the surface that appeared of interest, but he recorded them anyway.

And then with barely four days left before The Choralians were due to tranship to Lowell, came a transmission which set Homer tingling all over. He was eating a warm synthetic cheese sandwich at the time, doing another stint for Janek who wanted to see one last concert before his idols left. Unexpectedly, contact came over the ordinary Link, a conversation loaded with undercurrents – and a clear warning.

The transmitter was a Guido Servione in Sparta calling up Jay Raymer. The message came through on a limited access audio-only channel, an inconvenience Homer easily circumvented so he could pick up the visuals as well as Raymer.

Homer had never seen Servione before, but he was pretty sure he didn't usually look the way he did over the Link: his face had been badly readjusted, one eye was purple-black and swollen, and his lips showed signs of colliding with something seriously heavy.

"Jason – thought I should keep in touch," Servione was saying, trying to sound casual and not entirely succeeding: he was having trouble forming his words.

To Homer, the silent third party to this conversation, Raymer's response was what he could only describe as incredibly non-committal, registering the rearrangement of Servione's features with barely the flicker of an eyelid. "Trouble?" Raymer asked in what Homer took to be a masterly understatement.

Servione answered with a grunt and a slight nod.

"How much?"

"We've had a visit."

"When?"

"This morning. Sorry I couldn't let you know sooner. I've just got back."

Back from the MediCentre, Homer reckoned, going by the injuries.

"Any ideas?"

"Agents working for the Clinic."

Raymer paused, as if he were aware there might be someone else listening. "What were they looking for?"

"Evidence we'd been involved."

"Did they get it?"

"Probably. They did a thorough job – on Erasmus."

"Will it be enough?"

"Enough to follow a warm trail."

"How far?"

Servione shrugged. "Keep your eyes open, Jason, that's all I'm saying."

"Okay. Should we move?"

Servione shrugged again. "This agency has contacts everywhere – believe me."

Raymer just nodded, as if he'd picked up a hidden message. "Right. I'll watch my back. Thanks, Guido – and good luck."

Servione smiled apologetically, a lop-sided affair, then shut down the Link.

Homer punched the air. He re-ran the recording and savoured it, putting it into his memo-pad ready for transmission once the concert was underway. This was it! This was solid – and it had all the feel of something momentous. He flipped the recording back to the beginning. But he'd hardly had time to complete a second re-run before Raymer reopened the Link to an unidentifiable destination. It had a private audio-only and voice transcription facility with no visuals available. Homer swore.

"Are we ready to roll?" Raymer was asking.

There was a noticeable pause. "Ready and waiting," came the distorted reply. Homer cursed: it was impossible to tell whether the voice had originally been a man's or a woman's before it had been processed, or how many re-routed transmissions had taken place before it arrived on *Ivanov*.

His irritation was interrupted by the soft bleeping telling him there was a communication coming through on his private channel. There could only be one person making that call. Unscrambled, it came through on visuals.

"Hello, Strendl," Palatine said, smiling at him enigmatically from the screen. "I'm routing something to you that might be interesting. Do let me know if it is." She gave him a slight nod then disconnected the Link. Almost simultaneously, it sprang into life again and a crazy series of alphanumerics appeared on the screen in the shape of a decahedron.

By the time the transmission ceased, Homer discovered his hands were trembling with anticipation. Awkwardly, he fumbled in his top pocket to retrieve his decoding interface, and had to take a couple of deep breaths before he was able to plug it into one of the lesser-used back-up consoles tucked away in the corner of the room. Once he had the portable product, he'd be able to delete any evidence of the message ever having arrived.

He blew out his cheeks impatiently, waiting for the process to be completed. The data-slice eventually emerged from the console. Still shaking with excitement, Homer scanned it on the nearest available screen. He skimmed over it, hungry for information; so hungry it made no sense to him at first. He read through it twice more before the full implication of what it said sank in. It was a Global Search Notification – unusual in itself.

MISSING FROM GARRISON CLINIC, PELOPONNESE SUB-REGION

The following description is of an individual undergoing urgent medical treatment at the Garrison Clinic. This person was removed without authority on 23 March '56. Last reported sighting was at the Glyfada Terminal sometime in January '57. There is evidence to suggest he may no longer be Earthside.

A reward of DR250,000 is available for anyone with information leading to this individual's safe return to the Clinic.

Homer felt his pulse-rate quicken: the description of the missing person that followed matched the physical appearance of the Freak exactly!

He re-read everything again more slowly, aware it was all too easy in moments of an adrenalin rush to jump the gun, or to add two and two together and come up with 4.333 recurring. After all, he kept telling himself, he'd only seen the Freak for a few seconds, and if he *was* the missing person, he'd been missing for almost a year. That was a long time to be missing if you needed urgent medical attention, so it was hard to work out what was so vital about the treatment after so long. But the temptation of laying his hands on a quarter-of-a-million dollaroubles convinced him he should do something about getting that poor guy back to the Clinic a.s.a.p. He retrieved the data-slice, deleted everything else, and pondered on what to do next.

He didn't hear the door sigh open behind him, which was why he nearly climbed out of his skin when a man's hand with long, tapering fingers came over his shoulder and simply helped itself to his precious possession. He whirled round on his chair, scared out of his wits and angry at the brazen theft, both at the same time.

He looked up into the face of a tall, lean man wearing an all-black tight-fitting leisuresuit with silver piping at the neck and wrists. The stranger was a heart-stopping sight. Framed by collar-length platinum-coloured hair, the smooth-skinned, pale, angular features and hard unyielding mouth were partially hidden in the shadow cast by the man's brows. Homer swallowed hard as the man straightened slightly and his eyes came into view. Afterwards, Homer could honestly say that he'd suddenly felt very sick: the irises were so pale they were almost colourless, like ice on a frozen lake, and their uncompromising gaze chilled the soul.

There were people in Homer's life who'd been unpleasant; people he'd preferred to have standing in front of him so he could see what they were up to; people whose habits were unmentionable; and people who at the very first meeting gave off vibrations of such intense power and ingrained evil, they'd left him too weak to move. Standing in front of him was a perfect example of someone in that latter category: someone who represented ruthlessness at its most extreme.

The unyielding mouth wound itself up into a twisted smile. "I'd forget about this," the man said in soft, perfectly precise UniCom, his voice tinged with an underlying hint of menace. And the slender hand holding the precious data-slice closed round it and deposited it into the recyclation unit in the wall by the door. It disappeared with an audible hiss.

Seeing a small fortune disappear into the recyclation system, Homer was outraged. "Hey, that's mine!" he said, trying to sound full of righteous indignation. Somehow it didn't come out the way he'd intended: his voice had shot up an octave.

The stranger was clearly unimpressed. He ignored Homer's protest and sat down with careful dignity at Janek's workstation, swivelling the chair slightly from side to side, his gaze never leaving Homer for a second.

Homer licked his lips, wondering if this demon was a new breed of Security Bloodhound. "What do you want?" he demanded, summoning up his courage.

The man pondered the question but seemed disinclined to answer immediately. "I've come to have a little talk with you," he said after a suitable pause, casually riveting Homer to his seat.

Homer could feel sweat running down between his shoulder blades, and it wasn't because the room was hot. "What about?" he said, hearing his voice squeaking in his head, and hoping he could put this man into some sort of context without blabbing too much about his unofficial activities: it was unnerving enough to know he seemed only too aware of them already.

The twisted smile again – more of a sneer than a smile. "Oh – I think you know."

Homer shook his head vigorously and clutched the arms of his chair for support.

The man sighed and studied his fingernails for a moment.

"Look," Homer complained. "That message was private. You'd no right to -" He stopped short because the man was giving him that dead-eye stare again that nearly made him wet his pants.

"You've been monitoring transmissions," the man said, saving Homer the trouble of trying to lie his way out of the situation. "I know, because we've been monitoring you," he added, a long index finger extending in Homer's direction, looking horribly like a gun.

Homer opened his mouth to say something and closed it again.

"You're an interesting man, Mister Strendl."

Homer gulped and found his voice. "Who are you? Security?"

The man raised an eyebrow and shook his head.

"What then?"

"You saw what happened to Servione?"

Homer just managed to stop himself choking. He nodded rather than do nothing.

"You didn't see Erasmus?"

Homer shook his head.

That smile again, twisting its way up one side of the hollow cheeks. "Not a pretty sight."

"You?" Homer asked, fighting to keep the contents of his stomach in their rightful place.

The man paused for a moment, and then very slowly shook his head. "No. That piece of business came from the same source as your precious message. Quite a lady, Livilla Tullia Palatine, isn't she?"

Homer just nodded and made a positive effort to control his breathing, which seemed to have started a syncopated rhythm all of its own.

The man continued. "No. We're – how shall I put it? – we're the competition," he said, allowing Homer sufficient time to digest the implications of this information. "And the difference is we don't leave any evidence behind that can talk afterwards," he added.

Homer was beginning to turn to religion, praying that someone would come in and break up this cosy little chat. He realised however, the likelihood of this was remote: no one had any cause to interrupt them either now or for the next two hours – The Choralians were on-stage.

The man was still eyeing him, watching the sweat rolling down his face no doubt, and having the satisfaction of knowing why. "I want to persuade you to help us," he said at last, swivelling the chair from side to side again, his hands in the attitude of prayer, his fingertips lightly touching the thin, mocking lips. "It's worth more than a quarter-of-a-million dollaroubles."

Homer wavered. He was in Palatine's pay. He already had visual evidence of how she obtained information if she'd a mind to it. He didn't much like the prospect of what would happen to anyone who really crossed her. "I've got a contract," he said weakly. "It's more than my life's worth to break it."

This was clearly amusing. The man threw back his head and laughed. It was the most grotesque sound Homer had ever heard that dared to call itself laughter, and it was gone as quickly as it had arrived. "Your life? Your life isn't worth this much," and the man snapped his fingers a few inches away from Homer's face. "Your talent," he added. "Ah – your talent, Mister Strendl – that's something else."

Homer pulled himself back into his chair out of reach. "I daren't break the contract," he insisted, feeling marginally bolder if his talent was what the man was really after. "She'll take me out. You said yourself, Erasmus wasn't a pretty sight."

"She doesn't need to know," the man said. "Not if you play your cards right – and I'm sure you could manage that, Mister Strendl." He paused for effect. "Now, do you want to help us, or not?"

Homer wanted time to think. "What am I supposed to do?"

The man resumed swivelling the chair as if he had all the time in the world at his disposal. "Just keep quiet, that's all," he said, giving Homer the benefit of his smile once more. "Forget to mention you happened to notice someone – how shall I put it? – a bit strange on *Ivanov*. That shouldn't be too difficult for you. It's not exactly breaking your contract, is it?"

"I don't know who you're talking about," Homer said, hoping he looked suitably bewildered.

The smile vanished from the man's face. "Don't play games with me, Mister Strendl," he said, coming within uncomfortable striking distance of Homer if he'd a mind to do something unpleasant to him.

Homer frowned, pretending he'd just recalled the subject of the conversation. "Oh – you mean the Freak?" he said, trying to sound casual.

The man nodded.

"That guy should be back in that clinic, not running around loose. What happens if he goes Berserker without his medication?"

"Oh – he won't do that," the man assured him. "He doesn't need medication."

"What about the treatment he's supposed to have?" Homer objected.

"You don't believe everything you're told, do you?"

"That's all I've got to go on right now."

The man sighed indulgently. "Let's say we need him here and leave it at that, shall we? You don't need to know why."

Homer gave this some thought. "Okay, so I keep my mouth shut. What do I get besides saving my skin?"

"That rather depends on how much you're prepared to help us."

"Okay, so what else do you want?"

"Nothing complicated. Just keep monitoring. The difference is you'll let me have the data first. I'll decide what goes back to

Palatine and what doesn't. That shouldn't be too difficult, should it?"

"What would I be looking for?"

"The same as now. Anything out of the ordinary. We're putting a network in place, Mister Strendl. Once it's up and running we don't want any glitches. Do you get my meaning?"

Homer nodded. "Okay, so what's it worth to me – credit-wise?"

The man frowned a little, appearing to be engaged in mentally completing a long multiplication sum. "Oh – let's say something in the region of – around a million dollaroubles in the first six months. Probably nearer three million a year once the network's complete."

Homer felt his jaw drop. "Who's paying?" he demanded, deeply suspicious. "I like to know who I'm working for."

The man shook his head. "Not in this organisation you don't. You deal with the middle man. That's me. Any problems, I'll sort them out."

Homer had no doubt on that score. "How do I know you're not selling me a load of old recyclables?" he parried. "I want some proof before I agree to anything."

"Or you'll do what?" The contempt was clearly visible in the ice-cold eyes.

It was the only piece of self-preservation gadgetry Homer had to hand – his modified pocket torch. In one mode it was an ordinary torch like millions of others; in another a welder or drill with an auto-focussing beam control. It was unique; it was his, and it was lying next to him on his workstation. With a calmness he later marvelled at, he simply picked it up and pointed it straight at the man in the chair. "Or I'll drill a hole in your head," he said, feeling much calmer now he had the advantage.

The smile froze. Homer could see the man weighing up whether he was being threatened by a common-or-garden torch, or by something more sinister.

"I can demonstrate it – if you like," Homer offered, dropping his aim to the floor in front of the man's feet. He pressed the switch. The focal length of the beam adjusted and with a short burst of light, a neat hole smouldered in the polyplastic flooring. A thin wisp of smoke circled upwards towards the ventilation unit. The stink was abominable. Homer raised the torch again to aim it at the man's head. The pale eyes stared back at him. "Now," said Homer, "You give me a good reason to make the jump from Palatine to you."

The man considered the matter and then reached for his breast pocket.

"Slowly," warned Homer.

The man nodded. In slow motion he produced a credit film, holding it between two fingers as he extended his arm slowly in Homer's direction.

Homer took the film without checking it, more concerned there was sufficient distance between the two of them to ensure his safety. "How do I know it's valid?" he asked.

"You can test the source-code rating if you like. That would be child's play for you surely?"

"It could be a hologram honeypot. Nothing there in reality. Know what I mean?"

The man gave a slight shrug. "You could open a new account now and deposit it," he suggested.

"With you just sitting there letting me, I suppose. You must think I'm a Dummy."

"Do it later if you like. If it's no go, there's no contract. That's fair, isn't it?" He was swivelling the chair again.

For a brief moment Homer contemplated drilling a hole in the man anyway. The only thing that stopped him was the possibility there was someone else on-station, just a menacing, who'd be ready to act as back-up before he could blink. Tempted, he finally glanced at the credit film. Half-a-million! "Okay," he said, mentally adding this to his other income streams. "It's a deal. But what's your name? I told you – I don't do business with a Mister Nemo, middle man or not. So what's your name?"

"Anstrom. Axel Anstrom," the man said smoothly. "But you can call me 'Angel' if you like."

THIRTY-THREE

The last show before transhipping to Lowell was over. Outwardly Cassandra was displaying her usual elated self at the end of a run. Inwardly, she was deeply troubled. McMichael had been strangely silent on the topic of changing their repertoire, and she couldn't understand why. After the near-surger performance, it wasn't what she'd expected. He wasn't the sort of man to let a main chance slip through his fingers – and she'd offered him the perfect opportunity to grab it with both hands. So why hadn't he? Theo couldn't come up with any logical reason either.

The evening was getting late. Cassandra wasn't in the mood for company, but Raymer followed her out of the Bar when she excused herself from the after-show party. "Can I come in?" he asked when they reached her quarters. His easy-going bonhomie had evaporated as soon as they'd left the Bar. Maybe he knew his performance had been a shade less brilliant that evening.

He helped himself to a multi-juice cocktail and parked himself on the lounger opposite her, frowning into the contents of the beaker.

"Have you something to tell me?" she asked, because he was clearly anxious.

He downed the drink in one and avoided eye contact. "I don't know where to start," he said with an embarrassed shrug. "It's about Laz."

Was this it? – she asked herself. Was this the conversation they should have had in the diner at the Glyfada Ferry Terminal months ago?

"You need to know something," he was saying, addressing the empty beaker he was clutching tightly in both hands. "Because someone probably thinks you know already."

"Jason, I'm tired. I'm in no mood for riddles."

"Sorry – this is such a mess ..."

She lay back against the lounger and closed her eyes, ignoring him. He wasn't making sense.

"Cass, listen to me," he urged. "You've heard of the GRM, I suppose? The Genetic Rights Movement?"

"Yes," she said, wondering vaguely where this was leading and what it had to do with Lazar. "It's a bunch of self-righteous fanatics, isn't it?"

"Well – maybe," he conceded. "But I joined them – after I left social engineering. My way of atoning for my sins, if you like. I've been an active member for the last five years. Guido Servione is our Area Organiser. I should have told you."

She sat up, studying him more closely. Her tiredness was making it hard to concentrate. "What's this got to do with Lazar?"

"Give me a chance, Cass. I'm trying to explain."

"Okay. Get on with it."

"About a year ago, one of Guido's Action Units raided a clinic in the Peloponnese – the Garrison Clinic. It's run by a Doctor Elgar Garrison. It's very expensive – very exclusive. We'd got intel Garrison was carrying out unorthodox – possibly illegal genetic experiments on animals."

"And?" she said, just wishing he'd get to the point sooner rather than later.

"The Action Unit liberated three experiments. Two were mutated chimps we shipped undercover to a rehab centre in Central Africa. The third -" He stopped abruptly. "The third," he said, starting again, but clearly having difficulty trying to find the right words. "The third was more of a problem."

Later, she realised she'd half expected what would come next.

A pallor had settled on his face. "It was Laz."

There was a definite silence that sat like a solid block between them.

"Right," she heard herself saying as if talking to a very small child who needed tutoring on the basics of evolution. "But Lazar's a human being, Jason, not an animal."

"Yes, but the team didn't know that before the raid," he insisted. "All they had to go on was what one of Guido's Reps picked up from the Clinic – that there was a very special experiment on-site. When they discovered him, they decided to get him out anyway. It would have been the perfect opportunity for the GRM to blow the lid off the Garrison Clinic for using a human being as an experiment."

"But *was* he an experiment, Jason?" she asked politely, suspecting he'd no idea what he was talking about.

There was suddenly the old defiance in his eyes. "Oh yes, Cass – he was definitely an experiment."

"How do you know?" she said, challenging his certainty.

He paused, evidently working out the best way of coming up with an answer she could accept. "Because we discovered something," he began.

"Go on."

"There's no easy way to say this."

"Try," she said, now definitely beginning to lose patience with him.

"Okay – he appears to be a surgically augmented hermaphrodite with possible genetic modifications," he said, his self-assurance firmly back in its place. "Does that answer your question?"

It took a moment or two for this to sink in. "Does he know?" she asked.

"Yes – but I don't think he understands."

"So who is he, Jason?"

He shook his head. "We've no idea."

"What!" She was incredulous.

"Cass, believe me, we trawled every database we could get our hands on looking for relatives, friends – anyone who might know him."

"And what came up?"

"Absolutely nothing. Honestly, Cassie, we checked out every damned MediCentre admissions database we could lay our hands on. There wasn't a single trace of anyone with the injuries he was supposed to have."

"That's impossible," she objected.

"Cass, I swear, there wasn't a trace – anywhere. That's why Guido took him in."

She eyed him coldly: there was one very obvious hole in his story. "If no one knew who he was, Jason, how did he get an ID?"

He shrugged off her question. "Guido has contacts," he said, making light of it. "They manufacture IDs – for a price – and a reasonably in-depth history to go with them."

She denied him the luxury of her opinion at that moment.

"We used the only names we could think of," he was saying. "Lazar – short for Lazarus – you know, it seemed appropriate – and added his experiment number – forty."

She caught the drift. "The Roman numerals?"

He nodded. "Excell. It was as good a name as any."

"So why is he out here – with us, Jason?"

He got up suddenly and went over to the recyclation unit, shoving the beaker into it savagely. "To get him out of harm's way," he said, leaning heavily against the unit for support.

"What do you mean – out of harm's way?"

"Garrison's hired Agents to get him back," he confessed, finally screwing up enough courage to look her squarely in the face. "And they aren't too fussy about how they do it. Guido's been in touch. He's been beaten up pretty badly. So has the Rep who found out about Laz. Guido thinks it's possible he might have said something."

"That would lead them to us?"

"Yes. I'm sorry."

"You're sorry? Jason, what have you done?" Any vestiges of tiredness were now long gone. She was beginning to feel sick.

"Do you think I wanted this to happen? I don't know what to do. Laz needs protection."

"Call in Security."

"Cass, you know I can't do that!"

"Why not?"

"What could we tell them? They'd start digging into his past, never mind his ID."

"His forged ID, you mean," she corrected him.

He was irritated by her challenge.

"Surely Lazar doesn't have to go back if he doesn't want to," she argued, thinking the whole affair was ballooning out of control.

"It's not that simple. Garrison just needs to say Laz's treatment's not complete and it's vital he's got back to the Clinic a.s.a.p. If you were Station Security taking a long hard look at Laz, would you be asking too many questions?"

"No," she conceded. "I suppose not."

"And he's not likely to be given the chance to argue the point either, is he?"

Cassandra was beginning to feel a dull throbbing somewhere behind her eyes and the creeping nausea was starting to get the upper hand.

Raymer was back on the lounger studying his hands, busily chewing the inside of his right cheek.

Her incomprehension began to translate into something else – red hot anger at his crass stupidity. "So," she said, winding herself up because she simply couldn't stop herself. "Let me get this straight. You've got us involved in harbouring a hermaphrodite non-person with a forged ID who was a genetic experiment at a high-profile clinic that wants him back so much they're prepared to set a gang of thugs on our trail? Is that about right, Jason? Or have I missed some vital element?" She was aware she'd raised her voice.

He just nodded, raking his hands through his hair.

"I want Theo and Umo in on this – now!" she demanded.

"No, Cass – please!" he begged. "Let's keep it to just the two of us – for everyone's sake."

"For whose sake, Jason?" she challenged him. "Whose?"

"Everyone's!" he shouted back, a fierceness about him which caught her momentarily off-guard. "Can't you see? What the others don't know can't hurt them? They aren't involved."

"Oh, you think so, do you?" she said, openly mocking him. "And that's fine provided they can explain their non-involvement to the thug who's perfectly happy to beat them into a pulp – or worse!"

"Stop being so melodramatic!" he yelled back. "*You're* in danger because you're involved with *me* – that's all! And I never meant this to happen."

"Well it's a little late for that now, isn't it?"

"Stop it, Cass! I need your help. Don't make me feel any worse than I do already."

"How can I possibly help in a situation like this?"

"Because you're a survivor!" he fired back. "You know how to get out of bad situations. What are my options? Tell me – I have to find him a place of safety!"

"You're impossible!"

"Think for me, Cass! I don't know what to do!"

He looked pathetic, she thought. Useless and pathetic. He'd dragged poor Lazar out of one frightening situation into another and now he wanted her help! How could she? What possible answer could she come up with?

Agitated, she got to her feet and paced the room trying to clear her head. *You're a survivor, Cass.* Memories surfaced: memories of bolt holes she'd been dragged to by her mother *in extremis*; ancient crypts of deserted churches smelling of damp and decay; caves carved into rock faces with a rope ladder access; once even hiding out in an unregistered leper colony of Aberrants. Old fears die hard. Contagion the greatest of them all.

Contagion. The thought coalesced into an idea. "Is there an Isolation Unit on Lowell?" It was the only option she could come up with.

He looked up sharply. "No," he said, suddenly animated by her suggestion. "But there's one on Gio!"

His knowledge jarred. "How do you know?"

"Must have read it somewhere," he said dismissively, reaching out and clasping her hands to his lips. "Cass, you're brilliant!"

She watched his anxiety evaporate in front of her. Gone in a trice.

"And we'll need a tame Medic as well," he was saying. "Someone who'll give Laz protection on medical grounds without asking too many questions -"

"Jason – slow down. We're heading for Lowell, not Gio –"

He waved her objection aside. "That's not a problem, Cass. We can find out where Gio's Isolation Unit is once we're up on Lowell. It'll be easier to access Gio's databanks from there. I'll ask Laz."

Cassandra wondered if she'd heard him correctly. "Ask him what, Jason?" It was a very simple question to her way of thinking, but suddenly he was reluctant to be drawn. So she repeated her question.

"To access the emergency fire-fighting layout," he said with a shrug. "It'll show where the Isolation Unit is."

She searched his face for some hint of an explanation because she wasn't sure she'd understood him correctly.

His self-assurance slipped momentarily. He ventured a wan smile which quickly vanished. "Laz can do it, Cass," he assured her with that earnest expression he was so fond of bringing into play. "Honestly."

She pulled away from him, incredulous.

"He *can* do it," he insisted, sensing perhaps he'd over-played his hand.

"I'm not a Dummy, Jason. He wasn't born knowing how to access a databank, was he? He had to learn. Who taught him? Was it Guido – or was it *you*?"

His grey-blue eyes were pleading with her. "If it saves Laz from being bundled back to that Clinic, Cassie, does it matter?"

In the chaos she was suddenly inhabiting, the thought crossed her mind that it probably didn't.

THIRTY-FOUR

In amongst the silence that had risen up like a wall between them, the distant throbbing of the ventilation system came and went intermittently, fretful of some minor irritation. It echoed the drumming in her head.

They sat facing one another, remote and uncommunicative: they'd run out of words.

Raymer stirred himself. "Perhaps I'd better go," he said finally. Cassandra nodded. "Yes, you'd better get back to Laz."

He got up from the lounger slowly, uncertain how to take his leave. "Goodnight then."

"Goodnight," she said, making no move to see him out.

He hovered by the doorway, as if remembering something he'd meant to say, but seemed to think better of it and left.

She closed the door behind him, letting the room fall back into its perfectly enclosed silence. She needed time alone to think.

After a while, she pulled herself off the couch and closed down the lighting leaving only the hologram of Poseidon glowing softly and reassuringly by the door.

Automatically, she carried out the little rituals of retiring for the night: brushing her hair with long, sweeping strokes; buffing her teeth energetically, and swallowing the zygote blocker as a matter of routine. She caught sight of herself in the washroom mirror, scrutinising the reflection critically for a moment: it was like looking at a stranger.

Despite her energetic buffing and rinsing, a bitter taste lingered in her mouth. Gall rose in her throat, fermented by a combination of fear and disappointment. Jason had lied. Lied to her. Lied to them all. He'd had his reasons, she didn't doubt that, and she could persuade herself that in his position, she'd have done exactly the same. But he'd destroyed her trust.

Her reflection stared back at her. Would she ever feel at ease until Lazar was out of harm's way? Probably not. But he couldn't be lodged in an Isolation Unit for ever, and then what? She'd no answer for the myriad questions that kept bombarding her brain. And from what little she knew of Dr Elgar Garrison, he was clearly a man who'd circumnavigate any obstacle to get Lazar back. He'd a tenacity of purpose she'd find it hard to match.

She wanted silence in her head. Automatically, she reached for the SoundSleep, the first time she'd felt the need of it in months. She downed a half-dose, trying to persuade herself there was some merit in not succumbing to the full measure.

She turned down the washroom lighting and went into her darkened sleeping quarters. Snuggled under the coverlet in her sleeping robe waiting for the SoundSleep to let her drift away, she lay with her eyes closed conjuring up the calm expression of Athene's hologram, absorbing the peace and serenity the image offered.

Her pulse slowed. There was a gentle hum in her ears and the sensation of beginning to fall in delicious slow motion: down and down, like a snowflake.

Dreams. There were dreams where there should only have been nothingness. Her half-conscious self considered them remotely; curious about their existence. A door opening softly, its gentle hiss like spring rain on grass. The faint rustle of movement, like leaves whispering in the morning wind. A glimmer of dawn, its faint light still too feeble to push back the night. Scent. The heady aroma of warm resin: tangy, like pine trees in high summer.

She stirred, feeling a slight pressure on her wrist. Somewhere in the distance the faint glow of dawn had given way to a blaze of light. She tried to blot it out, but the brightness was too intense. She tried to cover her face, but found her hands refused to move: they'd become too clumsy to lift. In the space of a heart-beat, she felt heavy all over; no longer floating, but plummeting, dropping like a stone. She cried out, but there was silence except for the wailing in her head.

Strong hands gripped her and bore her up, carrying her with ease and placing her upright, doll-like on a seat: a rag doll, her head hanging forward, too massive to support its own weight.

And then, like a lightning bolt out of the blue, there was a tremendous slap across the side of her face. It crashed through her, knocking her head sideways.

The pain was real. She wanted to scream, but couldn't. Fear leapt up inside her. Consciousness awoke. She was *not* dreaming.

Her head was jerked forward. A vice-like grip held her jaw, fingers digging into the flesh of her cheeks. She struggled to move, but couldn't. The grip tightened. She cried out again, this time aloud, the sound distorted into an indistinguishable burble.

She strained to make her eyelids open against the brightness, unbearable in its intensity. A shape. The black silhouette of her tormentor. Her lids shuttered themselves against the vision.

A man's voice: elegantly rich in tone, terrifyingly precise. "You can't move," it informed her in UniCom. "You can't speak. Just listen."

The grip relaxed. She forced herself to keep her head from flopping forward. Anything to prevent him from hitting her again. The light remained full on her, making her eyes water, even through closed lids. She could feel the wetness gather at the corners and edge its way down her face: irritating; impossible to wipe away with unresponsive hands. She had no option but to sit, waiting for what she was supposed to hear.

Somewhere in her head her brain was beginning to unscramble.

She could feel the slight pressure on the inside of her wrist. A strip of sedatape – almost certainly doctored. A combo, she thought. Something not too strong perhaps – just strong enough to give this stranger his power over her.

A chair was moved and placed somewhere close in front of her.

"Are you listening, Cassandra?" the voice asked. "Nod if you understand."

She nodded promptly to prevent any reaction to her slowness. "Good."

A shadow passed across her face. She winced, but no blow followed. The voice, when it spoke, was much closer. The aroma of tangy resin came with it and etched itself deep into her consciousness.

"I know your secret," the voice informed her softly. "You and your partner are hiding someone. Someone somebody wants back very badly. Very badly indeed." The hand encircled her face, this time caressing her cheeks, her neck – playing with her.

Her stomach tightened into a knot. Was this Dr Garrison's emissary?

"You can help him," the voice insisted. "And yourself, if you co-operate." There was a significant pause. She sensed him moving even closer, so close, his breath was warm on her face. He kissed her neck gently, his voice lost in the depths of her hair about her shoulders. "If you don't, I can arrange an accident."

Something trailed across her throat. She gagged, the shock springing open her eyes. Her surroundings rushed in on her, familiar and yet unfamiliar with the stark contrast between blackness and blinding light. She was back on the couch in the main area of her living quarters. A man's face was only a hand-span away from her own, partially obscured by the deep shadows thrown across his features by the laser beacon set up on the side table. Around his head a halo of fierce white light encircled the edges of his shoulder-length platinum hair.

Angel, she thought. This is Angel.

This was the man who was able to move around and disappear at will. This was the sadist who used neuro-rods on Umo for his own pleasure. This was the man Karoli had met on the *Ptolemy* – who might have lured him to Hangar Six – who might have killed him.

Her anger was dulled by fear: fear fed by her miserably reduced state with no ability to retaliate or defend herself. This man – this demon – had denied her that.

The man got up from the chair, a threatening figure in a tight-fitting black leisuresuit, made more menacing by the brilliance of the side light illuminating the outlines of the sinewy body beneath.

How could this man disappear? – her brain was asking her? How could anyone so distinctive, so obvious in every way – disappear? The question demanded her attention but he was talking at her again.

"I want you to take something to Lowell," he was saying. "A package."

It was such a simple request, it unnerved her. What was the catch? What was so difficult about the task that her refusal could mean death? Instinctively, she put her hand to her throat, suddenly aware that movement was coming back into her limbs. The knowledge distracted her momentarily. Angrily, she tore the strip of tape from her wrist flinging it to the floor and tried to stand up, but there was no strength in her legs.

Her futility amused him. He laughed softly, the sound of it making her flesh creep.

She collapsed back onto the couch and willed herself to speak, her voice husky and still unsound; her throat parched and sore. "What sort of package?" she croaked.

He didn't reply. Instead, with a slow, very deliberate movement, he drew out from his top pocket a slim sheath. "This," he said, and with great care removed from it a thin strip of flexible polyplastic film barely a few centimetres long. It shimmered in

251

the brilliance of the laser, an insubstantial thing as fragile-looking as a dragonfly's wing.

"What is it?"

"It's new," he informed her. "Very new." And with a facile pleasantness he moved towards the VR facility at the end of the couch. "I could show you its delights, if you like?"

She recoiled from the notion. "No!"

He laughed at her reaction, returning the rainbow-coloured sliver to its protective sheath. "Another time, then," he said, sliding the sheath back into his pocket with evident care.

"It's mind-warp, isn't it?" she guessed.

He smiled, making a smile into an obscene act. "It's the best," he informed her.

With every ounce of strength she could muster, she pulled herself to her feet to defy him, her mind filled with images of her mother's terrible final hours lost in a grotesque fantasy, killing herself in an orgy of heart-stopping ecstasy.

He stood there in front of her like a wall. "You *will* take this to Lowell," he said very softly, "Otherwise I will have to arrange for your strange little friend to be found by those who are looking for him – and you and your partner will simply cease to exist." He pushed her roughly back down onto the couch and leaned over her. "Accidents happen out here," he added meaningfully. "Unfortunate, but fatal."

"Is that what happened to Karoli?" she asked, determined to confirm her guesswork.

"Karoli?" He made the name sound inconsequential.

"Karoli Koblinski. Shackleton Moonbase. Last September. Hangar Six."

He smiled at her lazily, a self-satisfied smile of someone who vaguely remembers a job well-done. "There have been others," he said nonchalantly. "Names are irrelevant."

"Why did you kill him?"

"He interfered," he said dismissively. "He destroyed something that didn't belong to him. He should have left things alone – then no one would have got hurt."

He pulled her up abruptly by the shoulders, tilting his head back slightly, forcing her to see the whole of his face lit up in the glare of the harsh white light. "Now – look at me!" he ordered. "Look very hard."

She looked, and knew she'd never seen such a face before: it took her breath away. So many contradictions: a smoothness of skin tone across harsh angularity; a compelling sensuality marred by an underlying, deeper brutality; perfect symmetry; an unforgettable face with ice-cold eyes, cruelly mocking, drilling through her and chilling her soul, utterly terrifying in their unrelenting gaze. He smiled at her – a demonic, hideous expression; the stuff of nightmares.

"Could you ever forget me?" he whispered, pulling her so close the tang of him tingled in her nostrils.

"No. Never."

"Exactly," he said with a stifled laugh, pushing her away, apparently unconcerned that she might try to escape. "Once seen – never forgotten." He smiled again, shaking his head over a private joke known only to himself. "Except," he added, surveying her from a distance. "I have more identities than you have ideas, Hurdy-Gurdy Lady. I could be the old man with a lisp sitting opposite you in a dining area. I could be the helpful young Seasian steward serving you on a flightcraft. I could be the dark-haired young woman in the front row of a performance. I can be anybody I choose. That's my talent."

"Then you don't need me," she said, allowing herself a hint of bravado. "You could take the product to Lowell yourself."

He was acutely amused by her apparent naivety. "I can't be everywhere," he said. "Besides, that's not my role. I organise. I direct. I recruit couriers – because that's what my organisation wants – and we want *you*. You're in demand. You travel. You can open up the entire system for us."

"I'll get caught," she countered. "The security sweeps will pick it up."

"You disappoint me," he said with mock seriousness. "How do you think it got this far? It's undetectable. Slim brilliance. MegaJoy has been working on it for years. It just needs to be put in the lining of a travelsuit and it can go anywhere. It doesn't show up on anything ConCorp have ever devised."

She remembered the cones on the surger costume – and Oliphant's interest in them. Had he suspected something like this? Had he even come close? Had he wondered if Karoli had died protecting the rest of The Choralians from precisely this situation? She hoped he had. But now it was her turn to protect them – and Lazar, who'd unwittingly become an innocent pawn in this terrifying game.

"You know that stuff kills," she said, feeling her strength of purpose grow by keeping him talking. "Out there – on stations – it could kill hundreds. Just one person warped out of their mind crashing a system – that's all it takes."

"Exactly."

"You want that? Hundreds of people sacrificed so you can market your beautiful product?" Her anger was rising as the drug began to loosen its hold.

"Of course not. But then, neither does ConCorp. They would pay an awful lot to keep MegaJoy off their premises."

"Blackmail?"

"If you like – but first we have to prove we can infiltrate every out-station – and you're going to help us do that, because – " he said, the dreadful smile fixing her again, " -because, my dear Cassandra, you really have no choice. But just to make sure of you, I'm going to give you a present. Something that will make you want to see me again – and again – and again."

His strange, cold eyes fixed her to the spot: hypnotic. She was spell-bound under his gaze, the tangy scent of him filling her brain. The essence of evil, she thought, and she could feel her willpower draining away, leaving her an empty husk. She couldn't move, even if she'd wanted to. She could only watch as he cleared the centre of the room of its furniture, his movements elegant and graceful, like a dancer. He brought up the sidelights on a low setting and extinguished the brilliance of the laser beacon. For a moment, he studied the hologram of Poseidon, then extinguished it. The strong silent presence of the god evaporated, leaving her feeling utterly alone and unprotected.

"Now," he said. "Come here."

She walked towards him in a trance, her consciousness barely aware of the floor beneath her feet.

"Give me your hand."

Obediently, she offered it and felt the firm pressure of sedatape against the inside of her wrist. She was powerless to stop him. "What are you giving me?" she asked, already aware that her voice sounded remote and unconnected to her.

Whatever it was, its potency was immediate.

"A bit of this – a bit of that," he told her. "You'll want more – later. When I want you to."

She could feel a warmth creeping into her veins. She was becoming as light as thistledown on the wind. And then she heard a distant rhythm softly thrumming in her ears and moving closer.

She looked across at him. He was strapping tape onto his own wrist and smiling at her with anticipation that made her feel weak. "You owe me something," he whispered.

Her head was filling up with exotic music: the faint but persistent trilling of a pipe; the deep swirling chords of a choraladian at full measure; an alphatron joining in, adding a deeper, richer dimension. Exquisite. Magnificent. All pervading music that sang in her soul. Her defiance glowed briefly. "I owe you nothing," she managed, barely able to think against the backdrop of the insistent beat. But somewhere, deep within herself a long way off, she could hear her mind saying, "But you owe me a life."

Her feet had begun to move her around the floor. She was swaying in time to the sound. Bright rainbow colours sprang in front of her from nowhere, outlining everything; shifting and shimmering in the half-light, casting strange and beautiful highlights along the length of her arms as she raised them above her head to sweep back her hair. She could make flames flicker from the tips of her fingers: soft iridescent flames that licked and lapped about her, consuming her with desire.

"You owe me a surger," she heard him say, his voice caressing her. "The one you never gave me at Shackleton. Now I want the real thing." And he pulled her close, fixing a small transponder disc to her forehead before kissing her fully on the lips, hungry for more of her, before pushing her away as he fixed a transceiver disc to his own forehead.

She moved around the room to the rhythm in her head, the music increasing in tempo, her robe turning this way and that with every step she took. She felt for the cord at her waist and pulled it free, trailing it behind her across the floor, twisting and contorting itself into multi-coloured knots. The robe fell open.

His eyes watched her as she approached, feasting on her, the rhythms in her head already making him sway as they soaked into his mind. He reached out for her and she spun around, avoiding him, letting the robe slip from her shoulders to the ground. She could hear him calling her back. She laughed, slowly advancing towards him again: swaying; seductive; tantalising him; running her hands through her hair sweeping it upwards from her shoulders, keeping her arms raised and moving her body in ways she'd learned to forget.

He urged her on, his hands pulling at the fastenings of his leisuresuit, his sleek torso emerging like a rare butterfly from its chrysalis: gleaming; shimmering in outlines of brilliant purples, blues and greens; incredibly strong and sinewy. Naked and aroused, he was beautiful. Superb.

The rhythm quickened with her desire. The pulse of it was now everywhere: in her eyes, her ears, the throbbing of her heart, her very core. The performance had begun. Her audience of one was waiting: she could hear his heavy breathing in her head. Give him what he wanted – everything.

She circled around him slowly, every movement choreographed: her hands sliding across her breasts, her belly, her thighs, drawing his eyes to them. Her body began to ache with the physical intensity of ecstasy laced with pain. Oh – to be touched! Now! She moved closer, dipping and stretching, letting him see what he wanted: a Salome for a Herod whose eyes couldn't get enough of what they saw. The music pounded on. She heard herself laughing like some maddened Bacchante as she slid her body fleetingly against him.

He pounced with the speed of a cat, his eyes and hair flecked with oranges and reds, his body the same: a glistening kaleidoscope of shifting light. His hands and tongue were suddenly everywhere, seeking her out: demanding; unhesitant; incredibly sensual. Sound and light combined with touch, whirling her into a vortex of orgiastic pleasure until she was only dimly aware of her own hands leading him on; of their sudden coupling; of his insistent frenetic movement within her. On and on, ecstasy upon ecstasy. She could hear her breath rasping in her throat in time with his: their total completion.

Then, without warning, the drumming in her head and the trilling of the pipe merged into one long, crashing, sustained note that seemed to drown her in sound. A huge black wave gathered itself up and swept over her, hissing and swirling in her ears, choking the breath from her. She was suddenly lost, carried away on a dark tide – a broken doll unable to save itself, at the whim of every passing eddy that flung her this way and that, until at last she was tossed helplessly onto a midnight shore, to be pounded over and over again by the remorseless beating of the waves.

THIRTY-FIVE

She came round slowly, aware of someone bending over her. There was the scent of patchouli. It was Raymer. He was trying to lift her off the floor.

A mind-numbing agony shot through her, sharp and sudden, like a high-voltage shock to her brain. "Don't move me!" she begged, choking on the words. "Pain. Everywhere." She could hear her breath coming in short, strangled gasps. Her throat was parched; her limbs were leaden. She just wanted to be left where she was, where she could drift back into nothingness. Raymer's presence troubled her.

His voice spoke to her from a long way off: urgent; pleading. "Cassie," she heard him say. "What's happened?"

What's happened? What *had* happened? She wasn't sure she could answer him. If she lay still, she felt warm and tingling all over. There were bright reds, yellows and blues behind her eyelids that lit up the darkness. When she partially opened her eyes, the colours were still there, shifting and changing, illuminating the room with the magical qualities of an aurora. And among the curtains of colour, vivid images danced and weaved before her: erotic, enticing, filled with an unfettered ecstasy and pain, passion and savagery all rolled into one. She ached with incompleteness.

She closed her eyes again. "Angel," she whispered. "Angel. Give me what I need ..."

But the warm, intoxicating scent of resin had gone. Now it

was patchouli and patchouli wasn't what she wanted. She wanted Angel.

Raymer's voice – intruding again – a long way off. "Cassie, wake up! You're in a mess!"

She knew she should pay attention, but her mind was elsewhere. She wanted to be drawn back into the world of exquisite interplay of light and sensation. A rainbow of intense colour coalesced, took shape and danced around her to the sound of distant music, lifting her again to melt at the prospect of completion. She sighed. "Give me what I need," she urged the image. "Come to me." She wanted to reach out and embrace the source of her pleasure, to bring him down to her, but she was helpless.

Had she slept? Why was she on the floor? She'd ignored the cardinal rule of survival. *Stay on your feet.* It worried her. She really should make the effort to do something about it. She tried to sit up, a lightning bolt of pain exploding again inside her head and she heard herself cry out as she fell back. Someone came padding quickly across the floor to kneel beside her. Patchouli again. Not resin.

"Lie still, Cass. I'll try to make you comfortable."

He was careful, lifting her head very slowly until the softness of a pillow cradled her and she sank back into it, letting herself float away again.

It must have been later. How much later she'd no idea, only a sense of time passing, as though in a dream. There was the dim awareness of Raymer still in the room and the warmth of a coverlet over her. And then other sensations: spasms that came in waves; a dull ache that occupied every cell in her body after they'd passed; the hardness of the floor beneath her.

She dared to open her eyes. No rainbows now. No music. Only the subdued lighting in the living area. Cautiously, she turned her head to one side.

Raymer was sitting on the edge of the couch, leaning heavily against his knees, watching over her. Seeing she was awake, he reached down and gently brushed a strand of hair back from her forehead. "Cass, someone's fixed you. You were off your head. Did you know that?"

"Yes," she said, vaguely remembering Angel's words. "It's new." She lifted her hand to her forehead, sensing something should be there. But there was nothing, only the lingering sensation of contact without the reality of it. A sudden spasm in her arm made her gasp.

"I'll call a Medic."

"No," she insisted. "No Medics. They'll ask too many questions."

He didn't argue.

"Just help me onto the couch."

He lifted her carefully to her feet, keeping the coverlet wrapped closely around her. The pain in her legs was almost unbearable until he eased her down onto the couch. He sat next to her. "Cassie, who's this 'Angel' you keep talking about? Did he do this to you? He's used neuro-rods, hasn't he?"

She just nodded – very slowly. It took several minutes before the pain subsided enough for her to speak. She kept the story short, from Umo's entanglement and Karoli's fatal meeting in Hangar Six, to the price Angel was demanding of her to keep Lazar out of Garrison's grasp. Told in such simple terms, the narrative lacked the fire she knew it deserved.

He listened in silence.

"Now do you understand what happened?"

"Yes," he said, his face carved in stone.

"He uses people. We're all just pawns in his game."

"Have you never seen him before?"

"No – never. Not as he really is." Images of him suddenly filled her mind again: the fine silver down on his body glistening in the sidelights, and the smoothness of his skin to her touch.

That was real enough. That was no elaborate disguise. "It's part of his power-play. Look at me. You can never forget me as I really am, but I've been shadowing you for months as someone else. I can shadow you again – how I like, when I like – and you'll never know who I am."

Raymer reached out for her hand but she avoided his grasp. "Cass – be honest with me. Were you conscious when he used the rods?"

"No," she said, relieved she could say this: it would have been torture. At least he'd spared her that.

"And – the rest?" Raymer was asking, his face betraying his reluctance to raise the subject. "Did he force you? It's a neutralising offence."

Her answer would bruise his ego, but that couldn't be helped. "I was surging, Jason. You know that's exempt." The visible hurt in his eyes stopped further explanation. How could she tell him? – that the drug had made her not just compliant, but hungry to consume the man? – that Angel's beautiful body had called to her and she'd answered? – that the thick sweet scent of this man Raymer could no doubt smell on her was now an addiction – and might be for ever?

"I need a shower," she said, wanting to make space between them. Keeping the coverlet close she struggled to her feet, trying to loosen the cramped muscles that cried out with every step. "Where's my sleeping robe?"

"Down the recyclation chute," he said, not looking at her. "I didn't think you'd want to wear it again."

No, she thought. You mean *you* didn't want me to wear it again.

He just sat, waiting for her to come back, his expression one of sullen resignation.

A quarter-of-an-hour later, she made her way back to the living area wearing her kaftan. They sat on separate loungers, a gulf opening up between them as tangible as if Angel himself had been standing there with all his dreadful physicality filling the space.

"You know I have to do what he wants," she said, filling the silence. "We need time to get Lazar to Gio – and we can do nothing until we're on Lowell."

"When do you think he'll bring the package?"

"I'm guessing just before we tranship from *Ivanov* – but I can't be sure."

"I want you to move in with me, Cass."

"No. If you put yourself in his way it would only complicate things."

"You can't go through this again."

"Maybe I won't have to. I think this was a demonstration. A warning of what he could do if I don't follow his instructions."

"You're grasping at straws."

"No, I don't think so. I'm hot property, Jason. If he stops me performing, he reduces my usefulness. He knew he could get away with using neuro-rods this time because we've no more performances here. It gave me time to recover."

"But what happens if you're caught by a security scan?"

"He didn't get caught, did he? I have to believe he was telling the truth – that it can't be detected. If we can get Lazar to safety quickly enough – I'll go to Security and hand it over."

"That's madness! They'll never believe your story – not for a minute!"

She got up, needing to keep her legs moving. "Jason, I'll have to take that chance. Let me deal with this my own way. You said yourself – I'm a survivor. I'll take Angel's fix. I'll take his product to Lowell – but I'll hold on to it. I won't be party to trafficking mind-warp."

"And what am I supposed to do? I got you into this." he said, sounding unnecessarily truculent she thought.

"You have to keep Lazar safe – in the meantime – whatever

it takes."

"And what do we tell the others? I made up a cock-and-bull story to keep Theo from checking up on you this morning. Everyone's asking where you are."

"What did you say?"

"I said you were feeling a bit down – and I was staying with you."

"Did Theo believe you?"

"Maybe he thought we were – otherwise occupied," he said, looking away from her, perhaps thinking of another man's occupation.

"Then let's leave it that way. I need time to think."

"Cass, how can you be so calm about this?"

"Because there's no other way to deal with a crisis, Jason. Believe me – I've had a lifetime's practice – I know. Angel's calling the tune right now but he can't control everything. I'll do my best to get Lazar safely out of the picture, but if I fail – it'll be up to you. You'll have to take over."

"How do you expect me to do that?"

She thought he was being particularly slow-witted. "You call in Security, Jason, because by then there won't be any alternative."

"And what happens to Laz if I do?" he said, getting to his feet, visibly angry. "Have you thought of that?"

She looked at him with fresh eyes. Had he really said that? After everything she'd gone through, and was prepared to go through to keep Lazar safe?

She turned from him to hide her disgust and began walking the room again with quiet determination. It was time to make her own plans, she decided – and they wouldn't include Jason Raymer.

THIRTY-SIX

Theo had become a Watcher. He wasn't sure why he was watching, he just knew instinctively it was suddenly important that he should.

He knew too the exact moment he'd taken on the role: it was when Jason had mysteriously reappeared from his visit to Cassandra, making an unobtrusive entrance from the R-corridor while the rest of the crew were heads-down crating equipment and costumes in the Ariadne Hall ready for transhipment. He'd seemed self-absorbed, unwilling to speak or be spoken to, and far removed from the image of someone who'd spent the intervening hours in the arms of his beloved.

Without drawing undue attention to himself, Theo had sauntered over to where Jason was studying an alphatron to no great purpose. "Where's Cassandra?" he'd asked casually.

Jason had looked up sharply and seemed lost for words.

"You look – troubled. Is she all right?"

"Yes. Yes – well – much better than she was," was the answer he'd got and it had sounded false – a ready-made excuse to deflect further interest. And with that Jason had pointedly walked away on the pretext of needing to help Lazar with crating the instruments.

Cassandra had remained shut away in her quarters, and Theo had consciously morphed into becoming a Watcher.

That evening, with transhipment scheduled within the next thirty-six hours, he went down to the loading bays adjacent to the central hub to talk through final arrangements with the Stores

Director, Remia Krusnik, a robust female of Junoesque proportions with a no-nonsense attitude.

The Minnow flightcraft *Tertia* had docked earlier in the day and was nearing the end of its overhaul and unloading sequence. When Theo arrived, the cargo bay was unusually quiet, caught between the hustle of off-loading and the bustle of on-loading. Brown-suited Stores Operatives sat around on crates in groups talking, or deep in concentration playing CrossTak on an InterLink board, waiting for the Flight Maintenance crews to give them the all-clear to start loading. He ambled between them searching out Krusnik. He found her in her small office off Bay Three, working her way through a checklist on her monitor.

"You worry too much," she said, eyeing him disapprovingly from beneath the peak of her brown cap.

"I usually have good reason," he explained, made to feel a little uncomfortable by her domineering presence. "Things tend to get lost – or left behind."

She glared at him fiercely. "Not on my watch," she stated flatly. "If your marker codes are on the right crates and everything is down here by twelve-hundred hours tomorrow, it'll be on the *Tertia* when you leave – you can bet on that."

Theo didn't feel he was in any position to question the veracity of her statement: it was quite plain such a suggestion would be met with considerable hostility. He excused himself politely and headed back towards the elevator shafts out of the hub. Passing one of the small eating areas usually reserved for operatives on duty, he was surprised to see Jason and Lazar hugger-mugger in one corner deep in conversation. Jason was leaning forward across the table and Lazar, hunched up more than usual with the hood of his leisuresuit pulled close around his face, was nodding in response to what he was hearing.

Theo lost interest in the elevator. Holding himself close to the shadows of a pillar, he watched their conversation. And the more he watched, the more uneasy he became, not just because he was playing the spy, but because there could be no doubt from the body language and taut expression on Jason's face, something serious was being discussed.

It was time to act, Theo decided. Something was wrong. Backtracking round the hub, he chose the more circuitous route to the elevator to avoid being seen.

In their quarters, he found Umo sprawled out on his bed listening to something on the periphones. "Just going to check on Cassandra," he said, loud enough to be heard above whatever was being listened to. Umo nodded.

With Umo preoccupied, Theo opened the internal Link and input Cassandra's room number. It was some time before she answered, and her voice sounded strange.

"I thought I'd find out how you were," he asked, using their mother tongue. It was an understanding between them. Over an open Link, a reply in UniCom would signal all was not well.

He heard her clear her throat. "A bit tired, Theo, that's all," she said, her precise UniCom hurting his ears.

"I'll let you sleep, then," he replied, slipping into UniCom so she'd know he'd received her message – loud and clear.

"Thank you." She disconnected.

He closed down the Link and waited a moment, listening to his heart-beat responding to the sudden surge of adrenalin. "Umo," he called through the closed door to the sleeping area. "Umo, I'm just going to have a word with Cassandra." There was a muffled response.

Theo was aware his anxiety had gone up a notch. Automatically, he activated the monitoring panel and was reassured to find no one waiting for him outside. Why he'd suspected anyone would be, he'd no idea, but he'd felt it important to check – just in case. Once out into the corridor, he walked briskly down to R-24 – a man with a purpose. As soon as he reached the door, it opened: she must have been monitoring his arrival. He stepped inside quickly and the door sighed shut behind him.

For a few seconds he was disorientated: the lighting was subdued, every wallpane blanked to a dull cream. For reasons he couldn't understand the furniture had been moved back against the walls with the exception of the couch which was dead centre opposite the door. Cassandra was sitting on it as a queen might sit on a throne holding court. She was wearing the outfit she usually kept for gala occasions: a full-length black chiton edged in gold, her hair loose about her shoulders. Her features were strangely smooth and drained of colour. Persephone – he thought, her image so strikingly evocative it almost took his breath away. Persephone, waiting for the God of the Underworld to come and claim her. The hairs on the back of his neck shivered.

She smiled wanly. "I'm glad you've come," she said, her voice oddly drained of vitality. "I hoped you would."

"You should have called me," he said, taking her hand in his. It was stone cold.

"I couldn't trust the Link. I've had a visitor, Theo – Angel."

Theo felt his heart lurch. "When?"

"After the last concert."

"But Jason was with you."

"No, Angel came later."

"How did he know where to find you?"

"Someone on *Ivanov* must be watching us." She glanced in the direction of the door. "Theo, you can't stay long. He's coming again. Sometime tonight. Sometime soon."

"Then I'll wait."

"No!" she said, visibly alarmed at such a notion. "He has to find me alone. Listen to me."

He continued holding her hand while she explained her reasons, all the more horrific for being told in such a matter-of-fact way.

He didn't know what to say: there was too much to absorb, and no easy answers.

In the silence that followed, she visibly withdrew into herself, her face unnatural in its stillness. He raised her hand to his lips and kissed it reverently. Her eyes watched him as if from a great distance, and then she turned away. "I hate this man to the bottom of my soul, Theo," she said in a whisper, " – and yet ... and yet I want him – do you understand?"

"You aren't in control," he said, remembering Umo. "Combos take you over."

Her gaze had begun to wander, fixed on nothing in particular. "He knew I would want him again. He was right."

He squeezed her hand a little tighter, struggling to hold his emotions in check. He was back on the *Ptolemy* wrestling with his memories – and something he'd tried to forget.

She appeared to be slipping into a trance.

"Cassandra," he said, raising his voice a little to attract her attention. "Cassandra, listen. This is important. Get Angel to put a name to what he's using."

She was only half paying attention.

He turned her face towards him. "Listen to me! After Angel fixed Umo on the *Ptolemy*, I asked a Medic for help. He gave me an alter-combo he was developing – to counteract the compliance drug – themaldrahine. It helped." He didn't go into the finer details of the price he'd had to pay – an unsavoury evening's entertainment requested by the Medic. "I still have some left."

She smiled at him fondly but he wasn't sure she could hear him.

"Cassandra!" he urged, trying to keep her concentration focussed. "Find out if he's using themaldrahine. I think he is. He wants you compliant and unconscious so he can indulge himself at leisure. The surger-fix is an add-on."

Her eyes were closing.

"Do you understand me?"

"Yes," she whispered, and then slipped out of his reach, her head resting against the back of the couch, her hair a dark halo around it. Her breathing slowed and there was no response to his touch.

For a few moments, he toyed with the idea of staying despite her insistence, until he realised it was nothing more than simple bravado. A light-weight Hurdy-Gurdy Man was nothing to Angel. Karoli had been a more formidable opponent – and Karoli was dead.

He kissed her hand and placed it tenderly in her lap. He could do nothing useful by staying.

He checked the corridor again before he left. It was empty, filled only with the burbling of the musi-tone and the faint vibrations of the filtration system. Unseen, he slipped back into his quarters relieved to find Umo already asleep. He fixed himself a multi-juice and discovered his hands were shaking. He downed it in one and quietly made his way into the sleeping area. Using the half-light shafting in from the open door, he retrieved his travelsack from the closet and brought it out onto the floor. In the side flap, he found the phial of colourless liquid that had cost him his dignity on the *Ptolemy*. He held it up to the light: there was very little left and he wondered if there'd be enough if it were needed. His hands were beginning to sweat.

He glanced across at Umo, peacefully asleep, the coverlet only partially across the broad sweep of his finely muscled back. He remembered how he'd found him after Angel had played with him.

An iron band tightened around his heart. He shuddered. He was angry. Angry that Angel was still able to abuse anyone he chose; angry at his own powerlessness to prevent him taking his pleasure of Cassandra; but most of all, angry at Jason for lying; for placing Cassandra in Angel's path and for making Karoli's sacrifice worthless.

He began to feel physically sick and just made it into the

washroom in time. Hanging over the basin, he felt as if the depth of his soul were being disgorged with every nerve-jangling spasm. Finally, he slumped onto the floor, exhausted, waiting for the agony of body and mind to subside.

It took a long time.

Thirty-seven

From behind closed eyes she heard the door sigh open and close quickly. She listened, her mind strangely alert now while her body remained devoid of movement. The air stirred with the opening and closing of the door, wafting a hint of his distinctive scent into her nostrils. She felt no fear at his arrival: an expectancy, perhaps; the thrill of anticipation, but not fear.

A curious thought struck her: had the SoundSleep distorted the effect of the combo-fix the first time around? It seemed strange she was so aware, so alive to the clarity of reasoning this time. Those parts of her brain devoted to intellect seemed intact, active and alert, the combo invading only those regions responsible for her most basic instincts and motor system. In which case ... in which case, she realised, smiling inwardly at the possibility, she might have greater control than she'd anticipated, even now, long after the SoundSleep had been filtered out of her blood stream. An interesting thought.

He was approaching. She heard the soft progress of his footfalls nearing the couch and the steady rhythm of his breathing as he bent over her. He remained motionless for a moment, then stepped back. Perhaps he was checking her reactions. The scent of him was muted, as though masked by something else: a faint odour of warm polyplastic – perhaps a body-form disguise – and the smell of a stationsuit impregnated with the sharper tang of fused metal.

He's a Techno, she guessed. It made sense: he'd the skill to open doors, an illicit extension of his professional expertise no doubt; a Techno who could move around from one job to the next; who could be on the *Ptolemy* and Shackleton, on the *Ivanov*, and who knew where else? Flight Maintenance perhaps? One of the short-term contract personnel on call to fill unanticipated gaps in the rosters? Someone who could be one identity on one trip, another on the next – and several in between when necessary? All the random pieces of the jigsaw that made up the man suddenly seemed to slip into place. The knowledge was almost as exhilarating as his presence.

She heard him place something on the table: a travelsack perhaps, or just an article of outer clothing. Her eyes still steadfastly refused to open and she was left with only theories and conjectures to play with. There were other sounds too, initially not difficult to identify. Almost certainly clothes were being removed: she could hear the rough sound of fastenings being undone and then long pauses in between. Then other, less easily identifiable sounds: something being peeled away, like a close-fitting second-skin, only much larger, and the exhalation of breath that went with it as though it had covered his face. Another pause, and then the rummaging around for something unidentifiable; the muffled sound of clothes being put on and fastenings being closed. There was a series of small grunts and then silence. His transformation was complete.

If she'd been able to open her eyes, she knew without any shadow of a doubt how he would appear to her – as she had first seen him: his lean sinewy frame in its black leisuresuit; his shoulder-length platinum hair falling in studied carelessness around his angular face; the thin lips with their cruel, twisted smile – and those eyes, devoid of colour, would be looking right back at her. This man would not be the man who'd stepped through the door a few moments earlier: that persona had been peeled away; disposed of until it was needed again; parcelled up out of sight.

He was approaching again. She waited with an even greater expectation, his closeness already lifting her heart-beat to a higher rhythm. His hand closed around her face, turning her head to one side, and she felt the brush of his hair on her cheek. The scent of him unhindered by his disguise left her weak and breathless.

He whispered in her ear. "Cassandra. In black and gold. Looking delicious. For me. I appreciate the thought." His hand moved slowly across her face and up into her hair, twisting it slowly around his fingers in a mixture of tantalising sensuality and potential violence. "Soon you can have what you want," he went on. "I know you want it. But first – listen and remember."

So, she thought, he knows I'm awake behind these shuttered lids; awake and able to think.

"I've brought the products," he whispered. "They're in a cover-slip on the side table. Take them with you to Lowell tomorrow. How you take them is up to you." He paused to kiss her neck with a mock gentleness. "On Lowell, you'll be given instructions on where to leave one of them. The other you'll take to Gio – when I say so." His tongue flicked lightly against her ear. "Don't worry, Cassandra, I'll be there in time for your next fix. Something for you to look forward to." And he kissed her neck again before loosening the clasps of the chiton at the shoulders and letting the fabric fall away to her waist. "Stand up," he said, lifting her to her feet and fondling her casually, his hands straying over her with calculated intent, lighting her desire for him. Did he know this? His touch was like fire and feathers so that she never knew which it would be from one moment to the next, her senses held in a permanent state of heightened expectation. His nails ran lightly across her with all the possibility of a more vicious progress later. She was aware, amidst the increasing vigour of his attentions, that he was somehow holding back. Why? He'd already aroused her and must have known it. She was ready for him, even if she couldn't move to draw him on.

He pulled away from her laughing, a sound that sent a chill of mingled horror and excitement up her spine. "I can do this later," he said brutally. "When you don't know what I'm doing. Now, I'd rather have you in action."

Still incapable of watching what he was doing, she heard him moving around the room and then return, taking her hand and exposing the veins on the inside of her wrist. She felt the slight dampness of the tape as it pressed against her skin.

She counted the seconds, and only reached three before she heard the humming in her brain and felt her eyelids flicker. She opened them, blinking for a moment against the unaccustomed light, even though the level was low, like an early dawn.

He was standing very close, looking exactly as she'd imagined he would. For all her preparedness, she couldn't help the sudden intake of breath at the sight of him: she'd forgotten just how potent his image was. A smile played around his half-open lips, and those eyes, partially hooded, expressed his full and unfettered anticipation of her.

"Now," he said quietly, "Let's start again." He removed the strip of tape from her wrist returning to a travelsack he'd left lying open on the side table.

She watched him prepare a fresh strip from two phials he'd removed from the sack: two drops of a colourless liquid from one, and three drops of a pale blue liquid from the other.

Theo's instructions filtered through her brain. "What are you giving me?" she asked, finding her voice at last, the words unusually slow in forming themselves.

He raised an eyebrow at such a question. "Does it matter?" he said.

She dared to move closer to him. "Themaldrahine?" she ventured, planting her feet squarely on the ground to maintain her balance. Sheer bravado. She knew its value. With her hands on her hips, she tossed her hair back from her shoulders and thrust her breasts forward, intent on distracting him.

It worked: his eyes fastened on her. "And something else," he said.

"A surger-fix?" she suggested, moving closer to him until she was barely a stride away.

He reached out and encompassed one of her breasts, manipulating its softness while his cold eyes regarded her with interest. "Of course." Her breast must have hardened at his touch because he smiled. "You're in a hurry, aren't you?" he said mockingly. "It's working better than I thought it would."

"Then why give me more?"

It must have been a challenge too far. His expression changed and he pushed her away roughly, almost causing her to lose her balance. "Because I want to," he said in a voice somewhere between a whisper and a snarl.

"To work me over with neuro-rods afterwards?" she said, surprised at her own temerity.

He laughed again. "That? That was just a warning," he said dismissively. "Or a promise. Whichever you prefer. Now – give me your hand."

"What is it?" she demanded a second time. "I want to know what makes me so hot for the man who killed my partner."

He yanked her forward, putting his face barely a handspan away from hers. "It's special," he said, his colourless eyes as hard as his grip. "Aphrochrome. Heard of it? No, of course you haven't. I told you. It's new. It's focussed. It's beautiful. And you'll take the VR version to Lowell because you want to save your little friend." Gifting her this knowledge seemed to give him enormous satisfaction. He fixed the tape to her wrist. "And you know what's the best part?" he went on, pressing the small transponder disc to her forehead, now clearly enjoying himself. "After tonight you'll be tuned into my pheromones – no one else's – until I lose interest." He fixed the transporter to her forehead and swung her away across the room so that she had to steady herself against the far wall.

Stay on your feet.

Satisfied she wasn't going anywhere, he turned his attention to doctoring a second strip with a few drops from the phial of pale blue liquid and fixing it to his own wrist.

He turned to face her, pressing the transceiver disc to his forehead, linking them together almost immediately, body and mind. The strains of distant music were already in her head, drawing closer with every heart-beat. Rainbow colours were beginning to flicker around the edges of the room. Images shimmered like a mid-summer heat filled with glorious iridescence. From where she was standing, she saw him beginning to listen to the music she was feeding him, his eyes seeing other images denied to her.

She started to experience the same effects as before – and yet not quite the same. Her body started to move and sway to the rhythms in her head as though it had a will of its own. She twisted and turned swishing the folds of the chiton around her hips. She dipped forward and then lifted herself up onto her toes, her arms raised, her breasts already burning to be touched, her whole core alight with the need to be filled. Yes, by him. But this time, her consciousness stood apart, as though watching the performance, not being a part of it, totally unconnected with the sensations running riot through her.

The SoundSleep, she thought. Was it possible it had unwittingly provided a blocking agent, immunising her against that first dose to safeguard her from all the others that might follow? The Aphrochrome was new. He hadn't known she'd taken SoundSleep. Perhaps he hadn't recognised her reactions had been different in some way from those he might have expected.

She swung round slowly pushing the half-discarded chiton down from her hips to escape its confines, stepping away from its descending raven-black folds with a sensuous, flowing motion. She gathered up her hair from behind her head and let it drift out of her grasp in slow, thick coils as she weaved and swayed before him, watching him undress. Give him what he wanted. Show him. Urge him on. He was already fully aroused, etched in a shifting kaleidoscope of colour. She twisted and turned again, cupping her breasts and offering them to him, seeing them encompassed by a blaze of orange and yellow flame that flickered from the tips of his fingers as he reached out. He held her tightly, moving against her, and then almost immediately into her. She consumed him, delighting in him, the pale bush at his groin mingling with her own dark hair in a fiery unison flecked with brilliant sparks of electric blue and green. The scent of him seemed everywhere. And all the time, the music swelled, soared and ran through every fibre of her body, overflowing into him. She arched backwards, letting him fill her, the ache she felt for him a deep purple gash in her soul.

For a few brief moments, she was lost in the ecstasy of their coupling like any surger-pop performance when alpha-wave stimulation overrode everything else. In the plateaux between, she was aware of an intense concentration, despite the incredible insistence of the music, the urgency of her physical needs, and the magical qualities of the flickering light that surrounded them both. Her eyes and hands coordinated in mapping him out. She knew every part of him so completely, she could have described him precisely down to the smallest detail, or picked him out from a dozen others blindfolded, simply by running her hands over his skin and the outline of the body beneath.

She discovered she could look into those awesome eyes, sometimes purple, sometimes deep crimson, sometimes frighteningly orange, and see the dilated pupils lost to everything except the sights, sounds and sensations heightened by the Aphrochrome.

Caught in the trap of compliance by the themaldrahine, she had no alternative but to go where the Aphrochrome took her.

But with her intellectual faculties intact, she quickly learned to pinpoint his erogenous zones with exquisite accuracy. Now, *he* was vulnerable. She could bring him to a swift conclusion whenever she wanted. She was in control – for as long as the Aphrochome and themaldrahine were in balance. It would not be long. This slim and wonderful advantage would be lost to her, she realised, as soon as the themaldrahine became dominant and induced unconsciousness. Until then she could afford to enjoy the luxury of using him to bring about her own satisfaction. A small revenge. For Karoli. For Lazar. For herself. It represented victory in the face of defeat; triumph in the face of degradation; mastery at the moment of enslavement. It gave her courage for whatever was to follow.

A crescendo was building again: the fifth, or was it the sixth? – she'd lost count. Once more their bodies fused in their combined heat and mingled juices, the rhythm intensifying. She wondered how many times the Aphrochrome would feed his lust, keeping him stiff and potent. How much was it taking out of his system? How much strain was it placing on his heart and lungs? He seemed insatiable.

He held her by the hips as she arched backwards again, his rainbow body streaming with sweat as he thrust into her with a savage intensity, his hair stranded and clinging to his face. She could laugh, and look into his unblinking eyes, now a deep impenetrable green, glowing like a cat's. With intense satisfaction, she realised if she were his, then he was indisputably hers. A bond: a terrifying bond.

She ran her fingers over him, revelling in the slipperiness of his breast and belly and her own ability to respond to him even then, listening to his breath rasping in time to the persistent beat as he pushed her downwards to the floor. Downwards and down. And then with the oncoming flood that gushed into her came the black wave that rose up and swept over her, taking her with it, rushing her away into a bottomless void. She heard herself cry out, not in pain or fear, but in anger, and then succumbed to the darkness.

THIRTY-EIGHT

She was awake. Cautiously, she opened her eyes and without moving, scanned her surroundings. From the walls, the sidelights still glowed on a low setting. The room had an empty feel to it. There was silence. He'd gone, leaving her naked spread-eagled on the floor: finished, like a discarded sacrifice.

Mild curiosity stirred. She had the sensation of disorientation, aware only of the slow, steady rhythms of breathing and heart-beat which somehow belonged to her, but not to her body. Her body seemed a distant entity, registering no particular sensation, and for a while she lay contemplating the strange non-existence of it, reluctant to move in case she triggered the bolt of intense pain she expected to tear through her. She drifted back into a half-sleep, memories of the man shifting and changing like a kaleidoscope, casting and recasting brilliant colours in her mind's eye.

She stirred again, this time aware of the sensuality still lingering within her. Her body was no longer asleep: it was murmuring softly to itself. There was no pain, just exquisite pleasure beginning to spiral upwards inside her. The scent of him was everywhere, filling her nostrils, the warm resin mingling with the thick aroma of his juices. With eyes still closed, she passed her hands over her breasts, her belly and thighs, remembering his hunger. Her hands echoed the urgency of his touch, the image of him as sharp as if he'd still been there. She heard herself crying out for him and her breath quicken as she abandoned herself to the urging of her fingers.

The swirling eddies of pleasure died away. At the edges of her consciousness, other sensations, only hinted at, hovered uneasily. She lay breathless and uncertain where the boundaries of reality and unreality merged. He was there, but not there. Unreality. Her hands were wet, covered in the warm slippery substance of him. Reality. She lay still, waiting for the dividing line to be drawn, her thoughts scattered; jumbled. A voice – her own – was trying to make itself heard. *Get up*, it said. *Get up. Slowly.* It was insistent.

She hesitated, still fearing the lightning bolt. But the voice was not persuaded.

Get up!

She clenched her teeth, preparing for the shock, and eased herself gently onto her elbows. But there was nothing. She stayed immobile for a moment or two, on the brink; waiting. But still nothing. Cautiously, she pulled herself up a little further, supporting her weight on her arms, and waited again. Still nothing. *Stand up,* the voice commanded. In slow motion, she obeyed, drawing up her legs and lifting herself onto her feet. Straightening and careful to keep her balance, unsure of what might happen next, she dared to turn her head slightly. Once again nothing happened. Growing bolder, she flexed her arms and legs and discovered the muscles moved easily and painlessly. Whatever else he had done to her, he hadn't used neuro-rods. A small triumph.

Tentatively, she made for the washroom and turned up the lighting, facing the full-length mirror prepared for the worst, half expecting to find he'd left her marked in some subtle way. The image that looked back at her was not a particularly pretty sight, but it wasn't what she'd feared. She was dishevelled. Her skin showed evidence of less that gentle handling: red marks were visible on her breasts and thighs, and with the lessening of the Aphrochrome's distortion of her senses, she was beginning to feel raw and over-used. Between her legs, his clinging wetness had gathered, curling the bush at her groin into sticky strands, and there was evidence of him smearing some of it across her face and into her hair where it had dried into spiky solid peaks that stood out above her forehead.

She turned slowly, twisting round to inspect first one side of her back and then the other. Here, there was nothing more than the raw friction marks on her shoulders and at the base of her spine where he had ground her hard against the floor. She studied herself with an air of detachment, wondering why he'd not abused her more thoroughly: he was certainly capable of it. Had he been too exhausted after she'd slipped into unconsciousness? Had the SoundSleep's intervention mistakenly led him to misjudge the ratio between the combo and the Aphrochrome? How much Aphrochrome had he given himself as a result? Questions she couldn't answer, but the prospect of him fixing himself with an overdose was deeply satisfying.

Her mouth was dry. She drank long and deep from the drinking fountain, ran the shower and stood beneath the stream of hot water feeling the cleansing needle-sharpness of it passing over her. She watched the mesh at her feet as it sluiced away the last traces of him, imagining him dissolving in his own juices and being sucked down into the bowels of *Ivanov's* recyclation unit, to be separated out into his component chemical parts and dispersed for use elsewhere. She watched for some time, revelling in the thought of it.

Dripping from head to toe, she finally activated the blowers and turned slowly in their balmy breezes, letting the softness of their caresses remind her again of the desire he could conjure up in her. But most of all, she could remember, with a satisfying clarity, her heightened control and the power this gave her over him.

She stepped from the shower unit, her hair still a little damp about her shoulders, and administered an aerosol salve to the pressure marks on her back as best as she could, watching in the mirror with a sense of satisfaction as the redness disappeared under the protein film. What would Theo make of her dispassionate reaction? – she wondered.

Theo!

Her daydreaming evaporated, bringing her up sharply. According to the clock, it was nearly 0650 hours. Theo would be wondering what had happened.

Snatching a kimono from the closet, she scrambled into it and called him up on the Link. In the few seconds before he replied, her eyes fell on the cover-slip with its deadly contents lying on the table where Angel had left it. A thrill of horror ran through her.

Theo sounded tense when he connected.

"It's Cassandra," she said casually in UniCom for the benefit of any Listeners. "Sorry to call so early. I've not finished packing. Can you help, or I'll be late?"

"I can come now if you like," he offered.

"I'll expect you then."

She felt exhilarated. The first move had been made: the rest would follow.

THIRTY-NINE

Theo had sat up all night, sick at heart and in a state of acute anxiety he feared was becoming a permanent part of his life. Half expecting Cassandra to call in the small hours, he'd felt it was essential to be ready to do whatever was required of him when the call came. He could sleep on the Minnow later, he'd told himself, although he wasn't sure he would.

As the hours drifted by, his anxiety had increased until it had almost reached breaking point. He'd even been tempted at the dread hour of 0400 to stand outside her door and demand entry, anything rather than live in a constant state of nervous expectation that exhausted his will-power and left him drained. And when she'd finally called, he'd found himself slumped on a lounger, fast asleep and thick-headed, panic ousting drowsiness in the blink of an eye.

He'd braced himself for what he might find when she opened the door, and found his expectations overturned almost at once. She embraced him, strangely unruffled and dignified, wearing her kingfisher blue kimono and looking magnificent. Her hair smelt sweet and newly washed, and there was an aura about her – an almost tangible sense of triumph: she glowed, her eyes shining with an unnatural brilliance – like a fever.

He returned her embrace, holding her gently as he might a fragile doll, bewildered by her apparent composure. He surveyed the room over her shoulder, seeking traces of violent activity, but there was none. Poseidon stood guard in his accustomed place, and for a moment Theo doubted whether Angel had ever been in the room at all.

She must have read his thoughts. "He came," she said simply, leading him to sit with her on the couch. "Don't look so worried, Theo, I'm fine. Honestly."

Angel wasn't usually so merciful, he thought. "Was it themaldrahine?" he asked, because this was uppermost in his mind.

She nodded. "And a new surger-fix – Aphrochrome."

It meant nothing too him.

She was caught up in the excitement of what she was telling him; about what she'd discovered that explained everything about Angel, but he wasn't listening, his limited supply of alter-combo troubling him more. "How much themaldrahine did he give you?"

She sat back, looking surprised for a moment, then laughed, a brittle laugh he found disturbing. "Theo," she said, heightened colour still suffusing her cheeks, "- we weren't having a scientific discussion."

He looked away, embarrassed by his thoughtlessness.

She touched his face, an incredible sadness in her eyes where fire had blazed only a few short moments before. "I told you – I'm fine. Please believe me."

He wished he could. "I've brought the alter-combo," he said, offering it to her, " – if you want to take some now."

She studied the contents of the phial in his hand. "There isn't much left, is there?"

"Not much," he admitted.

"Then I'll only take it when I need to – when I need total control."

Her tone had altered perceptibly: there was a definite edge to it that hinted at something dangerous.

"In four days we'll be on Lowell," she was saying. "Angel won't touch me again before our first performance, I'm sure of that. So, I think I've got ten clear days."

"To do what?" he said, hearing the anxiety in his voice as he said it.

"I've decided, Theo, so don't argue with me – I'm going to get Lazar to Gio before our first performance." She must have seen the look of horror on his face. Before he could interrupt she continued, breathless in her enthusiasm. "I know what I'm doing, Theo," she insisted. "But I need to act while time's on my side."

She was running ahead of him much too fast. "Cassandra, this is nonsense! – it's all guesswork!"

Her exhilaration turned to anger. "It's all I have to go on!"

"What happens when Angel finds out what you're doing?"

She laughed softly, a touch of menace in the sound of it. "Theo, don't you understand? Once Lazar is safe, things will be different."

"You can't make any difference – not with a man like Angel."

"With the alter-combo, I believe I can. And once *I* have control, I'll make sure of him – once and for all."

He was panicking. "You're just putting yourself in danger – either from Angel – or one of his back-ups. Let me call in Oliphant – now – before things get out of hand! I won't let you sacrifice yourself! And if it comes down to saving Lazar or saving you, it's you every time, I'm sorry."

She got to her feet, blazing. "And just how do you intend to do that?" she challenged him. "On an open Link? With all those Listeners out there? Just tell me – how? Don't you think I want to call in Oliphant? – because I do! I want to tell him I can prove I wasn't involved in Karoli's death – that I can guess how Angel works the system." She was breathless in her eagerness.

Theo could feel despair beginning to swallow him up. His head was spinning and there was a thick fog lodged where rational thoughts should be. He needed time to think more clearly; to find a way of alerting Oliphant to the danger she was in – and if possible, try to keep Lazar out of the picture. But at that moment, he could come up with nothing. Soon they'd be transhipping from

Ivanov to Lowell, swinging away from Earth – and from Oliphant, and any help he might be able to give. And meanwhile Cassandra would still be bound into the compliance Angel had placed on her, with only the slim hope that the alter-combo might guarantee some protection when it mattered most.

She was smiling at him, sure of herself, over-confident and determined to forge her own path. He knew nothing would stop her. But for all that, he had to find some way to keep her safe. Wasn't that what Karoli would have expected of him? Wasn't that what Karoli had died for?

Somehow he had to find a way.

FORTY

Spring was in the air Oliphant noticed as he strode across the quadrangle, the pink gravel still wet from an overnight squall scrunching beneath his feet. There was a hint of warmth in the Hebridean sun.

The familiar smell of newly polished flooring greeted him as the outer doors sighed open. He could feel himself relaxing almost immediately.

MacFadden was waiting for him in the reception area, looking pleased to see him. "Had a good break, Sir?" he asked, his approach lacking the stiff formality of a few months earlier.

"It had its moments," Oliphant conceded, not wanting to expand on an emotionally draining visit to Vienna which had marred the middle of his brief vacation. He'd made the trip out of a sense of duty. Now he felt thoroughly unsettled, old before his time, and in need of some solid work to get his teeth into.

It had all been that wretched woman Deneuve's fault. Always deciding what other people should do with their lives. Always interfering. Perhaps that's how she came to be a Station Commander. Anyway, she'd seen fit to get in touch with Lorraine after Oliphant's brief stop-over at Shackleton. Lorraine had hesitated to re-establish contact after so many years' silence, but Deneuve was, if nothing else, persistent.

Lorraine's message had arrived the first morning of Oliphant's leave. Their daughter, Vicky, now twenty-two, was taking out her first partnership contract in a week's time with a young man by the name of Feodor Bukhov, the twenty-six year old nephew of her mother's long-term partner Gregor. No gifts required she was at pains to tell him. Would James like to attend the ceremony and family celebrations afterwards? *James* – Lorraine still called him James, not Leo – and never Leonid: she said it made him sound too intractable – which in fact he was.

Oliphant's first instinct was to say 'no', but when it came to putting together a satisfactory reply to that effect it became altogether too difficult. The litter of half-finished notes which had cluttered his memo pad ranged from the brusque to the banal. So in the end it had been easier to accept the invitation – even with his serious misgivings. After all, he kept telling himself, it wasn't Vicky's fault her parents hadn't been able to make a go of it. And he was still her father. Nothing could untie that bond, however much he might prefer it not to exist.

So he'd gone to Vienna and suffered three days' personal torment.

It came as a shock to discover Lorraine had hardly altered one jot in all the passing years, except for the way she now wore her hair, a softer style to show off its silver highlights. Perhaps she was a little rounder here and there, but the old vitality and determination were still very much in evidence. So was the clear skin and bright-eyed enthusiasm that had first drawn him to her way back in '34.

Meeting up again had only been the start of what turned out to be an ever-increasing desire to leave as soon as possible. He'd discovered to his chagrin he actually liked Gregor: he was a vigorous individual with an open disposition and ready sense of humour. So it became only too obvious as to why this man had become a very satisfactory replacement to himself: the contrast in their personalities couldn't have been more marked, a contrast that had struck Oliphant with the force of a stun gun.

Then there had been the children – children no longer. Alex, eighteen, already as tall as himself and very much the young man conscious of his grown-up status and independence. He'd been welcoming, deferential almost, as though dealing with the formal visit from a much-respected high-ranking elder statesman, but noticeably wary. They'd met as strangers. For Oliphant, it was difficult to dislodge the image of him as the small struggling toddler he'd last seen, topped by a carrot-coloured mop of unruly hair. Now the hair had darkened down to almost the exact shade of his own, neatly trimmed and immaculately groomed. But the shape of his face was his mother's with her generous mouth, wide-set eyes and high cheekbones. There was none of his father's thick-set frame, with the exception of the broad hands, one of which was extended to shake his own when he was given access to the spacious Bukhov penthouse apartment in Zone Three.

And Vicky – a replica of her mother. She'd almost reduced him to tears by embracing him unselfconsciously, and introducing him with evident pride to her partner-to-be. For a few moments, Oliphant had experienced the odd sensation of arriving home a little later than expected having unexpectedly slipped into a time warp. He belonged, and yet didn't belong, a feeling intensified by the assembled company of more than a-hundred-and-fifty guests, the network of friends and acquaintances built up over the many years Lorraine and he had gone their separate ways. Many belonged to the mighty Bukhovsky drinks empire. He could pick them out from their similar facial features and easy laughter. Wealth seemed almost commonplace. The atmosphere was thick with it: the comfortable wealth of those who could afford not to be showy. They had the status to go with it – and they knew it. Oliphant was the stranger at the feast – a man of authority, equally high status, but out of place. Of everyone gathered in that apartment, mingling freely with one another, only Lorraine remembered him with any clarity, and even this, he decided, must have been dimmed by the passage of time.

His sense of discomfiture had been capped by Feodor: handsome, sleek, respectful but self-assured, and doing what was expected of him. Feodor was determined to make Oliphant feel welcome, introducing him to those he considered important enough to meet the father of his intended, and evidently seeking recognition that he'd be a suitable partner. His intentions had been well-meant, but by then Oliphant had wanted nothing more than to be quietly left to himself; to observe at a distance; to take part only on the periphery.

The contract had been signed and witnessed and the celebrations had continued. "I wish you both every happiness and success," he'd said as he took his leave, seeking the refuge of solitude elsewhere.

Vicky had hugged him and ruffled his beard. "It's been lovely to see you," she'd said. "Thank you for coming. Do try to keep in touch if you can." And the wistful look in her eyes had told him she meant it.

"Yes, please do," Feodor had added earnestly.

Lorraine and Gregor had said the same, and Oliphant had mumbled something to the effect he would try, knowing in his heart of hearts it would take something of a superhuman effort to repeat the experience. He'd fled Vienna and made straight for his original destination, Montevideo, where he spent the remainder of his vacation with an old Academy friend, trying hard to blot out memories which insisted on reasserting themselves at moments when he least wanted them.

Back in his office, his eyes were gladdened by the sight of familiar surroundings: the strident Gordenochek collages; the solid, comfortable feel of his desk and chair; and the fitful spring sunlight creeping in through the window. This was home: not the small apartment he rented in the township three kilometres to the south where he lodged when he was off-duty – and sometimes took the occasional casual partner; not the larger summer villa he rented on the Pacific Coast in California, where he spent his long-term vacations; not the countless stop-over places where he'd laid his head for one or two nights travelling from here to there on ConCorp Security business. Not Vienna. Here. On the wind-swept landing port of Benbecula. This was home.

MacFadden had followed him in with an air of enthusiasm that for an uncomfortable moment reminded Oliphant of Feodor.

"Down to business, MacFadden. What have you got for me?"

MacFadden settled into his favoured spot on the opposite side of the desk and took the liberty of repositioning Oliphant's monitor so they could both read it simultaneously, a liberty no other cadet would have dared to contemplate, but which Oliphant was content to allow in MacFadden's case. His JSO brought up the relevant logs. "Phoenix reported in from Lowell on arrival this morning, Sir. All The Choralians transhipped from *Ivanov* three days ago. No glitches."

Oliphant smoothed down his beard, Vicky's attentions still fresh in his thoughts, even when he didn't want them. "Nothing more?"

MacFadden was looking slightly perplexed. "No. Just the two reports – one recording the transhipment from *Ivanov*, the other reporting in from Lowell. Pretty basic stuff."

'Minimalist' was the word that sprang to Oliphant's mind.

"There should have been something more by now, Sir, shouldn't there?" MacFadden was asking.

"I'd have to agree with you. I'd not expected much action at Shackleton after my visit – but I was pretty sure something would come out of the woodwork on *Ivanov*."

"Do we have a problem, Sir?"

Oliphant didn't want to admit it, but it was looking increasingly likely. "Things aren't stacking up, MacFadden. Phoenix is supposed to be an ace operative. Someone who has the knack of sniffing out the little things – the little out-of-the-ordinary bits and pieces that make up a jigsaw – but it's not coming through. Lattimer will be checking this stuff and beginning to think I've laid out a scary scenario on light-weight evidence. He'll not be a happy man. He's put his name to Operation Misfit so he'll be scalp-hunting if we can't give him something soon."

"Then, what's gone wrong, Sir?"

Oliphant threw up his hands in exasperation, abandoning his desk for the view from his window. He let the sunlight stream in on him for a few moments, enjoying the sensation. Spring mornings shouldn't be marred by the sense of failure, he thought: it was almost sacrilege, but failure was staring right at him in his reflected image in the pane. He turned back to MacFadden. "There could be several reasons – and frankly I don't like any of them."

"Maybe, there just isn't anything to report," MacFadden suggested, trying to sound positive. "Or maybe he doesn't want to jump the gun until he's got something more solid to give us."

"At this stage I think we have to consider other scenarios."

"Such as, Sir?"

Oliphant returned to his desk, working through the possibilities. "He could suspect he's being monitored and he's keeping a low profile until the heat's off. Or – and this is where I'll start to lose a lot of sleep if we don't get some answers soon – his cover's been blown – and he's been persuaded to work for the opposition."

MacFadden's mouth gaped.

"Don't look so surprised, MacFadden. It's happened before. What worries me more is it could be something else – we could be faced with the possibility it isn't even Phoenix who's talking to us any more. He may have been silenced – or side-lined. Either way, we need to work out what we're dealing with – and we need to do it fast. The Choralians are getting further out of reach by the minute."

"What do we need to look for, Sir?"

"Anything else that might give us a lead. Has there been any increased global trafficking activity while I've been away?"

"No. Unusually quiet, if anything, Sir. Most of the Listeners are getting pretty bored. One of them even sent a scrambled communication she'd picked up on the Seasian network just to prove she was still alive. She only got part of it – a general call-out asking for sightings of a patient from a private clinic – somewhere in the Peloponnese. Nothing for ConCorp Security to get excited about, she said. Just something with a bit of curiosity value."

Oliphant snorted into his beard, his mind already discarding the information.

"A rum sort of message though," MacFadden commented casually.

"Why?"

"There was no name – just a description. Sounded like someone in need of a lot of treatment. Bit of a Freak actually."

Oliphant went back to re-reading Phoenix's last two-line report. "Not many of those around these days," he said, not entirely concentrating on what MacFadden was saying. "Anything else interesting?"

"Oh, just one thing that might be – a personal and private communication from SSO Srunam on *Ivanov*. It wasn't marked High Priority or Immediate Action, and came over the open Link, so I stored it along with the rest of the non-urgent memoranda and reports that came in."

Oliphant knew Srunam from way back. They'd been at the Academy together and kept in touch intermittently over the intervening years. But his tendency to indulge in gossip had always irritated Oliphant: it had all the hallmarks of a man with too much time on his hands and too many backwoods postings. But curiosity stirred. He brought up Srunam's message, half his mind still tuned into the prospect of it being little more than tittle-tattle about so-and-so and you-know-who.

A couple of paragraphs down, he realised he was reading

something entirely different, and promptly went back to the beginning, a bolt of adrenalin sharpening his wits.

MacFadden must have noticed a change in his expression. "Anything I should have actioned, Sir?" he asked anxiously.

Oliphant slewed the monitor round for him to read.

MacFadden read quickly. When he'd finished, he looked up, puzzled.

The message contained a first paragraph which was nothing more than introductory chit-chat. The second began casually enough, then seemed to have increasingly greater significance.

Incidentally, Leonid, it begun, I didn't know you were such a great fan of The Choralians! Can't blame you mind. That Cass Diamond really is something. I've never seen one of her surger-pop performances, but they say she knows how to give everyone a good time! Their new guy Jay Raymer isn't too bad either. They've really put some life back into this dead and alive hole. A real treat. We're all looking forward to their return visit. Booked my place for all their shows already.

Anyway – SO Jennard asked me to pass on a message. She was on duty when The Choralians transhipped over to Lowell. Theo Xenon – you know, part of the backing group, nice looking guy – asked if she knew whether you were coming up to the Mars Stations to see one of their shows. He said you'd promised you would, and they'd expected to hear from you while they were on Ivanov. Said they'd really be glad to see you. Well, naturally she said she didn't know what your plans were, but she'd make sure the message got passed on down the line. Said this Xenon was really pressing her about contacting you – so that's what I'm doing right now. Hope you've got a good excuse to go swanning off to the Quartet.

The rest of the communication was what Oliphant categorised as Srunam's usual 'burbling irrelevancies'.

MacFadden looked uncomfortable at being made a party to the information in the document. "I didn't know you were such a Choralians' fan, Sir," he said, smiling awkwardly.

Oliphant ruffled his beard re-reading the second paragraph with increasing apprehension. "I'm not," he said brusquely, determined to dispel any such notion.

"Did you say you wanted to see one of their shows?"

"No – and I didn't give Xenon any reason to suppose I would, or that I intended contacting them while they were on *Ivanov*. In fact," he added, wondering why he was suddenly feeling very hot under the collar, "I've not had any direct contact with any of them since last September. Under the circumstances, it was imperative I didn't." He pulled himself out of his seat again and returned to his earlier station by the window. He needed time to think. "MacFadden," he said after mentally deliberating with his reflected image for a few minutes, "I want you to get over to Communications. Start by running through the transmission surveillance records for *Ivanov* during the time The Choralians were on-station. Check out both sources and recipients. I want anything that's been transmitted to or from everyone in The Choralians' entourage – everyone. Recording crew, Technos – the lot. And anything else that might look a bit out of the ordinary. I'll join you after I've run through the rest of my inbox. This won't be something we'll be able to do in a day."

MacFadden got to his feet quickly. "Right, Sir."

With MacFadden gone, Oliphant continued to stare out of the window, sifting through his memories of that strange time at Shackleton Moonbase six months before. Theo Xenon. Theomenides Xenonopoulos. The name conjured up the image of the man; the man who wanted to protect Cassandra Diamantides from Oliphant's heavy-handed approach; the man who'd brought Umo Manaus to him voluntarily. And now this same man casually asking a question of a low-grade Security Officer in a by-the-by manner – a question that made no sense whatsoever.

What was it that made Xenon say he'd expected to hear from Oliphant while The Choralians were on *Ivanov*? Why did he say

The Choralians would be 'really glad to see him'? There was no obvious reason that made any sense – except, perhaps Xenon was sending a coded message in the safest way he knew how: a casual, off-the-cuff enquiry through the open Link, totally innocuous to any unofficial Listener or Watcher, but which would set alarm bells ringing in the mind of its recipient. Which meant Xenon must have had very good reason to believe an unofficial Listener was monitoring communications into and out of *Ivanov*, and more importantly, that this Listener was in some way dangerous – directly or indirectly. What did Xenon suspect? What was he really telling him? Was it Xenon who'd rumbled Phoenix?

They would be really glad to see you. The words jangled in his head. Was this a cry for help? It was beginning to look like it. Had Angel reappeared? This thought worried him most of all.

The sun had been swallowed up by a bank of angry grey Atlantic cumulus.

Oliphant returned to his desk and skimmed through the list of outstanding documents still waiting to be read. There was nothing that couldn't wait until later. He closed down the monitor and his Link leaving a message for any incoming callers to the effect he would be contactable in Communications in an emergency. With a sense of urgency, he took himself off in that direction with considerable haste.

FORTY-ONE

The afternoon slipped into the onset of early evening, triggering the automatic lighting in the manned areas of the Transmission Surveillance Section.

Oliphant had split the workload with MacFadden looking for general patterns of activity associated with Links allocated to Choralian personnel. "Let's start with the obvious," he'd said.

To begin with, progress had been deceptively easy. With the exception of the Link to R-27, where Maybourne and Banks were quartered, no one else seemed to have felt the need to have more than occasional contact with anyone Earthside – or anywhere else for that matter. On the face of it, the sweep of the entire *Ivanov* facility looked just as mundane and unexceptional, which Oliphant found dispiriting: he'd hoped at the very least to find a whiff of something looking not quite right. A second run-through to satisfy himself they'd not missed anything, only confirmed that it appeared they hadn't.

When the automatic lighting kicked in, the sudden increase in brightness stung his eyes and reminded him he'd been staring at the monitors longer than was recommended by Optical Regulations. He eased back his chair from the console and stood up, flexing his shoulder muscles to rid them of the accumulated tension around the base of his neck. His whole body felt stiff and leaden from prolonged inactivity.

In the adjacent booth, MacFadden was still pouring over the data, his expression one of deep concentration.

Oliphant leaned over him. "How's it going?" he asked.

MacFadden looked up, blinking hard. "Almost finished, Sir," he said, working his fingers into the corners of his eyes to readjust his vision. "I'm just waiting for authorisation to access the last five days before The Choralians transhipped to Lowell."

"Good. We'll need the whole picture."

"Anything else I can do?"

"No, that's fine. I've ordered details of times, duration and energy profiles of Phoenix's reports. They may give us a clue about what's been going on."

"Do you think we might be able to pin down which outlet he was using, Sir?"

"Possibly – but I'm not counting on it. I don't want to close down any possibility at the moment. I'm just banking on comparing total communication time on *Ivanov's* energy banks with total time officially logged that might throw some light on what we're dealing with."

MacFadden looked puzzled. "But they're bound to be different, aren't they, Sir? – if Phoenix is using illicit Link time?"

"Yes – but by how much?"

MacFadden's frown deepened. "By the amount of time Phoenix illicitly hacked into the Link," he said slowly and deliberately, as though he thought this was so obvious it shouldn't be necessary to explain it to a senior officer – unless there was a catch in the question.

"What if the disparity is greater than we expected?"

MacFadden looked troubled. "Other illicit usage?" he suggested.

"It's only a hunch, but I'm beginning to suspect there has to be. And if there is, then either Phoenix is relaying non-logged messages to unspecified destinations – or – someone else is."

MacFadden gave a low whistle. "How will we know the difference?" he asked.

"I've asked Communications R & D if they have any new gizmos coming on-stream that might be useful."

"Bit of a long-shot, isn't it, Sir?"

"It's the only one we've got, and I'm grasping at straws right now. But at least I can show Lattimer I'm not just scratching my head sitting around doing nothing if he starts pushing for action." He scanned the data MacFadden had left up on the monitor. "See this?" he said, pointing to a flat line on the graph. "It looks like zero usage, wouldn't you say?"

MacFadden nodded.

"Nothing very unusual in that. *Ivanov* isn't exactly a hive of activity, is it? There's a load of down-time all over this graph." And he pointed randomly at several of the flat lines showing no open communications on the Link. "This is what makes *Ivanov* different, MacFadden. There are no long-winded research reports being filed – or transcast conferences between boffins you'd see on BioTech mega-station logs. All you get on *Ivanov* are transmissions from incoming or outgoing Minnows, the occasional freighter, and the chit-chat between Spaceworkers on-station with their folks back home. That's about it. Down-time all over the place."

MacFadden swivelled in his seat to look at him. "But is it?" he asked, catching Oliphant's drift.

"That's what we don't know. Are there invisible messages in some of these gaps? Or – is someone riding on the back of an open Link?"

"Okay," MacFadden argued, "Suppose there is. Couldn't it just be a rogue Techno piggy-backing the Link to bag a free call back home? Nothing to do with Phoenix or The Choralians?"

Oliphant jabbed a warning finger in MacFadden's direction. "If it is, MacFadden, I'll have them anyway," he said brusquely. "That's theft in anyone's book."

MacFadden nodded, turning back quickly to face the monitor with exaggerated concentration as a rush of colour emerged suddenly from under his collar.

Reminding himself not to stay bent over for so long in future,

Oliphant went back to his own booth and retrieved the data-slice from the output tray recording energy consumption levels. "Re-route the logged transmission data through to my office, MacFadden," he called back over his shoulder, "Then take a break. I'll see you in half-an-hour."

"Right, Sir."

"And grab yourself something to eat on the way up," he added. "It could be a long night."

Several brisk circuits of the quadrangle and a hasty snack later, Oliphant was back in his office contemplating the data he'd transferred from the slice into the 3D graphics facility in his VR suite. He'd toned down the colour palette for the sake of his jaded vision, the intense scarlet tracks of peaks and troughs overwhelmingly eye-watering. The resultant dull red was preferable.

MacFadden joined him not long after. "The logged transmission data you wanted should be waiting for you, Sir. I gave Communications your access code."

"Do you know how to overlay it onto existing data, MacFadden?"

"Yes, Sir."

"Glad to hear it," he said, watching his JSO activate the comparison facility without a second thought, and feeling it might be time to consider taking early retirement after all.

A jagged neon lime-green trace sprang out of nowhere and flung itself against the data already displayed. MacFadden adjusted the axes scales to mesh together and toned down the colour to a tasteful pale lemon. Oliphant was grateful for his thoughtfulness.

It took only a cursory glance to see discrepancies between energy levels and the logged Link usage. The dull red line showed Link connectivity in several places where none was supposed to exist.

MacFadden whistled softly under his breath. "That's a lot of illicit communication time, Sir," he said.

Too much, Oliphant thought. "Can you give me how much?"

MacFadden ran a scan. "Two-hours-forty-six minutes and eleven seconds, Sir."

Oliphant could feel his stomach curling up into a knot. "Bring up the Listening Post data we have, will you? How long was Phoenix in contact with them during the time he was on *Ivanov*."

MacFadden complied. "Twenty-seven minutes and a couple of seconds, Sir," he said, staring glassy-eyed at the total that had come up in large white slabs at the front of the display.

"And now we don't even know if it *was* Phoenix talking to us."

"I could try doing a sweep to see if any of the outlets mesh in with the times Phoenix was reporting in, Sir," MacFadden suggested. "It could pin down whether he was using more than one outlet – "

"Or if he suddenly changed his routine, and then we have to ask the question – was it still Phoenix talking to us? Or even worse, was someone else piggy-backing on his transmissions at the time? Because if they were, MacFadden, Phoenix's communications will have been well and trully compromised. Let's get that possibility out of the way."

"Yes, Sir."

"Will it take long?"

MacFadden shook his head.

"Right, meanwhile I need more data," he said, quitting the VR suite and opening the internal Link at his desk. "We've only got part of the picture."

SO Gary Waterman answered his call. He was a rotund man in his early fifties who'd never wanted to be anything more than a squaddie, but whose integrity was cast iron. He also retained a gruffness that Oliphant appreciated.

"Sorry it's so late, Gary. I need you to chase up a couple of things for me."

"Anything to oblige you, Mister Oliphant."

"I'm checking on communications in and out of the *Ivanov* space station. I've already got details under Codes 457 and 779 for the period 29 January up to 21 March this year. Could you send me the equivalent security data for the six months leading up to 28 January and for the last three days since 21 March?"

"Is it priority?"

"Yes – absolutely."

"Any particular format?"

"Graphics. I can take a data-slice if that's quicker."

"No, I can route it direct to your facility if it helps."

"That would be useful."

"Logged in for action, Mister Oliphant. It should be with you shortly."

"Thanks."

MacFadden had clearly been listening. "What do you expect to find, Sir?"

"Something I'd not thought about, MacFadden – and should have. A long-term placement."

"A Sleeper?"

"Maybe more than one. Rotate the data one-eighty degrees, will you, and run a minute by minute visual breakdown for me."

The display turned as requested and began scanning. In some places the red line showed a series of separate spikes for periods when illicit transmissions were taking place.

MacFadden drew in a long breath and cleared his throat. "We're looking at more than one Whisperer, Sir. Different frequencies used by at least two different users simultaneously in down-time. Phoenix wasn't on his own up there."

It was what Oliphant had suspected, but it gave him no comfort that he'd been right. "You're sure?"

MacFadden nodded.

"Then maybe we're looking at the answer to some of the cases we've had to leave open."

"The accidental deaths on stations, Sir? Do you think a network might already be in place?"

"I don't think we can rule it out. But maybe – just maybe, it's only being strung together and not everyone's playing ball. Has the outlet sweep finished yet?"

"Yes, Sir."

"What have we got?"

"All the reports from Phoenix have the same transmission profile. They're all from outlet R-28."

Oliphant brought up the numerical list of *Ivanov's* outlets, identifying R-28 as a maintenance room. "There's only one official call registered to that outlet – 29 January. Duration – seven minutes."

"Does that tell us anything?"

"Only that it's an underused outlet, that's all. We need the rest of the data from Waterman."

Oliphant got up from behind his desk needing to stretch his legs again, and took up his favourite spot by the window. The earlier evening showers had moved on and he looked up into a clear night sky, searching for Mars without even knowing if it might be visible at that time of year.

Xenon's message resurfaced in his memory. Something was seriously wrong up there and he couldn't request operational action without knowing precisely what it was: Lattimer wouldn't stand for it. Going in too soon could jeopardise a successful operational outcome – going in too late could jeopardise lives. He could feel the familiar tightening in his chest – and knew precisely why – Cassandra Diamantides.

MacFadden had come out of the VR suite and was standing beside him looking up at the stars.

"Do you remember much about your space induction course, MacFadden?" Oliphant asked him casually.

MacFadden shook his head. "Not much, Sir. At the time I didn't think I'd have any use for it – being just a JCO."

Oliphant gave him a playful punch on the shoulder. "Well, it just goes to show how wrong you can be," he said, and watched MacFadden's face go pale at the prospect.

FORTY-TWO

Communications Officer Takemura in her crimson and grey uniform smiled briefly, acknowledging Oliphant's suggestion she should take the visitor's chair MacFadden had made available for her. Her self-contained air gave no indication she found the presence of a very senior Security Officer in the least bit intimidating, her expression radiating an exquisitely controlled composure.

Oliphant took to her immediately, not least because she was also remarkably pretty, and he needed something to distract him. "Thank you for coming back on duty at such a late hour," he said politely.

"I am on standby until twenty-four-hundred hours," she replied, inclining her head slightly as she spoke, her UniCom overlaid with a soft breathiness. He was completely charmed by it.

"Chief Communications Officer Dacosta said he thought you were the best person to translate all this latest wizardry into layman's terms," he went on. "Did he mention what we were looking for?"

She nodded, smiling again, this time including MacFadden, and lingering a little longer on him than was usual for a simple acknowledgement of his presence. Oliphant noticed the distinctive flush beginning to spread up the young man's neck. Well, he thought, it wasn't all that surprising: the two were very much of a similar age, and Oliphant couldn't delude himself that a young woman wouldn't prefer the attentions of a younger, more attractive man. Hadn't he discovered several grey hairs beginning to show in his beard only that morning? He dismissed the memory with some haste and returned to matters in hand.

"What can you tell us about the material we sent down to Communications earlier this evening?" he asked.

CO Takemura opened her case and removed from it a security data-slice folder. "This is the full documentation," she said, placing it on the desk in front of Oliphant. "It is very technical. I have a resumé with me," she added, producing a second data-slice. "But it was thought it would be easier if I explained what we have been able to discover so far – especially as you had emphasised it was important there should be as little delay as possible." A careful smile was aimed in Oliphant's direction.

"Thank you," he said, feeling this acknowledgement was necessary.

"Firstly," she said, back in serious mode once more, "you must understand the Unlogged Communication Identification Recorder – the UCIR – is still undergoing a validation period and has not yet been incorporated into the Communications Security System. It has however been designed to meet the precise requirement you are looking for in this case – the unauthorised use of ConCorp Communications – particularly by Spaceworkers. Off-Earth communication can be expensive," she added with another lovely little smile, this time in MacFadden's direction, which seemed to reduce him to a blob of embarrassment.

"CCO Dacosta tells me it can combine search results, but has additional features."

She nodded. "That is correct. We are able to identify unlogged transmissions as incoming or outgoing and whether they are Earth- or space-based. We can also identify the type of transmission – visual, audio or both. What we cannot do at the moment is provide translations of coded or scrambled content. But," and here her smile was positively radiant, "We can tell you what frequencies have been used, and whether a scrambling interface or non-ConCorp system has been in operation during transmission."

Oliphant smoothed down his beard. He was less than pleased he'd known so little of what new surveillance techniques were in the pipe-line. "Why wasn't I kept informed of these developments?" he asked, although he knew perfectly well she was the wrong person to bring to account for this omission.

Her smile faded under the intensity of his gaze and she appraised him warily for a moment. "I do not know," she said after considering the matter carefully. "The UCRI was developed at the instigation of the Fraud Division. They've suspected widespread communication abuses by Spaceworkers for some time."

Oliphant drummed the desk top with his fingers. He should have been notified. He'd take up the matter with Lattimer at the appropriate moment.

An uncomfortable silence had descended. MacFadden was studying his hands in his lap and CO Takemura had lowered her gaze to somewhere between herself and Oliphant's desk.

"Go on," Oliphant commanded her. "What else have you got?"

Her eyes remained fixed on the middle distance as she resumed her report. "We ran through all the data you had already accessed, including the additional dates you requested to bring everything up-to-date from the beginning of January."

"And?"

She lifted her head to look him straight in the eyes. "We have identified a total of sixty-three unlogged communication-related incidents on the *Ivanov* during that period," she informed him, without giving any sign she'd noticed the shock that he was certain must have registered on his face. "Of all types," she added. "All using non-ConCorp systems. Both incoming and outgoing. Earth-based and inter-space connectivity."

"Coded? Scrambled?"

"Both. We are working on refinements to separate out

individual patterns that might lead us to the users." She leaned forward and activated the second data-slice. "This is the summary page set out visually for you. You will appreciate the information better using the 3D graphics facility later."

Oliphant scanned through it quickly. "Hells bells! Have Fraud Division seen this?"

"No, Sir. Not yet."

"Well, we must be thankful for small mercies. The last thing we need is the Fraud Division tramping around in the middle of a covert security operation." He activated his internal Link, barely able to contain his anger. Dacosta's granite-hewn features came up on screen. "CO Takemura is just taking us through her report," he said brusquely. "It's loaded. I need a stop marker on this data being made available to anyone else until I've discussed the contents with Regional Commander-in-Chief Lattimer. Any queries from the Fraud Division – refer them to me."

"Understood."

"Thank you." He disconnected the Link and caught MacFadden casting a sideways glance at Takemura who was offering a shy smile in response.

Oliphant wasn't in the mood to tolerate dalliance. "If you two want to make any mutual arrangements, would you kindly do so outside my office," he snapped, reducing the pair of them into awed immobility. "Now, can we proceed?" He glared back at the summary, trying to concentrate. There were star-markers against the known transmissions from Phoenix. Other graph lines of assorted colours littered the screen, occasionally weaving together in twos and threes. Two vertical white lines marked the arrival and departure of The Choralians on *Ivanov*. Takemura was right: there was one hell of a lot of unlogged activity, more than he'd ever imagined. But what was more alarming was the presence of a regular weekly audio-only transmission from *Ivanov* to a destination somewhere on Earth even before The Choralians had arrived. The pattern disappeared while they were on-station and had been re-established as soon as they'd transhipped.

Takemura must have read his thoughts. "There is certainly one Listener in place on *Ivanov* – possibly two," she said. "Before and after the period The Choralians were on-station, the transmissions are little more than log-ons, perhaps confirming the Listener is still in place. They all last between thirty to thirty-five seconds as you can see from their band-width."

"So what's this?" he asked, jabbing at a series of purple lines scattered across the graph.

"Indications of unauthorised random scanning."

Oliphant frowned at her. "And all this was going on before The Choralians came on-station?"

"Yes. You may also be interested in the results from the latest version of the Communications Interference Monitor," she added, moving effortlessly through a series of overlays and finally selecting the one she was looking for. To Oliphant it looked like a bunch of neural response records all squashed together.

MacFadden came round to Oliphant's side of the desk to get a better view of the monitor.

Oliphant's eyes were beginning to ache. "What exactly am I looking at?" he asked.

"The CIM identifies indirect communication interference with the existing communication system," Takemura explained." It shows distortion in energy levels."

"Which means what exactly?"

"Possible re-routing or recording of a transmission. As you can see, when your Agent makes his first report on 29 January, there is already an unauthorised scan taking place, probably a general scan picking up anything useful. What is noticeable is that part of this report has been identified as interesting by the Listener and subjected to re-routing or recording, possibly for later evaluation."

Oliphant was bemused. "But it doesn't trigger any immediate action."

Takemura agreed. "As you can see, there is no unlogged transmission of any kind until twenty-one-forty hours when contact is made with someone on Earth. The blip on the graph suggests a simple acknowledgement the message had been received."

"Anything we can take from the timing?" Oliphant asked.

"I think I might have the answer to that one, Sir," MacFadden offered. During that period – from here to here – The Choralians were on stage for the first night of their tour. I checked their schedule this morning. I thought it might be useful."

"Good thinking, MacFadden. Can you upload it onto the monitor?"

"Yes, Sir. Just give me a minute and I'll bring it up as an overlay."

A series of straight orange lines came up cutting across the activity graphs at intervals for the period The Choralians were on *Ivanov*.

Takemura leaned in slightly to get a closer look.

"What do you make of it?" Oliphant asked.

She paused, evaluating what she saw before expressing any opinion. "One of the Listeners becomes a Whisperer and chooses to communicate when The Choralians are performing."

"Always? Or only sometimes?"

Another pause before she spoke. "Always."

Oliphant stared at the screen trying to get a handle on the whole picture; trying to spot obvious patterns of usage; trying to put some shape – any shape – to the volume of unauthorised activity in front of him. It eluded him. He peered more closely at the screen. Something caught his eye.

Takemura had stepped back, keeping out of his way, and when Oliphant glanced in her direction, he could sense she was trying very hard not to look at MacFadden. "What's this here?"

he asked her, pointing to the almost imperceptible smudging of the graph lines which started on 3 March and continued up to the end of the data.

She appeared embarrassed by his question. "We are not sure at the moment," she confessed. "There may be a fault with the equipment."

"Could it be anything else?"

She was in no hurry to answer him. "It might indicate a second independent group capable of scanning unlogged communications," she said, noticeably very reluctant to admit to this possibility.

"What!"

"It is possible," she went on, braving what must have been his visible anger. "There are some small discrepancies in frequency patterns which might suggest an additional surveillance operation."

Oliphant threw up his hands in frustration. "Hells bells, can't you be more definite?"

"It could still be an equipment fault," she said defensively. "But if I could draw your attention to the communication at eighteen-fifty hours on 18 March." She leaned forward again to indicate the precise location on the graph. "This was a charged incoming call on visuals to an outlet you identified as one allocated to The Choralians – R-25."

"Do you know the source?"

"Yes. There was no attempt at concealment. A public communication access point in the reception area of the Lysander MediCentre in Sparta. The smudging on the graph could indicate this message was double-monitored. Length, two minutes fifty-four seconds. The first Listener almost certainly stores this. There is a distortion in the interference pattern while the data is being stored, then the resumption of the normal scanning pattern. There is no subsequent external transmission, only a coded audio internal call made from R-25 to an unidentified receiver. The call lasts only four seconds. It is apparently monitored and stored. Again, no transmission. Then here," she indicated the spot, "within five minutes there is a trace – no more than that – two seconds at the most – of an incoming call. It arrives at *Ivanov's* Communications Centre then – disappears."

"Shunted somewhere?"

"Most likely to a frozen outlet. The energy patterns show the communication lasted only five seconds after it was diverted."

"Could you identify the source this time?"

She shook her head. "It came from an unregistered Earth-based source. We are seeing an increasing number of these being used. Detection counter-measures are currently being developed to combat them. But," she added, looking pained at having to mention this, "these sources can be highly mobile and difficult to pin down."

Oliphant leaned back in his chair and faced her. "So what you're actually telling me CO Takemura, is that putting aside the fact that there appears to be two independent non-ConCorp surveillance units operating on *Ivanov*, that it's entirely possible for someone to hack into our communication system from anywhere? – even a washroom in a sports centre in Siberia, for instance?"

She was unfazed by his incredulity. She gave a small nod in acknowledgement. "That is why the Fraud Division is involved."

"Anything else you can tell me?"

His question was tinged with sarcasm, but she showed no inclination to rise to the bait. "Yes," she said solemnly. "Only thirty seconds after the Link was broken, you can see there is a scrambled incoming communication from the same unknown source to *Ivanov's* Communications Centre lasting twenty-six seconds."

"And it's possible all these communications are being intercepted by a second surveillance team?"

"Yes, although my colleague, Armand de Rupe, has suggested the first Listener could be a sub-system installed in the Communications Centre, re-routing data elsewhere – without a Communications Officer even being aware of it."

"And then – " Oliphant said, knowing his tone betrayed his exasperation, "just random events. No pattern."

"No pattern," she agreed. "But a lot of unlogged activity until 22 March."

"When The Choralians left *Ivanov*. Back to normal, you might say – if we can call it that."

Takemura gave him an apologetic half-smile.

Oliphant allowed himself a moment to contemplate the very unpalatable truth – that ConCorp Security systems were wide open to every kind of interception. "CO Takemura, can we take it that everything – and I mean everything – including any scrambled messages from Security sent to *Ivanov* – could be open to scanning, storage and re-routing elsewhere for evaluation or decoding by a person or persons unknown?"

"It is possible, Mister Oliphant," she conceded.

"Well thank you for your time, Miss Takemura. It's been highly illuminating. MacFadden, will you please show CO Takemura out. And," he added as an afterthought, "if you do decide to make any mutual arrangements, you'd be well advised to make them sooner rather than later. I'm asking for an open-ended extension of your secondment to me, and we'll be heading out to the Martian Quartet as soon as I get operational clearance from the Regional Commander-in-Chief."

With a small sense of satisfaction, Oliphant noted MacFadden had looked anxiously in Takemura's direction and she'd had the good sense to acknowledge his interest with a discreet nod.

FORTY-THREE

The *Tertia* left promptly for its rendezvous with Lowell, its payload and The Choralians' personal belongings and equipment all accounted for, just as Krusnik had assured him they would be. For that, Theo was grateful. The nerve-racking moments of their departure when Cassandra stepped through the Security Zone had nearly undone him completely. But he needn't have troubled himself: as it turned out, the Security Officers were far more interested in the possibility of contraband in their luggage, than on their persons, and she'd passed through the scanners undetected. But throughout their flight, Theo could feel himself gearing up to repeat the process all over again. Beside him, Umo was trying hard to control a different kind of panic, not daring to look out at the blackness beyond the windows of the flightcraft and retreating to their interior cabin for most of the voyage.

Lowell hoved into view and in slow motion turned and lined up ahead of the Minnow, the docking manoeuvre completed with deceptive ease. With their bulky outer travelsuits left on board for decontamination, they emerged from the outer airlock in their lightweight versions and down the glidetrack to the inner airlock and the Reception Area. On their arrival, they found Station Commander Maurice Hautfort waiting to greet them. Suspicious now of anything even slightly out of the ordinary, Theo wondered why.

Hautfort was a striking figure in his titanium-grey uniform with its red and gold epaulettes. A tall man of medium build, he sported a neatly trimmed black moustache and wore his hair combed back from his high forehead in a severe style. His smile seemed genuine enough, if somewhat thin-lipped, but his eyes were restless, skimming over the troupe as if he were searching for someone. His sweep ignored Lazar, possibly because at the time he had his head down studying the fastening on the choraladian case he was carrying, and as usual, his features were largely obscured by his cap. But with an almost unerring accuracy, Hautfort's gaze settled on Umo, and Theo experienced the sensation of ice-water running down his spine. Hautfort's smile had become expansive. No doubt he had at least one Choralians surger-pop vid in his personal library.

"We have so much room on Lowell," Hautfort was saying brightly, his voice as crisp in its UniCom pronunciation as the creases down the front of his stationsuit trousers. "I've arranged separate accommodation modules for everyone in the newly refurbished B radial." He smiled again, well-pleased at the extent of his thoughtfulness and efficiency. "I hope this is satisfactory." There was an audible murmur of approval from the Technos who were becoming increasingly edgy with one another after four days' confinement on the Minnow.

Theo, more concerned at getting Cassandra safely through the security scans, didn't immediately spot the implications of what had been offered.

Raymer was quicker off the mark. He stepped forward, shielding Lazar from any further interest by moving over to where Cassandra was standing next to Banks. "That's very kind of you, Commander, but I hope you don't mind if some of us share." His meaning appeared to be unambiguous, but Hautfort's eyes swept over the assembled group once more, searching out the lucky individual attached to this evidently attractive man. Cassandra, with her hair jammed under her cap, escaped his notice – but so did Lazar.

Theo came to his senses. "I'd like to second that, Commander," he chipped in. And just to emphasise the point, he put his arm around Umo's shoulders and held him close. "We're official," he added, in case Hautfort thought otherwise.

The Commander's enthusiasm deflated with the speed of a punctured balloon. "Ah – well, if you insist," he said sadly. "We get so few Entertainers here." And with that observation, he smiled wistfully in Umo's direction in a way which suggested he was still contemplating the pleasures he would have to forego. "Well, no matter," Hautfort continued. "Whatever you decide. When you've settled into your quarters, please let Administrator Rainford know which modules you've chosen – just for evacuation purposes of course – not that we expect any emergencies." He smiled again, disappointment still tugging at the corners of his mouth. "Oh – and while I remember – your Agent, Mister McMichael has already provided Mister Rainford with your rehearsal and performance schedule. Could you please confirm this is satisfactory? Mister Rainford likes to ensure all facilities will be available when you need them." The Technos agreed.

Theo glanced back over his shoulder. Cassandra shook her head slightly. So neither of them had any idea why McMichael should provide their schedule in advance. He'd not taken the trouble to notify the Commanders at Shackleton or the *Ivanov*. So why now?

"Right then," Hautfort was saying, making a show of continued cheerfulness, "If you will all step this way, I'll hand you over to Security and then you can make yourselves at home. Do please join me this evening in the Visitors' Suite at nineteen-hundred hours. I'd like to take the opportunity to tell you about the special event I've arranged for you tomorrow. A rare treat before you have to concentrate on rehearsals et cetera." And with that he gave the Security Officers waiting patiently behind him a polite nod and took his leave.

To Theo's travel-weary eyes, the Security Zone seemed more

brightly lit than usual. Whether he was imagining this or not, he couldn't honestly say, but he knew he was sweating profusely, a situation he would have happily put down to the excessive heat of the place, except he knew it was fear: pure and simple.

Just wanting to get the whole dreadful business over and done with as soon as possible, he purposely placed himself at the head of the queue to go through the scanning process with Umo close on his heels. Krodalt and Farrance followed, eager to get the first pick of their respective quarters. Raymer had manoeuvred himself back to standing next to Lazar which made them next in line.

From inside the Zone, Theo watched, wondering if Lazar would come under closer scrutiny than he had on *Ivanov*, but neither of the Officers on duty showed the remotest interest in him. His ID tag was accepted with only the most cursory inspection, and it was easy to see why: Lazar's slight, shambling figure was dominated by Raymer standing behind him. So much taller, Raymer had removed his cap and allowed his hair to cascade onto his shoulders. The heavy scent he wore wafted ahead of him courtesy of the ventilation units. The finishing touch was his choice of turquoise and gold pendant earrings that couldn't fail to be noticed. They must have been painful to wear under the close confines of a travelsuit hood, but he'd clearly foreseen the need to distract curious eyes. So, there he was: intoxicating; bareheaded; laughing and joking with Ballinger behind him; his animation the focal point for everyone. It was a masterly show of bravado; of intentional attention-seeking carefully manipulated to appear perfectly natural. It left Theo breathless in its audacity.

Banks, always close to Cassandra, was next. With his usual eager smile and willingness to please, he deferred to let her through. Theo thought he might die of fright on the spot. Totally self-possessed however, Cassandra appeared unshaken. She looked the Officer coming forward to meet her squarely in the eyes. He was a solid, serious-looking man and he'd placed himself squarely in front of her. She moved unhurriedly towards him with an easy swing of her hips, and perhaps because she saw the effect Raymer had produced, she paused in her progress for a moment, and with great timing, removed her cap, shaking her hair free with a toss of her head as she stood before him. Another, almost imperceptible pause as she tilted her chin just a little and smiled up at him, her lips parting slightly as she offered him her security tag. He smiled back, his unyielding features suddenly softening, visibly entranced by her attention as he automatically took the tag from her and extended his hand, offering to lead her towards the scanners.

Theo watched with a dreadful fascination, his vision blurring at the edges. With masterly self-control, Cassandra graciously accepted the proffered hand, and adjusting the waistband of her travelsuit just enough to draw the man's eyes downward, allowed herself to be walked through the scanners. They registered nothing, not the slightest hint that Angel's deadly package was concealed in the lining of her suit.

She was through with a small nod of appreciation to the Officer for his trouble. He was suitably grateful. Theo just wanted somewhere to sit.

Then, almost before he knew it, they were all through, heading down the corridor for their quarters in the Accommodation Unit, and the immediate danger was over. Surrounded by conversation and oblivious of everything and everyone except Cassandra walking ahead of him, he wiped away the beads of sweat running down the side of his face and waited for his heart-rate to reach a level somewhere approaching normal, and wondered how many more heart-stopping moments like this he'd be able to endure. Beside him, Umo was oblivious of the drama, eager to find an enclosed space with wallpanes to help him forget he was in space.

Within a few minutes, all the Technos had dispersed. Theo could hear Raymer and Lazar talking in hushed tones behind him.

Then a door opening. "You okay, Cassie?" Theo heard Raymer calling out to her.

"I'm fine, Jay," she said with a brief wave of her hand without turning to acknowledge him. "See you at nineteen-hundred in the Visitors' Suite."

"Okay then." The sound of a door closing.

Theo and Umo had reached the next available empty suite. Ahead of them, Cassandra had stopped and was scanning the corridor. There was just the three of them. It was eerily quiet. No musitone.

"We're in here," Theo said, opening the door to let Umo through.

"I'm the next one down," she said, giving the corridor a second sweep.

"Are you okay?" Theo asked, because he wasn't sure she was.

"Yes, I'm fine, Theo. Don't worry."

But he did, because her face bore traces of the stress she was feeling.

Once inside their quarters, he dumped his travelsack onto the floor and threw himself onto the bed. He was adrift, and a persistent throbbing was setting up behind his temples, his mind on a permanent loop full of questions without answers. Would they find sanctuary for Lazar in time? Was Angel already on-station – watching them? Had he been one of the Minnow Flight Attendants? When nothing was certain, anything was possible. And then there was Oliphant. Had he received the message he'd been sent? Had he understood it? Would he sense the urgency Theo hoped he'd conveyed? But most of all he prayed he would come – if only out of curiosity.

He closed his eyes against the pain in his head, his mind only dimly aware of Umo's child-like voice drifting through the open washroom door lifting sweetly above the downpour of the shower. He was singing like a bird in a cage, untroubled by the complexities of life outside.

FORTY-FOUR

Station Commander Hautfort, accompanied by two Administrators in their light-grey stationsuits, had chosen to remain standing while the rest of the assembled company made themselves comfortable on the various loungers on offer in the Visitors' Suite. Most would have preferred to stay in their quarters to unwind from the journey. Oblivious of the lack of enthusiasm in the room, he made his announcement. "I thought that tomorrow, as you all have a few days' grace before the first performance, you might appreciate a day trip down to one of the most successful Martian field stations." And without the slightest awareness of the frisson of horror that ran through the majority of his listeners, he continued, "Of course, everything has been arranged to ensure your comfort during the tour. It will take approximately ten hours, and I will personally accompany you to answer any questions you may have about the terraforming project. If you could assemble at the Departure Zone at zero-eight-thirty hours, a scheduled ferry is due to leave for the surface at zero-nine-hundred." The two Administrators confirmed these arrangements with solemn nods at the appropriate moments in his speech. "I trust you will find the tour stimulating and rewarding, and a rare opportunity to see what has been achieved here over the last fifty years." His beneficent smile encompassed them all. Mission accomplished, he wished them a restful night and left, taking the Administrators with him.

The silence that followed his departure was brief, then almost everyone was on their feet talking at once.

Theo interrupted the general hubbub, aware the majority of voices were expressing reluctance. Only Argosti and Chimala showed any sign of enthusiasm for the idea. "I know – it's not what most of you wanted to hear, but we'll have to go."

"Why?" Ballinger cut in, red-faced with anger.

"Publicity," Theo explained, trying to sound reasonable. "It won't look good if we snub the generosity of a Station Commander."

"Bollocks!" Krodalt said, not caring who heard him.

"We can't afford to ignore what's being offered," Theo insisted. "This is a big thing he's organised for us. Don't you see?"

No one seemed to care. There was uproar again.

"We've just had four soddin' days stuck in that bloody Minnow, Xenon," Ballinger railed. "Why the hell should we want to have another day in spacesuits, just to keep that puffed up little dictator happy?"

Farrance chimed in. "We need to get the sound and lighting rigs set up before we start heading off for any jolly jaunts," he said, seeking support from Ortona.

Ortona nodded. "Hear, hear," he said.

Raymer positioned himself in front of Theo and eyeballed him. "I agree with Ballinger," he said. "We shouldn't feel pressured into doing something we don't want to do."

Cassandra had said nothing. She was the only one apart from Lazar who'd remained seated.

Theo's instinct was to go with whatever she decided. He knew her worries lay elsewhere. "Cassandra?" he asked, turning to seek her opinion. "What do you think?"

She stirred herself. "The Choralians will have to go," she said with an air of finality. "We don't have the same excuse as some of the Technos, Jay. We only need a quick run-through once the place is set up."

"Well I certainly want to go," Argosti said, visibly affronted by any suggestion to the contrary. "And so does Chimala." Chimala nodded.

Umo, perhaps feeling left out of the consultation process, chose that moment to turn difficult. "Theo," he said, his voice reduced to a whisper. "Too much space. Let me stay here."

Cassandra smiled at him. "There's nothing to worry about, Umo," she said gently. "No walkabouts. Come with us. Lazar needs your company."

A master stroke. Caught between his personal anxiety and the need to please Cassandra, Umo, casting a quick glance in Lazar's direction, and being rewarded with an uncomprehending smile in return, acquiesced reluctantly.

Raymer was furious. "We should stay," he insisted, his comment directed at Cassandra with noticeable animosity. She glared back at him.

Theo could almost feel the friction in the air: it was electric. If they had shouted it from the rooftops it could not have been clearer that a gulf had opened up between them. Whatever attraction had once held Cassandra and Raymer together, Angel had destroyed it. It was a visible fracture for all to see, and the possible effect on their future performances together was a catastrophe he didn't want to contemplate.

Cassandra continued to give Raymer a long, hard stare. Everyone looked uncomfortable. With great dignity, she pulled herself out of the lounger and indicated the discussion between them was closed. He turned, visibly angry, dragging Lazar out of his lounger and making for the door. Taking the hint, the rest of the company dispersed talking quietly amongst themselves. Theo, with Umo in tow, waited for the last of them to leave.

"Theo," she said quietly. "A word."

Umo, sensing he was no longer required, nodded and scurried after the rest. The door to the Visitors' Suite closed behind him.

Cassandra sat down again on the lounger and rested her head against the cushion.

"Please don't ask me why Jason is so angry," she said. "I've no idea."

"Is it something to do with Lazar?"

She shrugged, dismissing Raymer's show of petulance out of hand.

"Do you think he suspects Hautfort of something? Do you?"

"It's a possibility. I've got to consider he might be part of Angel's network. Or maybe I'm expected to meet up with someone down at the field station. Or someone might leave instructions in my quarters while I'm out of the way." She laughed mirthlessly. "Too many possibilities, Theo. Not enough answers."

"So, will you take the Aphrochrome with you?"

"No. I can't hand over what I haven't got. And I haven't had specific instructions."

"What about Jason? Will he come tomorrow."

"He'll come. I'll make sure of it."

"And Lazar?"

"Of course. We need to keep him close."

"Safety in numbers?"

She nodded.

The following morning there were more of them waiting in the Departure Zone than Theo had expected. Whatever Cassandra had said to Raymer the night before, it had worked. But he was in a foul mood, a reluctant tourist with Lazar in tow. Besides Umo, both Argosti and Chimala were present, along with Meriq and Banks. Maybourne had sent his apologies: Krodalt had insisted he needed him to help put up the lighting rig. Dunnock, Ballinger and the rest were notable by their absence.

Hautfort appeared punctually, the picture of a small boy on an academy outing, glowing with undisguised anticipation. "I don't often get the opportunity to go down myself," he explained to no one in particular.

"I'm sorry the others felt unable to take up your kind offer," Theo said, hoping he'd adopted the right tone to match the occasion. "Concerns over getting the rigs in place," he explained.

Hautfort was unfazed. "Quite understandable. Quite understandable," he said. "A smaller group will make the experience so much better," he added with a brittle smile. "Now, if you'll follow me, we'll get you fitted out with appropriate suits for the journey."

In the hub, their party was kept away from the twenty or so Technos and cross-discipline scientists going back to the surface after their regulation leave off-planet. There was some jostling to catch sight of the unexpected passengers on the ferry.

Hautfort looked pained. "You will have plenty of opportunity to see more of The Choralians in the next few weeks," he said, shooing them away. "Today is just for you," he added, turning back to his party and ushering them into a separate cabin marked 'VIPs Only'.

No one contradicted him.

The cabin interior was spacious, and could have accommodated the entire Choralian entourage and still had seats to spare. They spread out at Hautfort's suggestion while he selected one of the seats in the front row. Argosti and Chimala were chattering like finches one row back, filled with an almost childish delight at the prospect of something very much out of the ordinary. Raymer and Lazar sat two rows back, Lazar's gaze fixed on what was outside. Raymer was uncommunicative. Meriq and Banks had chosen the next row on the opposite side of the aisle to where Cassandra was sitting alone. Banks's body language betrayed his enthusiasm to engage her in conversation, while she smiled politely but made it clear she didn't want to talk. Tucked away at the back of the party, with Umo sitting next to him on an inside seat, his eyes clenched shut, Theo could watch everyone. But most of all he watched Hautfort.

The ferry slid gracefully out of the hub and turned on its course towards Mars gathering speed. They would cover the distance between Lowell and the planet's surface in under three hours. Within an hour, the curve of the horizon beyond the windows was visibly smeared with swirls of thin cloud gathering in thicker masses over higher ground, condensing into a thick fog. The northern ice-cap was already lost to view. Below them, the land mass, pitted with craters and scars of an earlier age, was still largely a dirty russet hue, dappled with occasional splashes of dark green where primitive forests were beginning to make their mark. These sprawled away from valley floors with their roots in water-ice trapped below the surface, and spread themselves out into more open areas seeking what limited sunlight they could find. Of the much hoped-for rivers and lakes, there was no sign, the atmosphere still too thin to allow water to flow continually without freezing. To Theo's eyes, it seemed a half-formed world still undecided about its future.

As the surface came closer, the sun lost its stark brilliance. Its light became diffused shimmering behind a thin purple haze, its disc noticeably smaller and less significant than when seen from Earth. Below them, Theo could make out well-used geotracker highways threading between smaller areas of vegetation. Closer still as the sun became obscured behind the jagged horizon, pin-pricks of light gleamed out from the shadowed sides of craters where field station biospheres with their seedling nurseries were located. Directly below, the Mars Alpha Landing Port at the southern end of the Aries Vallis came into view. A series of red and green lights in arrow formation surrounded the rectangular landing zone picked out by intensely white lasers – to penetrate dust storms – Hautfort informed them, pleased there was no imminent threat of any such hazard to make the landing difficult or to spoil their day.

Hautfort was an enthusiastic tour guide, eager to share his

knowledge and point out what he thought might be of interest. "Ah," he said, somewhat apologetically, "I should explain. Once we land, you will only be able to see the immediate area around the landing zone. The surrounding terrain is somewhat hilly and blocks the views – and the accommodation and administration facilities are underground, as you would expect."

"Like Shackleton Moonbase," Argosti chipped in, wanting to show he knew a thing or two and appreciated Hautfort's efforts.

Hautfort beamed. "Yes, I'm afraid until we can generate effective force fields, cosmic rays and solar flares remain something of a problem." His lightness of tone made these extreme radiation hazards sound as if they were minor inconveniences. "The main ferry terminal hangars are what you will see to your right. And on the left you will notice the manufacturing facilities housing the oxygen generating plant. You can see it quite clearly from this elevation," he added, moving across to a window and pointing out the vast industrial complex below.

From his window seat, Theo had no difficulty making it out. Illuminated from all sides by huge arc lights and surrounded by a necklace of immense gas collection tanks with interconnecting pipes, it reminded him of a badly designed octopus.

"The carbon monoxide by-product is utilised as one of the essential components of synthetic fuel, of course," Hautfort informed them, in case anyone was interested.

The retro-drive kicked in cutting short any further explanations as the whine of the engines reached ear-splitting level for a few moments and the speed of approach dropped back to a sedate pace. The lights of the landing port expanded and grew, appearing to reach upwards to embrace them and draw them down into the Martian dawn. There was a slight shudder as the ferry settled on its stabilisers, followed by the sudden diminution of noise to a faint humming which marked the shutdown of the thrusters. All vibration stopped. There was a brief pause, then a string of three geotrackers, headlights blazing, advanced across the landing grid from one of the hangars.

Hautfort stood up and coughed politely to make his announcement. "Please put on your travel helmets for transfer and attach the emergency airpacks. The Stewards will check they are properly in position before you leave. Purely a precaution, you understand," he added.

Umo turned white and Theo was preoccupied for a while reassuring him all was well while helping him secure his airpack. Looking up, he noticed Hautfort was fussing around Cassandra. She was watching the man with guarded eyes behind the toughened polyplastic visor, but he appeared not to notice.

By then the first geotracker had reached the ferry and was linking up to the airlock. The Spaceworkers from the other cabin were held back while Hautfort shepherded his group forward to leave first. As they lined up to transfer across, Cassandra hung back, waiting for Theo. She turned slightly as he stopped briefly by her and their eyes met. There was a slight shake of her head, indicating nothing had passed between Hautfort and herself – or at least nothing she was aware of.

They filed out of the airlock and took their places in the functional seating of the geotracker, Hautfort checking and rechecking everything like a distracted mother hen uncertain if all her brood were present. "We have to go through Security to be received," he told them. "Just a formality, you understand. Then after a little refreshment, a tourer will take us cross-country to the Ephesus Field Station. There we will be able to take a more leisurely look at the newly forested area by geotracker and go on to the Sagan Crater developments." He smiled at them briefly through his visor and sat down next to the driver. No one spoke. There was a sigh from the airlock and the tracker disconnected, trundling away towards the open door of the hangar. As they approached, the sun lifted above the distant eastern horizon, purpling the sky.

Umo sat rigidly next to Theo for the two minutes it took for the tracker to cross the grid to the main complex. At the disembarkation point, they followed Hautfort through the air lock and down the ramp to the security doors which opened automatically as they approached. Beyond, in the brightly lit Security Zone, three black-suited Security Officers were waiting for them. For no reason he could explain to himself, Theo felt his pulse rate surge. Why? – he asked himself. Hadn't Cassandra gone through every security check so far without a problem? Why should this be any different? The answer was simple – there was just something about the stance of these three men that frightened him.

Hautfort was unclipping his airpack and removing his helmet, indicating that everyone should do the same. The three black-suited figures stood immobile, watching, their eyes surveying the newcomers from under the peaks of their black caps with detached interest. With a heart-stopping jolt, Theo realised it wasn't Cassandra he should be worrying about – it was Lazar. Lazar minus his helmet and without his usual cap was bare-headed and very noticeable.

Hautfort greeted the Security Officers with a tight smile and introduced his guests. "Mister Carrigan, The Choralians," he said, addressing the Senior Officer and adding an unnecessary flourish for effect.

SSO Carrigan was a man of considerable presence with unsmiling, flint-hard features. He nodded in response to the introduction and let the Commander pass unhindered through the scanning process and into the Reception Area, signalling the rest of the party forwards.

It was all Theo could do to muster enough self-control not to fall into a dead faint. Cassandra, walking ahead of him, was unaware of Lazar's vulnerability, and within a few strides she was through the scanners and beyond the unblinking watchfulness of the Officers.

Raymer was next; then Lazar.

As Lazar's stumbling, awkward figure moved into view, Theo's worst fears were realised. Carrigan let Raymer pass without hindrance, then stepping forward placed himself squarely in front of Lazar. Raymer, sensing something had happened, swung round, alarm clearly registering on his face. Carrigan, looking over his shoulder as if he'd half expected some reaction, froze him into immobility, then turned back to regard Lazar with undisguised interest. Under such intense scrutiny, Lazar seemed to shrink into himself: his head bent; his shoulders hunched, and his arms folded tightly across his chest in an agony of defensiveness.

"ID," Carrigan demanded.

"Lazar Excell," Raymer blurted out from behind the man's vast bulk.

"His tag," Carrigan growled back without turning.

Raymer could do nothing. Lazar was beginning to sway and mumble incomprehensibly.

There was a terrible moment when all eyes were fixed on Lazar. Then something incredible happened: Umo suddenly pushed himself forward and stood beside him, two small figures overtopped by a colossus.

For what seemed like a small eternity, no one moved or said anything. Then Umo began opening the top pocket of Lazar's travelsuit hunting around for his identity tag. Still no one spoke: no one moved. Cassandra, standing next to Raymer in the Reception Area had turned to stone. Umo found what he was looking for and handed over the tag to Carrigan. "Here," he said, his voice stronger than Theo had ever heard it before under such intimidating circumstances.

The SSO took the tag without comment, his face expressionless as he surveyed Umo with an unblinking stare, no doubt already evaluating the reason for the unnatural pitch of his voice. He turned back to Lazar and put a hand under his chin, lifting his face upwards, ostensibly to check the hologram against its owner. A flicker of surprise crossed his face: either he recognised him, or he was genuinely caught off-guard by the strange features brought into sharper focus.

At that moment, Hautfort reappeared from beyond the Reception Area, no doubt concerned at what might be holding up his carefully organised schedule. Theo had never imagined he'd be so pleased to see him. "Is there a problem, Mister Carrigan?" Hautfort asked crisply, his small eyes skimming over the assembled company trying to identify the cause of concern. They alighted once again on Umo standing immediately in front of the Officer. "Leave the boy alone," he said with undisguised irritation, completely misinterpreting the situation and waving an impatient hand in Carrigan's direction. "Great heavens, man, these are The Choralians, not some bit-piece troupe of Hurdy-Gurdies. They've been scanned more times than you've got fingers and toes. Please don't delay us any longer than necessary. The tourer's waiting and no one's had anything to eat yet."

Carrigan raised an eyebrow at Hautfort's outburst, but let it pass. He put the ID tag through the scanner. It went through unhindered and he handed it back to Lazar without comment. From apparent paralysis, Raymer suddenly sprang into life, almost pushing past Carrigan to take hold of Lazar's sleeve, leading him through the remaining scanners at great speed. The rest of the group followed in their wake.

"We shouldn't have come," Theo heard Raymer tell Cassandra through gritted teeth as they settled into the tourer's luxury seating an hour later. He was steaming. "Carrigan knows something. He'll probably have a reception committee waiting for us when we get back."

"Relax, Jay," she said, her eyes critical of his lack of control. "I can feel your tension from here."

"Do you think I'm joking?"

"No – but what's done is done." And she leaned back to smile at Theo and Umo sitting behind her. It was a smile which registered a thousand contradictions.

Raymer continued to fume.

Umo had been silent since the incident with Carrigan. Theo was proud of him. "What you did before – for Laz – that was very brave of you, Umo," he said softly.

Umo's expression held traces of memories from other times and other places. "He was afraid," he said simply. "I know how that feels." And he turned his gaze back to the solid partition separating the pilot from the tourist cabin and kept it fixed there, blotting out the alien landscape from both his sight and his mind.

Theo reached out and held his hand. It was cold and clammy.

The hum of the turbo fans lifted slightly and the tourer eased itself out of the hangar following the red marker lights that led away from the landing port into the open ground beyond the perimeter. The hum increased, the tourer beginning to gather momentum. The marker lights came and went with increasing rapidity until they registered as a continuous red line that stopped suddenly, and they were away into a strange landscape of rust-coloured dust and rocks and towering crater rims bathed in the continual half-light of the Martian day. The distant sun hung in a butterscotch sky. On and on, until Theo found he could no longer sustain the visual agility to register individual landmarks in the landscape as they skimmed past. He leaned back and rested his head against the restraint, letting his eyes close. There were three more hours of this journey before they reached the Ephesus Field Station with its plantations of genetically modified conifers valiantly doing their best to absorb the carbon dioxide; then the geotracker expedition further north to the Sagan Crater and the first fledgling ice-ponds seeded with primitive algae to generate oxygen, according to Hautfort. And then what? The return journey back to Mars Alpha and the possibility of Carrigan and a reception committee waiting for Lazar.

Still holding Umo's hand, he let his mind slip into neutral. Inside his head, he allowed a well-loved melody to loop endlessly around on itself, keeping him company.

FORTY-FIVE

Around the time The Choralians were touring the Ephesus Field Station, Oliphant was rousing MacFadden over the Link. It was 0530 hours and Lattimer had finally been given the green light for operational and flight clearance at Baikonur on their arrival.

The young man appeared tousled and sleepy to acknowledge him.

An hour later, on the wind-swept Benbecula landing port in a brisk north-easter, MacFadden was his more usual well-groomed self, trying to put a brave face on the suddenness of their departure. Out on the grid, a supersonic lightweight passenger Dart, used exclusively by ConCorp Security personnel, was already splitting the gale with the high-pitched whine of its engines.

Oliphant handed his travelsack to the Steward and led the way up the steps into the warm interior of the passenger cabin. They were the only passengers. A priority flight. Immediate. He made himself comfortable in the nearest seat and fastened the restraints. "Made the most of it last night, did you?" he asked MacFadden as the lad wrestled with the fastenings in the seat opposite him, all fingers and thumbs in his haste to comply with the Steward's instructions. The external door closed with a thump and the engines lifted to screaming pitch.

MacFadden looked up, a warm flush spreading across his fair complexion that had nothing to do with the temperature in the cabin. He mumbled something inaudible and looked away at the fast-receding landscape beneath them.

Oliphant felt a twinge of guilt: he hadn't meant to embarrass the lad so obviously – although a senior officer had done exactly the same thing to him as a novice cadet. He remembered his own discomfort at the time, smoothed down his beard and realised he was jealous: jealous of MacFadden's youth, not specifically because he'd spent the night with CO Takemura – lovely though she was – but because he, Oliphant, had simply not had the energy, nor the will, to seek out a casual partner for himself. He'd been too distracted by anxiety and it had drained him. Every minute waiting for the operation to receive the go-ahead had seemed like an hour and he'd paced his office like a caged tiger desperate for release.

In the small hours of the morning, Regional C-in-C Lattimer had gone into conference with the Emergency Strategies Group to consider Oliphant's request for an urgent operation to be put in place with the resources he'd asked for. He'd kept it simple, asking only for MacFadden to accompany him on the grounds he was *au fait* with the case, with the additional request that a policy of direct operational silence be maintained until their arrival on Lowell. Any essential communication with him, he suggested, should be routed indirectly through InfoNet taking into account the usual channels were potentially compromised. He would, he insisted, enlist any additional manpower needed from available personnel on site and asked only for authorisation to mobilise whatever back-up was needed. He suggested the investigation into the communication abuses on *Ivanov* could wait.

When the authorisation finally came through just before 0500 hours, he'd fallen into an exhausted sleep at his desk. He awoke with a start to the beeping of the Link, his neck stiff, and his head still full of strange and unsettling dreams. Pulling himself together, he'd acknowledged the message and headed for the washroom before waking MacFadden. It had seemed a small thing to give the lad half-an-hour more under the circumstances.

For himself, under the needle-sharp spray of the shower,

Oliphant had come to terms with his agitation: it wasn't Phoenix he was worried about, although his possible defection or worse represented an operational disaster; it wasn't the knowledge that ConCorp Security was potentially under constant outside surveillance. What continued to worry him to the core was the message from Xenon and what might lie behind it.

His distraction had only served to remind him for the umpteenth time that Xenon was only part of his disquiet. Everything about the conversation between himself and Cassandra Diamantides on that fateful visit to Shackleton Moonbase had chased around his brain until his head ached: the strange attraction he'd felt for her from that very first moment; the scent of her; the way she moved; the touch of her hand against his; the look in her dark eyes, penetrating his inner thoughts. If there'd been any means known to humanity to propel him to Lowell within the space of a few seconds, he'd have used it. Sitting in the comfortable Dart recliner, the sense of powerlessness however, ate into his soul. Now more than ever, he felt certain Cass Diamond was in danger, and there was nothing he could do to accelerate his reaching her beyond what he'd already done. Time and space stood immovably in his way. He gazed out of the window, seeing nothing, locked into his private frustrations.

Two hours later, the Dart had travelled through four time zones and touched down at the Baikonur Cosmodrome in time for lunch.

In the Kazakhstan plain it was a bright, late spring day, with evidence of newly fallen snow on the steppes far to the east. There was deep chill in the air and Oliphant saw MacFadden pull up the hood of his travelsuit as the Dart's door slid open, letting in a blast of icy wind.

On the grid a hover-car bearing ConCorp Security markings was waiting for them. They were ushered inside and driven across the vast spaces of the landing port to the Space Embarkation

Zone. Captain Igor Orlev greeted them warmly and introduced the six other members of the crew and four stewards over a light lunch, every last one of them a seasoned Spacer for whom this latest assignment was just another job. Oliphant wished he could feel the same.

The *Oryx* was a sleek craft built for speed, a larger version of the Dart class designed to tranship up to thirty security personnel to any of the inner stations in an emergency. Her larger dimensions housed the Duval booster drive for enhanced acceleration, and tucked away behind the payload bays, five containment modules for detainees.

Lunch over, the Chief Steward showed them around the accommodation suite for their journey, ensuring they were securely fastened into the take-off and landing modules before leaving them with the standard safety procedures.

Oliphant's earlier disquiet resurfaced in the claustrophobic environment of the modules, heightened by the increased tension he always experienced before lift-off. "My maternal grandmother came from these parts," he said in a long-shot attempt to distract himself and thaw relations with MacFadden. There'd been little conversation between them since his earlier blunder. "Irgiz – over to the west," he added. "Haven't been back there for years."

MacFadden's only reaction was a slight nod. He was unnaturally still, his face chalk-white against the backcloth of the deep plum-coloured fabric of the seat, his freckles suddenly much more visible. His knuckles, Oliphant noticed, stood out starkly against the back of his hands that were holding the restraint buckle in a vice-like grip.

"Nervous?"

"Yes, Sir," MacFadden informed him, turning his head to address the triple thickness of the polyplastic laminate which in less than quarter-of-an-hour would separate them from the vacuum of space. He clearly had no wish to engage in conversation.

Taking the hint, Oliphant checked his watch. Roughly five minutes before lift-off. He eased himself back into the recliner letting the autocontours embrace him, and began the deep-breathing exercises he'd learned several years before to help him through those first ten minutes. He'd never totally conquered the fear – he knew he never would.

There was a shudder and a muffled roar as the engines built up their power. Strange, almost sensuous light vibrations ran through the entire fabric of the craft, tingling every fibre and nerve-ending in his body. Then with an elegant slowness, the ground appeared to sink away from them until around 500 metres a new sound began drumming in his ears and G-forces pushed him backwards into the seat. Outside, lakes were suddenly puddles; vast plains no more than patches of spare ground; towns and cities like micro-boards. He glanced briefly at MacFadden and saw the lad had his eyes tight shut. And then the secondary thrusters kicked in and with them the adrenalin-pumping, heart-pounding acceleration that signalled the sudden surge that would give them escape velocity. It had an orgasmic quality. Thrilling, all-consuming and exhausting. For a moment, Oliphant indulged his fantasy. He closed his eyes, listening to his heart thundering, imagining more than he would ever confess to. And all the time, her name was repeating itself over and over again. Cassandra. Cassandra. Cassandra.

He pulled himself together and opened his eyes. Earth was receding fast, the horizon curved and edged in the pale blue light that marked the outer limits of the fragile, life-sustaining atmosphere. Barely a minute later and Earth had become something else – the Blue Planet – set in unfathomable darkness pitted with an unimaginable number of stars. "Look," he shouted across to MacFadden. "You'll want to see this."

The lad unclenched his eyes, blinking for a moment against the brilliance of the blue and white jewel framed in the window. His lips parted slightly, but he said nothing, just stared. "It's beautiful," he said at last, his voice charged with emotion. "I never imagined I'd ever see it for myself."

They watched it recede rapidly to become little more than a marble, and then the roar subsided into a hum as the Duval thrusters took over and it vanished from sight as the *Oryx* turned, heading for Mars.

"We are now at maximum thrust," Captain Orlev's well-manicured UniCom informed them over the speakers. "You are now free to make yourselves comfortable in your accommodation suite. Please relax and enjoy the entertainment options on offer. The Chief Steward will attend you shortly with today's menus. Thank you."

Relieved to escape the restraints, Oliphant unclasped the buckle and let the straps retract into the squab.

"When are we due to reach Lowell?" MacFadden asked, still wrestling with the mechanism to release himself.

Oliphant got up and stretched. "In roughly six days," he said, heading for the more comfortable, open environment of the accommodation suite. "We're lucky, Earth and Mars are almost in opposition."

The wall-mounted screen that housed the communication and entertainment facilities suddenly blipped into life. Communication Officer Janaghar's hadsome features slowly coalesced into a sharper image. "There's a redirected restricted access call for you, Mister Oliphant," he said. "Do you have the necessary activation and decoder codes?"

"Yes, thank you. I'll take it now."

"Redirecting," Janaghar said and the screen went blank for a moment.

Oliphant input the codes and settled himself in a lounger. "Come and join me, MacFadden," he called back over his shoulder. "Might be something interesting if it's being re-routed."

The screen cleared and a bright green message informed them

'This message has been recorded and re-routed through InfoNet.'. The message dissolved and Constance Imogen, Senior Security Officer in charge of the Mars Quartet, dark-skinned and blue-eyed, sat facing him, although in reality, she'd simply been delivering her message to Central Communications. Someone there had put a marker on it and sent it chasing after him – Dacosta perhaps, or maybe CO Takemura.

"Senior Security Officer Tariq Carrigan has reported the following incident on Mars Alpha, twelve-fifteen hours standard time, 25 March 2257," she informed him. "SSO Carrigan was present at the arrival of The Choralian party of nine on a tour organised by Lowell Station Commander Maurice Hautfort, who was also in attendance. The tour comprised a visit to the Ephesus Field Station and an onward inspection of the Sagan Crater developments. One member, a Lazar Excell, appeared unwilling to talk directly to Security personnel. SSO Carrigan challenged this man who seemed unable to speak UniCom and was of a sickly appearance. There was also evidence of facial reconstruction and the suggestion that mental impairment might also be present. This individual's ID tag passed through scanning procedures with no adverse reading. SSO Carrigan has since completed a further scan of this man's security data and felt it necessary to raise a report. Since receiving this, I can confirm that Excell's biodata, although apparently genuine, shows possible less solid documentation on back referencing. This would seem to indicate a manufactured history. He may therefore be of interest to Security. Request guidance."

The image of Constance Imogen faded, the screen cleared and a further message in bright green appeared – 'Suggested covert surveillance but no overt action at this time." It was signed by Lattimer.

Oliphant dropped any pretence of remaining calm. "Hells bells! That's all we need," he said, tugging open his travelsuit collar which had suddenly become irritating tight. "A security alert in the middle of a covert operation!"

MacFadden was looking puzzled. "Who's this Lazar Excell?" he asked. "He wasn't on the original tour list."

"My thoughts exactly." Something was lurking at the back of his mind that was prompting him to pay attention. "Remind me, MacFadden – what was that scrambled communication you picked up on the Seasian network?"

"About the patient lifted from the private clinic in the Peloponnese?"

"That's the one. How did you describe him?"

"As someone needing a lot of treatment. Do you think this could be him? With the Choralians?"

Oliphant raked his hands through his hair. "I think we should consider it a possibility."

"Could *he* be Phoenix, Sir?"

"I don't know, MacFadden, but if he is, Lattimer's keeping his cards close to his chest. Maybe he's not so sure himself."

MacFadden was frowning. "But would you pick someone like that to be a Freelance, Sir?"

"No, but then I'm not Lattimer. Maybe Servione's come up with a real blinder. Picked an unlikely individual with specialist skills and a basic understanding of what's expected and let him loose. Right now, I'm not discounting anything. If Excell's acting nervous, maybe he's under pressure – or knows he's in danger."

"What can we do? We've nothing much to go on?"

"We know he's almost certainly travelling on a false ID, so let's start by getting the full picture to work from. Use your personal Link, MacFadden. Get all the info you can on that report from Seasia – description of patient – precise details of the clinic he's missing from. Anything. I'll go into the security files and see how far I can chase this Lazar Excell back through the system."

FORTY-SIX

"You look done in," Raymer said.

Cassandra would have given anything to let sleep take over, but there were urgent things to discuss. The ferry had returned them to Lowell shortly before 2300 hours and she'd existed in a state of heightened anxiety the whole day. It was now almost midnight.

"Where's Lazar?" she asked, dropping onto the nearest lounger and pushing her hair back from her face.

"In there," Raymer said, indicating the sleeping area.

"Asleep?"

Raymer helped himself to a multi-juice from the dispenser and brought one over for her. "No," he said, pausing before adding. "He's accessing Gio's databanks."

She ignored the incongruity of this statement. Instead, she swirled the tangy liquid around the beaker and gathered the courage to ask the question she hardly dared to ask. "What do you think happened today – down at Mars Alpha?"

He sat on the lounger opposite, leaning forward. "I don't know," he said, studying the floor in front of him. "I almost got the feeling Carrigan was waiting for us."

"Do you think he was watching out for Lazar? Or was I just imagining it?"

He shrugged. "I've no idea. Cass, I'm getting so jumpy, every puff of wind has me looking over my shoulder. Look – I'm sorry about – well, you know – losing it – yesterday. I've no idea how you're coping with all this."

"When you've no option, you learn fast."

"Is there still no message?"

"No. Nothing. It looks like Hautfort's trip to Ephesus was just that – a day out."

"So what about Carrigan?"

"Jay, it's just possible his interest was inevitable. Lazar's appearance – his behaviour – our behaviour – everything looked so – so suspicious."

Raymer downed his multi-juice in one and stuffed the empty beaker down the recyclation chute. "Then why was there no welcoming committee when we got back from Ephesus?" he wanted to know. "We got nodded through – no trouble at all. It doesn't add up."

"It doesn't to me either, but what can we do about it?"

"Have you said anything to Theo yet?"

His question almost caught her off-guard. "About the incident with Carrigan?" she asked, choosing the less troubling topic on her mind.

He nodded.

"No – not yet. There's been no opportunity." She sipped her drink, keeping her wits sharp, wondering what was coming next and deciding to take the initiative. "Perhaps," she volunteered cautiously, "nothing's happened because Carrigan has another paymaster besides ConCorp."

"The Clinic?"

"No – if he was in their pay, he'd have lifted Lazar straight off, no question, I'm sure."

"So what's left?"

"Maybe he's one of Angel's Watchers," she said casually. "Just checking we're all here. You – me – Lazar."

Raymer glanced up briefly. Just for a moment, Cassandra thought she could see a hint of panic.

From behind her, she could hear sounds of muffled activity

coming from the sleeping area. Finishing her drink, she abandoned the beaker on the side table and made for the door. She was curious to see if Lazar was as capable as Raymer had made him out to be.

In the sleeping area, the beds had been pushed aside, and Lazar was sitting cross-legged on the floor, his head encased in a lightweight VR helmet oblivious of his surroundings. In front of him was a supplementary transputer access board and a hand operated pathfinder. To one side was a mini-vid screen; on the other, several assorted pieces of equipment Cassandra couldn't identify. She turned back, closing the door behind her: it was difficult to believe what she'd seen.

Raymer had sat down. "He'll do it," he said. "Don't worry."

"I'll try not to," she said, her thoughts drifting. They'd lost a whole day to Hautfort's well-intentioned but misguided tour, and the first performance date was that much closer. Meanwhile, she was sitting in an accommodation suite on Lowell, while Lazar was hacking into the database of another Mars station in search of an isolation unit. It was too bizarre for words.

Another thought crossed her mind. "Jay," she said, adopting a mildly interested tone that was a long way from her sense of unease. "None of that stuff Lazar's using is standard issue, is it?"

Raymer was leaning forward again, arms buttressed against his knees. He shook his head. "No," he said glancing up at her briefly. "It's Guido's."

"Guido's? Quite a man, your Guido," she said, and wondered if he caught the rich sarcasm she'd added to her observation.

Behind her, came the sound of the door opening and she turned to see Lazar emerge helmetless with an unexpectedly animated expression on his usually dull features. "I got it," he announced triumphantly and beckoned them both to follow him.

Together they went through into what had now become a Techno workshop rather than any semblance of a sleeping area.

"Sit," Lazar said, indicating the bed nearest his work station. "I show you," and he pointed to the vid-screen with a delicate finger. Filling the screen was a chequerboard of squares, each containing what looked like vastly reduced floor plans. He picked out one of them. "Isolation Unit here," he said, smiling at both of them with a sense of achievement.

"Which is where precisely?" Raymer asked, screwing up his eyes in concentration.

"Next to MediCentre," Lazar said, bringing up an enlarged version, and then for good measure, said to Cassandra, "I take you there. Then you know the way when we go." And before she'd a chance to say anything, he'd pulled up a swivel stool from the side of the bed and indicated she should sit on it. "You put this on," he added, handing her the VR helmet and sensor gloves.

She looked down at the offending items and felt her insides turn to jelly: the VR helmet represented everything she'd most feared for years, the image of her demented mother flashing in front of her.

Lazar must have sensed her reluctance. "I help you," he said, suddenly serious again, as he pushed her hands into the gloves, and with a gentleness it was hard to imagine from such a damaged individual, he lowered the visor carefully over her face.

There was the sudden but very real sense of claustrophobia as he fixed it securely, before the sensors adjusted to the contours of her face and the imager aligned itself to match the symmetry of her vision, guaranteeing her the perfect illusion she was standing in a Reception Area beyond the Security Zone. It was a basic program: all that was needed for Emergency Units to evacuate personnel in a crisis. No frills attached.

"I set up tour now," Lazar informed her over the headphones. "You on Gio remember. I follow you on screen." And with that, she felt him place the pathfinder into the palm of her left hand. "You ready to go?"

"Yes," she said, turning her head slowly to take in the surroundings. It was the usual Reception Area found on every station, sparsely furnished with low tables and casual seating to the sides leaving an open area through the middle leading to the exit. The décor was the standard cream and brown, with stark black stencilled alphanumerics on the walls giving an instant location bearing in an otherwise anonymous layout. The scene was deceptively realistic – except there was no one else in the place, and the ubiquitous musi-tone was missing. It gave her the scary sensation of being stranded alone on an abandoned station.

"Exit ahead," came Lazar's instruction over the phones. "Go through. Turn left in corridor."

She obeyed hesitantly, showing her inexperience in the way it took her a little while to move the pathfinder smoothly without jerking or rushing, while trying to stop herself physically taking a step forward.

The door in front of her slid back into its casing as she approached. She went through into the curving corridor beyond and investigated it to get her bearings, turning her head slowly.

"Turn left," Lazar repeated. "Press button on pathfinder. It fixes new direction."

She did as she was told and progressed down the corridor with care, presuming Lazar was still following her on screen. Two elevator shafts appeared on her right. She paused. "Do I take these?" she asked.

"No," he said. "First radial elevators. Go to next pair. Not far."

She moved forward again, continuing round the corridor. The second pair of shafts came into sight. She stopped and turned to face them, remembering to fix the direction.

"Go in. Select Level 2."

The doors opened automatically as she approached to reveal the standard elevator interior. There was a control panel where she expected to find one. Gingerly, she extended her right hand

and pressed for Level 2 feeling the slight pressure against her finger tip, then turned and fixed her new direction. The doors closed but there was no sensation of movement. The doors opened again revealing the bold alphanumerics L-2 on the wall opposite. To the right and left were additional information boards. The MediCentre was listed to the right. She stepped out of the elevator and went through the motions of stopping and turning right, pausing for a moment to get her balance.

"Intervention Unit," Lazar informed her as she scrutinised the red door which was closest to her. "Not here. Three more doors – all brown. Next one red. Isolation Unit."

She was feeling more confident now and kept going, counting off the doors as she went and checking what was written in UniCom on the information boards next to them. The next door was marked 'Reception – Please Enter'; the next couple were security coded doors marked 'Private – Medical Staff Only'. She indulged herself by the simple expedient of accessing each in turn, something quite impossible under normal circumstances. "Just curious," she said, warding off any queries from Raymer.

The next door down was red as Lazar had predicted, and the words 'Isolation Unit – Unauthorised Entry Strictly Forbidden' were emblazoned in stark white lettering across the doors themselves. On either side were security coded access panels and directly above, a scanner unit providing 180° surveillance of the corridor as an added disincentive to anyone not authorised to access the area.

Cassandra moved forward through the doors. There was something deeply satisfying about breaking so many restrictions without any consequences. Immediately inside was a changing area leading to the Decontamination Zone. Access and exit routes were separated by polyplastic dividing walls and automatic doors. To her right were banks of lockers. Intrigued, she opened the one nearest to her, turning the non-existent key with ease. On the inside of the door hung a sterile oversuit, the sort she'd had to wear to go into the mortuary at Shackleton when SSO Davron had taken her to identify Karoli's body. She shut the door quickly and must have confused the pathfinder, inadvertently finding herself inside the Decontamination Zone. It was a long rectangular shape with six cubicles on either side, each sealed off from the central area by airlock-style doors. Inside each cubicle was a treatment couch, basic life-saving equipment she recognised and a separate sealed section for Medics and Technos dealing with whatever problem they were presented with. There were security cameras everywhere.

"Where will find the Chief Medician, Lazar? What's his name? Do you know it?"

"Yes – Mehari. Ibrahim Mehari. His office off Reception Area. Private access. You want me take you there?"

"No, there's no point, Lazar. We'll have to go through Reception anyway. You can bring me out now, if you like."

He obeyed her without question, and the image vanished before she had time to shut her eyes. There was sudden total blackness and a terrible sensation of dropping into oblivion, like a painless, but terrifying death. It lasted only a moment, but jangled her nerves nonetheless.

Within seconds Lazar was loosening the helmet fastenings and she emerged from it, blinking and disorientated. Raymer had already taken the pathfinder from her hand and was starting to remove the gloves.

She got up unsteadily from the stool, running her fingers through her hair. She felt dishevelled and hot, and the visor had left pressure marks on her skin as if it were still in place – like Angel's disc on her forehead. "Download a visual onto my personal Link, will you, Lazar?" she said, feeling her way back to the living area. "Just to remind me when we get there," she added finding the nearest lounger to sit on as a matter of some urgency.

Behind her she heard Raymer say, "Pack all that stuff away out of sight, Laz," before closing the door and joining her.

She gave herself a few moments to recover. Raymer was waiting for her opinion. "I think I should get him over to Gio as soon as possible," she said. "There's no point in delaying."

"We've got rehearsals the day after tomorrow, Cass," he pointed out.

"Make some excuse for me not being there if I don't get back in time."

"Like what?"

"I don't know. Think of something. This is your mess I'm dealing with, Jason, so it's up to you. The incident with Carrigan leaves too many questions unanswered. If he's holding off – for whatever reason – I'm not going to sit around waiting for him to pounce."

Raymer didn't like the idea. "And what happens if you go into withdrawal?" he said. "How's that going to play out?"

"I won't go into withdrawal before the first performance."

"How can you be so sure?"

"Because Angel knows our schedule," she said.

"Come on, Cass, you're not making sense. We didn't know our schedule 'til we got here."

"But Commander Hautfort knew it," she pointed out.

Raymer studied her for a moment, catching her meaning. "Smiler?"

"Yes, Smiler. He probably communicated our schedule on an open Link, available to anyone who was interested – probably even before we left the *Ivanov* – which gave Angel all the information he needed to fix me with the right dose. The more I think about it, the more I can see Smiler's hand in everything that's gone wrong for The Choralians since we came back from the Uranus tour."

"In what way?"

"The surger-pop performances – before your time, of course.

The last gig at Shackleton I was supposed to do with Karoli to please a well-placed 'client'. Forcing us to do another space tour against our better judgement. Even you, Jay, brilliant though you are – you were forced on us."

"Thanks," he said, looking less than delighted by her observation.

"He's played us all – like fish on a line, Jason, and I'm not going to play his game any more."

"Do you think he's in with Angel?"

"Yes, I do – and I think he's had me lined up as a courier right from the start."

"What makes you say that?"

"My history, Jason. Ancient history. I was sixteen when I joined his stable. I was flattered, I suppose. A big-time agent looking for new talent. I'll give him his due – he coached me and launched me straight off as a solo act on a small circuit in Seasia." She paused, remembering some things she'd preferred to forget. "I met some strange people on that tour, Jay, and I don't think I met them accidentally. He knew my mother used mind-warp. At the time, he probably thought I either used the product – or had contacts he'd find useful. I must have looked like a present – gift-wrapped." She laughed at the thought. "I must have been a bitter disappointment to him when he realised the truth, which is why," she added as a terrible thought came to her, "he must have brought in Karoli to be my partner."

"Cass, you can't mean that!"

But she did, with a terrible sense of betrayal this new-found understanding gave her. It suddenly became horribly clear why she'd been teamed up with him in the first place. In that empty time after his death, she'd not been able to think so clearly. But now it all seemed so obvious a small child could have worked it out.

Raymer was staring at her.

"I knew Karoli kept his past from me. I never asked. We don't, do we, we Hurdy-Gurdy folk?" She paused, aware for the first time and in sharp focus that Angel and his Aphrochrome had wiped the slate clean, not just of Raymer, but of Karoli as well: he'd become just someone else she'd known in the distant past. Their lives had crossed briefly, and nothing more. "All I know is that Smiler had some sort of hold over him – and he didn't like it." It was suddenly so easy to talk about him and she wondered at her lack of anger that he he'd gone out of her life: it was a tragedy that no longer touched her emotions.

"Did Karoli know about your mother?" Raymer was asking, cutting across her thoughts.

"Yes, and I told him that's why I'd never touch mind-warp – ever."

She could remember when she'd told him. He'd been lying next to her after they'd made love, sometime very early in their relationship. It had been dark and his voice had come to her across a pillow in a whisper. "He said we should swear always to protect one another – and we did. He kept his word, Jay. He was murdered trying to stop Smiler turning me into a courier."

Raymer was studying his hands. "So, you think Smiler only takes on Folksters he can blackmail?" he asked quietly.

"Would you disagree?"

He shook his head.

She didn't ask him to explain: she didn't need to. "I think Smiler calls the tune and Angel does whatever's necessary to make us dance. And I'm guessing they're only part of a much larger network – which is why I want to get Lazar out of the picture while I can – while I still have time. I'll take tomorrow's shuttle to Gio, Jay. No fuss. Nothing high profile. I'll make it look like another day trip off-station."

"You're running way ahead of me here," he objected.

"I'm calling the tune this time, Jay. Just get Lazar down to the hub in time for the first shuttle. I'll tell Theo I want a break, that's all."

It was a lie: she knew she would be telling Theo a lot more.

"Keep Theo out of it, Cass. It won't help."

"I *have* to tell him. He's the one who contacts McMichael with progress reports. If anything goes wrong with the plan, he's the one who'll have to do the explaining – and I won't have him trying to cope with that without knowing the truth. Do you understand?" And quite suddenly, as she looked at the disapproving expression on his face, she didn't much care whether he did or he didn't.

FORTY-SEVEN

When his door buzzer sounded, Theo had fallen into a deep, but troubled sleep. He forced himself awake easing his arm from underneath Umo and slipping noiselessly off the bed, trying not to disturb him. Collecting his bathrobe from the floor, he wrapped it round himself and padded through into the living area, closing the door softly behind him. Cautiously, he lifted the lighting level to an early dawn and activated the visitor monitoring panel. In the brightly lit corridor outside Cassandra stood looking anxiously around her. She was still wearing her light travelsuit, although the trip to Mars Alpha had ended almost two hours earlier. He let her in quickly.

"Umo asleep?" she asked, brushing past him quickly, keeping her voice low.

"Yes. I'm guessing you've not been to bed."

She nodded, "I've been talking things over with Jason."

"What does he think? – about Carrigan?"

"The same as I do. It doesn't add up."

"No. It was strange – no one waiting for us when we got back. Do you think he's operating with Angel?"

"Who knows?" she said, looking at him in that scary way of hers which always warned him she was going to do something that would make his hair stand on end. "But I'm not waiting to find out. So this is my plan."

He sat listening to her as if he were in a dream, making no real sense of her conversation with Raymer and the VR journey she'd taken to Gio under Lazar's guidance.

"So you see, Theo, I don't think I've got any choice," she was saying to him while he struggled against contradictions in his sleep-befuddled brain. "I'm taking the first shuttle out to Gio this morning. Jason and Lazar will come down to the hub to see me off – or that's the way we're going to play it. All very casual. Then Lazar will join me – a spur of the moment decision. Nothing obvious. In a couple of hours we'll be on Gio. And," she added, "I'm taking the Aphrochrome with me." She must have seen the look of horror on his face. "No – there's been no message, but with Lazar safe, I can clear my head and work out what to do next."

"Angel could be watching your every move, you know that."

"If he isn't, someone else will be," she said philosophically. "I'm prepared for that."

"Are you?"

She laughed off his concern. "As prepared as I'll ever be." Her defiance was breath-taking and somehow chilling. "Now," she said, taking hold of his hand and looking deeply into his eyes, "I want you to do something for me. I don't know how things will play out on Gio. I may not get back in time for rehearsals – or even the first shows – " and before he could interrupt her, she pressed on. " So I want you to tell Smiler I'm exhausted and taking a break."

"Will he buy that?" It seemed highly unlikely.

She shrugged it off. "I know it's not perfect, but it's the best I can come up with. Can you manage that? You don't need to tell him for at least twenty-four hours. I should know how the land lies by then."

"All right, I'll bluff my way through it – somehow. Does Jason know you're asking me to do this?"

"Yes. It makes sense as far as he's concerned – you're managing the tour. You send Smiler our regular updates. But Theo, that's all I've told him," she emphasised. "He has no idea you know anything else. Understand?"

"If that's the way you want it," he said seeing her heightened animation and being almost afraid of her intensity.

"Good," she said, patting his hand affectionately.

"But why? Why haven't you told him I know everything?"

"It's better that way," she insisted. "I don't want him relying on you to bail him out if things don't go according to plan. This is his mess – he'll have to shift for himself."

"You make it sound so simple."

She was suddenly serious. "I think he's afraid, Theo. He's got out of his depth – and knows it. I look at him and I see someone who's starting to panic. So if anything goes wrong, look after yourself – and Umo. No one else."

"I think you underestimate him."

"No, I know him for what he is and what he isn't. He's not really one of us, is he? Not a true Folkster, just a Songster. Brilliant – yes, but still only a Songster. We're Hurdy-Gurdy folk, Theo, you and I. We're survivors. We've seen and done things he's never experienced. That leaves him open and raw when things get out of control. Don't be tempted to rescue him. Promise."

He nodded, raising her hand to his lips and kissing her fingers lightly, hesitating over what he was about to say. But he had to tell her now, before she committed herself to any dark undertaking she might plan when he wasn't there to help her. "Cassandra," he said, "I have to tell you something. Don't be angry with me."

"Should I be?" There was a hint of caution in her tone.

"I've contacted Oliphant."

"What!" she said, pulling her hand away as she got to her feet, a flush of colour suddenly flooding into her cheeks.

"Hear me out – please. I sent him a coded message when we left the *Ivanov*."

"How?"

"Through one of the Security Officers – a casual enquiry that's all." He could see her temper rising and he pressed on before she could interrupt him. "I made it sound as if Mister Oliphant had said he'd wanted to catch one of our shows, that's all – and I said we'd be very glad to see him if he ever made it up to the Quartet."

She was frowning now, her head tilting a little in disbelief at what he was saying. "He didn't, did he?" she asked, and he wondered in that moment whether she'd half-hoped that he had.

"No," he assured her, "That's the point. And he'd know that. It would sound wrong and it was the only way I could think of to tell him we're in trouble." At that moment he expected her to rage at him for his interference, but the storm never came. Instead, he saw the briefest flicker of relief cross her face.

"Is he coming?" she asked, her voice betraying the forlorn hope it might be true.

"I've no way of knowing," he confessed.

She let out a small exasperated sigh. "So he might never have got the message," she said and looked away. She's hiding her disappointment, he thought.

"Perhaps he had his reasons," he suggested.

"Maybe – but what if he comes before I've got Lazar safely out of harm's way? – or before Angel makes contact again?"

"Cassandra, forgive me, Lazar isn't my priority – you are."

She turned her back on him, her arms folded across her chest, hugging herself close.

"You said it yourself, Cassandra," he said, getting up to put his arms around her and give himself comfort as much as to reassure her. "Carrigan knows something. We have to face it – perhaps no one can help Lazar now. In the end, saving yourself from Angel has to become your priority."

She twisted round, looking up at him, the familiar fire in her eyes again. "I don't just want to save myself from him, Theo. You know that. I want to destroy him – and everyone who's part of his network." She meant it, he could see that, but it was something he knew was well beyond her power to achieve.

356

"If Oliphant comes," he said quietly, "You can leave that to him."

"If," she said, suddenly looking exhausted.

For a few moments they just stood together, his arms wrapped around her giving her the only protection he could until she gently pushed him away. "I have to go," she whispered. "Give me the alter-combo – in case."

He nodded.

With his mind in turmoil, he collected the phial from his travelsack in the washroom. He studied it for a moment before closing his fingers around it, feeling the polyplastic cold against the palm of his hand. The familiar tightness in his chest began to encircle his heart. Something dreadful would come of this, he thought, quickly casting the idea from his mind. Better not to think at all.

"Take care, Cassandra," he said as he handed it to her.

She nodded, taking the phial from him and slipping it into her travelsuit pocket as if it were nothing of any great importance. A trifle. Reaching up, she kissed him lightly on the forehead, held his hands in hers for the briefest of moments, and then made for the door.

She looked magnificent, he thought. Wild, defiant and unshakable. "Send word to me when you can," he whispered.

"I will." She smiled sadly and let herself out into the brightness of the corridor leaving him wondering what price Smiler would exact if she failed to return for the first performance. And behind that, an even larger concern he hardly dare give any thought to – would he ever see his beloved Cassandra alive again?

FORTY-EIGHT

When Cassandra arrived at 0830 hours, the hub was quiet, with only the usual musi-tone for company. Raymer and Lazar had not yet arrived. From the waiting area and the partial concealment offered by a pillar, she surveyed the shuttle in the embarkation airlock, scanning the activity around it. The Flight Maintenance crews in their dull khaki stationsuits went about their business with polished efficiency. She studied each of them in turn, an unseen Watcher, searching for the vital clue that might mark out one of them as Angel in another guise. It was a futile exercise, she knew: he would move and respond to those around him as any Actor would, shaping himself to become the part he was playing. But for all that, she could not prevent herself trying to seek him out; to have that adrenalin rush of seeing some sign, however small, that would betray one of the mannerisms she'd come to know so well. Too well. She wanted to see him – to have that sense of connection. But there was nothing.

Below the waiting area, a couple of Stores Operatives in brown stationsuits were stacking crates of boxed cargo onto loaders ready for transhipment. From their easy-going rate of progress it was clear they were in no hurry to complete their task, but were sufficiently engrossed not to notice her. She'd taken care not to draw attention to herself. Dressed in a commonplace travelsuit, her mass of hair stuffed under her grey cap, there was nothing about her that would draw a second glance.

The door into the waiting area sighed open and a small group of project personnel ambled in and took up the seats on the far side of the room, talking earnestly amongst themselves. Cassandra kept her back to them, apparently continuing to gaze out across the embarkation bay. But her eyes were focussed on their reflections in the polyplastic laminates in front of her. None of them seemed remotely interested in the apparently unremarkable figure leaning against the pillar opposite, a travelsack slung across her shoulder.

The numerals on the time board at the far end of the bay flicked over to 0845 and the stream of unrelenting musi-tone was interrupted by the announcement that passengers wishing to take the zero-nine-hundred inter-station shuttle from Lowell to Gio should present themselves at Door Three.

She hung back, letting the others go ahead of her. She saw the numerals flick over to 0846. There was still no sign of Raymer and Lazar. She began to suspect they might not come. 0849. She was having difficulty now not looking round to see if there was any sign of them. Where were they? Doggedly, she waited until the numerals flipped to 0850. Now she had no option: she would have to make a move.

The corridor to Door Three was empty by the time she turned into it from the main access. By the door itself two male Security Officers were waiting to check ID tags and mark their owners as being off-station in the event of emergency head-counts. She took her time to reach them and fumbled in her top pocket for the ID tag. There was still no sound of anyone behind her. She began to find herself working out how she might find some excuse to disembark if Lazar didn't get to the hub in time.

The nearest officer took the tag and studied it for a moment before transferring his interest to her, his stiff, on-duty expression changing as he recognised the identity of the anonymous-looking traveller. "Cassandra Diamantides? That's Cass Diamond, isn't it?" he asked, weighing her up with undisguised curiosity. "You look different."

She smiled at him, but not too much, hoping that when she spoke her voice wouldn't betray her nervousness. "Just having some time off," she said casually.

"Well don't forget to come back," he said, appreciating her all the more. "There's a good hundred of us booked in to see your first show."

She kept her smile in place. "I'll do my best," she said, accepting the tag back from him after he'd run it through the scanner. "But it's nice to get away occasionally," she added, securing the ID tag in her pocket before stepping forward into the boarding tube.

From the far end of the corridor there was suddenly the definite sound of footsteps and somebody calling her name. When she turned, it was Raymer, bare-headed, hair flowing free. "Hi – Cassie, glad we caught you," he panted. "We just wanted to see you off." Lazar was some distance behind wearing a peaked cap that helped obscure his face.

Both officers transferred their interest to whoever was approaching. Her heart skipped a beat. One of them put out a restraining hand, taking her by the arm to prevent her leaving the tube. "Sorry," he said firmly, "You can't walk back in, I'm afraid. We'd have to book you back on-station if you do."

She smiled to indicate she understood, and felt the pressure of his hand unwilling to loosen its grip.

"Want some company, Cassie?" Raymer was asking as he drew level with the officers, his joviality excessive, she thought. It sounded forced and horribly false. What was he playing at? "I'm offering," he added in a jokey, off-hand manner, including the officer nearest to him in his brazen, full-on availability mode. A wave of patchouli scent wafted through the air.

Gathering her wits, she shook her head, trying to pick up on the light-hearted banter he'd chosen to adopt. "Not yours," she said, thinking at any moment she might just be violently sick.

Lazar had finally caught up and was suddenly stepping out of

Raymer's shadow. He was actually laughing. How he achieved this was beyond her understanding, but she made the most of it. "I said Lazar could come," she said, hoping he could maintain the cheerful grin on his face while the Security Officers gave him the once-over. "And I wouldn't mind your company either," she gushed, patting the Officer's hand that was still restraining her, and diverting his attention very definitely back in her direction. The Officer blushed openly and let go of her, his companion laughing at him and slapping him on the back enjoying his discomfort.

Raymer was still piling it on. "Just listen to her," he said, engaging both Officers simultaneously with a toss of his head while he casually removed Lazar's ID tag from his travelsuit top pocket. "I sing all my best songs for her – just for her – and she treats me like this." He winked at the Officer nearest him who took Lazar's tag and passed it through the scanners without so much as a cursory glance. "It's always the same," Raymer continued in a pseudo-confidential manner, accepting the tag back when it was handed to him and replacing it in Lazar's pocket. "She never takes me seriously," and he laughed heartily to emphasise the point while Lazar slipped between the Officers and made his way unhindered down the tube.

They were both on stage now – acting out a closeness that no longer existed. She took up the theme and dazzled the Officers with her most winning smile. "He doesn't deserve to be taken seriously," she said playfully. "Go away. I need time off from you."

Both the Officers agreed with her and waved Raymer back down the corridor.

"'Bye," he called back, "Have a good trip."

"'Bye," she said, keeping herself under control, and turning quickly, ushered Lazar ahead of her into the shuttle. Raymer's ploy had worked, but it had been too high-profile for her liking. It wasn't how they'd agreed to handle things. She was so angry with him, it was all she could do to master herself.

The shuttle's interior was stiflingly warm, a seemingly essential requirement of all shuttles. She paused at the access door to loosen the neck of her travelsuit and pull herself together. Lazar waited patiently for guidance. His smile was still in place. Quickly surveying where the other passengers had chosen to sit, she selected the block furthest away from them, noticing they remained too engrossed in their own conversations to take notice of anyone else. There were four empty seats close to the main exit. "In here," she said, guiding Lazar ahead of her and encouraging him to sit with his back to the central walkway. He complied without question.

She sat on the seat opposite, facing outwards, prepared to charm anyone who came too near. The Stewards would be the first and perhaps the only obstacle with their constant fussing over the comfort of passengers. Trying to remain as invisible as possible became her main concern. To that end, she kept her cap firmly in place, despite the heat, and encouraged Lazar to do the same.

They'd barely had time to settle before a rich bass voice came over the speaker announcing the shuttle was clear for departure, and passengers were reminded of the emergency evacuation procedures and the necessity of following instructions very precisely. There was the dull thud of the door closing as the boarding tube retracted, and then the sensation of increased pressure in the ears as the hydraulic rams eased the shuttle platform out of the airlock and into the central hub. There was a pause for a moment. An expectant stillness, and then without any sense of movement, the shuttle had disengaged and was easing out of the brilliance of the hub into the vast blackness of the void. Lowell, its myriad lights blazing, slipped silently away, the speed of its going increasing with every heartbeat until it was no larger than a pin head, and then entirely lost to view. Disconcertingly, at an angle close to the vertical, the curve of the Martian horizon

362

appeared in the window on the opposite side of the walk-way and hovered uneasily within her view.

The bass voice came over the speaker again, informing passengers that departure procedures had been completed and anyone wishing to take advantage of the various on-board entertainment facilities was welcome to do so. Passengers were also advised Stewards would be available shortly.

The bright young woman in a grey and blue uniform was eager to please. "Breakfast is available in the refreshment area," she informed Cassandra, flashing a set of beautiful white teeth in her direction, "or can be served at your table, if you wish."

Cassandra smiled back. "Thank you, we've both eaten," she said, irrespective of whether Lazar had or not. He said nothing to the contrary.

The Steward gave him a cursory glance and nothing more: from behind and sitting down, there wasn't much to give anyone cause to look twice. Satisfied her services weren't required, she moved on down the walk-way towards the other passengers.

Once she was out of earshot, Cassandra eased herself forward. "Laz," she said, keeping her voice low. He looked up. The smile was no longer in place – just a blank expression hovering on expectation. "When we get to Gio, keep near me – but not too close. And don't, whatever you do, hold my hand. Do you understand?"

He nodded, a small frown creasing the crazed skin across his forehead.

"Don't worry, Laz. I'll look after you."

He nodded again, but the frown didn't lessen. "Frightened," he said after some thought.

She reached out and patted one of his hands lying inert in his lap. It felt cold to touch. A flicker of gratitude registered briefly and then equally suddenly vanished. "You'll soon be safe," she reassured him, wishing with all her heart she could be so sure.

"Yes," he said, his gaze sinking to where his hands were lying inert. The sight of them seemed to disturb him. With great concentration he began twining his fingers around one another, slowly at first and then with more determination.

She watched him anxiously for a minute or two as the movement became more frenetic. It would draw attention to him. Quickly, she put both her hands over his, stifling the activity. He looked up, startled. "Have you anything you can do to pass the time, Laz?" she asked him. "Anything at all? A game? Scroll? Anything?"

"Not mean to worry," he said, anxiety written clearly in his eyes. And he fumbled in one of his pockets and brought out a small slim black box. He opened a compartment concealed along one side and extracted with great care a curved band that expanded into a smooth, full-face black visor with tiny phone attachments.

Her curiosity was stirred: she'd never seen anything like it before. "What is it?" she asked him.

And with perfect pronunciation, he trotted out the words, "Transputerised Entertainment System. Make it myself. Doctor help me." He had an almost wistful look on his face as he said it.

Why this piece of information should have added to her sense of unease, she couldn't say, but it did. For a moment she was almost tempted to ask him more, but thought better of it, so she confined herself to saying the obvious. "Clever device, Laz. You must be proud of it."

He nodded, and placed the black opaque visor across his eyes, the phones slipping effortlessly into his ears. For a moment he was motionless, and then his fingers began feeling their way across the soft-topped surface of the box in a strange pattern of ceaseless movement.

She watched his fingers for a while, fascinated, wondering what sort of images he was conjuring up, and what could keep him so totally preoccupied. And when her own concentration wavered, she found herself looking at the wreckage of his face, somehow made more grotesque because half of it was hidden by the visor. His disfigurement was a physical pain to her. She turned her head away and felt ashamed.

In the window on the far side of the walk-way, the Martian horizon had righted itself. She pushed her seat back a little and readjusted the restraint she'd left in place, feeling more secure leaving it holding her in its embrace. Her hand paused for a moment as she settled into the warm contours, straying lightly over the fabric of her travelsuit where Angel's deadly product lay nestling against her heart. She closed her eyes and forced the memory of him out of her mind: there were other, more pressing matters demanding her attention.

What was she going to tell Chief Medician Ibrahim Mehari? – a man about whom she knew absolutely nothing and would need to entrust with everything. The stakes were ridiculously high. Would he be prepared to give her a hearing, or would he simply find her story too ridiculous to accept and immediately alert Security? Anything was possible and as the questions ebbed and flowed, weaving themselves into an ever-tightening knot, she came to the conclusion it was better not to think at all, beyond the necessity of having to think on her feet when necessary and acting accordingly.

I'm prepared, she told herself. I'm prepared to be whatever I need to be: the straight-talking no-nonsense persona; the slightly nervous – not hard in her present state of mind; the I-really-need-your-help-in-this-situation part; the tartar not prepared to take 'no' for an answer; or the beguiler – anything that worked – except that of being a liar. If this unknown man was to be Lazar's saviour – and perhaps her own, unravelling whatever horrors lay ahead to free her from the Aphrochrome, she couldn't afford to lie to him.

Just as she couldn't afford to lie to Oliphant, she thought. If he came.

Forty-nine

The disembarkation procedure was purely routine: ID tags were run through the scanners to record their owner's presence on-station and nothing more. The two Security Officers showed only a passing interest in the flow of passengers, content in the knowledge they'd all been scanned only a couple of hours before.

As they exited the New Arrivals tube, Cassandra held back, waiting a few moments until the other passengers moved on and only the musi-tone was left behind. Lazar stood quietly next to her with the patience of a well-trained dog.

For those few moments, Cassandra experienced the unsettling sensation of never having left Lowell. The only confirmation that they hadn't been travelling around in circles for the last couple of hours was the clear black stencilled lettering in UniCom on the wall opposite welcoming them to Gio.

They went through the door into the curving corridor she remembered from the walk-through, the image in her memory and in reality merging seamlessly. They passed the first set of elevator shafts and moved on to the second.

"Swing your arms, Laz," she whispered to him, seeing them hanging lifeless by his sides. "Like me," she added, giving him an impromptu demonstration. He managed to perfect it just as three crimson-and-grey-suited Communications Officers advanced towards them. One turned his head as they passed, and with practised artifice, Cassandra acknowledged him as though they met every day, and would stop for a chat if they both weren't so busy.

The second pair of elevator shafts came into view. A solitary Administrator dressed in pale-grey was waiting patiently outside one of them. Cassandra reckoned it was better to continue walking than stop with the possibility of being inveigled into an unnecessary conversation.

The shafts were only a few paces ahead of them now and the Administrator was still waiting. It suddenly became imperative to warn Lazar they would need to keep walking. For a moment Cassandra had the heart-stopping image of him obstinately refusing to obey, creating a scene perhaps, and the inquisitive eyes of the Administrator would fall on both of them.

"Laz," she whispered urgently. "Walk past the elevator with me. We'll have to come back when the Administrator has gone. Understand?"

He was instantly covered in confusion. He opened his mouth to say something.

"Yes, I know," she said, cutting him off abruptly. "But we want to be alone if possible, don't we?" She beamed at him.

Obediently, but confused, he kept by her as they passed the shafts and continued down the corridor. A few strides further on, they heard the elevator doors sigh open and close again.

Certain now the coast was clear, she turned, Lazar following suit, and both of them came face to face with a solitary Security Officer resplendent in his black-and-gold uniform. He was overpoweringly tall.

For a split second, Cassandra thought her heart had stopped dead. It was as if he'd appeared from thin air, his silent progress along the corridor behind them masked by his soft-soled station shoes.

Her evident shock amused him. "Are you lost?" he asked, stopping directly in front of her, his UniCom shaded with a hint of lilting Italian.

She summed him up quickly. No animosity. No suspicion.

Curiosity – definitely. He was a youngish man interested in a good-looking woman. She smiled at him, knowing how. "I'm still not used to station layouts," she said, engaging with him more positively. "I think I should have taken the last elevator."

"Where do you want to be?" he asked, his interest firmly fixed on her.

"The MediCentre."

"Well, you're right," he said graciously. "You needed the last elevator. Level Two. Would you like me to show you the way?"

"Thank you," she said, hoping to decline his offer as delicately as possible, "but that won't be necessary. It's to the right, isn't it?"

"Indeed it is," he said, and she had the definite sensation she felt every time Staines came too close to her during rehearsals.

She smiled up at him and made an intention movement to walk around him, keeping Lazar slightly in front and out of the man's focus of attention.

The Officer stepped to one side and let her pass with a smile.

Only when they reached the shafts and stopped in front of the doors did she dare to turn and see if he was still watching them, but the corridor was empty.

The elevator arrived almost immediately at her summons and the doors slid open to reveal a mercifully empty interior. Ushering Lazar ahead of her, she closed the doors quickly and pressed for Level 2. There was a brief surge and almost immediately the sensation of slowing down, something that had been missing in the walk-through. The doors sighed open and they stepped out into the corridor, following the direction signs to the MediCentre Reception.

They pushed open the door into an area with an antiseptic tang to its atmosphere. It was busier than she'd expected. White-suited Medics and ancillary personnel of all grades, Administrators and Maintenance Operatives mingled with off-duty Spaceworkers reporting for their regular medichecks, treatment or medication.

Choosing the shortest of the three queues lining up in front of the reception screen, she steered Lazar towards it, joining the four others waiting to be attended to. In front of them was a scarlet-suited Power Operative who was evidently nervous. Shortly afterwards, a woman in a striped purple and green leisuresuit stood behind them. Cassandra turned briefly, sensing her closeness, but the woman was consulting her personal Link, seemingly lost in thought. There was a low buzz of continual conversation and the occasional name being called. Lazar, head lowered, kept close, his stillness making him seem almost invisible.

The Power Operative was dealt with and moved away. Cassandra stepped forward to the grille, keeping Lazar behind her out of the direct line of vision. The Receptionist consulted the list on her monitor before looking up. She was a woman of an indeterminate age, somewhere between thirty and fifty, with her dark hair pulled back from her face. Everything about her spoke of crisp efficiency down to the precise angle of the name tag on her ample bosom which identified her as Katerina Moderna.

"Can I help you?" she asked in a way which served to remind Cassandra of the ugliness of functional UniCom, and her flint-hard eyes registered the potential patient was wearing a travelsuit and wasn't on her list.

Cassandra adjusted her tone to suggest extreme confidentiality was required. "I've just arrived from Lowell," she explained carefully, "and I need to speak with Chief Medician Mehari as a matter of urgency."

The Receptionist was unfazed by this information. In her clipped UniCom and without any hint of emotion whatever, she replied icily, "Doctor Mehari is off-duty until tomorrow afternoon. You would have known this if you'd made an appointment. His deputy, Doctor Velasquez is available, if required – for medical advice." The emphasis was very precise and the cold stare brooked no contradiction.

Cassandra stalled. In all their planning, they'd never once considered the possibility Mehari might not be available when he was needed.

The Receptionist was waiting.

Cassandra needed time to think, resorting to repetition to give herself space. "I need to see Medician Mehari," she said firmly. "It's most important."

"You cannot see him if he's not here," Moderna was at pains to point out, noticeably raising her voice so that Cassandra was aware that the woman standing behind her might hear what was being said.

"Could you tell me how to get in touch with him?"

"Does he know you?"

"No."

Moderna was adamant. "Then I can't possibly give you access to him," she said, and then, possibly because she suspected there might be another reason for the urgency of the request, she asked, "Do you require medical help, or not?"

There was nothing for it but to say she did.

"Then you would have been better advised to attend the MediCentre on Lowell," came the brisk response.

"I couldn't."

A very definite chill emanated from the other side of the screen.

"I need protection," Cass informed her, keeping her voice as low as possible, and maintaining a steady eye contact to emphasise the problem. "Medical protection – requiring high level consent," she added for good measure. "I can't say any more."

The Receptionist scrutinised her, perhaps recognising someone vaguely familiar beneath the grey cap. "Name?"

Cassandra handed over her ID tag. The Receptionist compared the likeness to the person standing beyond the polyplastic screen and decided to run it through her desk scanner, studying the data it threw up on the monitor beside her. "Ah," she said in a nuanced tone that hinted at contempt. "The Entertainer."

"Yes."

"Would you be prepared to discuss this – whatever it is – with his deputy?"

"Under the circumstances – yes."

"I'll see what I can do. Take a seat in the last bay on the right. There's no guarantee Doctor Velasquez will be available for some time, of course. She may be in the Intervention Unit."

"I understand. Thank you."

The Receptionist acknowledged her thanks with a slight nod, beckoning the woman who'd been waiting patiently behind Cassandra to step forward.

Dismissed, Cassandra ushered Lazar quickly away, conscious the Receptionist's gaze was following them.

The end bay was empty. With her back to the rest of the Reception Area, Cassandra sat down, indicating to Lazar he should do the same.

Time passed, and while Lazar sat patiently staring ahead at nothing in particular, Cassandra found herself going over and over the story she had to tell until it became a meaningless jumble of words. She was no longer going to relate it to a complete stranger, but to someone entirely different, who might, or might not have the authority to act on it, or even be prepared to consider it.

After half-an-hour Lazar was becoming restless and increasingly anxious. "We go," he announced suddenly, making a move to get up from his chair.

She restrained him. "No, Laz, we have to stay."

"Not coming," he said flatly.

"We have to be patient. The Medician is probably busy right now."

Reluctantly, he sat down again and stared at the wall.

Another half-hour passed. Lazar's nervousness was starting to rub off on her too. Leaving, she thought, was beginning to become an attractive option. There was noticeably less conversation taking place, and when she turned to see how many others were still in the waiting area, she wasn't unduly surprised to find it was almost empty. There was only a handful of people at the Reception screen and no one was sitting in any of the bays adjacent to them.

Suddenly, the door to the side of the Reception screen opened and Katerina Moderna emerged, walking purposefully in their direction. Lazar shrank into his travelsuit. Cassandra got to her feet to shield him.

"Doctor Velasquez is available now," Moderna informed them. "Please follow me." And she led them through into the inner corridor, passing one door bearing Mehari's name and stopping in front of the next one along. She announced her presence to the communicator, a warm contralto voice answered, and the door slid back with an exhausted sigh.

Cassandra muttered her thanks and propelled Lazar through the door without a backward glance, the Receptionist denied any further interest by the door conveniently closing behind them.

Medician Velasquez got up from behind her desk and surveyed them with the curiosity Cassandra had grown accustomed to when meeting strangers who knew her as an Entertainer. She was younger than Cassandra had expected, possibly only a little older than herself, her hair the colour of dark chestnut worn in a short bob that emphasised the slender neck and slight upward tilt of her chin that gave her a commanding air. But there was no aloofness in her open expression, or the generous curve of her mouth. "Sit down," she invited them in UniCom, indicating the chairs to one side of her desk. "It isn't often we have the company of celebrities," she added, "but you must forgive me, I don't altogether understand what it is you want."

"I wanted to see Chief Medician Mehari," Cassandra said, regretting this sounded both monumentally rude and unhelpful.

Velasquez nodded. "Why was it so important to see him?" Her attention was shifting from Cassandra to the silent figure slumped in the seat next to her, his face partially obscured by his peaked cap.

"I think he might be the only person who can give his consent."

"Because he's the Chief Medician?"

"Yes."

Velasquez raised an elegant eyebrow. "What are you looking for?" she asked casually.

Cassandra looked her straight in the eyes and said it. "Sanctuary." It sounded bizarre enough to her own ears. What Velasquez would make of it, she'd no idea. "Not for me," she was quick to point out. "For Lazar – here." And she indicated the huddled individual next to her. "This is Lazar Excell. He's a Techno on tour with our group – and he needs help."

Velasquez's gaze shifted back to Lazar who remained sitting with his head down, motionless. "What sort of help?" she asked, referring the question back to Cassandra, perhaps already aware of Lazar's limitations.

"Protection," Cassandra explained, the story unravelling haphazardly and not at all the way she'd intended. "I can't involve Security for the moment – for reasons I can't divulge. But he needs a safe haven – and a monitored medical environment – with a high level of restricted access."

Velasquez wasn't slow in picking up what was being asked for. "You mean the Isolation Unit?"

"Yes."

"Are we talking about a potentially serious medical problem here – or something else?"

"I think Lazar might need treatment – I honestly don't know what – but it's his safety that's more important. There are people determined to forcibly repatriate him if he falls into their hands."

Velasquez gave this considerable thought. Casting a quick glance in Lazar's direction, she input several codes into the Link on her desk and for one terrible moment, Cassandra was convinced she'd called up Security. She half rose, ready to make for the door.

Velasquez motioned her to stay seated. "Doctor Mehari," she said, watching Cassandra's reaction. "Apologies for intruding on your down-time."

A softly-spoken voice came over the open Link. "Is there an emergency?"

"Not exactly. But I would be grateful if you could come to my office, Sir. There's something I can't discuss on an open line."

"I see. Give me ten minutes, will you?"

"Thank you, Sir." The Link disconnected and Velasquez leaned back in her chair, her dark eyes fixed on Lazar's disordered features.

FIFTY

Cassandra wasn't sure what she'd expected of Chief Medician Ibrahim Mehari – except he didn't turn out to be anything like the person she'd imagined from his biodata on the Link. His image hadn't done him justice. He had presence – a definite gravitas.

A man of medium build, somewhere in his late forties perhaps, he appeared casually dressed, as was to be expected of anyone who was not officially on-duty, and the faint tang of sandalwood followed him into the room. He was dressed simply in a white robe which hung freely from his shoulders in deep folds, giving him the appearance of belonging to a religious order, and the stillness that surrounded him was that of thoughtfulness and careful consideration before he spoke. He was also remarkably handsome. At a guess, Cassandra surmised his fine sculpted features belonged to the ancient peoples of the Aethiopean Triangle, and his smooth skin was the colour of bitter chocolate. His hair, untouched as yet by any sign of grey, a glossy ebony tinged with midnight blue in the sidelights, fell softly to his shoulders, framing his face. His eyes, compelling, intensely dark brown and liquid, would have charmed the stars from the heavens if he'd cared to look at them.

Velasquez had briefly introduced him when he arrived in her office, and with careful courtesy he'd shepherded Cassandra and her companion into his consulting room in the adjacent suite. His wallpanes had been programmed to an exotic courtyard setting with a background of birdsong, and a delicate hologram fountain sprinkled water into a small pool in one corner.

Lazar was visibly confused by his sudden emergence into an environment he hadn't expected.

"My apologies," Mehari said, turning off all the programs and returning the room to a functional cream and brown. "I was here on my own yesterday. I like to be reminded of home, but it's not to everyone's taste. Do please take a seat," and he indicated the loungers set a little way back to one side of his desk. He made no distinction between his visitors. Lazar had fallen under his gaze only briefly, as anyone might, without the slightest hint at curiosity.

Mehari himself remained standing, apparently in no hurry to begin the interview. "Please forgive me," he said with a slight bow, keeping to UniCom as a matter of routine, but giving it a softer tone than Cassandra had ever heard before. "I understand you have both been waiting to see me for some time. May I offer you some refreshment?"

He input their requests into the dispenser and brought their drinks to them on a small tray of elaborately decorated metalwork, serving them in a strangely deferential manner for someone whose position gave him every right to dictate rather than be dictated to. Yet he was in no way demeaned by his hospitality; if anything, he gave this simple act the appearance of grandeur it would have been difficult to equal.

Cassandra was mesmerised.

Satisfied he'd been an exemplary host, he retired to his seat behind his desk and paused before speaking. "I have never been asked to give someone sanctuary before," he said, leaning forward slightly, his slender hands clasped in front of him on the desk. "It is to say the least – an unusual request." He smiled, as if it were also a great honour. "Please tell me everything I should know."

He listened impassively, his stillness rock-solid; something permanent in a shifting world. Occasionally, he would indicate with a slight raising of a hand that he wished to speak, seeking elucidation on this point, or that. The pattern changed only when she began to relate Lazar's history in greater detail. Then, he wanted to know more.

"When you say Lazar was a genetic 'experiment' at the Garrison Clinic, do you know what type of experiment was involved?"

Lazar, unable to follow what was being said in UniCom but catching his name being mentioned, looked anxiously in Cassandra's direction seeking reassurance.

"No," she said, reaching across to hold his hand and smile encouragement, only to find herself stumbling over what she was about to say. "I – I think," she paused wondering what Mehari's reaction would be to such a bizarre notion. "I think," she began again, "he might be an engineered hermaphrodite." She was embarrassed to confess such obvious nonsense.

Mehari's only immediate reaction was one of profound silence, the expression on his exquisite face unaltered by the revelation. After a moment's reflection, he observed with some gravity, "Then he is indeed someone very special."

"Yes, I understand that."

"As I'm sure you know, such conditions are rare these days. Any genetic dysfunction would be modified before birth, if possible. To engineer such a condition would indeed be a very serious infringement of medical ethics." He paused to add weight to this observation. "Miss Diamantides, will you please translate for me? I'd like to ask Lazar some questions and my English is not as fluent as it might be."

"Yes, of course."

"Thank you." And he turned to Lazar with a kindly smile. "Mister Excell," he began, honouring him by addressing him formally and respectfully, "Do you remember anything about your life before the Clinic?"

Cassandra translated and Lazar shook his head vigorously. "No memory," he stated flatly.

377

Mehari turned back to addressing her. "And all you know is that he was involved in a possible construction site accident?"

"Yes."

"And when the Genetic Rights Movement checked Universal MediCentre records, there was no trace of anyone being admitted to any Intervention Unit with his injuries, is that correct?"

"Yes."

Mehari gave this some consideration before deciding to question Lazar further. "Was Doctor Garrison kind to you, Mister Excell?"

Hesitantly, Cassandra translated again.

To her astonishment, Lazar nodded enthusiastically, a shy smile registering for a fleeting moment before it was gone, over-ridden almost at once by underlying anxiety.

"He never hurt you?"

"No," Lazar assured him, adding, "He my friend."

Cassandra stopped translating, "Laz? Are you sure?" she asked, wondering if he had understood what he'd been asked.

"Yes, he my friend," Lazar insisted, and to prove it, he nodded to Mehari so there could be no mistaking what he meant.

Cassandra felt as if the ground beneath her feet was threatening to swallow her up. "I'm sorry – Laz has never mentioned this before," she said, recognising she'd been wrong-footed and didn't know what to make of the revelation.

Mehari glossed over her ignorance. "Well, even if Doctor Garrison is his friend, it's clear he's gone to some extreme lengths to get Lazar back to the Clinic – but hasn't been able to call on the services of the Enforcers for obvious reasons. And you are in a similar position, are you not?" he observed, stating a bald fact without implying any criticism of her predicament. "You know for instance that Lazar has a forged identity, and that he's been supplied with the necessary adjuncts to give him an acceptable history to bypass security checks."

"Yes."

"And do you accept this makes you an accessory to a criminal offence?"

"Yes."

"And you are now asking me to give Lazar sanctuary in the Isolation Unit to protect him from forcible repatriation – or, as it would seem in his case – forcible reclamation?" He was studying her closely. "You are asking a great deal, Miss Diamantides."

"Yes," she said, with as much defiance as she could muster.

"So tell me – why are you prepared to go to such lengths?"

"I don't believe he should be taken back to the Clinic without any questions being asked. He should know who he really is – why he's there – and what's been done to him. He's a human being, isn't he!" Her sense of injustice had put fire in her voice and she was glad of it.

Mehari leaned back in his chair and considered her argument. "I know something of the Garrison Clinic," he said, a faint smile on his lips. "It has a strange reputation and there have been many questions raised in the past about Doctor Garrison's research programmes. From what you've told me – and from what I can see – here," he added, casting no more than a fleeting glance in Lazar's direction, "I believe it would be right to protect Lazar until enquiries reveal his true identity – and the circumstances surrounding his admission to the Garrison Clinic. I am therefore prepared to accede to your request."

If it had not been wholly inappropriate, Cassandra would have willingly embraced Ibrahim Mehari. Instead, all she could do was struggle to find the right words to thank him repeatedly.

Lazar, suddenly aware all was well, smiled broadly.

Mehari got up from behind his desk and came forward to take Lazar by the hands and lift him to his feet. They made a strange, ill-matched pair. "Can I call you Lazar?" he asked, speaking a little hesitantly in English.

Lazar nodded.

"I can keep you safe. Will you stay with me?"

Lazar looked serious and nodded again. "Cass stay too?" he asked nervously.

"Of course," she said, wondering at her willingness to agree to such an open-ended commitment, and to whatever consequences might lie ahead.

"Cassandra won't be able to stay in the Unit with you, Lazar," Mehari explained gently. "But she can visit under supervision whenever she wants. Is that all right?"

Lazar seemed less certain, but Mehari was at pains to remove any doubts from his mind. "My Medics speak English better than I do. You will be in good hands." And turning to Cassandra, reverted to UniCom, "I intend to keep the true reason for Lazar's admission strictly limited to myself, my Deputy and the Isolation Team. For the purposes of a wider audience, however, I will say Lazar has a possible viral condition that has the potential to be dangerous and highly contagious. Such a diagnosis is almost certain to ensure his complete safety from outside agencies while he remains with us, and under the circumstances, I shall arrange for him to be admitted immediately. Please wait here while I instruct Doctor Velasquez and Unit personnel on the protocols that need to be put in place as a matter of urgency. I shall return shortly to advise you on the procedures to follow to maintain the sterile environment of the Unit. Look after Lazar until I get back."

"Of course. Thank you – thank you for everything."

He bowed slightly to acknowledge her thanks and left.

Cassandra felt the adrenalin rush die away. Lazar was safe. The rest was up to her.

FIFTY-ONE

It was Ortona who unwittingly drew attention to Cassandra's absence. The recording equipment had developed a glitch, and he accused one of the rigging Technos of carelessness without naming anyone in particular. He then made matters worse by implying Krodalt wasn't being helpful, recalibrating the lighting rig without discussing integrating the visual effects with the sound systems.

Theo had wandered into the Masursky Hall earlier to keep an eye on things and discovered he was witnessing a rapidly deteriorating situation. Ortona and Krodalt were squaring up to one another, and the remaining Technos were showing signs of being drawn into the argument. The only person clearly keeping himself to himself was Meriq, standing apart as usual, lost in his own world with phones clamped over his ears.

Krodalt, hands on hips, was eye-balling Ortona across the space of little more than an arm's length. "It doesn't make a damned bit of difference," he was yelling back at him.

Ortona was having none of this. "You have no frigging idea what you're talking about!" he bawled back, not remotely intimidated by Krodalt's aggression. "If we run through a couple of numbers, you'll see *exactly* what I'm getting at!"

Whatever was going to happen would happen in the next few seconds. Krodalt backed down. "Okay," he said, dismissively turning away. "*You* want a run-through? *You* ask Cass to satisfy your over-sized ego – not me." There was an ominous silence. Krodalt scanned the hall. "Where the hell is she anyway?" he wanted to know as the realisation dawned he'd not seen her around for at least thirty-six hours – or maybe more. And when no one came up with the answer Theo found himself the centre of attention, his determination to keep Cassandra's absence out of the picture for as long as possible blown clean out of the water.

"Hey, Xenon – what's going on? Where is she?"

He'd rehearsed how he'd deal with this question more times than he cared to remember and decided on keeping things simple. "She's taking some down-time," he said, making light of it.

Raymer, who'd come into the hall half way through the confrontation chipped in. "No big deal," he said, evidently prepared to put his own gloss on the situation. "She's bunked off to Gio – can't blame her either," he added jokingly without any apparent understanding of the effect this might have.

"She's what?" Krodalt's animosity was firmly back in place: he was going red in the face. "How long for?"

With Raymer an unexpected loose cannon, Theo could see no way around the question without lying, and there didn't seem much point in making matters more difficult. "I'm not sure," he said, opting reluctantly for delaying tactics.

Krodalt said something thoroughly obscene, disengaged himself from Glaister and thrust his face up close to Theo's. "You're not sure! Are you managing this tour or not, Xenon?"

Theo braved the man's sour breath and managed to maintain as much dignity as was possible under the circumstances. "If you're getting rattled this early in a space tour, Krodalt, what do you think it's like for her? – after what she went through last time?"

At which point, Ortona tried to apologise for involving Krodalt, while Farrance, perhaps sensing this wasn't going to end well, decided to intervene. "Lay off, will you Krodalt," he said, yanking him by the arm to get him from under Theo's nose. "We're all under stress."

Krodalt, still glaring at Theo, allowed Farrance to pull him back. "Okay," he said grudgingly. "But we should know when she's going to turn up. This is our show as much as hers." Other heads were nodding and there were mutterings of agreement from one or two others. "Well?" Krodalt demanded, "When *is* she coming back?

Theo stuck it out. "I can't tell you what I don't know. Do you have a problem with that?"

Farrance had stopped yanking at Krodalt's arm and was showing signs of taking up the argument himself. "Are you telling us she mightn't make the first performance?"

Theo's lack of an immediate response confirmed the possibility and there was uproar.

Krodalt burst out laughing. "Good luck telling Smiler," he said viciously.

"Rather you than me," Farrance said, and started walking away. "Come on," he said to the rest of the crew. "We're wasting our time. May as well crash out until Xenon can get some answers." And they trooped off, a truculent bunch of men in no mood to be pacified.

Raymer was left standing in the middle of the hall, looking embarrassed.

Theo faced him, trying not to show his anger. "That wasn't helpful, Jason," he said, thinking he'd have liked to say a lot more.

"Sorry, I didn't realise they were so wound up."

"Not everything can be passed off as a joke."

"No, I realise that," Raymer admitted, stuffing his hands in his pockets. "I'm worried about her too, you know."

Theo didn't bother to reply. Smoothing down Raymer's conscience wasn't high on his list of priorities. He turned to go.

"What will you tell McMichael?" Raymer called after him.

"Only what he needs to know. That Cassandra needs a complete break. That I'm hoping she'll be back in time for the first performance."

"At least Lazar's safe."

"And no one's noticed he's missing yet. Try to keep it that way for as long as possible, Jason."

Raymer followed him out of the hall. "Look," he said, "I think perhaps I should tell you something -"

Theo cut him off, determined not to give him the opportunity to reveal Cassandra's involvement with Angel if that was his intention. "Leave me out of any problems you and Cassandra might be having right now," he said, successfully stifling whatever Raymer had intended to say, adding for good measure, "I've got too many other things on my mind." And with an air of controlled irritation, he left Raymer looking suitably chastened.

Back in his quarters, he shooed Umo into the sleeping area to give himself time to think. Keeping McMichael at bay until the last possible moment was his preferred option, but careless talk in the Artistes' Bar could alert him much sooner. He needed another stratagem. Mindful any accommodation Link could be open to a Listener, he called up Administrator Rainford and asked if he could speak to him privately. Within ten minutes he was in Rainford's office trying to spin an acceptable story as to why he was there. On the surface at least, keeping Rainford abreast of the situation had some semblance of the truth.

"So you think you'll need to cancel the first performance?" Rainford was asking.

"I thought you should know in advance – in case there are any problems with disappointed ticket holders."

Rainford looked pained. "I'm sure there will be," he said. "Commander Hautfort for one. I'll alert Security so they can be on standby if there's any trouble."

Rainford was being very helpful, and with that in mind, Theo played the only card left in his hand. "I wonder – could you let Mister McMichael know as well?" he asked innocently. "I think he would appreciate being kept up-to-date with the situation."

The request must have struck Rainford as unusual. He looked up from his desk and frowned. "Won't he expect to hear from you?"

Theo gave this a moment's studied consideration. "I think it would be more appropriate coming from you, Mister Rainford. A courtesy, if you like – as Mister McMichael contacted you regarding our schedule before we came on-station."

Rainford swallowed the bait, and Theo returned to his quarters wishing his heart would stop bouncing around giving him the jitters.

Cassandra's message via one of the Medics on Gio to a counterpart on Lowell had said simply, "Please let Mister Xenon know everything is fine but I might need to stay a few more days." It had told him everything, and nothing. It almost certainly meant she'd not be back for the first performance. And now McMichael would be alerted to the possibility via Rainford. What would happen next was something Theo had to wish to contemplate. He knew only one thing – that Smiler would exact a price for Cassandra's absence.

FIFTY-TWO

On the *Oryx*, time seemed to have found a new dimension in Oliphant's estimation. Seventy-two hours into a flight travelling at 160 km per second seemed twice as long as it should have been.

MacFadden had found himself a useful preoccupation digging around for more data on the missing patient mentioned in the scrambled report picked up in Seasia, and the leads were looking promising.

Oliphant meanwhile had turned his attention to the mysterious Lazar Excell, and come to the same conclusion as SSO Carrigan – that the available data didn't stack up when probing into it more deeply. However, what there was of it showed a considerable amount of energy had gone into weaving a credible back-history, cross-referenced where necessary with essential details to produce what was known in security circles as 'hologram infobunk' – data that looked solid enough on the surface but in reality was completely illusory. Details of his date and place of birth checked out with registration lists; so did those of his father, mother and even his grandparents, both maternal and paternal. But the generation before that was where the holes started to appear. There were names and ID numbers, but not much else and it soon became clear that Excell's great-grandparents had never existed. There it was – the screen message – 'Input data not valid'. After that it was like pulling out a single domino from the bottom of a carefully constructed edifice. He'd uncovered a monumental identity fraud revealing a whole tribe of people who only existed as entities in a highly sophisticated program, nothing more than insubstantial ghosts. It must have cost a small fortune to manufacture such a complex history, but it made one thing very clear – whoever Lazar Excell was supposed to be, he was *not* Lazar Excell.

MacFadden interrupted him. "I've managed to track down the original scrambled report, Sir. Do you want me to send out a general request to our Listeners to check their random scanning logs for the transmission time in question?"

"I think that would be useful. Ask them to report back via InfoNet if they have the complete message."

In less than an hour, three scrambled reports had been forwarded to the *Oryx*.

MacFadden alerted Oliphant as soon as they arrived. "Look at the description, Sir. That patient has got to be Lazar Excell."

"Agreed. Do we have the source of the original message?"

"A dead end, Sir, I'm afraid. The source was mobile, but there's only one clinic in the Peloponnese likely to be dealing with something like this – the Garrison Clinic. It's a private facility run by a Doctor Elgar Garrison. I've checked him out. Looks like he keeps his medical practice under pretty close wraps."

"That might explain the size of the reward. So there's not a cat in hell's chance of accessing their admissions records."

"No, Sir. I'm afraid not."

"Well, thanks for getting this far. Take a break. I'll see what I can find working backwards from what we already know about him."

"Right, Sir."

Left to his own devices, Oliphant went back over Excell's movements, starting with Carrigan's report from Mars Alpha. Gradually, a picture began to emerge. Transhipment data showed Excell had travelled with The Choralians to Lowell from the *Ivanov*, to the *Ivanov* from Shackleton, to Shackleton from Kalgoolie, and to Kalgoolie from the Glyfada Ferry Terminal. Significantly, his ID tag had gone through every scanning process without so much as a hiccup.

The small doubt that MacFadden had lodged in his mind became a very real possibility – that two of The Choralian entourage were travelling on forged IDs, unless Excell really was Phoenix, inserted as a last-minute blinder by Lattimer to put Oliphant's well-known dogged persistence off the scent. To get the answer to that, Oliphant knew he'd need to interrogate Guido Servione, and he equally knew he hadn't a cat in hell's change of ever getting the opportunity to do it. Firstly, Lattimer would never agree to it. Secondly – and more importantly – such an interrogation would be Enforcer territory, not ConCorp Security.

While he was mulling over what to do next. the Steward came round to take details of what they would like from the menu. MacFadden took his time over what was on offer. Oliphant picked a selection at random, ignoring the Steward's raised eyebrow at some of his choices.

After a half-hearted interest in the food when it arrived, and for want of anything else to do at the time, Oliphant went back to his favourite occupation – accessing the security data on Cass Diamond. It was an obsession, he accepted that, but it kept drawing him back. He felt a compulsion to read and re-read everything until he could almost recite it off pat. It was a personal weakness he'd never admit to anyone.

Settling back into the autocontours of his chair, he started where he always began, way back when Hippolyta Diamantides had taken in the abandoned babe-in-arms in June 2230, and registered her as Cassandra Diamantides in the Budapest Registration District.

Cassandra and Lazar Excell, he thought. Both mysteries in different ways: one without a known parentage; the other without anything at all.

He scanned her data, enjoying the sensation of indulging himself unobserved. And then he saw something he'd read, but glossed over time and time again – her blood group – category 1052 – and he experienced a very definite surge of elation, he was reluctant to acknowledge – even to himself.

Such a high number could only signify one thing – an extremely rare sub-group. Closing down her security file, he accessed the Link OmniTool for the number of recorded individuals still extant who had the blood group 1052. It was a surprisingly small number of 287 individuals. The Geographical Distribution Databoard showed them to be largely concentrated in the area east of the Danube in the old province of Hungary with very few elsewhere. With his curiosity stirred, he pursued what category 1052 meant in medical terms. The data that came up was an unintelligible combination of biochemical and genetic jargon that was beyond him. He closed down the enquiry, mulling over his discovery, and absent-mindedly input the security code for Theo Xenon. Suddenly, staring him in the face was Xenon's blood group – 1052. His vision momentarily blurred, but the image in his mind's eye was as clear as when he'd first seen Cassandra and Xenon together in her quarters at Shackleton. Two peas in the same pod – but not quite.

With the bit now firmly between his teeth, he went back onto the medical data site and input a query on genetic relationships. The advice on the screen directed him to an interactive layman's guide to genetics. He opted for a female tutor.

The screen cleared and the introductory music faded with the titles. "Hello," said a crisp female voice in UniCom. "To access the guide, please indicate your preferred language and state the nature of your enquiry."

The female voice continued the tutorial when the screen cleared to provide a Mercator projection of what had once been known as Eastern Europe. "This group is largely to be found in the area immediately to the east of the Danube," the voice informed him, and a helpful pale blue wash spread out over the area in question. "The limited spread of this blood sub-group is largely due to the concentration of a few hundred families in the area during the last century who had ancestral links to the Hungarian Romany culture. Socially, they occasionally interbreed with the indigenous population which has diluted inheritance numbers. Larger pockets existed for a limited period elsewhere in the Balkan region, but these did not survive the Great Purge of 2203. Do you require any further information?"

He did, but none of the options he was offered. He jabbed in an over-ride and closed down the file.

Lifting Xenon's security file back onto the monitor, Oliphant went back to the original data. Xenon was six years older than Cassandra, and his parents, Margaretta Nearchos and Ianos Xenonopoulos were resident in Delphi at the time he was born – an anomaly if they were supposed to hail from east of the Danube.

Oliphant input Ianos's identity code and suddenly found a whole new world opening up in front of him which explained everything. It preoccupied him for some time.

Ianos had been born Janos Szechenyi in 2193, the second son of an established Entertainer partnership, and had been registered at Debrecen in the Hungarian region. He'd been a tearaway by the look of things and at sixteen he'd had an unauthorised liaison with one Anna Katona, a local girl of the same age with an equally rickety lifestyle. The result was the birth of a daughter registered as Anna-Maria. With neither parent considered suitable, Anna-Maria had been placed under the oversight of a Judicial Guardian as soon as she was born, and according to official records, the couple had been prohibited from either contacting each other, or trying to make contact with their daughter. Perhaps the seriousness of this injunction had made Janos take life more seriously. Just two years later, he'd taken out a four-year partnership with a Margrit Tormay, the younger daughter of another Entertainer family. Two years into their first partnership, they'd moved south into the Hellenic Peninsular to an Aktichoria near Delphi and officially became known as Magaretta Nearchos and Ianos Xenonopoulos. Margaretta had died there from a brain haemorrhage in 2249 at the comparatively young age of 56. Ianos had committed suicide three months later. A sad end, Oliphant thought, for a man who'd probably moved away from his roots to spare his official partner his disgrace as a younger man.

Xenonopoulos. Oliphant pondered the choice of name. Xenonopoulos. The stranger in the city. Ianos had labelled himself for what he had become – a stranger in a strange land.

Out of little more than idle curiosity, Oliphant accessed the history of the luckless Anna Katona. With her child taken from her at birth, Anna's record became a catalogue of bouts of depression, clinic admissions and final containment in 2232. She outlived her one-time lover by almost thirty years, in what was diagnosed as a state of extreme melancholia, unresponsive to any long-term medical intervention.

Oliphant eased himself out of his chair wondering on the advisability of pursuing the strange histories of the minor characters that lay behind the present drama. He considered disturbing MacFadden just for the want of filling in more time, but his JSO had taken his advice and was sound asleep in his quarters when Oliphant went looking for him.

Helping himself to the odd assortment of food he'd left unfinished, Oliphant mooned around for a while until, almost inevitably, his curiosity drew him back to the world he'd uncovered earlier. What had become of the motherless child Anna-Maria? He soon found out. She'd clearly become an equally ungovernable handful for her luckless guardians. There were a string of Compulsory Restraining Orders from the age of eight, all for minor criminal offences, and as soon as she reached eighteen in

2227 she was on the loose, moving from one Entertainer group to another, occasionally going off the official registration radar altogether and attracting the attention of the Enforcers. And then, in late 2229 Anna-Maria had joined the travelling band of Entertainers moving north from their usual Hellenic circuit into the Hungarian district looking for fresh fields to conquer. The Kallistoi, as the group were known, were on tour in the area around Budapest when Anne-Marie left them in June the following year, moving on to another destination, another life and managing to achieve what was officially said to be impossible – dropping off the registration radar altogether. What the data didn't reveal to any casual enquirer however, was what she had left behind.

MacFadden was standing at the door, looking slightly dishevelled. "Sorry, Sir. Fell asleep longer than I meant to."

Oliphant felt too self-satisfied to make a caustic comment: he was still quietly enjoying the sensation of having found the direct connection between Cassandra and Xenon that he'd always known was there, but couldn't put his finger on. And now he knew something else. Anna-Maria was almost certainly Cass Diamond's real mother.

"Do you want me to carry on with the search for Excell, Sir?"

Oliphant swivelled back to face the screen and brought up a familial connection diagram. "No, lad – just take a look at this," he said, highlighting names and dates and drawing them together. "What do you see?"

MacFadden, still half-asleep squinted at the monitor. "Am I reading that correctly, Sir?"

"You are. Theo Xenon and Cass Diamond are related. There's the connection." He pointed to Ianos. "Father of one – grandfather of the other."

"Do they know, Sir?"

"No, I don't think so. At least, not in the way we can see here." He closed down the file, and feeling quietly self-satisfied with what he'd uncovered toyed with the prospect of being able to reveal it to both of them at a more propitious time in the future.

He was still indulging in this fantasy when a scrambled incoming message rerouted through InfoNet cut across his speculation and the image of SSO Constance Imogen came into focus. "For your information, transhipment data on Lowell shows Cassandra Diamantides and Lazar Excell as passengers on the zero-nine-hundred hours ferry from Lowell to Gio yesterday. Subsequent report from Chief Medician Mehari, Gio station, has logged the following: 'Lazar Excell admitted to the Isolation Unit on Gio at 1330 today with possibly dangerous and highly contagious viral condition. Tests ongoing.' Cassandra Diamantides remains on-station. No contagion reported in her instance. All Security personnel on standby." When the screen cleared, Lattimer's observation in bright green lettering simply said. "Review possible courses of action and report back."

Oliphant found himself just staring at the screen. "Hells bells," he heard himself saying under his breath, the warm glow he'd experienced a few moments before chilled into non-existence.

There was an audible intake of breath from MacFadden. "What's going on, Sir?"

"I've not the faintest idea, MacFadden."

"Are we looking at a diversion?"

"Whatever it is, it isn't anything we bargained for. And we need some very specific answers from Doctor Elgar Garrison – fast. If someone from his clinic's been on the loose with a potentially dangerous medical condition, he's got one hell of a lot of explaining to do." Angrily, he opened the scrambling facility. "MacFadden, forward that missing patient report over to me."

"Yes, Sir."

"If Lattimer wants me to come up with all the answers in short order, I'm going to suggest to him, whether he likes it or not, that he alerts the International Enforcement Agency. Ask them to investigate as a matter of urgency the possible connection between the Garrison Clinic and Lazar Excell. Let's see if that flushes him out."

With MacFadden gone, Oliphant realised his increased adrenalin level was far more to do with his concern over the safety of Cassandra Diamantides than his desire to resolve the mystery of Lazar Excell.

FIFTY-THREE

Time dragged. MacFadden had retired to his sleeping quarters hours ago while Oliphant tossed and turned waiting for news. They were still three days away from reaching Mars and for him it may as well have been Eternity.

The evening had been spent in scrambled discussions with Lattimer on the situation as it was developing. It was no longer a single-pronged investigation into a mind-warp network being set in place, but also the manufacture and distribution of forged IDs, and the containment of a possible plague carried by an unknown person currently going by the name of Lazar Excell. Between these three strands there was a fair bit of flak flying around in various corridors of power. But to Oliphant it was as nothing compared with what might be going on around The Choralians, and Cass Diamond in particular.

High-level discussions were currently still taking place between ConCorp Security and the International Enforcement Agency. A Deputy Regional Commander and his team had been assigned to go hot-footing it to the Garrison Clinic with Powers of Interrogation. Meanwhile, Leonid Oliphant was lying on his bed, thrashing around in a permanent state of restlessness, his mind refusing to let him sleep.

Eventually, he gave up. He threw off the coverlet and emerged from his cramped sleeping quarters in his crumpled sleepsuit, seeking the more spacious area designated for 'daytime' living. His throat was parched and his temper frayed. Ignoring the lighting options, he stumbled around the furniture in the semi-gloom of the emergency lights, still unused to the layout of the place, and ordered himself a Bukhovsky beer, slumping down with it onto the nearest couch.

For the umpteenth time, he checked his watch. It was not quite 0400 hours. He wondered how long it would be before the Enforcers got what they wanted out of Garrison; how long it would be before their procedures allowed ConCorp Security to be informed; and how long it would take Lattimer to get the details back to him. Another eternity, he thought, downing the Bukhovsky Beer and getting himself a refill which did nothing to liven up his jaded palette.

"You're a bloody fool," he told himself slumping back onto the couch and closing his eyes wondering if he'd sleep better there than in the confines of the cubby-hole passing for a bedroom. But it was useless. She was there again – in his mind – her dark eyes fixed on him; the scent of her as she glided past; the touch of her fingers on his.

Troubled by the memory, he could only find one solution. "What the hell," he said to himself. "Why not?"

He accessed the entertainments list and found what he was looking for under Folksters – 'The Choralians – Uranian Tour on Herschel Minor'. His hand hovered over the selection button almost furtively, like an adolescent about to be caught out accessing dark data. Pure guilt, he thought. If there was such a thing.

The confirmation message flashed on-screen. He allowed himself one brief moment of reflection before accessing the recording.

He lay back on the couch, letting the VR visor settle around his face. It pressed lightly against his beard. For a moment, its closeness and the complete blackness troubled him – like space.

"Begin," he commanded the voxbox. "Standard decibels."

The introductory titles came and went. There was darkness and silence again, then the faint sound of the absent audience talking in whispers in the seats behind him. The front row where he was 'sitting' was unlit, but the stage, barely four paces away, was ablaze with a circle of intense blue light. Into this circle stepped Cass Diamond with a clash of music and a startlingly high bird-like trill from a paparingo pipe which sent shivers down his legs as far as his toes.

He held his breath, absorbing the sight of her as the music shimmered in time to the swish of the silver robe she wore, its sequined girdle pulling the fabric into her waist. Her eyes had been outlined in metallic aqua-marine and her lips were a troubling deep ruby-red. In amongst the dark mass of her hair, curling silver ribbons twisted and turned as she moved, reflecting the intense blueness of the light into his eyes.

The music built on itself, her voice entwining around it, winding into his brain. A song of storms and lightning; of primitive fears; of gods and demons. And the gods and demons were there in the basic rhythm that trapped his heart and snatched at his soul until he wanted to reach out and hold her.

Silver pools of light began to form around her, bringing the other members of the group out of the darkness as their voices joined with hers in an almost paralysing combination of human sound and instrumental music. He had never experienced anything like it before.

The crescendo came suddenly. The stage lights shifted from blue to gold and The Choralians stepped forward to acknowledge the wild applause and cheers from the audience: Umo Manaus, his face painted silver to match his scaled costume, and looking strangely self-assured in the comfortable world he knew, a different person from the terrified individual who had stood before him at Shackleton; Xenon, dressed and painted the same, smiling and relaxed, glancing occasionally in the direction of Cass Diamond, oblivious of the connection that bound them together; and lastly, and most painfully for Oliphant's peace of mind, Karoli Koblinski, strikingly handsome and forceful, with silver studs in his ears, his hair pulled into a tight knot at the back of his head. He was vibrant, alive, dressed from throat to his bare ankles in a figure-hugging outfit that said everything there was to know about his physical attractiveness as far as Cass Diamond was concerned – a far cry from the lifeless corpse Oliphant had seen in Shackleton's mortuary six months earlier. A far cry too, he realised, from the likes of himself, his own heavily built frame, although equally powerful no doubt, embarrassingly cumbersome in comparison.

The stage lights dimmed and Karoli and Cassandra came into the centre light, which softened into a pale mauve, then into pink and finally to peach. The silver of their costumes mellowed and glowed; their skin tones shifting to reflect the warmth of a late afternoon sun. Xenon and Manaus remained in the shadows providing the instrumental backing to a duet, Koblinski's fine tenor rising and falling in close harmony with Cassandra's as she moved effortlessly from the warm depths of a contralto to the spine-tingling upper reaches of a clear soprano. It was beautiful. It made him want to weep.

For a fleeting and terrible moment, he wished he'd seen one of their surger-pop performances. And in that brief moment, the thought of sharing the vicarious pleasure of surging with her through Koblinski was dangerously attractive. He strangled the notion, ashamed of it, but the guilt remained.

The duet ended. More applause and cheering, interrupted by an instrumental piece with Menaus and Xenon coming centre stage. He skipped through this, stopping the recording in time as Cassandra reappeared in a different costume: high-necked, a close-fitting short-sleeved bodice in deep purple with pantaloons edged in gold pulled in at the ankles. Her feet and arms were bare except for two slim golden bangles on each wrist, and she wore a tiara of purple and gold that framed her cheeks and formed an artificial widow's peak on her forehead. The song had an ancient feel to it, wavering and high-pitched but melodious, and she glided around the stage with a flowing, sinuous motion. Transfixed by sound and sight, Oliphant watched her moving closer and closer in his direction and felt a definite stab of pain when her dark eyes looked directly into his.

He closed his eyes, letting the combined sound of her singing and the plaintive accompaniment insinuate itself into his senses.

He opened his eyes in time to see her receive the applause. The lighting changed to a fiery red. With one quick movement, she freed her hair from the tiara and swathed herself in a fringed golden shawl which had been draped over a side-stool outside the pool of light. The rhythm changed and she began to sing again. The brilliance of the lighting gave her features a molten heat, her voice dropping to a low, husky contralto. The words were unintelligible, but the meaning was very clear. She turned to face him again, moving closer across the virtual space between them – singing to him; for him, and he was lost.

I'm like a million others who've ever watched this, he thought, hearing his heart picking up the beat of the music and feeling his desire for her rising. He was being seduced. Like Davron, he supposed, who'd seen her give a live performance. Like any man who'd ever wanted to make love to a woman.

Out of passion came anger. Anger at Miles McMichael; at his manipulative manoeuvrings; at his ability to keep himself just out of reach, but close enough to benefit from the unsavoury trafficking he dealt in; and most of all at his capacity for depravity. Smiler McMichael, who had a network of thugs who did his dirty work. Smiler, who didn't care what happened to those he ensnared, as long as they fulfilled the role he'd marked out for them.

Oliphant cast his mind back, remembering the others who'd died before Koblinski. All perfectly explicable accidental deaths – except like Koblinski's, they were not accidental at all.

Damn McMichael. Damn him to hell.

FIFTY-FOUR

The sound of the buzzer to her quarters in the Visitors' Accommodation Unit made her start, and she hesitated long enough for the caller to press again, this time with greater urgency. Heart pounding, she activated the door monitoring panel. It wasn't Angel.

"Jay! What are you doing here?"

He was wearing an anonymous travelsuit with his hair stuffed inside its grey cap. He looked nervous. "Quick, Cass, let me in. I've got to get the next shuttle back in an hour."

She closed the door quickly behind him.

He surveyed her living quarters as if expecting someone else to be with her. His nervousness was starting to rub off on her, and she was edgy enough already.

"What's wrong?" she asked.

He tugged open the top fastening of his travelsuit as if it were choking him, his concentration not fixed on any one object in the room for very long. "I wasn't sure I'd find you here," he said, engaging eye contact for the first time. There was a fine slick of sweat on his upper lip. "I thought they might keep you in the Isolation Unit."

"There's no need."

"There's rumours. I've tried to squash them but Security know he went off-station with you. Mehari's laid it on a bit thick. Why would he do that?"

"That's what we wanted, wasn't it?" she said, noticing he

didn't appear to be paying much attention. "To keep Laz out of harm's way."

"Can we trust him?"

His questioning was becoming irksome and deeply troubling. He'd helped himself to a multi-juice but seemed in no hurry to drink it.

"He's what we hoped for," she said, still trying to work out where this strange conversation was going.

"Good," he said, showing no obvious sign that it was anything of the sort. "When were you planning to come back to Lowell?"

"I don't know. Not until Mehari can give me answers about Lazar. I thought we'd agreed that."

He sat down on the nearest chair clutching the beaker, his jaw muscles working hard.

"What's the matter, Jay? Has there been any contact I should know about?"

He nodded.

"When?"

"Last night. There was a message on the memo screen when I tuned in."

"Who for?"

"You – through me."

She felt the stab of momentary panic. "Was it Angel?"

He shrugged. "It didn't say."

"What *did* it say?"

"Whoever it was, they want one of the products tonight – on Lowell."

"So Angel must know I'm not on-station?"

"Yes – looks like it."

"Which is why you're here."

"And why I've got to get the shuttle back on its return flight." He looked up sharply. "Cass, I've had one hell of a job finding where you were. Reception referred me to Security. They weren't all that keen to give me your room number until they'd checked me out." He sounded thoroughly rattled. Something else was clearly bothering him.

"What are you not telling me, Jay?" she asked, trying to sound matter-of-fact.

He gave an embarrassed shrug and was suddenly very interested in the contents of the beaker. "The message said I have to put the product in Umo's costume."

Her heart missed a beat. "Has Smiler been in touch?" she asked pointlessly.

Raymer nodded. "He's changed the schedule."

"It's surger-pop, isn't it?"

Raymer couldn't look at her. "He told Theo he couldn't cancel the shows. If you didn't make an appearance, the punters were entitled to have something else for their money. Something more 'exciting', as he put it." He got up and deposited the beaker and its contents into the recyclation chute.

"But we've no surger costumes," she protested.

"That doesn't matter – because he wants a total strip – and he wants the shows recorded. Says there's a huge market right now for surger material."

A high-pitched hum was filling her ears. "Do you have to take part, Jay?"

He shook his head. "I don't know why he's kept me out of it."

"Because it's me who broke the contract – not you. And he knows how to get back at me. Did Theo say anything?"

"He said there was no alternative."

She sat down heavily on the nearest chair, choking back the rancid taste that was filling her mouth.

Raymer was breathing very rapidly. "I'm sorry," he was saying, "I don't know what else to say. This is my fault – not yours."

The urge to throw up was suddenly overwhelming. She fled to the washroom. Bent over the basin with the water fountain on maximum, she thought the retching would never stop. Raymer tactfully kept out of the way.

Eventually, the dreadful heaving subsided. She raised her head, catching sight of herself in the mirror. Her reflection looked back at her, accusing and dark-eyed. "Forgive me, Theo" she whispered. "Forgive me."

Raymer was standing by the outer door when she returned. "I need to be going," he said, glancing briefly at his watch. "Can you get me the product?"

She nodded.

Retrieving one of the cover slips from the lining of her travelsuit, she hung the suit back in the closet, closed the doors and returned to the living area. The process felt oddly mundane and automatic. A kind of mind-warp in itself.

Raymer let her fix the cover slip under the lining of his collar without making any move to help her. She could smell the faint scent of patchouli on him, a vague memory from the past.

"There's something else," he said, when she'd pressed the lining back in place. "You've to stay here. At least four days."

She nodded. "For Angel?"

"It looks like it. Will you call in Security?"

She eased herself away from him "No – not until I know Lazar's safe."

"How long before you know?"

She shrugged. "It's impossible to say. Mehari's still running tests on him."

"What about you – and Angel?"

"I'll survive," she said, her mind already wheeling away wondering when she should use Theo's precious gift to its best advantage.

"Are you sure?"

"Yes," she said, wishing him away. "I'm sure." And she was.

FIFTY-FIVE

She disliked the close confinement of the small MediCentre anteroom: it reminded her too much of the exact replica at Shackleton with its comfortable pastel-toned furnishings, soft lighting, the hologram of a crimson and bronze potted Croton, and mood musi-tone designed to help those coping with bereavement. Simply by asking her to meet him there, Cassandra had steeled herself to accept Mehari had bad news of one sort or another.

For two days she'd lived in a permanent state of agitation, but Mehari would not be hurried. "We have several more investigations to pursue," he'd told her when she'd pestered him repeatedly. "Be patient. I will let you know as soon as we have everything we need." And he'd bathed her in his glorious smile, placing a reassuring hand on her shoulder.

But horrors would rise up in the small hours to haunt her, and seeing her agitated state, Mehari had offered medication. She'd tactfully refused, afraid it might distort her finely-balanced metabolism. There were moments now when she could feel the Aphrochome begin to stir and Theo and Umo were paying the price for her continued absence. Distracted as she was, all she'd managed to express the guilt that racked her was to send Theo the simple message – "I'm sorry." It seemed shamefully inadequate.

Now the four days she'd been instructed to remain on Gio had shrunk to two. Her desire for Angel was growing; building on itself with every passing hour. Soon, she must find the courage to stick to her resolve to destroy him. There were times when her rage was hot enough to fuel hell's furnace; times when she doubted her determination; times when she'd dared to believe Oliphant might save her. But she'd nothing to pin her hopes on; no White Knight riding to the rescue – just an empty silence. She must accept salvation lay in her own hands – no one else's.

Already anxious, she'd arrived early, hoping Mehari would too, but the ante-room was empty. He'd come at the appointed time and not a moment sooner. Why had she thought otherwise?

She checked the numerals on the wall clock for the fourth time in as many minutes willing them to move faster. On Lowell, she thought, the audience would be settling into their seats, the previous evening's entertainment a boost to potential sales, no doubt. Commander Hautfort would be present: immaculate, filled with anticipation, eager to experience the vicarious pleasure he'd been denied first hand. He would enjoy Umo through Theo.

Sickened, she forced her mind from the scene, trying to concentrate instead on what Mehari might have to tell her. The mood musi-tone had begun to intrude. She would have preferred silence.

Mehari arrived, resplendent in his pristine white stationsuit marking him out as a Medic, the red and gold epaulettes, embellished with three stars, distinguishing him as the senior officer on-station. He was carrying a portable modeller. He placed it carefully on the table by the Croton before electing to sit on the couch next to hers, his delicate hands clasped together, lying strangely inert in his lap.

Beyond his initial respectful greeting, he was in no hurry to speak, apparently gathering his thoughts.

Cassandra could sense his disquiet. "There's something wrong, isn't there?" she said.

"Yes," he said, after a moment's hesitation, speaking slowly and precisely in his careful UniCom. "But not perhaps in the way any of us imagined." His eyes were filled with compassion.

She felt a shiver run through her. "Is he very ill?"

He shook his head, venturing a small embarrassed smile. "No – no, not at all," he said emphatically. "Lazar is an extremely healthy individual. But you must understand that what I am about to tell you may not be what you want to hear. Are you prepared for this?"

She had no idea what he meant.

Taking her silence as consent, he continued. "Perhaps it would be better if I showed you the diagnostic simulacrum we constructed. Please bear with me." With a few deft movements, he activated the modeller, bringing a hologram springing to life between them. It revealed the bizarrely shaped interior of Lazar's skull. "Firstly, large parts of his frontal lobes are missing," he said, using a location indicator to highlight the area in question. "Intelligence can be well preserved despite extensive removal, but there will always be some intellectual impairment and limited emotional responses. The left perisylvian region," he went on, showing her the precise region for her to study, "is the language centre. Damage to this area results in language problems of one sort or another. This explains why Lazar is unable to cope with UniCom grammar and syntax. Do you follow me so far?"

"Yes," she lied, wondering if Mehari saw through her deception.

He only smiled sympathetically. "Then I will continue." He turned back to the hologram, careful not to rush his explanation. "His thalamus – here – is intact – so Lazar can feel pain, or whether something is hot or cold. The optic nerve to his right eye has been reconnected and is functioning well. Other scans however, reveal major repairs not just to his cranium but to most of his skeletal framework."

She pressed him for details, knowing she'd have little proper understanding of what he told her.

The cranial hologram dissolved and he brought up a whole-body simulacrum for her scrutiny. "I think I can best describe the reconstruction work on his body as 'extensive'. It includes the replacement of eight of his vertebrae and the revival of his spinal cord." Again, he mapped out the areas for her before moving on. "Other reconstruction work arising from severe fractures is evident in the rib cage, the right humerus, clavicle and scapula, the pelvis, both femurs, and to a lesser extent minor work elsewhere." He seemed reluctant to be more specific on that topic. "All his injuries are consistent with a considerable weight falling across his body from somewhere above and to the right. Only his left arm, lower legs and feet escaped the impact."

"So, he *could* have been in an accident on a construction site?"

"Oh yes. This would also explain the damage to his vital organs." He paused before continuing. "I should explain. He only has one lung – on the left side – and his right kidney is missing. His liver is a successful porcine transplant – and his circulatory system functions because he has an exceptionally efficient artificially constructed heart. There is also a considerable length of sophisticated synthetic intestine – and other anomalies." He got up and began a sedate progress around the room, avoiding the hologram.

Cassandra sat, mutely watching him, aware she'd already disengaged from his explanations.

"Your assumption concerning his hermaphrodite status was correct," Mehari went on. "In that regard, he has indeed been 'engineered'." He must have caught her reaction to the word. "I'm sorry, I don't like the term either."

"So – what is he?"

"It's more a matter of what *was* he, I'm afraid," he said, shutting down the hologram before resuming his steady progress around the room. "He was originally male, but adapted – or should I say 'modified' – to include the female elements. These have been provided with hormonal stimulus to keep them functioning to a high level."

The musi-tone was now definitely intruding on her concentration.

407

"To put it bluntly," Mehari was saying, "two ovaries have been implanted and nurtured by adjustments to his endocrine system. As a result, he produces female quantities of oestrogen and reduced quantities of androgens. There is no womb and a low sperm count. Nonetheless, we still expected his gene map to register the twenty-third gene as a XY pair. However, it does not. He has a mutated aggressive gene XXY which has replaced the original male chromosome in every cell of his body." There was a brief moment of reflection before he continued, a slight frown marring his otherwise smooth forehead. "Then – there is his blood," he observed enigmatically .

"His blood?" she heard herself repeating like a sad echo.

"Yes. To put it simply, it contains an inbuilt mechanism which 'reads' the blood type of any variant mixed with it and adapts accordingly. It also contains a parcel of antibodies and enhancements that trigger phagocytosis." And seeing her bewilderment, he hurried to explain further. "Forgive me – this is the process whereby hostile invasive micro-organisms are attacked by white blood cells in order to destroy them."

"Oh," she said weakly.

"It also contains a quantity of mutated viruses and liposomes designed to activate deficient immune systems, and something else quite extraordinary – the capacity to manufacture thrombin to convert a plasma protein into fibrin – essential to facilitate blood clotting in haemophiliac conditions. Truly remarkable."

She stopped him mid-flow. "I'm sorry – what does all this mean?"

He was about to speak, stopped himself and started again. "I don't know of any other way of putting this," he said, casting an anxious glance in her direction, "but Lazar is – in medical terms at least – forgive me – what can only be described as a Eugenic BioTech Reconstruct." And he looked her full in the face as he said it. "Putting it simply," he added, seeing her complete lack of understanding. "the injuries Lazar sustained would have been fatal."

The meaning behind his words refused to solidify. Even the gravity of his expression failed to convince her. "But he's alive," she protested.

"Only as a living entity," he said quietly. "You must accept that whoever Lazar was – that person ceased to exist. He's a reconstruction built from the shell of a shattered brain and body."

"Then what is he?" she wanted to know, feeling her anger rising: she was risking her life to keep him safe, and Theo and Umo were degrading themselves to satisfy the perversions of others.

"He's an experiment," Mehari said quietly.

His words struck her with the force of a physical blow. No, she would not have him reduced to the cold, scientific description of an *experiment*. Lazar was Lazar: yes, a sad, disfigured and complicated individual who could show affection one minute and deal with the complexities of sophisticated hacking the next, but *not* an experiment. The incomprehensible catalogue of his body's inner workings seemed hideously remote from the gentle, frightened person she knew

"Medically," Mehari was saying, although his voice seemed a long way off, and possibly might not be directed at her in any case, "we are looking at a unique resurrection never before witnessed in medical history."

She pulled herself together. "Forgive me, I don't understand half of what you're telling me."

"Do you know about the process we call Vindegaard Intervention?"

"I've heard of it."

"Its discovery was a tremendous breakthrough in the prevention of brain death – but only if it was applied within the vital six minutes after the heart stopped beating. Let us say for the sake of argument, when Lazar was rescued from whatever happened to him his heart had stopped beating – but no one knew for how long. At that point he would have been declared dead. But – and here I am just hypothesising you understand – perhaps a Medic thought it worthwhile to give him the necessary dose of Vindegaard – or even an overdose. Who knows? But almost certainly, if this is what happened, the drug was administered on the very edge of survival. It may not have produced any signs of revitalisation – and in any case, the state of his fractured skull must have raised the question – how could this man survive such injuries?"

"But if he was declared dead, he'd have been taken to a mortuary surely?"

Mehari agreed. "But the effect of lowered temperature combined with the Vindegaard could have put him into a state of comatose hibernation, suspended at the point of death. If no relatives came forward to claim him, the body would have become legally available for clinical purposes. Perhaps Doctor Garrison was alerted to the circumstances of the case and thought it worth investigating."

"So there'd be no record of Lazar being admitted to any MediCentre."

He nodded. "Somewhere in the Central Registration Files however, there will be an entry for the real Lazar Excell recorded as an accidental death. But I am afraid where and when this occurred is something we will probably never know. We may also never know the techniques Doctor Garrison used to resurrect him. We just have to accept, however much we disapprove of his methods, his Clinic is famous for its successful interventions. It seems he has made an astonishing medical breakthrough that would never be countenanced under current medical regulations. It may be it was just a chance event – never likely to occur again. But whatever it was, Miss Diamantides, he did *not* revive the individual involved in the fatal accident – he reconstructed him from the body of his former life. This is why Lazar only remembers from the time of his revitalisation. His body has become a repository for a range of complex modifications which medically, I have to admit, could offer a range of specific therapies – all of them highly beneficial." He looked embarrassed at having to admit this.

"But he's still a human being, isn't he?" she argued. "He still has a conscious will. Surely he has all the rights of a human being? He's not a 'thing'."

"I would agree with you on that point – he is not a 'thing'."

"Then surely he can't be reclaimed by the Clinic as an 'experiment', can he? That's grotesque!"

"I think that would be the basis for profound medical and philosophical argument," he said with a thin smile. "The concept of Eugenic BioTech Reconstructs has long been regarded as an unacceptable avenue for medical ethics to follow. The Guardians of Life Party saw to that almost twenty years ago. But Doctor Elgar Garrison has never made any secret of the fact if the end justified the means, he would be prepared to ignore any ethics imposed by those he regards as the self-appointed self-righteous, who, if I remember correctly, he said 'prefer ignorance over progress'."

"But Lazar is still human!" Cassandra insisted. "We can't ignore that."

"Lazar is certainly sentient, but I am not sure that makes him human – within the precise medical understanding of the term."

"Then how can we stop him being repatriated to the Clinic?"

"Only by seeking a definitive ruling from the Medical Ethics Council."

"Will you?"

"You must accept such action would have repercussions. Firstly, he would not be allowed to stay here – and finding him an alternative place of safety could prove intractable and leave him vulnerable to forced reclamation. I can foresee protracted discussions, arguments and counter-arguments. The hearings could go on for months – possibly years before any decision is made – with no certainty as to the outcome."

"But he wouldn't *have* to go back to the Clinic," Cassandra insisted. "Would he? Surely the Council would give him some protection in the meantime?"

"I can't guarantee anything, Miss Diamantides. I am sorry. This case would be the first of its kind, and we cannot lose sight of the fact that Doctor Garrison will not sit idly by and wait for other people to argue the endless pros and cons. He has already gone to extreme lengths to reclaim him. Lazar is obviously a very precious experiment – a commercial venture, if you will pardon me for saying so. He will provide the Garrison Clinic with the means of providing sophisticated therapies for years to come. Doctor Garrison is not likely to give him up without a fight: it would be commercial suicide. You must see the problem."

"Yes, I do," she said, increasingly angry and frustrated by her own impotence. "I just don't want to accept it."

Mehari considered the situation in thoughtful silence for a moment. "Out of curiosity, Miss Diamantides, have you ever asked Lazar what he wants?"

"No," she said, embarrassed to admit it.

"No? Then how do you know, if you have never asked him?"

She felt the sting in his words – and the truth of them.

"You say Lazar is human. In which case, he should have the right to decide for himself, should he not?"

"Yes," she said, sensing she was being trapped by her own cleverness.

"Then I suggest we ask him."

She nodded mutely, following Mehari out of the ante-room and down the empty corridor to the red door of the Isolation Unit.

FIFTY-SIX

Oliphant read through the unscrambled report several times while MacFadden stood behind him, anticipating he would say something. They'd been waiting three long days for this reply: three uneasy days while Oliphant's moodiness increased with every passing hour, the confinement and inactivity only adding to his ill-humour.

"What do you think, MacFadden?" he said. "When you read this, what's your gut reaction?"

"There's not much to go on."

"You're damned right there isn't! All the International Enforcement Agency's come up with is what we knew already – Lazar Excell is the missing patient! Bloody useless!" He heaved himself out of the lounger and paced the living area barely able to contain his anger.

"At least they've been able to confirm that whatever's wrong with him, it isn't infectious or contagious."

"Oh yes, they've done that all right. Except it's sufficiently worrying for the Chief Medic on Gio to slap him straight into the Isolation Unit and keep him there. It doesn't add up, MacFadden – none of it."

MacFadden agreed but didn't offer any explanation.

"Those half-baked squaddies didn't even question how he'd managed to travel on a false ID! – And this damned Excell's got more hologram background than we give our own Freelances! It's damned ridiculous!"

"Is there anything we can do, Sir?"

"Well, not according to this, MacFadden. None of our business, apparently. Garrison's contacting Gio direct and we're just supposed to get out of the way and crawl back into the woodwork. Excell goes back to the Clinic, finishes his treatment and everything's just fine. Except I'm *not* having him disappear without some questions being asked about his ID."

MacFadden looked doubtful. "We've been told to lay off, Sir. Maybe if Excell is Phoenix, the Clinic story is just a cover he's been given for Operation Misfit."

"If Excell *is* Phoenix – which I'm seriously beginning to doubt – he's effectively been taken out. What use is he to us or to anyone else – if he was ever any use in the first place – if he's stuck in an Isolation Unit on Gio? No bloody use whatever!"

"The Regional Commander must have had his reasons," MacFadden insisted. "Or maybe Director Mendoza – "

Oliphant rounded on him, raising his voice more than he meant to. "And you think because the Director of Security – or anyone else at the Board's top table for that matter – might have a buddy-buddy relationship with the Garrison Clinic, that makes it all okay, do you?"

"I was only saying, Sir – "

"Nobody tells me to lay-off a security problem, MacFadden, not on ConCorp property. Right now we've a whole string of people – not to mention this so-called 'Angel' – running rings around ConCorp's security systems. We're up to our ears in forged IDs, the occasional dead body, and suddenly no one seems remotely worried. But you can bet a month's credit, MacFadden," he added, feeling considerable heat generating under his collar, "they'll be looking for heads to roll if there's a Red Alert and a station goes down. And you know whose heads they'll be, don't you? Yours and mine!"

MacFadden had backed off.

Oliphant eased the collar of his travelsuit away from his neck and consulted the wall clock above the communications console. Almost 1640 hours. "How long before we're due in?"

"Captain Orlev said ETA is nineteen-thirty tomorrow, Sir."

"Right. Who's SSO on Gio?"

"Bekka Gordon, Sir."

"Ask Orlev to contact her and tell her to meet us when we arrive. Don't make it sound too high-powered – just a spot-check visit. That'll get all security personnel on their toes without raising too much dust. I'll give her the low-down once we're on-station."

"Right, Sir." MacFadden turned at the door. "Will we need our stun guns, Sir?" he asked tentatively.

"Hells bells, MacFadden, what do you think, lad? That we've come haring out into the depths of space for a tea party?"

"No, Sir."

"Right then. Get on with it."

"Yes, Sir."

When he'd gone, Oliphant glanced through the report again. "Hells bloody bells!" he yelled at the empty room, and in a state of melt-down, shoved the report into his junk file, mentally screwing it up into a tight little ball and throwing it across the room in disgust.

FIFTY-SEVEN

Cassandra lay on her bed, tears coursing down her cheeks. They gathered in sad little groups, staining the fabric of the pillow into dark blue circles.

She'd turned off the lights, seeking the enfolding darkness as protection. Everything had happened – was happening – so fast; she could no longer fight back the effects of despair.

She hugged the coverlet closer, praying the alter-combo would take effect in time to numb the themaldrahine. As soon as the first stirrings had become more than stirrings, she'd followed the instructions exactly as Theo had given her. Afterwards, she'd taken the half-dose of SoundSleep as a simple precaution. The rest was waiting. Waiting for Angel. Waiting for Fate.

And while she waited, the jumbled memories of the previous hours harried what was left of her peace of mind: the revelations; the disbelief; the sense of futility and meaninglessness, all mingled together, disordered and random, interleaving themselves with the rising tide of heightened sensuality flowing through her: fierce; demanding.

Anger rose above her despair, bright and hot, shining like a beacon in the darkened pit of hopelessness. Her humiliation; Theo and Umo degraded – and all for what? For the sake of Raymer's stupidity: crass, unforgiveable stupidity.

Fresh tears flowed; unchecked, hot and scalding against her skin.

Mehari had led the way to the Isolation Unit. She'd followed, hardly daring to imagine what the outcome might be. They'd waited a few minutes in the sealed-off area of the visitors' booth while one of the Medics on duty went to fetch Lazar from his cubicle. He came through the door, his blank face lighting up a little to see her, his small voice distorted even more by the communicator.

And Mehari had been so kind, so gentle, talking through what little of his past Lazar could remember with Cassandra translating. Taking him back. Back to the Clinic – and Dr Garrison.

The interview had barely begun when the communication arrived to say there was an urgent transcast from Earth and Doctor Mehari was needed immediately. He'd excused himself, leaving Cassandra asking silly, unimportant things about how Lazar was feeling, and expressing the hope he wouldn't have to stay much longer in the Unit. And then Mehari had returned, and nothing afterwards made sense.

Without any explanation, Lazar had been taken through the decontamination process and the three of them had returned to the anteroom where Mehari had spoken with her earlier. The vid-Link had been activated, and Mehari had instructed Lazar to sit in front of it motioning Cassandra to stand back, out of sight.

She'd watched, half-fascinated, half-repelled as the features of Dr Elgar Garrison had appeared: gaunt, taut, momentarily austere until Lazar's image was linked back to him. To Cassandra's horror, he'd smiled: a nervous smile filled with anxiety and hope – and then in defiance of everything she'd come to believe – a kind of love; a visible tenderness. And Lazar had responded, the blandness of his expression suddenly suffused with an unexpected animation, and even joy.

"My dear fellow," Garrison had said, tears in his eyes. "Are you all right?"

Lazar had nodded.

"I've missed you dreadfully."

Lazar had snuffled and hugged himself pitiably. "I missed you too, I want to come home. Too many bad things. Nice people sometimes. Not always."

"I know, but don't worry. I'll get you home. Doctor Mehari will look after you until I can sort things out."

And Lazar had smiled happily while Cassandra sat listening to the thudding of her heart trying to make sense of everything, and nothing would resolve into anything meaningful: not the madness of Lazar's kidnapping, nor his artificial existence with Servione; not his removal from Earth under Raymer's misguided philanthropy; not the grotesque blackmail she'd endured at Angel's hands, nor the anguish she'd caused Theo and Umo in seeking to give Lazar a place of safety. The irony of it struck her with the force of a physical blow. The safe pair of hands had been there all along – at the Clinic with Dr Elgar Garrison. She'd allowed herself to be blind: he'd been Lazar's creator and protector. There was a bond between them no one should have severed – and no one should have ever tried.

And now she must face Angel. The deep longing for him had started to throb in her veins. Soon he would come for her. He'd be angry she'd tried to out-manoeuvre him. There was the potential for violence if he had a mind to it – and he probably had. He would take pleasure in it.

Her mind ceased its tumult. The tears ceased to flow. Her limbs were lightening, like feathers caught in a summer breeze, floating on air as the SoundSleep took hold, easing her gently from the turmoil of consciousness into the blissful ignorance of sleep.

FIFTY-EIGHT

Voices. A long way off. Low conversation, rising a little at times. Not quite an argument, but almost. She knew them both but could put no names to them, just a familiarity that produced a contradiction of emotions: contempt and desire. A simplistic response.

The scent of resin. Her mind cleared a little and focussed on the thought. Angel. Here. Now. One of the voices. The one that brooked no interruption. Coldly decisive. Deadly, even when it wasn't raised in anger.

She felt his breath against her cheek as he leaned over her, his need for her now as great as hers for him. She would have embraced him, but she couldn't move. She had to wait. He kissed her neck, his soft hair brushing against her face, his hands pulling back the coverlet, eager to begin.

Her wrist exposed. The pressure of the tape against it. His voice in her ear. "You tried to be clever, Cassandra. That was naughty." He pulled her up roughly against him so the scent of him filled her nostrils and thrilled her. "You should have known better," he scolded, his grip on her waist not to be fought against.

Still wrapped in half-sleep, her eyes closed, she could do nothing – except listen. The other voice spoke, a little closer, muffled and indistinct. It began to worry her. Her plan had not included someone else. A small panic pricked her thoughts, unable to lift itself into anything more than a reminder she had no contingency to fall back on.

"I've brought a friend," Angel was saying softly into her ear.

"To watch. He likes to watch. And when I've finished, he can begin. Do you understand? Open your eyes."

She obeyed, the themaldrahine ordering her compliance.

He led her through into the living area, his grasp on her wrist like a manacle. The room was in darkness save for the pale blue light glowing from the wallpane opposite: moonrise over a low horizon. The edges of the room were cloaked in shadows, hiding the figure of the unexpected guest. But she could hear him breathing: quick, shallow breaths; nervous; anticipating the delights ahead.

In the middle of the space, Angel turned, the light from the moon reflecting in his eyes echoing the paleness of them and making a halo of his platinum hair. The rest of him was masked in blackness. "Where's the product, Cassandra?"

"In my closet."

"Bring it here."

She obeyed, following his instructions in a trance. "You could have brought it to Gio yourself," she said, feeling strong enough to defy him as she handed it over.

He threw back his head and laughed. Then just as suddenly stopped and took hold of her jaw in a grip of iron. "But we wanted *you* to do it. To make sure of you." It was little more than a whisper but it sent a chill through her. "Now, let the performance begin," he said and she felt the tape pressing against her wrist. "Make it special, Cassandra. Remember, we have an audience."

Like a helpless rag doll she let him fix the transponder to her forehead, placing the transceiver on his own and throwing a second one across to his accomplice in the shadows.

"Catch," he said with a laugh. "You may as well get in the mood."

How quickly the Aphrochrome began its work, she thought, as the colours and music sprang into her head and began to weave their magic. Her eyes had grown accustomed to the paleness of the light and the shadows of the furniture had become clearer, etched now in flickering shades of blue and purple. The outline of the figure standing in the corner shimmered in a rainbow.

She turned in time to the rhythm in her brain, peeling away her sleeping robe and letting Angel's eyes feast on her. That's what he wanted, wasn't it? He was naked now, brilliant in orange and red. As hot as hell, she thought, lifting her breasts for him to touch, the swelling ache inside her intensifying with every twist and turn of her progress towards him. The music was swelling, each crescendo more demanding than the last; exquisite.

He played with her, his hands sliding over her as she passed close to him. "Just watch and listen," he was saying to the figure in the shadows. The accomplice said something obscene and Angel laughed viciously. "She'll do anything," he said. "Anything at all, won't you?" he added, throwing his contempt in her face.

No, she heard her mind say behind the din of the music. No, not this time. This time I will perform, but only on my terms. And she knew it: beneath the initial shock to her system, the combo was losing its power to overwhelm her. She could abandon herself to the Aphrochrome until she was ready – and then she would act, regardless of the consequences. She would kill him, but she would enjoy him first. I am the Black Widow, Angel. That's what you made me.

She swayed closer to him again, tempting him. He pulled her close, the scent of him almost overpowering. She heard herself laughing as she reached for him, consuming him quickly, urgently; watching the blues and greens in his eyes shift to turquoise and gold. He was already lost in the drug, drowning in the sensuality of the experience; drowning in music and lust.

She led him on, her fingers tracing lightly over his back and hips, down between his thighs, mapping him out and urging him on. The alter-combo was working – she was using him, and he had no idea it was happening. It was an exhilarating thought.

Now there was only the magnificent music in her head, and she could cope with that. She pulled away from him, compelling him to follow, his desire unabated. Cold logic sat behind her eyes, calculating how many times she could make him climax while her body urged him on in every way she could imagine, however bizarre; however demeaning. And there was no stopping him.

He laughed suddenly in the middle of his frenzied, terrible motion within her. "It won't be long," he cried out to the silent, unmoving figure in the shadows, his voice a husky, rasping thing that grated in his throat. "Then we'll both play. Teach her to be a good girl. Yes?"

No, her mind said firmly. No.

She started to collapse, feigning how she remembered it had been as the great wave of blackness had swept over her at other times. She must act it well.

Crying out, she sank to the floor and he came with her, his body slackening for a moment before the Aphrochrome demanded more.

Now, she thought. Now! But she'd barely formed the thought and not even begun to reach for the pressure points in his neck when he jerked violently, his breath coming in sudden, strangled gasps that quickly became choking, garbled cries. He flung himself free of her, one arm reaching out to the figure in the corner, standing like a stone, too frightened it seemed to make a move. The other hand clutched at his chest as if trying to rip it open. One more terrible rattle and he pitched sideways onto the floor and was still.

She stayed motionless, weighing up what she should do now. The music had ceased. In its place was a sublime silence. The Aphrochrome and themaldrahine had succumbed – and so had Angel. She had loved him to death. She'd not expected it would be so easy.

Now there was the other one. From barely open eyelids, she

saw the figure in the corner emerge cautiously, bending over Angel's grotesquely sprawled body, searching for signs of life. There were clearly none. The figure straightened slowly, unsure for a moment what to do. Perhaps he would flee rather than chance being found. Perhaps she wouldn't have to deal with him after all. But then he turned, his attention now fully on her, perhaps finding her apparent vulnerability too tempting to ignore.

She remained motionless; watching; from her prone position only able to see the lower half of him.

He moved towards her, in no apparent hurry, his figure outlined in the eerie silver-blue glow of the rising moon. A pace away from her, he stopped, while she held her breath, ready for anything. His hands hovered for a moment and then plunged into his hip pockets – for what, she didn't know, but she couldn't afford to wait a moment longer. With all the speed she could muster, she rolled away and sprang to her feet, couching like a cat ready to take whatever action was necessary.

At the suddenness of her movement, he scrambled back into the safety of the shadows.

Savagely, she yanked the transponder from her forehead and threw it blindly in his direction. It rattled against the wallpane and vanished, rolling away across the floor.

For a moment there was silence, each weighing up the other. Then he sprang at her with a speed which almost caught her off balance: a blur of action; a body hurtling out of the darkness. She ducked and dived past him, seeing the sprawled lifeless body of Angel too late to save herself from tripping headlong across him. Half-winded, she rolled herself into the shadows and back onto her feet, the demon following behind her.

He paused, weighing up his next move, then edged closer.

Her racing heart missed a beat. Her finely tuned senses, still heightened from the Aphrochrome, caught the scent of him. Patchouli. *Patchouli!*

"Raymer!"

He laughed softly, barely an arm's length away from her, his face still in darkness, but his voice unmistakable. "You fooled him, didn't you? You fooled both of us. You're cleverer than I thought, Cassie – and that was clever enough. But now I have to finish the job."

Adrenalin was pumping through her. This was a nightmare. It had to be. She would wake up soon, she kept telling herself. "Why?" she heard herself asking him. There had to be a rational explanation.

"It's part of the contract," he said, his voice stone-cold.

"What contract?" She could feel herself starting to shiver.

"My contract with Smiler. Redundant social engineers have to make their way as best they can. Jobs don't come easy. You take what you can get."

"And what did you get?"

"The chance to help set up the network. To tie in with Angel – and the others."

"And where did I fit in?"

"Angel thought you'd make a first-rate courier."

"You let him use neuro-rods on me!"

"I'd no say in the matter, Cassie. You must know that. Angel always did what he wanted. Smiler promised he could have you at Shackleton last September. He's just been collecting his debt."

His indifference appalled her. "But you didn't need me! You could have run the network without *me*."

He shook his head. "Oh no, we couldn't. You'd have worked out what I was up to sooner or later. Look how you handled the little problem over Lazar. I have to say, that was brilliant."

"You filthy Toolman!" she spat at him. "You used everyone!"

"Laz was a bonus," he said without any sign of emotion. "I guessed early on you'd do anything to protect him." He seemed to find this amusing. "Sometimes, Cassie, you're too straight for your own good. Apparently, Koblinski was the same." He couldn't have said anything more likely to incense her to a point beyond reason.

She glared across the space between them and hated him.

"Well – that's enough chit-chat – as I said, I've got to finish the job. Sorry about this, Cassie. Nothing personal."

She caught sight of what he'd taken from his pockets – two slim tubes, the ghostly light from the wallpane running the length of them. Neuro-rods. She backed away, trying to work out how she could wrestle them from his grip.

"If you do as you're told, I won't have to use them."

"Meaning?"

"Meaning, I need to make you dependent – totally dependent. VR dependent."

"No!" But she knew the sight of her, naked and visibly shaking, was going to give him all the confidence he needed to carry out his threat.

"I don't know how you've overcome the combo," he was telling her. "You must let me know sometime – but after tonight's little session, my pheromones will overlay his. You'll be hooked into me for ever." He smiled: an ugly, self-satisfied, nauseating smile. "Come here," he said. "Don't fight me, Cassie. It'll hurt if you do – I can promise you that."

She leapt back, avoiding his grasp.

"You can't win, Cassie," he taunted her. "You haven't called Security – I got that much out of you two days ago – and after tonight, you'll need me too much to think of doing it any time in the future. Then we can work as a team. The most amazing Folkster duo in history," he added with a malicious flourish.

"And what about Theo – and Umo?"

"They can tag along – if they like. But it's best if they don't, of course," he added, and she knew exactly what he meant: they'd be expendable.

He caught her off-guard, springing across the space between them with lightning speed and catching her arms with the rods. The pain was indescribable. She sank to her knees, gasping for breath.

He towered above her. "I warned you, Cassie, this is going to be rather painful." And he put both rods against her jaw.

An explosion lit up inside her skull, reverberating in her ears. Blinding lights flashed and died behind her eyes and her whole face froze as her voice was stifled in her throat. Wanting more, he touched her thighs, felling her like a stunted tree to lie twisted and broken on the ground, a mass of uncontrollable spasms, her limbs twitching and writhing as though they had a life all of their own. The pain had become unbearable. It swallowed her up, wave after wave of it, merging into one long agony. She was screaming inside her head and no one could hear her.

Almost leisurely, he examined his handiwork and moved away from her, turning up the lighting level a little. She watched him through half-closed lids as he placed the rods to one side and stripped off his leisuresuit, throwing it deliberately onto the floor beside her so she should know precisely what he intended to do. Then, with studied slowness, he sauntered back and scooped her up, her spasms lessening to a miserable quivering in his arms.

"Now, you just lie down there," he said, laying her out like a sacrifice on the couch, his hands running over her indiscriminately, touching her as an object of casual desire; without love, or any trace of affection. "I promise you," he whispered, "you'll forget everything that's happened here tonight. I'll make sure of that. And then? Then you'll want me like you've never wanted anyone before." And he repeated his loveless mauling, lingering over the pleasure he found in abusing her while her whole body rebelled at his touch.

With a nameless horror, she heard the VR visor sliding out from its recess on the couch above her head and felt the claustrophobic sense of suffocation as it slipped downward over her face. "You'll enjoy this, Cassie," she heard him say out of the darkness.

A burning, screaming fury raged inside her head, her body still immobile, unresponsive to her commands. She would *not* surrender, she kept telling herself. She would *not* surrender. *Never!* And then the alpha-wave music began, and the hypnotic, dancing lights, merging and tumbling behind her eyes and in and out of her brain, finding their way into every corner of her thalamus. MegaJoy. MegaJoy. The words coalesced from a wreath of colours before melting away into a kaleidoscope of pure delight.

She was floating, light as thistledown. There was no pain now. Just exquisite pleasure. She could feel a soft breeze against her skin, caressing her, rousing her. She wanted more.

I can fly, she thought. Yes – merely by wanting to – she could fly. She could do anything: anything her conscious or unconscious self wanted. She could dance on a beam of light shafting through an immeasurable vista of weaving patterns; she could whirl and turn, wrapping herself in the veils of an aurora; she could feel the tingling of the colours as they touched her; smell them; sense the thrill of them assimilating themselves into her body. The scent of the colours was everywhere. Patchouli. Patchouli. Evocative. Delightful. She was on fire. A liquid fire that ran through her loins. A glorious fire that heaved itself up inside her. A coupling with life itself. She could fly. Was flying. Higher and higher …

Then a sudden blackness. A terrible blackness. Tumbling downwards through it. Unfathomable. The very depths of eternity. Down and down. Into hell itself. She heard herself screaming endlessly, unchecked and uncheckable inside her head. Loss beyond words.

Suddenly voices. Urgent. Commanding. Half-remembered. A dull thud somewhere, followed by another. Banshees in the wilderness. Demons let loose in the dead of night.

Hands touching her. The agony of being touched. A chill

that struck at her very core. A shuddering that would not stop. Crying again. Trying to move. Pain racking her limbs. Someone wrenching the visor from her face. A scream that escaped and she couldn't contain.

Voices again. New ones. Half-remembered ones.

Someone close. The scent of sandalwood. A quiet, comforting voice she recognised, but could not name. An aura of calm after the turmoil of the storm. Tape against her wrist. Another voice, commanding, forceful – somehow familiar. The warmth of a coverlet wrapped around her. Firm hands lifting her. The tingling of anticipation. The closing in of peace. Silence. Oblivion.

FIFTY-NINE

She became aware of her surroundings slowly: the warmth of the coverlet; the newly-laundered scent of sanitised bedding; the softness of the fabric against her bare arms. She listened, eyes closed, to the silence inside her head, conscious of echoes straining to fill the void which refused to be filled; conscious of being alive but unable to register more than the simple experience of living the moment; conscious that the wheel had somehow come full circle, and brought her back to the same beginning.

But not the same. Theo was absent. Somewhere else. Out of reach. In his place was an aching emptiness. But she was safe. She knew that. Why she was so certain, she couldn't say: she only knew she was.

Somewhere deep within her consciousness, she could feel pain; physical pain that was being controlled. It was there, and yet not there. A strange sensation. The mental pain was somewhere else; subdued; waiting its turn. Emotionally, she was numb.

Someone had moved to the side of her bed; was leaning over her; had taken her hand and was smoothing her hair back from her forehead. Not Theo. Someone else. Incredibly gentle. Incredibly kind.

"Cassandra," a man's voice said softly in careful UniCom; calming. "Cassandra, if you can hear me, squeeze my hand."

She tried. She wanted to please him, all her thoughts directed to the task. But nothing seemed to work: her fingers were remote things; distant, as if listening to other voices – other commands.

His presence seemed to fade into the distance and she was alone again, standing in a wooded glade, listening to a breeze whispering through the tree tops; watching shadows playing on the grass below.

He had come to her again. Or had he ever left? She didn't know. She wanted to open her eyes. She wanted to see him.

"Cassandra, can you hear me," he was asking her again.

She squeezed his hand.

"Ah," the voice said, directed away from her now. Perhaps someone else was in the room. Did it matter? Not if the voice stayed close. The someone else spoke, but she didn't hear the words. "Yes, she can hear me, but her response is still very weak. You will have to be patient."

She squeezed his hand again to bring him back to her, willing her fingers to close around his. "Stay with me," she begged, her lips frozen, barely able to form the words.

"I'm here," he said. "You have nothing to fear. You are in the Gio MediCentre. Psy-Medic Han and I are looking after you."

The image of Ibrahim Mehari drifted out of the mists in her head and solidified. A kind of hope leapt momentarily within her. "Thank you." Had she spoken? She wasn't sure. She felt herself drifting away again.

Had she slept? It seemed she had.

She opened her eyes.

The room was in semi-darkness. Mehari was still by her bed, holding her hand, his beautifully symmetrical features partially lit by a golden glow thrown into the room from an open doorway on the right. She turned her head slightly. A man was standing in the doorway silhouetted against the light. She focussed her attention on him. A large man, filling the doorway, legs slightly apart, hands planted firmly on his hips. A vivid image, reinforcing an earlier one. From when? How long ago? She felt her heart flutter for a moment.

"Will she recover?" the man was asking.

She heard the gruffness of the voice; the rich baritone beneath; the slight rolling of the 'r's. She savoured the sound, and felt herself transported back through time and space: Shackleton – a lifetime ago.

She didn't listen to Mehari's answer. Her mind was elsewhere, tingling softly, singing to itself. Strange emotions swirled through her: stirrings of exhilaration; joy mingled with delight. Her body had answered.

Oliphant had come.

SIXTY

It was two days since the raid on Visitor Accommodation Suite E-3. Oliphant had forced his way through the door with MacFadden, SSO Gordon and three squaddies close behind. Mehari and two Medics had been on hand to pick up the pieces afterwards.

The last twenty-four hours of the flight had catapulted him from comparative inertia to an adrenalin-fuelled blur of nervous energy. A simple re-routed message from Xenon had lit the fuse. It screamed *Help* without actually saying so.

"I thought I should tell you Cassandra is taking a break on Gio. We all hope she will return fit and well. Theo Xenonopoulos."

Oliphant's blood pressure had shot through the roof.

The scene that greeted them in E-3 had imprinted itself indelibly on his brain ever since. In the half-light of the interior, the body of a man was sprawled out naked on the floor, hideously contorted in death – Axel Anstrom – as they'd later discovered, who had a string of aliases as long as your arm, but was better known as Angel. On the only couch, a naked woman was stretched out like a lifeless rag doll, her face encased in a VR visor. Above her, his weight braced by his arms and well-muscled shoulders, was an equally naked man, deeply absorbed in ramming her.

With the hiss of the retracting door, the man's head had whipped round, registering the cause of the interruption. His reaction had been incredibly swift. In the blink of an eye, he'd yanked himself clear of his pleasure and lunged for a pair of neuro-rods on the table beside him. He'd scooped them up, leaping backwards out of immediate reach, half-crouching, ready to pounce.

What followed had barely filled the space of a minute, but in recalling the scene, Oliphant experienced the sensation of witnessing everything in exquisite slow motion. All the dots had suddenly joined up: Lattimer; Servione – and this man – Smiler's protégé, conjured out of nowhere – a Freelance from Hell.

"Phoenix!" Oliphant remembered yelling, his voice catching in his throat; strangled; unnatural.

And Jayson Raymer had actually laughed in his face. "CSO Oliphant, I presume," he'd said, mocking him. "You're a bit late."

A split second later, MacFadden had pushed past and fired without hesitation, leaving Oliphant with the abiding knowledge it should have been his own finger that had pulled the trigger.

With the laughter knocked out of him, Raymer had grabbed at his solar plexus, gasped and fallen, a crumpled heap of disorder, stunned into sudden unconsciousness, the neuro-rods slipping from his grasp.

Somewhere between the dull thud of MacFadden's stun gun discharging and Raymer hitting the floor, Oliphant had thrown himself across the room to immobilise the VR facility, wrenching the visor back and snapping the delicate mechanism from its mounting. Beneath it, Cass Diamond, her eyes glazed, had stared blindly up at him. And then her lovely features had suddenly contorted into an expression of blind terror. She'd started to scream; a terrible hair-raising wail sufficient to waken the dead, while her arms and legs began jerking uncontrollably like a broken mechanical doll. The Medics had rushed forward and held her steady while Mehari had fixed the sedatape to her wrist, keeping her head still until the medication took hold. The screaming had stopped as suddenly as it had started, and Oliphant remembered careering through into the sleeping quarters and dragging the coverlet off the bed to hide her nakedness.

How many times had he dreamt of holding her naked in his arms? Over the last six months, he'd lost count, imagining how he'd look at her, caress her – yes, even make love to her. No fool like an old fool.

In E-3 his adolescent dreams had come true – in part: he'd held her as he'd always wanted, and for those few precious seconds before concealing the beautiful body he craved so much, he'd looked. It had only been a moment of guilty pleasure before he'd hidden her from the inquisitive hunger of his eyes, and the eagerness of his hands to touch. But he *had* looked.

He'd carried her to the MediCentre, oblivious of her dead-weight, cradling her head on his shoulder, her wild, dark hair cascading over him, its fragrance suffusing his senses, just as it had the day he'd first laid eyes on her and she'd set his soul on fire. The scent of her was still in his nostrils when he closed his eyes and remembered.

Just two days ago. And since then he'd been existing in a kind of trance somewhere between supervising Raymer's interrogation and sitting next to her bed in the MediCentre.

Sometimes her treatment sessions lasted for hours, but he'd remained patiently in the anteroom until they were over on the pretext he was waiting for her to be strong enough to answer his questions. He might have fooled Mehari – which he doubted – but he couldn't fool himself. He wanted to be near her. To watch over her. It was as simple as that.

With time on his hands, he'd devoted some of its ponderous minutes to searching for something to salvage from the disaster of Operation Misfit – because operationally it had been a disaster: Lattimer's refusal to share Phoenix's identity with him had contributed to the confusion, and would possibly cost Lattimer the chance of filling Mendoza's shoes.

That something good had been salvaged was a small consolation: authorisation for Raymer's interrogation had been swift in coming. Initially, he'd been a reluctant talker, but the series of Statement Ratings he'd been subjected to had revealed a treasure trove, not least his true identity – Dawson Haynes – ex-Social Engineer with a history of dubious contacts. A Freelance who'd gone to the bad. He'd finally named four other Spacers, and their rapid interrogation had fingered six more contacts still on flightcraft to outer stations. The distribution network had been successfully unpicked before it became fully operational. That at least gave Oliphant some satisfaction.

Earthside, the International Enforcers had lifted Miles McMichael off Philomos. Within hours, he'd unburdened himself of his role in distributing MegaJoy products, enthusiastically naming his contacts higher up the chain. The mere mention of a Statement Rating had loosened his fat tongue. His assets had since been seized pending Judicial Oversight, his Entertainment Agency had ceased to exist, and he had been incarcerated at a secret location for his own safety.

For ConCorp, there had been added kudos from exposing the GRM's involvement in the manufacture of forged IDs and hologram histories. Besides Servione's operation, three other production centres had been identified and closed down in Calcutta, Amsterdam and Hong Kong. Servione himself was facing the likelihood of confinement in an Aberrant colony for a very long time. Only the illicit communication usage on *Ivanov* remained unresolved. Once the general alert had gone out, there'd been a sudden deafening silence. Someone had pulled the plug. ConCorp's Fraud Division were already on the case.

Oliphant sighed and shifted his position slightly in the bedside chair, his thoughts circling back to the reason for his vigil, watching the slow, steady rhythm of Cassandra's breathing, her lovely profile outlined by the pale glow of the night light beside her.

Cassandra and Xenon – the link between them yet to be revealed to her.

After the incident, Xenon and Manaus had been brought to Gio on the first available shuttle and Oliphant had been at pains to meet them in the Security Zone. Their appearance had shocked him. Xenon had looked drained and both men carried their public humiliation written on their faces. But at least he could assure them that Cassandra was safe and in good hands. "Thank you for your messages, Mister Xenon," he'd said, wanting to acknowledge Xenon's part in her rescue. "She owes you her life."

"I hoped you'd understand them," he'd said, a wan smile registering for a moment before vanishing. "Cassandra is very dear to me."

And to me, Oliphant had thought, seeing her features echoed in the man's face. "Will you bear with me? I've something I think you should have." And he'd handed over the transcript of the family connections he'd discovered.

Xenon had read the notes, absorbing the information without comment. When he'd finished, he'd offered Oliphant his hand, said his thanks, and left quickly, close to tears. Umo had put a comforting arm around his shoulders.

For Cassandra, the revelations would have to wait.

Oliphant leaned forward, his eyes never tiring of looking at her. Sometimes, the urge to stroke her hair, or simply to cradle her head on his shoulder, was almost unbearable. But surveillance eyes were watching.

Occasionally, he wondered at his dedication – or fixation – whichever it was. Maybe it was neither. His thoughts always came back to that moment when they'd first met. That spark. Had she felt it too? But then he'd admonish himself for indulging in self-delusion. After all, what was there for her to admire – or be attracted to? Just a man in his middle years who always thought he knew best; who no longer had any confidence in suggesting even a short-term partnership with a woman; whose temperament was better suited to a career contract than an emotional one; a man who'd indulged in casual short-term partnerships in place of a lasting and meaningful relationship.

Once, he'd thought of her as little more than a Hurdy-Gurdy. Now he knew better: whatever the casual relationships of her youth, Koblinski had remained her one and only official partner. Oliphant remembered them together on the vid. She'd truly loved him. Raymer had been little more than a distraction; Anstrom, a grotesquely manipulated physical experience; and E-3 – E-3, an unforgivable enforced defilement.

Yet still he hoped; still remembered the moment their fingers had touched and she'd stayed his hand, her warmth passing into him – that gift of touch which lingered. When she'd looked into his eyes, had she seen more than a brusque Security Officer? Had she seen something behind the bluff exterior? Or was it nothing more than the product of his fevered imagination?

He was still not prepared to say it was. Still not prepared to damn himself completely. Still prepared to sit; and watch; and wait.

There was no fool like an old fool.

SIXTY-ONE

Oliphant eased himself into the visitor's chair. "I wanted to check the de-animation procedures had been completed," he said, trying hard to concentrate on matters in hand. "Is Haynes ready?"

Mehari offered him refreshment which he refused. "Yes. He's ready. What time are you leaving?"

"The *Oryx* is due out at thirteen-hundred."

"Doctor Velasquez will supervise the transfer."

"Thank you."

Mehari had raised an enquiring eyebrow. "I thought you might have delayed until Miss Diamantides was fit enough to make the journey with you."

Oliphant studied the man's face. "My first responsibility is the transhipment of the detainee, Doctor Mehari."

The Chief Medic remained unruffled. "So you are leaving your star witness behind." It was a statement, not a question.

Oliphant cleared his throat. "Until you give the go-ahead she can travel."

"I see. Give her two – maybe three weeks. She is very resilient but we need to be certain the detoxification programme has been successful."

Oliphant readjusted his position. Conversations with anyone other than Xenon which mentioned Cassandra always left him uncomfortable. "Just give me the word and I'll arrange a direct flight."

Mehari nodded. "Mister Xenon and his partner are staying on, I believe."

"Yes. I think it's best if they stay with her. They can travel back together."

Mehari nodded. "Have the others left already?"

"Yes, the Technos left Lowell on a freighter due to dock with the *Ivanov* in ten days' time."

"There will be many disappointed Spaceworkers, I believe."

"Yes, but there was no way the tour could continue."

"No, indeed. But I'm told the Choralians were the best Entertainers on the circuit."

Oliphant shifted in his seat again, eager to drop the subject and pursue another that was bothering him. "What do you know about this Lazar Excell, Doctor Mehari," he asked. "Are you absolutely sure he doesn't pose any threat to station welfare? – because I'm not getting any answers I'm happy with."

Mehari's expression didn't alter one jot. "I've already told you as much as I can," he said, which implied more than he was saying. "He has a blood disorder, but I can assure you, it is not contagious, infectious, or in any other way a potential hazard."

"Then why all the secrecy? And who is he – really?"

The Chief Medic remained unfazed. "It is not for me to answer that question, Mister Oliphant," he said smoothly. "A patient's right to privacy in this situation is inviolable."

"That may be, but Doctor Garrison seems to know some pretty important people who can work the system."

Mehari's courtesy knew no bounds. "It would seem so. I understand one of ConCorp's Directors has offered a personal flightcraft for the specific purpose of returning Mister Excell to the Clinic as soon as possible."

"I'm not comfortable with that. Do you know why I wasn't allowed to interrogate him? He was travelling between ConCorp's stations using a false ID."

"That is something you will need to discuss with your superiors."

"I don't like loose ends."

"Can I suggest, Mister Oliphant, that if your superiors are happy that the matter should be dealt with in this way, you cease to think of it as a 'loose end'?"

Philosophy wasn't Oliphant's strong point, but he knew when he was being stonewalled, and Mehari had the most charming way of doing it.

"If that is all, Mister Oliphant, I presume you would like to see Miss Diamantides before you go. There is still time, I believe?"

Oliphant tried hard to appear unmoved by this observation. "Thank you," he said, wondering why he felt like a child receiving a gift from an indulgent parent. "I had it in mind."

Mehari led the way through the MediCentre to the convalescent modules. "Mister Xenon is with her, of course," he informed him casually as they progressed through the maze of confusing corridors.

"Of course."

"The news of their family connection was most beneficial. It came just at the right moment for her. She was badly adrift at the time." Mehari had stopped outside the sepia door with her name illuminated in white above the communication panel. He buzzed, announced himself and Oliphant, and the door slid back.

It was a comfortable room, not the basic functional accommodation elsewhere on-station, even in visitor suites.

Mehari went in first, Oliphant finding himself unaccountably holding back.

Xenon stood up as they entered. He'd been playing a rehearsal choraladian and was cradling it in his arms, like a child. Hardcopy sheet music from it lay in untidy clusters here and there on the floor, as one piece had been discarded in favour of another.

On an adjacent couch, framed in the wallpane behind her filled with snow-covered peaks and pine forests, sat Cassandra, relaxed and dressed in her red kaftan, her hair falling loosely onto her shoulders: an image as remote from the screaming entity he'd rescued a week ago, as Pluto was from the Sun. There was a sheet of music in her hand. Perhaps she'd been singing: there was a lovely heightened colour suffusing her cheeks that Oliphant had never seen before – except on the vid. She was captivating.

"CSO Oliphant has come to say goodbye," Mehari announced in a matter-of-fact tone.

Oliphant noticed her eyelids flicker slightly at the news.

Xenon briefly exchanged glances with her and lovingly placed a hand on her shoulder. "I'll come back later," he said, and tactfully began to follow Mehari out of the room. "A safe journey, Mister Oliphant," he said as he reached the door. "No doubt we will see you again at the Judicial Enquiry?"

"Of course."

The door sighed shut behind them and he and Cassandra were alone. He found himself standing awkwardly under her direct gaze feeling foolish and suddenly at a loss for words.

"Theo thought it might help if we composed some new songs," she explained, indicating the scattered music and filling the silence that had come between them.

"An excellent idea," he said, his brain empty of whatever he'd originally intended to say. At a loss, he sat down on the couch Xenon had quit earlier and tried to gather his scattered wits. "You're looking better," he said, feeling this was at least a reasonable comment to make.

She acknowledged his observation with a smile. "Thank you. I feel it. Doctor Mehari is pleased with my progress. He tells me the mind-warp program hadn't been running long enough to do lasting damage. For that at least, I should be grateful – as I am for your very prompt action," she added with the most radiant smile ever bestowed on him by another human being.

He looked away, studying the hardcopy strewn across the floor at his feet. "What will you do once the Enquiry's over?" he

441

asked casually. "Any plans?" He had no idea why he was asking these questions.

She gave her answer some thought. "We may give up touring. The strain is too much. Perhaps we'll put all our energies into composing in future. Maybe even open a Folkster Academy."

"No more Choralians?"

She shook her head. "No. We'd need another male soloist ...."

She'd left the observation hanging in the air, and he understood why.

"What will happen to Raymer?" she asked suddenly.

"You mean Haynes," he corrected her and immediately wished he hadn't.

"Forgive me, I have difficulty thinking of him as anything other than Raymer."

Oliphant held himself in check before he answered her original question. He wondered if she realised the extent of the felony he'd witnessed in E-3, or its likely consequences. Sometimes, he decided, it was better to be economical with the truth. "Probably psycho-realignment and a twenty-year community service programme," he lied, keeping his face devoid of expression.

"Will he ever sing again?"

"I don't know," he confessed. It wasn't a question he'd ever been asked before, but he doubted Haynes would feel much like singing after psycho-realignment, not to mention ...

"No," she said, cutting across his thoughts. "I don't suppose you do." She looked down quickly at the music still in her hand, a sadness enveloping her which possibly threatened to become something more emotional: something that might demand action from him; something that might compel him to comfort her. But the moment passed. She seemed to recover her composure, and the opportunity to embrace her was lost. She looked up, making an obvious effort to control herself. "You know, Mister Oliphant," she said, "I can never forgive him. I want to see him punished, but I can't forget how beautifully he could sing. Whatever they do to his mind, I hope they'll leave his voice alone."

He couldn't answer her. What happened to the voice after neutralisation? – he wondered. But he could guess.

"I didn't love him, you know," she confessed, apparently thinking it was necessary to clarify this. "We were unofficial for a while, but I never loved him – not like I loved Karoli. Perhaps I always knew there was something about him – something about the way he came into our lives – too sudden, too convenient, too charming." She turned her attention once again to the sheets of music on the floor.

Oliphant leaned forward and contemplated the sheet nearest his foot, not because he had any particular interest in it, but simply because it was something to do. He'd come to say goodbye – and more, and yet here he was, tongue-tied and wasting time. Seconds were ticking away. He knew it, but seemed powerless to act. When they next met, she would be a Judicial Witness. Communication between them would be forbidden until after the Enquiry. Yet now, when she was so close, when he had the opportunity to act, and in those few precious moments to say what was on his mind, his obstinacy was leaving him mute.

With care, she placed the sheet of music she was holding on the couch beside her and addressed him directly. "Theo always said you'd come," she said simply, her gaze fully on him. "I hoped – but I wasn't sure."

Caught out by the directness of her statement and its potential implications – which he might be misinterpreting – he fell back on the safer ground of officialese. "Operational silence prevented taking you into our confidence, I'm afraid."

She reached out across the space between them, unexpectedly placing a warm hand over his. The shock almost knocked the breath out of him. "I'm partly to blame for what happened," she was saying. "I should have followed Theo's advice. I should have contacted you as soon as Angel ..." She looked away, withdrawing her hand and leaving him bereft.

It was warm in the room. He was starting to sweat. Automatically, he loosened his collar a little and checked the time on the wall clock. Twelve-fifteen. There was still time before he had to leave, except he'd let two golden opportunities to reveal his feelings slip through his fingers: a third was unlikely to manifest itself in the short time left available. He stood up to avoid further complications. Delaying his departure was pointless.

"Do you have to go now?" she was asking him.

"I think I must," he said, unwilling to read too much into the intonation of her voice, which seemed to suggest a hint of regret. "MacFadden and Captain Orlev will be waiting."

"Then you must go," she said. With great dignity she rose from the couch and moved closer so that he began to experience real physical pain. "But before you do, please tell me something."

"If I can," he said, conscious of an audible thickness in his voice.

"Something has troubled me since we first met – that night at Shackleton." She was looking straight into his soul as she spoke. "When you were questioning me about Karoli's death. Do you remember?"

Hells bells – how could he ever forget?

"Did you think I was involved in any way? Or that I was trying to bribe you for some reason – making you a very obvious offer?"

His mind rolled away, filled with the memories that haunted him: the red kaftan with its gold tassels – why did she have to wear it today? Her hands emphasising her lovely body; the body he'd now seen – and held – in such different circumstances from those he most wanted – and still wanted. "No," he said lying effortlessly despite the boiling in his brain. "Never," he added, taking a defensive step backwards and smoothing down his beard as if to emphasise the point more forcefully. "Now, you must excuse me. MacFadden will be waiting."

He was running away and he knew it. Leonid James Oliphant was a coward. Afraid to let her know the truth. He straightened his uniform and made for the door.

She called after him. "You haven't let me thank you," she said. "For discovering who I really am."

He'd reach the door, his hand raised to the control panel ready to open it. But it remained poised, paralysed. He heard her moving closer, the swish of the kaftan filling his ears as it had at Shackleton.

"You are often in my thoughts, Mister Oliphant," she informed him softly. "More often than I understand."

He swung round, wondering if he'd heard her correctly. She was standing within arm's reach, her head tilted slightly, her face looking up at him, her eyes large and liquid, dissolving him. Thunder hammered in his head until he thought his skull would split apart with the din. Yes – her meaning was quite clear: it was written in her eyes. If he was to act, it had to be now, or never. He paused to collect himself. "And you in mine," he confessed at last. "But perhaps you knew that already."

"I thought it possible."

"I'm really just like all the rest who find you irresistible, you know." His voice was clogging in his throat. "You've heard – and seen it all before."

"No, I saw something else. I wasn't always asleep while you kept watch – by my bed. I saw the way you looked at me. It wasn't the way others have looked. There was more."

He leaned heavily against the casing of the door for support. "Cassandra," he rasped between gritted teeth, "I care what happens to you. I can't help it. But I also recognise the simple fact you are without doubt a very beautiful, sensual woman, and I'm like any other man with an interest in the female of the species. I'd have to be made of stone not to want to make love to you."

"I know that – but there *is* more. I can feel it."

445

"Don't mock me!"

Her hand was suddenly on his shoulder, a tenderness of touch that would undo him if it stayed there much longer. "I'm not mocking you," she said earnestly. "I knew from that first moment I saw you. There's a connection I can't explain." There was anxiety in her eyes at having made so open a confession. "Perhaps in a few months," she suggested tentatively, removing her hand from his shoulder, "When I can understand myself a little better. When I'm no longer a Judicial Witness – perhaps we could spend some time together? Unravel the mystery? Would you come? – to Athens – if I asked you?"

This is a dream, he decided. This strange conversation was a figment of his over-heated imagination. He shook his head. "I don't belong to anything good in your life."

"That's not true. You saved me. You gave me a history. You gave me a greater reason for the love I have for Theo. All these things are very precious to me."

He could give her no answer – and MacFadden and Orlev were waiting.

"Will you come? – to Athens?" she repeated. "I want to know why it is I feel the way I do. To understand the attraction. To spend some time with you."

The thunder in his head pounded on. Memories of all his wasted years came flooding back; all the wasted possibilities. "No," he said, determined not to suck her into his destructive world. "You'd only regret it."

"Why?"

"Because I don't have a good record with personal relationships, that's why. I'm a Security Officer. Security Officers put their careers first and everything else a long way behind. It's the way we survive – because we're like the Enforcers – we usually see the worst side of people."

She smiled faintly. "A bit like being a Folkster," she said quietly.

446

It wasn't what he'd expected her to say. "Perhaps," he conceded, reluctant to agree too readily.

"Then will you come?" she insisted.

He could have said no again, and been done with it. He could have said no and got on with his life. Except for one small, but significant fact – his resistance had crumbled. He needed no prompting to tell him he could no more say 'no' to her a third time than he could perjure himself at the Judicial Enquiry.

Slowly, he reached out for her hand, daring to take hold of it, feeling its living warmth; imagining it holding him. He raised it gently to his lips, capturing the image of her at that moment to imprint on his memory until they met again. He yielded graciously. "Yes, I'll come," he said softly, the scent of her pouring into him.

Now she has me, he thought. Body and soul. Every last atom of my being is hers for the taking. And the thought was strangely liberating.

~~~~~~~~

Lightning Source UK Ltd.
Milton Keynes UK
UKHW020739110822
407164UK00007B/408